WH^T PEOPLE ARE SAYING ABOUT

PAN[

CH(

This uplifting, highly enjoya)UNT
series by Carolyn Mathews
duction to the main character, Pandora   act I
hadn't read *Transforming Pandora* or *Squa.*   *..es* didn't
prevent me from the appreciating the book.

The author's style is light and breezy, with deft characteri-
sation and expert use of snap-shot descriptions, combining an
energetic approach with mystical themes. The main character is
both likeable and complex enough to carry the story, her flaws
balanced by honesty and humour. Throughout the book she is
torn between three potential love interests...yes, three!

Initially believing I was reading a hen/chick-lit crossover, I
was stunned when the author dropped a bombshell in the
middle of the novel that had me reeling. I was expecting a bitter-
sweet ending but was left with something altogether different,
hard to describe but satisfying on an emotional level.

R. J. Dearden

Pandora's Gift

Pandora Series – Book Three

Pandora's Gift

Pandora Series – Book Three

Carolyn Mathews

ROUNDFIRE
BOOKS

Winchester, UK
Washington, USA

First published by Roundfire Books, 2015
Roundfire Books is an imprint of John Hunt Publishing Ltd., Laurel House, Station Approach,
Alresford, Hants, SO24 9JH, UK
office1@jhpbooks.net
www.johnhuntpublishing.com
www.roundfire-books.com

For distributor details and how to order please visit the 'Ordering' section on our website.

Text copyright: Carolyn Mathews 2014

ISBN: 978 1 78535 175 4
Library of Congress Control Number: 2015941049

A CIP catalogue record for this book is available from the British Library.

Design: Stuart Davies

Printed and bound by CPI Group (UK) Ltd, Croydon, CR0 4YY, UK

We operate a distinctive and ethical publishing philosophy in all
areas of our business, from our global network of authors to
production and worldwide distribution.

CONTENTS

Enlightenment is absolute cooperation with the inevitable.

Anthony de Mello

Acknowledgements

My thanks to Marianne Holland, Nathalie Mathews and Jessica Moss for being such fine test pilots.

And to my family and friends for bearing with me until I reached the end of the story.

Last but not least, my grateful acknowledgement to the team at John Hunt Publishing, with special thanks to Dominic James, publisher of the Roundfire imprint.

Chapter 1 – May Day 2009

'Fancy a drink, Pansy?'

Gina's reflection appeared in the illuminated mirror in front of me. She stood at my dressing-room door, small patches of beige make-up clinging for dear life to her face and neck, her cheeks smudged with blusher, giving her the appearance of a badly-painted puppet.

'You look like Aunt Sally,' I said, turning to face her. 'I wouldn't be seen dead going *anywhere* with you in that state. And don't call me Pansy.'

Parking herself in the seat next to me, she picked up a powder brush and began dabbing at her cheeks. 'All right, Miss Goody Two-Shoes. Life's too short to waste valuable drinking time hosing that muck off.'

I ignored her and continued cleansing.

'Come on, *Pandora*, I'll stand you a pint and a bite.'

My studio car was booked for one-thirty. 'I'll miss my ride home.'

'Since when has that bothered you?'

I laughed. She knew I had nothing much to rush home for when my partner, Jay, was out of the house, especially since my neighbour, Olivier, had taken the dogs under his wing. As long as I boarded the train before the rush hour, I was quite amenable to unwinding in the pub for a couple of hours before heading to Marylebone station.

Scraping the last vestige of foundation from my face, spray-painted on at eight-thirty that morning by a make-up artist, who insisted we needed it 'to be HD-ready', I applied an ultra-revital-ising moisturiser while Gina performed an autopsy on the morning's *Straight Talking* show.

'Kay came down a bit hard on Trevor when he defended the May revellers, don't you think?'

She was referring to our choice of articles from the day's newspapers. Trevor had picked one about a group of nature worshippers who'd lit a bonfire to celebrate Beltane Eve. It was too close to the maypole, had got out of hand, and a concerned member of the public had called the fire service.

'I thought we were all supposed to be singing from the live-and-let-live *politically correct* hymn sheet these days,' she moaned. 'Calling them "irresponsible nutters" wasn't exactly PC. If they leave it in, there's bound to be a backlash.'

Kay was the *Straight Talking* anchor whose contempt for neopaganism and the like was legendary.

'They won't cut it out, Gina. That's what they want, something a bit provocative. If it makes the newspapers, they might get a few more viewers.'

Gina glanced at her watch. The programme aired at one o'clock. We'd finished recording at twelve-fifteen and had emerged relatively unscathed from the post-show rundown. Neesha, the executive producer, could be forensic in her dissection of who said what to whom, and wasn't above scolding us if she thought we weren't being sufficiently entertaining.

'We'd better get a move on, before we have to fight our way through disgruntled druids.'

I'd finished my own primping so I waved a heavy-duty moisture wipe in her direction. 'Only if you let me perform a bit of restoration work on you first.'

Heaving a sigh, she allowed me to begin renovating her face and neck.

In her day, she'd been a promising young actress, linked to several A-list actors. She'd even married one of them. But drink had done for both of them, and here she was, the wrong side of forty, single, and scraping a living from daytime TV and the odd supporting role. Despite all this, on a good day she still scrubbed up well.

'I've never danced round a maypole but I've been to some

similar shindigs in Glastonbury,' I admitted, as I rubbed away the remnants of her face paint. 'That's the sort of thing my mother was into.'

Gina swivelled her eyes away from her own reflection to meet mine. 'Didn't you tell me once *you* were some sort of alternative therapist?' Before letting me confirm this, she steamed on. 'Why didn't you put in your two penn'orth? It would've shaken things up.'

'Didn't think it would get past Kay. Too New Agey for her.'

She nodded. 'It's a fine art, darling. Being expected to have an opinion on everything, yet toeing the party line.'

Jay had also commented more than once on my reactions and interactions on the show. He felt I'd started off okay, but had recently become a puppet of the programme makers. I explained to him that ratings dictated content and daytime viewers on that channel preferred altogether lighter entertainment than we'd been giving them. But he still accused me of playing a part, of not being true to myself, at which point I'd had to bite my tongue.

'I can't afford to lose this job, it's what we live on,' I declared, saying out loud to Gina what I hadn't been able to say out loud to Jay.

'You and me both, darling,' she replied, without a shred of sympathy.

Feeling there was a danger of getting into a *I need/deserve this job more than you do* contest, I focused on the task in hand. 'Do you want to go *au naturel* or have you got some make-up with you?'

We both scrutinised her reflection in the mirror. Even in the unforgiving light of the illuminated mirror she didn't look bad. Her grey eyes were finely outlined in black liner with pearl-grey shadow, still intact. After my efforts, her complexion was now clear with a natural hint of pale rose in her cheeks.

'Just a bit of lippy,' we said, almost in unison.

Once we were done, after cancelling my ride home, we

jumped into the car booked for Gina, getting the driver to drop us off at the Raglan Arms in Fitzrovia, round the corner from where she lived. She favoured this pub because it meant she could drink as much as she liked and be home to sleep it off within five minutes.

I let Gina order the food, as she was footing the bill. We ended up with a baffling array of bar snacks, rarely seen outside of the pub's Quick Bites menu. As I bit into a Cajun rarebit and Gina tackled a Bangkok Scotch egg, I noticed a man in a crumpled suit at the bar staring at us. 'Do you know that man? He's looking over here.'

She peered in the direction my eyes were pointing and shook her head. 'Never seen him before. He's quite fanciable, don't you think?'

Gina was into her second cocktail and her tongue was loosening. I giggled nervously. 'Sshh, he'll hear you.'

'He probably thinks he knows us but can't think where from. *I* get that all the time.'

Her insinuation that she was much better known than me didn't escape my notice. It was true. She was. But I didn't need reminding of it.

The man had started walking towards us. When he reached our table, he stopped. 'Excuse me, are you Gina Fraser by any chance?' he said, regarding her with a pair of large, soulful eyes edged with thick, dark lashes.

He was well-spoken, of slightly above average height and indeterminate middle age. His dark grey hair, long enough to be arty but short enough not to be hippy, was brushed back from a wide brow, framing a face which had the nut-brown hue of someone who regularly spent time in the open air. Although he glanced away every so often in a way which suggested he posed no threat, this was belied by his cleft chin and wiry frame. I could see that Gina was intrigued.

'Yes, guilty as charged. I am Gina Fraser.'

I half expected her to add, *Who's asking?* But she left it at that.

'My name's Andrew Truman. I wrote to you about Raymond Stone.'

Gina looked blank but motioned him to sit down all the same. He put his glass of beer on the table and leaned forward, giving her his full attention.

'I've just started writing his biography and I'm interested in talking to people who knew him and may be able to contribute some memories, anecdotes. I was given your address by your ex-husband.'

Gina let out a snort, her vacant expression swiftly replaced by one of fury. 'That bastard! He's got some nerve putting you on to me.'

The silence that followed could only be described as charged. Truman looked uneasy, his glance towards the door indicating he wanted to be anywhere but here. He must have needed contributors badly, because he sat tight and waited for her anger to subside. 'Can I get you ladies a drink?' he said, finally.

This was very timely as I'd drained my lemon and lime seconds before.

'I'll have a Gin Fizz,' said Gina, 'and my friend will have a Piña Colada.'

This had been a favourite of mine, before I'd found out how calorific alcohol was. Since then, I'd been on the wagon.

I hesitated.

'Okay, just this once.'

While he was at the bar, I quizzed Gina about the letter Truman had written to her.

'I ripped it up. He said Brett had told him I'd been a friend of Ray Stone's. I thought he was insinuating I'd had some sort of a fling with him while I was still married to Brett.'

'And did you?' I said, my curiosity aroused. Raymond Stone was an American film director, famous, not only for his artistic vision, but for his playboy reputation rivalled only by the likes of

Jack Nicholson.

'Of course I did. How else would I have got the job? But I don't want the world and his wife to know that, do I? If I ever decide to spill the beans it'll be in *my* book, not his.'

Truman arrived at our table with the drinks and a grilled cheese sandwich which he quickly polished off. I took a sip of the drink he'd bought me. The coconut and pineapple flavours were easily identifiable, unlike the white rum and triple sec which usually hit the back of my throat at the first mouthful. It crossed my mind that maybe he'd economised and gone for the non-alcoholic Virgin Colada, instead.

I saw him eyeing our plate of snacks and told him to help himself. I'd been gaining weight lately and was having to watch every morsel. In no time, he'd devoured the last Clonakilty black pudding croquette, sitting back with a contented sigh.

'So was it a coincidence meeting Gina today,' I said, 'or were you lying in wait for her?'

Gina tittered.

'It wouldn't be the first time I'd been stalked.'

'Not exactly. As I hadn't heard from you, I took the liberty of knocking on your door. No reply, of course, but your neighbour came home as I was leaving and told me where you might be.'

'Man or woman?' said Gina, almost sweetly, cradling her Gin Fizz.

'Man. Oldish.'

'That's Morrie. I'll have his guts for garters when I see him.'

Actress that she was, Gina could do almost any accent, and she'd lapsed into Eliza Dolittle cockney for her last line. I was used to this, but Truman looked startled. Taking pity on him, I decided to move proceedings along. 'Gina, for goodness' sake, put the poor man out of his misery. Can you help him or not?'

'We-ell,' she said, coquettishly, 'it depends what you want to know. I only worked on one film with him.' She paused, eyeing him up. 'But if you like, we can go back to my place and see if my...memory...can be jogged.'

Truman's grip tightened on his glass and I felt myself blush on Gina's behalf. But to my surprise he went along with it. 'No time like the present, I'll be happy to escort you back.'

His smile was thin but it fooled Gina.

I was the first to move, almost knocking over a glass in my haste. It was illogical, but the prospect of them going off together consumed me with a feeling of being left out, even if it wasn't something I wanted to be in.

I held out my hand to him. 'Goodbye, Mr Truman'.

'You're not coming?' he said, tilting his head slightly and holding my hand for a second too long.

While I was trying to work out whether he wanted me there: a) for a threesome, b) as protection against Gina's sexual advances, or c) was just being polite, Gina cut in, making it quite plain she was riding solo.

'Gimme a break. We've been together since eight o'clock this morning, we're not joined at the hip.'

She struggled to her feet, teetering slightly. Gina always kept a small bottle of gin in her bag to top up the pub cocktails, which explained why she was bordering on smashed. I, on the other hand, felt completely sober.

'I'm off to the loo,' she slurred. 'When are you in next week? Or, should I say, which day *aren't* you in?'

Gina had always held it against me that I was on a maximum four-day-week contract while hers was only three.

'Tuesday onwards.'

'See you then, ducks.'

Gina had gone all cockney again so I answered in the same vein. 'Okay, gal. Don't get locked in the lav, will you?'

She chortled her way to the ladies and Truman and I exchanged wry smiles.

'I'm afraid I'm completely lost,' he said. 'Do you two work together?'

'Yes, as panellists on a daytime talk show. When Gina's around I sometimes end up here.'

'Really? What's the show called?'

'*Straight Talking*. Probably not your thing. It started out being fairly serious but it's changing. Not completely frothy yet but it's getting there.'

'I haven't seen it, but I'll make a point of watching it now,' he said. 'Sorry – I didn't catch your name.'

'Pandora Armstrong. But I answer to Pandora Fry and Pandora Jay on Google, as well.'

The implied expectation that he would go home and look me up had slipped out before I knew it.

'You can find anyone and anything on the web these days, can't you?' I said, to hide my embarrassment.

'Very true,' he replied, delivering his line with a downward sweep of his thick, dark lashes.

I don't know why, but I was suddenly filled with a desire to help him. Maybe it was his slightly hangdog air, or the fear that he might tar me with the same brush as Gina. Whatever it was, I found myself informing him of her intention to keep any revelations for her own book.

'That's what they all say,' he said, seemingly unperturbed. 'I'll still give it a go. Her ex-husband said she more or less lived with Stone while they were making *The Red Galaxy*. It was a defining moment in his career, so I'd like to flesh out that period in his life. Who knows, it might give her a boost. From what I've heard, she needs it.'

This was all very well, I silently speculated, but how was he going to stop her from jumping his bones as soon as she closed her front door?

'I hope you get away unscathed,' I gabbled, wanting to get it off my chest before Gina got back. 'After an hour in this place, she casts all inhibitions to the wind.'

There, I'd said it. I'd committed the most heinous crime of all

– undermining a fellow female's chances of getting laid by labelling her a loose woman.

He looked away, at first I thought in embarrassment, but when he raised his head he was smiling broadly.

'Sweet of you to warn me, but don't worry, I *can* look after myself.'

Seeing Gina coming towards us. I waved in her general direction and, Judas that I was, blew her a kiss before speedily exiting stage left into the May Day sunshine.

* * *

When I got home to Phoenix Cottage I searched for Andrew Truman on my computer. Isn't technology wonderful? His potted biography was there for me to see on his own website.

How times had changed in just four years. When my one and only book came out in 2005, no one had pressured me to become 'an online presence'. Interviews and articles arranged by the publicist had done the trick, plus a few photo shoots, usually with Jay. But I was never under any illusions. If I hadn't been married to, divorced from, and freshly reconciled with my rock star, the book would have no doubt sunk without trace.

I looked in my desk drawer for some file paper to make notes on but found only paperclips, Tipp-Ex and elastic bands. I was about to walk to the village newsagent when I remembered the file I'd used for a spiritual correspondence course in the bottom bureau drawer. *I'm not going to start reading it,* I thought, *it'll just make me feel guilty,* so I deliberately opened it from the back. My idea had been to extract some unused sheets of paper but, in the end, I simply placed a page divider between the course notes and the blank pages. Then I began copying an abridged version of Andrew Truman's details from the computer screen.

Andrew Truman: born 28 July 1953 (55 yrs old)

Education: Bristol University, History degree.
Career: publishing until 1992, left to pursue a full-time career as ghostwriter and biographer, specialising in creative artists: actors, musicians, directors, authors.
Family: married 1980, one son, divorced 2005.
Resides: Reigate, Surrey, and S. W. London.
Hobbies: sailing, fishing, squash.

There was more, but I was beginning to feel like a stalker, so I switched off the computer and went to get the dogs from Olivier's house, a short walk from my cottage. The back door of The Cedars was locked, so I opened it with the key Olivier had given me. In response to my whistle, Oscar and Fritz appeared from the direction of the large dining room, where they liked to go when the room wasn't being used for filming or functions.

After our joyful reunion, I put my head round the door of Olivier's office on the off chance he was there. The room was empty, which meant he was probably at his cake boutique in the village, so we made straight for the woods. I needed a jog to separate my London self from my Chace Standen self, although these days I wasn't particularly keen on either of them.

Chapter 2 – Losing It, Autumn 2008

I can trace the start of my decline back to one day last September. I was in my study at Four Seasons when the house phone rang. A man's voice asked for Mr James Jay so I said I'd see if he was available. I wasn't sure whether he was in his recording studio or in the packing shed with Hugh, helping him get the fruit and veg deliveries ready. I didn't have to search far – I found them both in the kitchen having a coffee break.

'Someone from the bank's on the phone for you, Jay.'

The panic on his face tempted me to hover in the background when he took the call, but instead I did the polite thing and stayed to chat with Hugh. When Jay came back, he sat down at the table and clutched his head with both hands. I asked him what was wrong but he was so distraught he couldn't speak.

Hugh got up to leave, looking embarrassed.

'Sit down,' said Jay. 'This affects you, man, as well as us.'

Jay reached across the table and took my hand, his eyes pleading.

'I'm sorry, Andy. I didn't want to worry you. I was hoping there'd be some way out of it.'

He started shaking and I got the cooking brandy out of a kitchen cupboard and poured some into a small tumbler. He emptied the glass in one gulp and helped himself to a second shot.

'Fact is, I'm skint. I've lost everything in the crash.' His voice broke and he wiped his tears away impatiently with an upward sweep of his hands. 'The guy on the phone said it'd take a miracle for me to hang on to the business...or the house.'

He looked wildly around, as if expecting a good fairy to fly in the kitchen window and make everything all right.

Hugh and I sat in stunned silence, trying to absorb the consequences of this news. Jay started to explain, his eyes downcast, his hands still trembling.

'Five years ago I was advised to invest in property. There was this guy who did it all for me. He just used to ring up for my go-ahead and I let him get on with it. This isn't his fault, by the way. He warned me about the subprime defaults in the States, but I never thought it would affect this country.' He crashed a fist on the table. 'Those greedy, bastard bankers! More like bloody gangsters.'

I stroked the knuckles of his hand, trying to sooth him, telling him it would be all right.

'I thought I was being clever...remortgaged this place to build up the portfolio. Shouldn't have put all my eggs in one basket.'

My brain jerked to attention. I had no idea he owed anything on Four Seasons. Fighting down a rising feeling of exasperation that he hadn't thought to mention it, I forced myself to concentrate on what he was saying.

'...I got a letter from the bank last year, didn't take much notice. It said their commercial mortgages had been sold on to Lehman Brothers.'

'That's the American bank,' I said, with a sinking heart. I'd followed their demise in the papers so I knew there was no hope.

'Lehman Brothers crashed,' said Hugh, a split second ahead of me.

Jay's face creased in pain.

'Yeah. Tell me about it. On top of that, the guy I just spoke to told me if I don't pay the mortgage arrears on this place, they'll be taking me to court to repossess it.'

'How many payments have you missed?' I said, holding my breath.

'Must be about five now.'

'But what about the business?' I said. 'Doesn't that make enough to pay the bills?'

Jay looked glumly at Hugh and shook his head.

'Only partly. I was using the rental income from the properties for the rest. That was frozen by the bank months ago. I've only just been managing the school fees, allowances...'

He stopped. He didn't need to go on. I was only too aware of how much money flew out of Jay's pockets to keep his five children, his mother, the two of us, plus various livestock, in comfort.

But maybe there was a way out. I still owned two properties. Ashley and Linden were living in my flat in Fulham but I could sell Phoenix Cottage. The present tenancy was due to end soon.

'Why didn't you tell me sooner, Jay? I would have put the cottage up for sale. I still can. Would the bank wait if I did that?'

Jay put up his hand to stop me.

'I've already had the standard interview, babe.' He flicked his head back as he always did when he was stressed. 'All avenues have been explored. This is my final warning. There's no point in selling either place...that's where we'll be living.'

I groaned. Much as I loved the cottage, I couldn't see us, his mother and whichever of his children needed a roof over their heads shoehorning into a three-up, three-down. I was about to ask him to expand on this idea when Hugh intervened.

'What about the business, Jay?' he said, almost apologetically.

Considering his livelihood was at stake, Hugh was showing admirable restraint.

'Afraid I'll have to wind it up sharpish, mate. I've got to get shot of the house...can't afford to complicate matters by selling it as a business as well. The way property prices are diving, I'll be lucky to break even.'

Hugh's chin was almost on his chest; he looked the picture of misery, as we all did at that moment.

Jay continued in confessional mode, his voice low and full of gloom. 'My priority has to be scraping together enough to pay off the arrears and stay out of debt until the house sells. That way, I keep whatever equity there is *and* my credit rating. The only assets I've got left, apart from the furniture, amount to a couple of delivery vans and any fruit trees that can be sold off.'

Hugh shook his head as if he still couldn't believe what was happening.

'So when should I start looking for a job?'

'I wouldn't waste any time. The vultures are circling.'

The two men continued to sit staring at the table, lost in their thoughts, until Jay finally broke the silence. 'We might as well go out and start making a list now, then you can get in touch with the organic farm, see if they're interested in taking anything off our hands.'

Jay got up and walked out into the garden and Hugh followed him, nodding in my direction.

I'd rather Jay had stayed with me to talk about how we could raise the money for the mortgage arrears and where everybody was going to live. I wanted to run after him but I suspected he was avoiding me, out of fear that my initial sympathy had shunted into reproach.

At that moment, Jay's mother appeared.

'Hi, Pandora. I thought I heard Hugh. I wanted to ask him to keep some asparagus back for me. I wanna make some soup. It's got great slimming properties.'

Since Sharon had become close to my stepfather's friend, Pete, she'd made an enormous effort to lose weight. But Sharon's weight-loss programme consisted of combing magazines for slimming tips in search of a quick fix which never came quick enough to fix her fat problem. Being in love suited her, though. She would never be a sylph again, but her eyes held a newfound sparkle and her skin glowed.

'Wait, Sharon,' I said, as she made for the back door. 'Sit down. Jay's had some bad news. It's about the house.'

* * *

After dinner that night, we all assembled in the sitting room for a pow-wow. Jay's whole tribe was there – Rowan, still at school, Willow, waiting to take her place at university, Cherry, about to start her third year, and the two oldest, Ashley and Linden, who'd driven down from London after an urgent phone call from Sharon.

Once she'd got over the initial shock, Sharon had valiantly taken up the reins and arranged for three estate agents to come the next day to value the property, for which I was exceedingly grateful, since both Jay and I had been in a daze all afternoon.

Sharon kicked off the meeting. 'You're all gonna have to grow up fast. Your dad needs to pay his mortgage arrears so he'll get something out of the place when it sells. If he doesn't, the bank will take it and he'll be left with zilch. So we'd welcome some suggestions from you. How do you think you can help him save money?'

I looked over at Jay and pulled a face. He looked as mortified as I felt. None of the kids had any source of income: they all depended on Jay. What did she expect them to do, run off and join the circus?

'I can leave school, if it helps,' said Rowan, finding the silver lining.

'Yeah, boy, that's likely,' said Linden, ruffling his hair.

'Okay,' said Sharon, 'that's a very good suggestion. You can go to a free school and that'll save on school fees.'

Rowan's face fell.

'Not the local comp, Gran.'

'Once they know you're one of the poshos from King George's, they'll eat you alive,' said Cherry. She stared accusingly at Jay. 'Anyway, if you're selling up, it won't be the *local* comp, will it, Dad? Where are *you* going to live?'

Jay was sitting with his head in his hands so I explained that Rowan could come with us to Phoenix Cottage and Sharon could have the third bedroom if she wanted.

'So if you four are going to live in Pandora's tiny house, what about me and Willow, where are we supposed to go?'

Jay's expression, ever since he'd got the news, had been one of tight-lipped despair. Normally he would have told her not to worry, that he would sort it out. But he could only groan and shrug his shoulders.

Unusually, it was Sharon who reassured Cherry. 'In a couple of weeks you'll both be in university digs anyway. Other times, you can stay with Ashley and Linden.' She looked enquiringly at me. 'It only means moving in two more single beds.'

Ashley didn't look too pleased at the prospect of having his younger siblings as roomies. Nevertheless, I was glad that Sharon had stated it as a fact, rather than an option.

Sharon glanced at Rowan, who was also looking glum.

'Rowan can use the sofa bed in the living room when he visits, can't he?'

I nodded, the image of my once immaculate flat being overrun by juveniles diluted by my relief at the thought they wouldn't be squeezing into Phoenix Cottage every weekend.

'And you're always welcome at ours,' I said, all the while thinking, *As long as you don't all come at once.*

Willow smiled weakly. She was trying to be brave and not succeeding very well. I felt the sorriest for her, having her milestone experience of starting university blighted by the family's descent into comparative penury.

'What about our clothes and stuff?' she whispered.

This was a logistical problem I had no answer to. I couldn't even see how Sharon, Rowan, Jay and I would fit all our clothes into two double and two single wardrobes, let alone accommodate Cherry and Willow's personal effects. And there wouldn't be much spare storage space at the Fulham flat, either.

'I should have hung on to The Cedars,' I fretted, wishing that I'd rented it to Olivier instead of selling it to him.

'Woulda, shoulda, coulda won't get us anywhere, Pan,' Sharon said sharply. 'We have to get moving, starting with a car boot sale on Sunday. You girls won't be needing your riding gear for a start.'

'That's a point,' said Ashley, 'what's happening to Midnight and Beau and the rest?'

'I've no idea,' I said, looking at Jay. 'Any suggestions?'

The thought of losing Beau, a Poitou donkey I'd grown very fond of, had lent a hard edge to my tone which I immediately regretted when Jay started to sob. Seeing how much this distressed the three younger siblings, I sent a flashing-eyeball SOS to Ashley, directed at the door. Luckily, he got the message and took Jay away to the kitchen, presumably to dose him with hot, sweet tea.

As soon as they'd gone, Sharon played her Get Out of Jail Free card. 'I've got something you should know, Pandora. I haven't told Jay yet in case he gets too upset.' She paused dramatically. 'I won't be coming with you. I rang Pete this afternoon. I asked him if I could go live with him in Glastonbury and he agreed. Plus he said he'd ask farmer Steve if he'd take all or some of the livestock.'

I could have kissed her. In fact, I did. But when we parted, I noticed the faces of the three younger Jays failed to reflect my relief.

'You're just *abandoning* us,' cried Cherry.

'Taking all our pets away,' moaned Rowan.

'Nothing will ever be the same again,' wept Willow.

I was glad Jay wasn't present because it would have crushed his heart into even smaller pieces.

'Listen here,' snapped Sharon, bristling with impatience. 'You kids don't know you're born. I had a baby at sixteen and went off to Canada at eighteen to find my way in the world. You've been pampered long enough. It's time you stepped up to the plate and gave your dad a bit of support instead of take, take, take all the time.'

Even though I half agreed with what she said, I still felt for them. The consequences of this catastrophe were clearly freaking the life out of them, especially as they'd led such protected lives up to now. And Cherry had a point – Sharon was a bit of a bolter. Hadn't she abandoned Jay when he was only two years old?

Linden, who was comforting Willow and Cherry, gave me a beseeching look. 'This won't affect their education, will it, Pan? They can't be expected to give up now.'

'Of course not. That's what student loans are for. And I've just paid off the labyrinth, so I can cover their allowances.'

'Good news, girls,' said Sharon, dryly. 'You won't have to work your way through college after all.'

While the girls were digesting my offer and their grand-mother's sarcasm, I weighed up Linden's situation. He'd been working as an unpaid intern for a PR company but this luxury was no longer viable. 'Sorry, Linden. I wish I could help you, but your dad and I will need my salary to live on.'

'That's okay,' he said, evenly. 'I've got enough experience now to freelance until I find something more permanent. If necessary, I'll flip burgers in the evening or something. It's Ash that needs help. He's still got two years to go and he's never wanted to do anything else.'

I felt proud of him. Both in looks and personality, he was the image of Jay when I'd first met him and today he was showing himself to be the most composed of all of us.

Sharon had been listening intently and moved to sit next to him, ordering Cherry into another chair. She took his hand. 'Linden, you're the only one of my grandchildren who's so far volunteered to stand on your own two feet. I'm proud of you.' He angled his cheek for a kiss and she duly obliged. 'I have a little bit of savings of my own. Don't worry, my darling, I won't see Ashley go short. Or you, for that matter, if you need a little time.'

'Thanks, Gran,' he said, a huge grin on his face. 'I'll go and tell Ash and Dad the good news.'

'You do that,' said Sharon, winking at me. 'Tell Ashley there's no way I'll be cheated out of having a doctor in the family.'

'What are you crying for?' she chided, when she saw me dabbing my eyes.

I was crying for all of them: for the loss of their home – the only home Jay's children had ever known. I was crying for the labyrinth, installed barely two years ago; for my beautiful geodesic dome, sadly neglected since I'd started my TV job; for my beautiful blue shepherd's hut where I used to write my online dispatches; for Four Seasons itself, which Jay and I had chosen in our second year of marriage when the band had really taken off; and for all the mistakes we'd made which had led us to this point. But most of all from an overwhelming fear that the family was breaking up and would never be as close again.

I brushed the tears away, forcing a smile. 'I'm crying because I'm happy that things aren't as bad as they seemed. Thank you, Sharon. You're an angel.'

Chapter 3 – Straight Talking, May 2009

'So, do you think he slept with her?'

It was a week after our afternoon in the Raglan Arms and Gina and I were in the studio restaurant grabbing a coffee before our pre-show briefing. She'd been quizzing me about Jay, who'd had the mad idea of re-forming the Jaylers, improbable whichever way you took it.

He'd contacted bass player Eddie first, who wasn't too keen on prising himself away from his trout farm. Jay had asked him to sound out his fellow guitarist, Ian, but they'd lost touch. To my surprise, though, Donny on keyboard and Clive on drums said they were up for it. Consequently, Jay spent most weekdays at Donny's place in Hampstead, plotting a comeback and 'rehearsing'. They'd even constructed a website in preparation for the grand resurgence in their popularity.

Jay's manager, acquired last year when he and Gaby Laing were supporting Sammy Wilson, had leaked the planned reunion to the *Daily Express*, using the angle of trying to find Ian's where-abouts. He said it was a way of 'testing the water' – to see if the public gave a damn, basically. Gina had chosen the article as one of her newspaper cuttings, hence the questions.

I'd confided that the voluptuous Gaby had propositioned Jay when they'd spent time together working on her material, and was now wondering if I'd been a bit rash. Gina wasn't known for her discretion.

'Pansy,' insisted Gina, 'did he sleep with her or not?'

'I've got no idea. He said he wasn't interested. But he'd never tell me anyway, would he?'

'Does he still write for her?'

'No. That all fizzled out. She went down like a lead balloon. I almost felt sorry for her. Jay got good reviews, but Sammy was furious with his people for booking her.'

'You're not too keen on him going on tour with his buddies, is that what I'm sensing?'

I sighed, remembering how much pain I'd felt during the weeks Jay had been away rehearsing and touring, knowing he was in Gaby's company every day and maybe every night as well.

'He needs the money.'

'But you downsized, didn't you?'

Gina knew about our financial wipe-out – how could she not? We'd been widely featured in the press as casualties of the crisis, alongside ex-millionaires living on benefits and a celebrity couple whose £20 million property debt ended up in the hands of Lloyds (partly owned by the government following a bank rescue package), so effectively shifting the burden on to the British taxpayer. At least Jay had managed to emerge from the whole mess without owing anyone a penny.

'Yes, we downsized to my old place. No mortgage, thank God. I can easily cover all the bills. But he feels so guilty about losing everything...he's desperate to be successful again. He says he wants to have something to leave the kids.'

'The male-pride thing.'

'And there's not enough to keep him occupied where we live.'

'Mmm, while the cat's away... He's probably better off in Hampstead with his Jayler mates, darling, than being bored witless in suburbia.'

'Hampstead can be pretty suburban,' I shot back. 'Just because a terraced house goes for a million quid, doesn't make it any less bourgeois.'

'All right, all right, keep your 'air on.'

Gina was up to her old tricks of adopting one of her accents so she could be rude by pretending to be humorous. Before I could reply, we were called to the briefing. The company drew on a cast of about ten regulars in a pick 'n' mix formula. Our appearance days were variable, the idea being that the panel wouldn't be too predictable or the panellists too cliquey.

Today the other two panellists were Trevor and Trudy, a comfortably built agony aunt with silver hair who wore a lot of lavender and reminded me of a plump pigeon. After Neesha had gone over the schedule, we took our places in the studio ready for recording.

When my turn came for the daily papers, Kay had to ask me twice for my selection because I was so distracted with thoughts of what Gina might say when it was her turn. Today I'd selected an item on swine flu. Another, about a minor actress who'd appeared in porn movies to pay for plastic surgery, had been given to me by Neesha.

During the subsequent discussion on the porn star, I caught Trevor's eye and we shared one of our *oh dear* looks, which had become increasingly common of late. He, like me, had been told to be more in tune with popular taste and to cut back on anything too serious. A former TV horticultural pundit, he was now on the compost heap as far as gardening presenting went, having been edged out by younger, more vigorous climbers. He needed this job, so he spent most of his time playing the role of jocular old gent – a wasted talent, in my opinion, because he was naturally witty and would have made a much better anchor than Kay.

'What have *you* got, Gina?' asked Kay, after every avenue of speculation about which areas of the actress's body had been altered had been explored.

'Well, I have here an article of *special* interest to a certain member of our panel. It's from the *Daily Express* suggesting that James Jay and the Jaylers may return to rock another day.' She proceeded to read it out, which didn't take long, after which she aimed her gimlet gaze at me. 'It's so nice to have the horse's mouth here, so to speak. Is this true, Pansy? Is your partner, James Jay, likely to be gigging again soon?'

I took a deep breath. How the flipping heck did I know? Jay had sunk into depression the day he got the call from the bank about having to sell Four Seasons and hadn't completely surfaced yet. For all I knew, this talk about getting back together was Clive and Donny's way of cheering him up.

But I wasn't paid to be noncommittal. Gina, Kay and Trudy were waiting, necks thrust forward, for the horse to talk.

'They're definitely thinking about it. But they've lost contact with Ian and they want him to get in touch.' I paused, not sure what to say next. 'It wouldn't be the same without him,' I ended, vaguely.

Trudy wound her beak in slightly so her double chin almost disappeared into her breast. 'How is Jay coping now?' she cooed, composing her face into a mask of concern. 'He's been through a lot lately, hasn't he? Did he consider having therapy?'

The audience grew hushed; all eyes seemed focused on me.

'Jay hasn't got much time for shrinks,' I parried. 'He thinks music is the best medicine.'

Trudy blinked her beady eyes at me in disapproval, so I blocked her with a cheap laugh.

'You know that joke? How many psychologists does it take to change a light bulb?'

Gina and Trudy remained silent, refusing to feed me the line.

'How many?' said Trevor, coming to my rescue.

'One. But the light bulb has to want to change.'

Over the audience laughter I added, 'Maybe he needs to deal with it in his own way.'

Gina barely waited for the audience to settle down before she came out of her corner. 'And you, too,' she said. 'You've been through a lot. You lost your home and your livelihood as well, didn't you? What was it you did – some sort of healing with bowls and bells?'

I had a suspicion she was setting me up to expose me as a dilettante with questionable skills, and therefore no right to be on the panel, so I wasn't sure what to say to this.

I caught Kay's eye and saw she was giving me her fast-blink, hurry-up signal. Still not sure how to spin my answer, I ignored the *What was it you did?* question and stalled them with some lines about a lot of people being in the same boat. Then I brought the topic back to Jay: how he'd never stopped writing music, still had a lot to give, and was hoping to build on his success last year on the Sammy Wilson tour.

'Talking of that tour,' said Gina, her lips smiling but her eyes hard, as she got me on the ropes. 'He was singing and playing with Gaby Laing, wasn't he?'

The suggestive way she'd said 'playing with' drew some sniggers and I felt my cheeks burn.

Surveying the audience with a knowing look, she continued. 'We've heard about other bands and what they get up to on the road, do you ever worry when he's away from home?'

I was about to deny this when I heard a whisper in my left ear. *Tell it like it is, Pan. Turn the tables on her.*

This was my mother, Frankie, speaking. She occasionally visited me from whichever dimension she'd landed in when she'd popped her clogs, dishing out 'guidance' which wasn't necessarily helpful, even if it was from the Great Beyond.

But today she caught me in the right mood, so I took her advice, which weirdly was Jay's advice too, and told it like it was. 'Jay and I split up in the first place over another woman. They had five children together so it wasn't a casual thing. In the end, I didn't really blame him, because I couldn't have children.'

At the mention of my infertility, there was a chorus of *aaahs* from the audience. 'But when we got back together he said there had been others, mostly on tour, although they hadn't meant anything.'

Both the panel and the audience lapsed into uncomfortable silence. Even Gina held back, probably because I clearly had the audience's sympathy.

The silence was finally broken by Kay. 'And you still stayed with him, knowing that? That's more than most women would do.'

It struck me that if I was being wholly truthful, I'd have to admit to my own infidelity: initially with someone back when we were first married, and more recently with someone a mere four months ago. I decided discretion was the better part of valour and adopted a brave smile.

'Yes. But let's face it, most men can't keep it in their trousers, can they, given the opportunity? So why be surprised if they stray when they're away from home?'

I glanced at Trevor, expecting disapproval, but he was actually grinning from ear to ear.

'What do you think, Trevor,' I said, delighted at his obvious willingness to take over. 'Can we trust you men or not?'

Taking the baton and running with it, Trevor proceeded to treat us to an earthy discourse, as befitted his status as a man of the soil, on the male brain and its biological imperatives. As the audience responded, so his language grew more colourful. When 'on the job' the 'gardener' had to make sure the 'furrows' were 'well-ploughed', give the seeds a good 'hosing' – all that and more. Once he got into his stride, he had the crowd in stitches.

Kay must have been receiving orders from above in her earpiece because she let him have his head, her brittle smile and tapping foot confirming my suspicions that she resented him getting the limelight he deserved.

But I wasn't out of the fray yet. Kay must have been given the go-ahead to move on from Trevor, because she waited for him to draw breath and nipped in quickly to ask Gina if she would put up with a wandering husband or partner.

'You're asking the wrong person, darling. I think marriage is an obsolete institution, and the idea of monogamy totally outdated. It's not natural for two people to be together for that length of time and still fancy each other. Look at Ronnie Wood – he's left his wife for a twenty-year-old Russian girl. What chance does the more mature woman have when girls that age are willing to sleep with wrinkly old fossils? How long have you been with Jay, Pansy?'

I was fully aware she already knew the answer to this and was just asking me so she could prove her point in public. 'We were married for ten years, then we divorced, and we moved back in together five years ago.'

Some of the audience reacted by making little squawks of surprise which prompted Gina to go for the knockout. 'So he wants to re-form his band, which will, no doubt, involve going on tour, knowing he can get away with a few little...transgressions, because you've already taken him back in spite of his track record.'

By now I was wondering if Jay would see today's transmission. The old Jay would have had a good laugh and said 'there's no such thing as bad publicity', but since his depression, I could never be sure how he'd react. I felt the prickle of sudden tears at the thought of him being hurt by our conversation, so I tried to rescue his reputation in the only way I could think of. 'Give him a break, girls. He's a broken, sixty-one-year-old man who's lost his home and his business in the space of a few months. He wants to go on tour because he needs the money – not for sex, drugs and rock 'n' roll. He can manage the rock 'n' roll, but as for the rest, forget it.'

The audience laughed and clapped. Trudy and Gina laughed too but not before I saw a glint of disappointment in their eyes, like dogs whose bones had been snatched away just as they were about to sink their teeth into them.

I heard Gina mutter, 'He's the same age as Ronnie Wood, you'd better look out,' but Trevor jumped in and saved the day by joking that if Jay needed any help in 'a certain department' he knew of a very effective South American herbal remedy. Not that he needed it himself, of course, wink wink.

'As always, the answer lies in the soil,' he finished, to the accompaniments of whistles and cheers from the handful of men in the audience, most of whom seemed to be over sixty.

Hearing such a warm response to Trevor's words of wisdom, Kay sprinted on to the next item, leaving me bursting with relief that the Jay debate was over.

On our way back to the dressing rooms I tackled Gina about why she'd put the boot in. 'That's the last time I tell you anything personal,' I said icily. 'Okay, you could say that Jay needs the publicity, but if I was Gaby, I'd be on to my solicitor.'

'Come on, Pansy, it was only for the telly.' She took hold of my hand but I snatched it away. 'If you want to hang on to this job, you'll have to roll with the punches. You heard what Neesha said this morning, we have to give the punters what they want...which is basically gossip, scandal and well-endowed boy bands. Otherwise ratings drop, advertising dries up, they get new people in and we're out of a job.'

'That's not what I signed up for,' I said, slamming my dressing-room door behind me.

'Well, bully for you,' she shouted, through the crack in the door. 'If it's not good enough, go and be a pundit on some other show. Oh sorry, I forgot, you don't actually have an area of expertise, do you? You got the job on the strength of your old man's faded career. I doubt if it'd work a second time.'

Crossing the room at the speed of light to fling open the door, I let rip right back. 'You cow! You don't know what the hell you're talking about. I'll have you know I was *headhunted* by a researcher who found my online ANONYMOUS column and traced me through that. It had nothing to do with Jay...'

We were interrupted by a member of the production crew who asked us, very politely, to accompany him to the executive producer's office. This was usually where we assembled at twelve-thirty for the post-mortem, but it was only twelve-fifteen. We followed him in silence. I had a feeling in my bones of trouble ahead.

Neesha greeted us and asked us to sit down while her

assistant fetched some tea.

'Now, ladies,' she said, looking at her watch. 'First of all, I'd like to congratulate you on your discussion this morning. It went down well with the audience and even trended on Twitter.'

'Hashtag ageing rocker?' said Gina, with a smirk.

'What about the bit insinuating that Gaby Laing may have been sleeping with my partner?' I said, baring my teeth and aiming them at Gina. 'I wouldn't want Gina to be sued for hashtag slander.'

Even though she was late twenties at the most, Neesha surveyed us as if we were two schoolgirls brought to the headmistress for cat-fighting in the playground.

'The legals have had a look at it. It's okay. We'll definitely be keeping that segment in.'

Gina and I exchanged cold stares.

'So,' said Neesha, waiting while our plastic cups of tea were set in front of us. I had the feeling she was in the act of delivering a criticism sandwich: a slice of good-news bread first, then a bad-news filling followed by more empty carbs.

'I sense a "but" coming,' said Gina, catching the same train of thought as me.

Neesha still didn't crack a smile. It was clear she thought the 'talent' had it easy compared to her task of managing the hectic whirl of the whole operation.

'We're trialling some new panellists, which means, as your original contracts have expired, you'll both be working on a freelance basis from next Monday, getting paid for the hours you work.'

'Does that mean we might not be called in?' I said, with a sinking heart.

'Possibly,' said Neesha smoothly. 'We're aiming to give you both two days a week but, ultimately, it depends on how the new panellists get on.'

'Why us?' I cried, unsure whether it was performance or age-related indignation I should be feeling.

'It's not just you – it'll affect all the panellists. It just happens that you're the only two who were given contracts. All the others started out as freelancers.'

'So that's why Oven Ready haven't renewed my contract,' said Gina. 'It was due two weeks ago.'

'And mine.'

Gina and I looked mournfully at each other, instantly united in misery. This was our worst fear – death by a thousand cuts. From now on we'd never be quite sure whether we were going to be re-employed: worried that if we put a foot wrong they wouldn't ask us back.

'Please don't think this is any reflection on your performances,' Neesha said, metaphorically serving us our finished sandwich and bringing our lay-off interview to a close. 'Engaging freelancers has become standard practice, I'm afraid.'

One or two crew members had started to trickle in, so Neesha got up and we followed her to the adjoining meeting room.

As soon as Neesha had delivered her final verdict on the morning's show, not that I'd listened to a word of it, I made a beeline for the exit. There'd been something I'd wanted to ask Gina, but that would have to wait. I could hear her clip-clopping behind me down the corridor but I didn't stop. She probably wanted us to bury the hatchet so she could spend the afternoon in the Raglan Arms, drowning her sorrows with me for company. But I had other fish to fry, so I picked up speed and hid in the ground-floor ladies' room till I knew she'd be safely out of the building. Then I went to Reception to say I was ready for my car. When it drew up, I got in. 'You're reprieved today, Bob. There's no need to take me home. Can you just drop me at the Oven Ready offices, please?'

Chapter 4 – Crossing the River

On the way over, I rang the office to see if Zac Willoughby, the Oven Ready CEO, was there. I could have rung his mobile number but, as I was on official business, I felt it best to go through the proper channels. His assistant answered and told me he was just about to go out.

'Could you ask him to wait until I get there, Portia. I'm about five minutes away. I just need a few words with him.'

She asked me to hold on and I heard some distant conversation but couldn't make it out. I was half hoping Zac would come to the phone but the voice that came on the line was hers.

'He's on his way to meet a client but he'll wait for you in the atrium.'

Portia would normally have exchanged a few pleasantries but today her 'goodbye' was so quick that I hardly had time for mine. My persecution complex was persuading me that she didn't want to get involved with disgruntled employees whose hours had been cut, when Bob brought the car to a halt.

'Here we are, miss. See you tomorrow, bright and early.'

Thanking him, I launched myself out of the car, almost flooring a passing pedestrian. With a hurried 'sorry' I dashed into the building, panning wildly around for Zac. I was just about to ask at Reception if he'd left a message for me when I felt a tap on my shoulder.

'Pandora. Is it me you're looking for?'

I turned round to find him grinning at me. I'd been avoiding him since Christmas and was surprised to see how lean and fit he was. He'd updated his look, too. Instead of a Barbour jacket over a shirt and tie, he was wearing a slim, grey blazer, pale-grey polo shirt and black jeans. Rather than a briefcase, he was holding a leather holdall.

'Yes, of course it's you I'm looking for, Zac. And I expect you know why.'

I could feel myself going hot with embarrassment at having to beg him not to put me on short time. At least that's what I told myself, trying to block out how much I fancied him.

'Don't take it personally, Pandora. The show's just not doing well enough, I'm afraid. That's why we're trialling some new blood. If that doesn't work...'

The two of us were getting in the way of the flow of bodies passing back and forth, so he took my arm and propelled me out the door. 'Let's discuss this over lunch.'

'But Portia said you were meeting a client.'

'You're so naïve. That's her standard reply if someone wants to see me without an appointment. She knew I was on my way out to the gym.'

'Oh, well, don't let me stop you.'

He laughed. 'Don't be so grumpy. We'll get some sushi and you can unburden yourself.'

I wasn't very keen on eating sushi at a long counter. I preferred face-to-face eating, and fish had been disagreeing with me lately, but Zac seemed to be on a health kick so I went along with it.

Despite what he'd said about me unburdening myself, it was actually he who took the floor, bemoaning the state of the economy and accusing 'the bloody politicians' of 'fiddling their expenses while Rome burns'.

He complained that the public were curbing their spending, with a knock-on effect for advertising. Consequently, commercial TV channels were becoming more conservative about the sort of programmes they were commissioning because they couldn't afford to get it wrong and lose advertising revenue.

'Do you think *Straight Talking* was a mistake, then?' I said, turning my head to see his face. I was getting a crick in my neck from this sideways seating.

'It was a good concept, but uh...' He gave me a guarded look.

'...the wrong channel.'

I wanted to blame Oven Ready for getting it wrong in the first place; on the other hand, if I said that, he might accuse the panellists of not being up to scratch. I wasn't in the mood for a performance critique, so I bit my tongue.

'How long do you think we've got before it folds?'

'If the BARB ratings don't improve by the end of June, they'll pull the plug. Keep it under your hat, mind, there's a slim chance it could be back in the autumn.'

I expected to feel agitated but, in a funny sort of way, felt liberated instead. The early mornings had been harder than I'd expected.

Zac patted the top of my arm. 'I'm sorry. This sort of thing happens all the time in our business.'

I'd set out with the intention of telling him how much we depended on my earnings and asking if my hours could be reinstated, but there was little point now I knew the show was probably doomed anyway.

We'd finished eating and I was wondering what would happen next. He and I had been lovers for a fairly brief period in 2003, just before I got back with Jay and, I was ashamed to say, had slept together after the Oven Ready Productions Christmas party, four months ago.

Halfway through that evening he'd asked me for a dance. Being nicely oiled by then, I'd enquired about his love life, and he said he'd met someone when he was on a trip to New York. I'd heard about the singles scene there, and how long it could take to get from dating to the holy grail of exclusivity. So I wasn't surprised at what he told me next. 'We've kept in touch but she's still seeing other men, so I regard myself as technically single.'

Later on, both full to the gills with champagne, we were on the dance floor again. I'd already booked a hotel room in London and it seemed the most natural thing in the world for Zac to suggest joining me later.

If I'd been getting some action at home, things might have been different, but Jay couldn't manage any more than a cuddle since the crisis, so what with that and Zac being tall, blond and handsome, I was easily persuaded into his arms.

The morning after the party, Zac and I had made love again. It was Christmas Eve and I was in no hurry to rush away. Sharon and Rowan were staying with us over the Christmas holiday and when I got home I could hardly look them in the eye – not to mention Jay's eye.

There was no house big enough now for the whole family to assemble and eat together, so I'd booked a Christmas meal in a hotel within easy reach of the Fulham flat. Sharon had been going back and forth there on the train most days, so she could catch up with what her grandchildren had been doing. Linden had finally managed to get a job and the girls were on vacation from university, staying at the flat. Rowan was happy to hang out with Jay, learning to play the guitar under his tuition.

He was doing his A-levels at a college in the vicinity of where we used to live. He'd been quite anxious about leaving his friends, so when his best mate Tom said he could stay at his house we didn't see him for dust. All in all, the kids had adapted to the simple life surprisingly well.

'What would you like to do now?' said Zac, interrupting my reverie.

That's exactly what he'd said to me in the hotel room on Christmas Eve morning and I wondered if it was his way of reminding me of our last meeting.

I suddenly felt very sad. 'I'm not coming to the gym with you, even though I need it,' I said, my voice cracking slightly, giving me away.

He sighed. 'I feel I've let you down by getting you into all this.'

'Don't,' I said. 'It's not your fault we went broke. I just wish I could shake off this feeling of hopelessness. There's no point in blaming you when I know it's coming from inside me.'

For a moment, I saw a glimmer of recognition in his eyes.

'Are *you* having any reaction to the show closing down, Zac?'

He always gave the impression of relaxed self-assurance but maybe the *Straight Talking* situation was taking its toll. 'I'm okay,' he replied, with the hint of a shrug. 'But I know what you mean. I felt like that once.'

I waited, but he didn't elaborate.

'How's the girl in New York?'

A muscle in his left cheek twitched. 'Lauren? Fine. I think. Last time we spoke she was trying to get a transfer to her firm's London office.'

'She must be keen,' I said, trying to keep my tone neutral. 'If *you're* not, you'd better run for the hills.'

I was hoping he'd open up about his feelings for this woman but instead he resolutely placed his hands on the counter and turned his gaze on me. 'Shall we go back to my place?'

Knowing what this would mean, I should have said no, but the morning's bad news had made me reckless. I might be worthless as far as Neesha and co. were concerned, but someone still wanted me. What's more, that 'someone' was looking exceptionally hot: who better to draw a little comfort from than him?

So I nodded, without pretending I had to think about it, and followed him out of the restaurant to Shaftesbury Avenue where he hailed a cab.

I'd never been to his apartment before. It was just the other side of Chelsea Bridge, in Battersea. The lift took us up to the second floor and he led us through a small hall into a large, open-plan room with a kitchen at one end, filled with light from floor-to-ceiling windows displaying a panoramic view of the Thames. It was furnished in minimalist Scandinavian style – blond wood, natural fibres, angles everywhere – and remarkably spick and span for a bachelor pad. On the way in, we'd passed a bathroom and what I took to be two bedrooms either side of the small hall, which was occupied by a collapsible bike.

'Is that part of your fitness regime,' I said, as I navigated my way round it.

'Absolutely. Only takes me thirty minutes to cycle to work from here, less if I avoid the rush hour. I try to do it a couple of times a week at least.'

I imagined Zac striding around the office in figure-hugging lycra shorts and jersey. 'Do you bother to change when you get to work?' I said, grinning at the thought.

'Don't need to. I wear my usual stuff. Just have to remember to take my bicycle clips off.'

This made me laugh and I could feel myself relax. Pressing home his advantage, Zac took my hand and walked me to his bedroom to show me how far the wraparound balcony extended. After sliding the full-length window half-open, he started to undress. I sat on the side of the bed and watched him. He didn't seem to mind – I'd seen him naked before and he was obviously proud of his newly toned body. I didn't take my clothes off because I knew he liked to undress a woman.

'You've got a six-pack now,' I said. 'Your abs are almost as chiselled as your cheekbones.'

He raised his arms and inhaled to give me a better view. 'I'm back to my fighting weight.'

'You're a lean, mean machine,' I said, giggling at how pleased he was with himself.

He climbed on to the bed and started kissing the back of my neck. Giving myself up to the pleasure of his firm lips, I remained sitting on the side of the bed as he undid the buttons of my blouse and cupped my breasts, still encased in their bra. I badly wanted to turn round and crush them to his chest but the thought of appearing overeager stopped me.

Leaving my bra in place, he manoeuvred me backwards on to the bed and undid the zip of my trousers, expertly pulling them off. He grasped the top of my briefs but then changed his mind and left them on. His lips started exploring the area just above them and I felt my back automatically arch but he still didn't hurry.

'Your skin's so silky,' he murmured, stroking my torso.

'I'm getting fat,' I said. 'It's the price you pay for sleeping with a woman of a certain age. Fat accumulates round the middle, as you can see.'

He laughed. 'You don't look anywhere near your age. What's your secret?'

'The elixir of life.'

I'd said the words before I knew it. To my relief, he laughed, taking it as a joke. Rosemary, the dentist slash high priestess who made the elixir, was very strict about who took her potion and why. I didn't want Zac enquiring about stockists.

He resumed his slow exploration of my body, his mouth pulling down my bra straps, his fingers finally undoing the clasp. By this time I was fairly aching with desire for him, so I took matters into my own hands in the hope he'd pick up pace.

'Mm, that's nice,' he murmured and a familiar thought flashed through my mind: how unimaginative a man's sweet nothings can be.

'I can barely remember what to do,' I said, rashly. 'I haven't had sex since the last time I was with you.'

I'd kept Jay's impotence from Zac at Christmas, thinking it was only temporary, so no wonder he jumped to the wrong conclusion.

'What, you mean, you're not with Jay now?'

'No. I mean yes, I *am* still with Jay, but he can't...'

'...Get it up,' breathed Zac.

At that moment, there was a knock at the bedroom door and a woman's voice came floating through. 'Mr Willoughby. Are you in there? Your phone's been buzzing away like crazy for the last five minutes.'

He leapt out of bed, grabbed a dressing gown and shot out the door, closing it swiftly behind him. I guessed that he'd gone straight to his phone because I heard snatches of what sounded like a work-related conversation. Then I heard him call out 'Goodbye, Jana,' followed by the sound of the front door closing. When he came back, he was looking worried.

'Sorry about the interruption. I've sent Jana away...forgot this was her day to clean.'

Miffed at having to start all over again, I showed my discontent by rolling my eyes, the way Cherry did when something hacked her off.

'That was Portia on the phone,' he said, apologetically. 'The panellists are revolting about their reduced hours. Sounds like Gina's been stirring them up. They've been on to Equity and they say they'll picket the studios next week if we go ahead with trialling the new blood.'

The thought of the likes of Trevor and Trudy bearing placards and shouting anti-Oven Ready slogans made me laugh and Zac was soon joining me.

'Well, at least you know I wasn't in on the putsch,' I said.

'Hmm,' he answered, pseudo-seriously, 'for all I know you might have been sent to distract me while they forged their plot. I was thinking of taking the rest of the afternoon off, but it looks like I'm needed at the front. Sorry, Pandora.'

He left the room and I heard the gushing of the shower. When he came back I hurriedly took his place in the bathroom, trying hard to disguise my disappointment.

* * *

Leaving me to continue on to Marylebone station, Zac pecked my cheek and got out of the cab, heading for an afternoon of phone-schmoozing the *Straight Talking* 'talent' so they wouldn't go on strike and thus render the show bereft of experienced panellists.

He'd even made a couple of calls in the taxi, while I tried to avoid my reflection in the window. There hadn't been time to do anything with my hair after showering. With no hairdryer to hand and Zac intent on hurrying me out, I'd had to go with the *pushed through a hedge backwards* look.

I'd been curious to know if anyone else lived in the apartment so I waited for a break between phone calls and asked him. He told me that it was sometimes used at the weekend by friends and family.

'So where do *you* spend the weekend?' I asked.

'In Kent. I inherited a place from a great uncle who had no children of his own. My sister and her family live there, so I get my fix of family life. And it's close to a good golf course.'

'Don't tell me. You love them all dearly but two days a week is enough. And you'd be lonely if you stayed here anyway.'

Sometimes a thought popped into my head and popped out of my mouth, bypassing my internal editor and occasionally causing offence. This was one of those occasions.

He turned his head sharply in surprise. 'Are you trying to read my mind, Pandora?'

He'd never been keen on my extrasensory side. In fact, that was why I'd chosen Jay over him, because Jay had believed me when I said I'd been contacted by a supernatural being called Enoch, while Zac had made it plain he thought it was all hogwash.

'Everyone can tap into their intuition, Zac. If you'd made use of yours, you might have avoided having to sack people right, left and centre.'

At this, he'd flushed to his flaxen roots, and we sat in uncomfortable silence for the last few minutes of his journey.

Alone in the taxi, I examined why I felt so rattled, and a quote came to mind which I'd heard from my mother's partner, Charles, whenever he was describing an unsatisfactory social occasion. He'd say it had deprived him of the solace of solitude without affording him the satisfaction of good company. That's how I felt about my truncated afternoon with Zac, especially the bit about satisfaction.

Then my internal therapist asked me the million-dollar question.

So what exactly do you want?

When I answered myself, I tried to be honest.

I want to feel happy and satisfied. I want to get rid of this yearning for something that's missing in my life. Either that, or find the missing element to make my life complete.

Chapter 5 – New Blood

On the train, I took out my phone. I'd switched it off earlier, because I hadn't wanted any distractions from what I'd been anticipating. Had I known our *coitus* was doomed to be *interruptus*, I wouldn't have bothered.

There were three missed calls from Gina, no doubt to muster support for the strike. I composed an excuse for not answering and rang her number.

'Pansy, I've been trying to get hold of you. Why did you rush off? Are you still on your high horse?'

I was momentarily confused by her last question, then I remembered her slurs on Jay's reputation. Since then, although I still thought she'd gone too far, I'd mentally conceded that she'd only been giving the producers what they wanted. As for accusing me of getting the job because of my connection to Jay, I was happy to let that lie – let's face it, it *was* my connection to a man which had secured me a full year's contract, with the maximum number of working days. But the connection had been with Zac, not Jay.

'What? No, I had some shopping to do. Wassup?'

I knew very well what was up, but had to play dumb.

'We're not putting up with the reduced hours.'

I let my mind wander as she ranted on, only reconnecting when she said, 'You are with us, aren't you? You will refuse to work next week unless they cancel the new panellists.'

'Um, I suppose so, if that's what everyone else is doing.'

Gina tutted in exasperation. 'Haven't you been listening? I've just told you, Trevor's not onside, nor wotsername, the woman who used to jump up and down on *The Good Morning Show*.'

Gina was referring to a keep-fit goddess whose iron will had kept belly fat at bay well beyond the age it should have invaded and settled, so it wasn't surprising that Gina hadn't been able to sway her.

'Zac got to them,' she snarled. 'He's been oiling everyone up so they'll behave like good little girls and boys. Did he contact you?'

If only you knew, I thought, but I just mumbled something about a missed call, my peeved inner voice complaining, *That's not all he missed.*

'So can we count on you, then? You don't sound very enthusiastic.'

Having heard from the head honcho that *Straight Talking* had a dubious future, I found it hard to match Gina's campaigning zeal, so I changed focus to distract her. 'What about tomorrow, though? My car's coming to pick me up...it's all right if I work, isn't it?'

There was a pause before she went on. 'I suppose so. We've given notice of action from Monday, so you might as well. I'm not in anyway.'

I suddenly remembered what I wanted to ask her, so I blurted it out before it flitted out of my mind. 'By the way, what happened last week with Andrew Truman? Did you tell him anything about Raymond Stone?'

What I really wanted to know was if they'd slept together, so I waited with bated breath for her answer.

'Oh God, I was so pissed. And feeling horny, I might add. I remember opening a bottle of wine...we were both drinking and he was asking me questions and making notes. I must have fallen asleep. When I woke up he wasn't there. What happened is anybody's guess.'

'So you think you might have slept with him?'

'Who knows, darling, all I'm worried about is if I told him too much. But I suppose I'll have to wait for the book to come out to find out.'

Annoyed with myself for slipping into the role of teenager grilling a school friend about her date with someone I fancied too, I decided to be a grown-up and dig no further. 'Okay then, old girl. See you on Monday on the picket line.'

'Yes, see you, comrade. Give me a ring tomorrow and let me know what the atmosphere's like – what Neesha's take on it is. You never know, she might be on our side.'

From the way she'd been regarding us over the top of her spectacles earlier in the day, I doubted that very much.

* * *

I took a taxi home from the station, expecting the house to be empty, but I found Jay and Olivier chatting in the conservatory. Today Jay had forsaken Donny's for a day in the garden; Olivier had heard the mower and popped by.

My friend Olly divided his time between the Cool Cake Boutique and his office in The Cedars, the house he shared with his partner, Justin. They'd developed it as a wedding venue as well as a location for recording cookery programmes. In fact, Oven Ready Productions had been the first company to film there. I'd owned the house then and that was how I'd met Zac.

'Hey, babe,' said Jay when he saw me. 'Had a good day?'

They were both beaming at me and I wondered what their expressions would be like if they knew how I'd spent the afternoon. I guessed that Jay's would be one of impotent rage and Olly's would be pursed lips, rolling eyeballs and an implied *I told you so*. If my memory served me right, he had expressed surprise when I'd forsaken, in his words, 'a very delectable morsel' (Zac) for 'an ancient rocker' (Jay) more than five years earlier.

'Not bad,' I replied automatically, then pulled myself up short. 'Actually, no, they're cutting our hours.'

Olivier got up and gave me a hug. 'Oh, Pandora, I'm sorry. But this is your life recently. You go up, you go down...like a yoyo.'

'Is that supposed to comfort me, Olly?' I said, breaking away. 'If so, it's not working.'

He looked hurt, his clear blue eyes searching mine to see if I was serious, so I smiled to make him feel better.

Jay took my hand and gently pulled me down to join him on the two-seater. Once we were all in place, Oscar and Fritz relaxed, settling down to bathe in the warmth of the sun filtering through the glass.

'Tell me all about it, Andy.'

So I described our interview with Neesha, leaving out the bit about heading straight to Zac for help immediately afterwards. Although Jay was aware that Zac ran Oven Ready, he also knew that my arrival on the shortlist for the job had been anonymous and coincidental. And he was savvy enough to realise that Zac wasn't based at the studios. Nevertheless, I'd been careful never to mention his name and I wasn't going to start now.

'Gina's got this crazy idea of us going on strike and picketing the studios next week.'

The three of us were having a good laugh at this when Jay's mobile rang. 'Hey, Donny.' There followed a series of exchanges which, annoyingly, I could only hear one side of. 'You're joking...she's here now...no, mate...I'll have a gander later...thought he was somewhere in Wales...Eddie as well... fantastic.'

Olly and I exchanged quizzical looks and I began to worry that Donny was alerting Jay to his reputation being dragged through the mud on today's *Straight Talking*.

'Okay, Don, see you tomorrow. Looking forward to it, mate.'

Jay pocketed his phone and stretched his arms upward in a sort of *Praise the lord!* gesture. 'Good work, my pretty,' he said grinning at me. 'Ian's mum saw the show and told him we were looking for him. He rang in and left a message that he'd be interested.' Jay got to his feet and punched the air. 'Donny let Eddie know and he said if Ian's in, he's in. The boys are back in business!'

He then did his comic running-on-the-spot victory routine

which I hadn't seen for months and which caused the dogs to thump their tails on the floor in approval. It was great to see him so elated, but how would he feel when he heard what Gina had implied about him and Gaby, not to mention what I'd said about him being deficient in the bedroom department?

'If you'll excuse me.' He grinned. 'I'm on my way to watch it on Catch Up. I hear you sprang to my defence when others were blackening my name.'

While I was relieved that Donny seemed happy with this morning's show, I was still nervous about Jay's reaction to the sensitive subject of his missing sex drive. This had been the last straw for him. He'd eventually taken himself to a doctor, but after refusing therapy, had been sent on his way with a prescription for antidepressants, which he'd put straight in the bin.

'I hope you'll still be talking to me afterwards,' I said, giving him a soft look. 'Just bear in mind, we were all being pressured to be more controversial.'

He left the room, shaking his head and chuckling to himself, looking the happiest I'd seen him since the 'banksters', as he now called them, had 'shafted' him.

Olly and I regarded each other like concerned parents, worried that our boy's fantasies of becoming a rock star would end in tears.

'What's going to happen when it all goes wrong?' I moaned. 'Who do they think's going to promote a tour at their age?'

'You never know, sweetie, look at the Rolling Stones. They're old as the hills. Seventy, at least.'

'Hardly, Olly, they just look it. The difference is, the Stones never really stopped. But the Jaylers haven't performed together for twenty years. Jay and Clive are the only ones who stayed in the music business.'

He shrugged. 'He needs *something*. Who knows? They might succeed.'

I tried to look convinced but he saw through me.

'What's wrong, Pandora? You seem more stressed than usual.'

'You mean I always seem stressed? I thought I was disguising it.'

'Sorry, chérie, it's in the way you move...so quick. Your head jerks, your fingers tap.'

'Oh God,' I moaned, 'you're going to tell me next that I've got frown lines.'

He stared at my features and shook his head.

'Actually, I can't see that...surprising, given your age. But your jaw is set and your expression is not very 'appy.'

I went to the mirror in the hall to see what my jaw was doing and was met by the sight of my poor, neglected hair which had dried flat as a pancake. Seizing a brush and hair dryer from the console table drawer, I performed an emergency repair by spraying it with styling mist and blasting it into a semblance of its former self.

When I returned, Olivier nodded his dark head approvingly.

'That's better, Pandora. When you came in you looked like you just got out of bed.'

I almost told him about my dalliance with Zac at that point, but an inbuilt safety mechanism kicked in, prompting me to steer the conversation back to my finances.

'We rely on my money now, so any threat to it is bad news. That's why I'm worried.'

'Then don't go on strike.'

His logic was impeccable but he wasn't in full possession of the facts.

'It probably won't make any difference in the long run, Olly. *Entre nous*, I've heard the show may be on its way out...we're not getting enough viewers.'

His face expressed sympathy but little surprise. He'd started his media career as a chef with Oven Ready Productions, so he knew all about BARB ratings.

'Who told you that?'

I paused to consider my answer. It wouldn't do any harm to tell part of the truth.

'Zac. I went to see him today. He's not very hopeful.'

True to form, Olly's eyes were now twinkling. 'Ah, now the Greek tragedy unfolds. You throw yourself on the mercy of your former lover and 'e rejects you, as you rejected him. Did you feel any *frisson* between you?'

'Sounds more like a Victorian melodrama to me,' I said sharply. 'And anyway, it wasn't like that. It's not just me, it's all the *Straight Talkers*.'

He was still smiling.

'But did you feel anything for him? I had a meeting with him last month. As Justin would say, he's looking very *buff*.'

'Never you mind. Anyway, forget Zac, I have to concentrate on keeping Jay cheerful, so I won't tell him I'm out of a job until it's absolutely definite.'

Olly put a finger to his lips to indicate they were sealed. 'So you might be looking for a job. Remind me what you did before you joined Oven Ready. Were you involved in Jay's fruit and veg business?'

Olivier and Justin had visited Four Seasons soon after I'd moved in with Jay and marvelled at the organic garden which supplied restaurants all over the county. But Olivier had become immersed in his budding TV career, so our paths had diverged until we'd arrived back here last December.

'Good heavens, no. I used to do sound healing. You never saw my geodesic dome, did you?'

'Your geo-*quoi*?'

So I gave him the lowdown on the dome and the labyrinth, and how much the healing clients had benefited from them, and was in the middle of telling him about my online magazine blog from the shepherd's hut, which had resulted in me being headhunted for *Straight Talking*, when Jay wandered back into the conservatory.

With a pretend serious face, he announced, 'As a broken man who's lost his home, his business and his libido, I'd like to say thanks for defending me – I think.'

I got up and kissed him full on the lips, filled to the brim with relief that he hadn't taken offence. The snog went on for longer than I'd anticipated and, when our bodies parted, I saw that Olivier had got to his feet.

'This programme sounds interesting. I need to watch it,' he said, his eyes twinkling. 'I leave you to it. Bye-bye, lovebirds.'

As soon as the front door closed, Jay beat his chest like Tarzan and made for the stairs. 'Race you upstairs, doll. Something's stirring down below.'

More than ready, I followed him upstairs and, let's just say, the following *coitus uninterruptus* was very satisfactory indeed.

* * *

On Monday morning I had to make my own way to the picket line outside the studios. I'd been feeling tired lately and finding it harder to drag myself out of bed in the mornings so I didn't hurry in. There was no point, anyway: I knew it wouldn't get us anywhere. When I arrived, I saw Gina and three others grouped at the entrance, being filmed for a local news item.

'Where've you been?' she hissed, when she saw me. 'Quick! Take this and I'll ask if they want you to say a few words. We've all done a vox pop.'

Bearing the placard she'd shoved into my hand – an A3 laminated sheet attached to a stick of bamboo which read: WE'VE BEEN STUFFED BY OVEN READY – I waited at the end of the line until a young reporter shoved a mike in my face and asked whether I felt we'd get anywhere by taking this action. 'Um, well. We hope so, otherwise we wouldn't be here.'

His head was nodding away like billyo, willing me to give him some usable footage. I couldn't think of anything more to say, so he asked another question. 'What's your objection to the new panellists, Pandora? Don't you think some younger faces would attract more viewers? Isn't it true that ratings have been dropping lately?'

'I don't object to younger people at all, but neither do I think people over fifty, especially women, should be put on the scrap heap. Between us, we've got a lot to offer...a lot of, er, experience of life.'

I'm glad to say he interrupted me at that point before I chugged to a complete halt. 'Talking of "veterans", I understand your partner, James Jay, is planning a reunion with the Jaylers some time soon. Any more news on that?'

Out of the corner of my eye I could see Gina exchanging eye signals of irritation with the other strikers because I'd allowed him to veer off-message. But so what, I thought. At least this was something I could talk about with conviction. 'Yes. Now that Ian's turned up they're going into rehearsal very soon. Jay and Donny have written some new material which they're itching to showcase. And if any of their fans want to support them, there's a website – just google James Jay and the Jaylers – where you can find out what they've been up to and leave a message to say whether you'd like to see them performing together again.'

'Great,' said the young man, barely concealing his relief that he'd got something worth broadcasting. 'You'll have to keep us posted.'

When he and the crew had packed up and gone, I asked Gina what the day's schedule would be. I didn't fancy standing outside like a lemon all day, with people smirking and staring at us.

'We wait till they leave the building. After that, we can disperse.'

I looked at my watch. It was eleven-fifteen. 'If they stay for the rundown, which they're bound to, they won't come out before one. Can't we go for a coffee and come back?'

The others had huddled round and added their voices to

mine, so we sent in former soap star Gary to chat up one of the cleaners to let us store our placards in the cleaning cupboard.

On the way to Starbucks, Gina told me that seven people, including herself, had opted to join the picket line but only five had turned up.

'So that means it's fifty-fifty,' I said. 'Half of us demonstrating, half of us not. It's hardly going to win our cause is it?'

'Is Kay doing anything to support us?' asked Ivanka, a pin-thin ballroom dancer who looked as if a puff of wind would blow her away.

The rest of us knew this was highly unlikely, Kay being a dyed-in-the-wool Oven Ready *apparatchik*.

'Not on your nelly,' said Gina, with a curl of her lip. 'Nobody told *her* she was on short time.'

'She could have come out in sympathy,' I bleated.

'Pansy, you should have learned by now, in this business it's every woman for herself. Or, in her case, dog eat dog.'

We spun out our time in the coffee house as long as possible before Gina ordered us back on duty. I'd assumed our protest would be conducted in polite silence but a few paparazzi had turned up and when the first of the new panellists emerged – a young soap actress who'd recently met her fictional end in a blazing warehouse – Gina couldn't resist playing to the gallery.

Waving her placard, she shouted, 'Out, out, out!'

The poor girl looked terrified as the photographers, vying for the best shot, blocked her way to a waiting car which roared away like a bat out of hell when a security guard was finally able to bundle her inside.

'Come on you lot,' said Gina, glaring at the rest of us accusingly. 'Let me hear you – this is why we're here. To PROTEST!'

'Wouldn't it look better if we reasoned with them?' said Trudy, glancing over at the paps. 'If we explain to them that what they're doing impacts upon our very lives, our standards of living...'

'Yada, yada, yada,' jeered Gina. 'How far do you think that would get you?'

At that moment, a young man I recognised as an erstwhile Blue Peter presenter came through the revolving doors. Trudy approached him, smiling like a loon, parting the photographers like the Red Sea. 'Good afternoon. Um, I'm sorry, I don't know your name. I was wondering if you realised that if you accept employment with this company, you're virtually taking our jobs.'

'Sod off, grandma,' he snarled, snatching Trudy's placard, snapping the bamboo support like a twig and hurling it to the ground. 'It's time you lot of old has-beens moved over and let the *real* talent in.'

'Scab!' cried Gina, the cameras flashing fit to bust, as a guard rushed forward to prevent the Blue Peter lout from snapping *her* in two as well.

Once the offending new panellist had been escorted to his vehicle, the security man gave us a proper talking to, advising us to picket silently or he'd have to call the police.

At the mention of the 'p' word, Trudy, Gary and Ivanka decided they'd had enough.

'Are you coming tomorrow?' demanded Gina, as they abandoned their placards.

'Doubt it,' muttered Gary. 'This is a waste of time. I'd be better off signing on.'

'Don't you think I've been insulted enough?' huffed Trudy, as she linked arms with Ivanka and headed in the direction of Waterloo station.

So it ended up with Gina and me standing mutely by, as Trevor and Kay left the building along with the last of the day's 'new blood', a Page Three pin-up girl and Big Brother contestant. They must have been told not to communicate because Kay put her nose in the air and ignored us. Trevor caught my eye and gave me a sympathetic wink, but I still felt ridiculous.

Predictably, Gina and I ended up lunching in the Raglan

Arms. She drank too much but I stuck to fruit juice. I didn't want to fall asleep on the train and miss my stop, as I had once before after an afternoon session.

The following day, nobody turned up to picket and Oven Ready Productions issued a statement saying they were sticking to their guns, but the strikers were welcome to return. So in the end, we swallowed our pride and drifted back to our reduced hours.

But one good thing came out of it. The Jaylers' website was inundated with fans clamouring to see and hear them again, which augured well for the comeback which Jay and his gang were hoping for.

Chapter 6 – Making Contact

I was chatting to Ivanka in her dressing room about a new tanning treatment she'd been testing for a feature in a celebrity magazine, when I got a call from Portia.

'Hello, Pandora. How are you?'

Pausing just long enough for me to say 'Fine,' she cut to the chase.

'There's a letter here for you. I was clearing out my in-tray and found it tucked away under a pile of expenses claims. I was wondering what you wanted me to do with it?'

'That depends,' I said, making a face for Ivanka's benefit, 'whether or not it's a redundancy letter.'

There was a pause followed by an impatient sigh. 'If it were, it wouldn't be in *my* in-tray, it'd be hand-delivered to you at the studio.'

'Okay, that's good to know. Any idea when I'll be getting that one?'

It was three weeks since the strike and Kay and Neesha had been noticeably cool towards those of us who'd protested. This had infected us with a *nothing left to lose* bravado, which extended to our dealings with the Oven Ready office as well. To say we were *personae non gratae* would be putting it mildly.

Ignoring my last remark, Portia pressed on. 'Would you like me to forward it to your home address or do you want to collect it in person?'

'What's the handwriting like? Does it look like it's from a nutter?'

The fan mail I'd received since I'd been a *Straight Talker* had been easily dealt with by a personally signed letter, thanking them for their interest. But one or two correspondents had been quite creepy. A man in Birmingham had sent me a picture of himself lying naked on a fur rug, describing what he wanted to do to me when we met up. For a laugh, I showed it to Jay who sent it back to him with a picture of a chainsaw, saying what he'd do to him if he wrote to me again. It makes you wonder who took the picture in the first place and what he told them he wanted it for.

'It's typewritten.'

'What's the postmark?'

'Oh for goodness' sake, Pandora, it's so faint it's impossible to make out. You'll be asking me to open it and read it to you next.'

I felt a slight sensation between my eyebrows. If my third eye was stirring, this must be something important.

'No, no need. I'll pick it up on my way home.'

'Good. I'll probably be at lunch so I'll leave it on my desk.'

'Tha...'

Before I had a chance to finish thanking her she'd rung off. I couldn't blame her. The Straight Talking show and its plunging audience figures were probably making life in the Oven Ready office fraught enough without cheeky, soon-to-be-ex employees wasting her time.

There were whispers going round the studios that the new 'young turks' weren't saving the sinking ship as hoped. It wasn't just their general gaucheness on camera, but the obvious enmity between us and them. Whereas before the shake-up Neesha had been encouraging us to be more dynamic and forceful, in the last three weeks Kay had been breaking up more on-air rows between back-biting panellists than she had in the history of the programme.

'I'd better shoot off,' I said. 'Go easy on the tan, Ivanka. Mahogany face, platinum hair – not a good look.'

She grinned, her teeth almost blinding me with their brilliance. 'You should try some, darlink, you're pale like a ghost. See you.'

Almost as soon as I'd asked Reception to call my car, it appeared at the kerb, chauffeured by a driver I hadn't seen before. I told him where I wanted to go and we sped away. As we neared the building, I asked if he could drop me and come back in five minutes, my plan being to pick up the letter and make a quick getaway home. But my voice was drowned out by the siren of an ambulance approaching from behind, now stuck behind us while the jammed-up road tried to rearrange itself to let him through.

I jumped out, lunging towards the front passenger door to knock on the window and give the driver my instruction, but the car accelerated away so quickly that I missed my chance.

Flustered at losing my ride home, I took the lift up to the second floor and walked into Portia's office, where my fluster level rose even further. Sitting at Portia's desk was Zac, conducting a phone call and jotting down notes on the back of an envelope. His office was at the end of the corridor so I hadn't expected to see him. He nodded in my direction, not looking in the least surprised to see me. We hadn't communicated since our chilly parting, following our curtailed session in his apartment, and I found myself blushing at the sight of him. He really was a dish. He motioned me to sit down, finishing his call shortly afterwards.

'Good afternoon, Pandora. To what do I owe this pleasure?'

Was I imagining it, or had he deliberately lingered on the last word?

'Portia rang me,' I said, trying to sound businesslike. 'She had a letter for me that came here. I've come to pick it up.'

Portia's desk was empty except for a computer and a tiered document tray which Zac began to search.

'She said she'd leave it *on* her desk.'

Leaning forward, I flipped over the envelope that Zac had been writing on. It was addressed to Ms P. Armstrong, c/o Oven Ready Productions.

'Whoops,' he said winningly. 'Do you mind if I keep the envelope?'

He opened a drawer and found a paperknife which he handed to me along with the envelope. He seemed as curious as I was about its contents, so when I unfolded the single sheet of paper it contained, I was careful to elevate it so he couldn't see. Today was June 1st – the letter was dated May 4th. It turned out to be something far more intriguing than a fan letter.

Dear Ms Armstrong,

We met recently in the Raglan Arms when I was looking for Miss Fraser. I hope you don't mind me contacting you – in fact, I'd like to ask you a favour.

As I'm close to completing the final draft of the Raymond Stone biography, I will soon be starting my next project, which is to take a selection of four or five musical groups popular in recent decades and write a section on each.

Have you guessed yet why I'm contacting you? I was wondering if you could have a word with your partner, James Jay, to see if he and his fellow musicians might be interested in being featured.

You can reach me at the phone number above. I hope to hear from you soon – otherwise I might have to track you down.

Yours,

Andrew Truman

I smiled when I read the tracking down bit. That's how he'd finally cornered Gina.

'Good news?' asked Zac when he saw me smiling.

'Possibly.'

Enjoying the opportunity to be mysterious, I handed him the envelope and put the letter in my bag.

We sat across the desk from each other, our smiles getting wider as we relaxed into the moment. My spirits had lifted since reading Truman's letter and I could sense Zac's energy responding to mine.

The lift pinged and two men, who I recognised as joint

Directors of Production, passed by the open door of Portia's office, waving when they saw us. The meaningful grins they exchanged with Zac weren't lost on me.

'Don't rush off,' Zac murmured to me, as he got up and followed them.

Five minutes later he appeared in the doorway, beckoning me outside.

'I'm on my break now...got a meeting with Ben and Greig at three. Fancy joining me for lunch?'

The hypothetical moral dilemma I'd been considering while he was away, of what I'd do if he wanted me to go back to his apartment again, disappeared in a puff of relief tinged with faint regret. It was getting on for two o'clock, so when he said 'lunch' he could only mean that.

I felt my left ear twitch.

You should have been nicer to him last time, whispered my mother. *This could be your redundancy interview.*

Feeling apprehensive, I followed him to the lift. 'If my car hadn't taken off before I could stop it, I'd be on my way home by now,' I said, in case he thought I'd hung around for illicit sex.

'Chace Standen's loss is my gain,' he said, with an engaging smile, as we descended.

He took me to an Italian place, close to the office, where the waiter greeted him by name and led us to a quiet table at the back of the restaurant. After we'd ordered, Zac clasped his hands and regarded me like a benign judge. 'So, Pandora. I'm sorry to say that something I told you in confidence seems to have found its way to the ears of the masses and become common knowledge. Rumours are rife about *Straight Talking* being on its last legs. What have you got to say for yourself?'

I felt myself go hot with guilt, which was crazy because I hadn't told anyone but Olivier.

'You mean, the bit about the TV channel pulling the plug at the end of June? I didn't leak it, Zac. The reporter who interviewed me on the picket line raised the subject of low ratings, not me.'

'Ah, the picket line. What on earth possessed you?' He clicked his tongue in mock disapproval and shook his head.

'Gina pressured me. You know what she's like. And it wasn't fair, bringing in the new people. It was bad manners – it made the regulars look like incompetents and we're not.' Bringing to mind a couple of veteran panellists who were borderline, I added, '...on the whole.'

He looked slightly taken aback. Maybe he'd expected me to hold up my hands and go quietly. 'You realise you've shot yourself in the foot for any further work, don't you? The others might emerge intact, their agents will do their best to rescue them but...'

He paused. I sensed he didn't want to hurt my feelings so I said what he was thinking. 'Don't worry, I've had that home truth from Gina. They're professionals with long CVs whereas I'm a nobody. I'm just somebody's wife, and not even that, really.'

A quagmire of self-pity was looming so I skirted round it and went for bravado. 'Anyway, who cares? It's all so trivial and tedious. And I'm fed up with getting up early.'

That made him laugh but I didn't join in.

'Quite frankly, I'm sick to death of the whole stupid business and the end can't come quickly enough for me. Anyway, with Jay getting the band back together, things are looking up.'

Zac took a sip of mineral water.

'Well, I'm glad *something's* coming up for him.' The look on his face told me he wasn't talking about career opportunities.

'As it happens, Zachary, normal service has now been resumed in that department, thank you very much.'

'So you won't be needing *my* services in future?'

His voice was ice cool but his eyes held a flash of fire.

I didn't answer immediately because I was too embarrassed. Sophisticates might be able to have sexual liaisons without strings but, if our last meeting was anything to go by, conducting a relationship along those lines didn't work for me. *Especially when there wasn't much sex to the liaison*, my inner voice carped.

'I'm sorry if you thought I was using you,' I said finally, a feeling of wretchedness engulfing me.

For the first time that day we touched, his hand reaching out and taking mine across the table. 'And I'm sorry if you felt the same,' he said, the expression in his eyes confirming the honesty in his words.

Then some people came and sat at the next table so we withdrew our hands and continued eating.

We spent the rest of the meal talking about our lives: in his case, how the business had grown and whether or not to sell out to the latest big fish who'd approached him; in my case, comparing the Jay family circumstances before and after the crisis.

'So how do you think your maternal experiment went?'

He was referring to my stint as a substitute mother to Jay's five children.

'They seemed to like me, but I don't know how much they actually needed me. Jay's mother was always the alpha female, although I *was* close to the two youngest.'

I felt a pang of loneliness when I thought of the busy household we'd had and the empty house I usually went home to now.

'Rowan's still only seventeen,' I sighed.

'But not living with you, you said.'

'No. We only see him every couple of weeks in term time. He splits his weekends between us and his brothers in Fulham. And I hardly see anything of the girls now. Actually, I began losing them once I started working for you.'

He looked concerned. 'In a roundabout way, I seem to have caused quite a bit of disruption.'

'Of course not, it was my decision. Anyway, the kids leaving home was bound to happen sometime. Nothing stays the same.'

He nodded, observing that his two older nephews going off to university had altered the household dynamics for his sister's family.

'Did you ever want children, Zac? Wouldn't you have liked an heir?'

He looked surprised at the question. 'No need. Luckily my sister's been very productive – three boys and a girl. Anything I've got when I turn up my toes will be divided between them.'

By now we were on to coffee, so I asked him a question I'd often seen in the celebrity gossip magazines I always pounced on at the hairdresser's. 'How would you sum up your life?'

'Let me see. Uh, happy childhood marred by boarding school; wine, women and song which started at university and more or less continued until recently; mediocre degree; rescued by uncle who took me into the business; good circle of male friends; broken engagement; broken heart; middle-aged and feeling it.'

I found the romantic history the most intriguing part of this summary. 'Who broke off the engagement?'

'Me, I'm afraid. I was into rugby then...she expected me to cancel matches for lunches with her parents. I just couldn't hack the idea of domesticity. Didn't seem like much fun.'

'So who broke your heart, the American girl?

He studied the tablecloth.

'Lauren? Good lord, no. It was someone I was keen on who went off with another bloke.'

'How long ago was that?'

'Five or six years.'

It must have happened just before or after we met. But before I could delve any deeper, he turned the spotlight on me. 'What about you? How would you sum up your life?'

'Grew up as an only child; parents divorced in my teens; met Jay, lived the high life, desperately tried to conceive; divorced Jay; married first love; widowed three years later; got involved with a spirit in the sky; got back with Jay; found I had a secret half-brother; am now in reduced circumstances, might be forced to go on the game.'

I'd only added the last bit to see if he was listening. He was, because he opened his eyes wide and tutted at me. 'What about starting up your therapy business again? Could you make a living out of it?'

Being a non-believer where the supernatural was concerned, Zac said this in the tone of someone who considered that any healing administered by a person without MD after their name was witchcraft.

'It's not that simple. I need the right space and a regular clientele.'

'You could go back to writing. A novel about warring panellists on a TV chat show, perhaps?'

'And what do I use for money while I'm writing it? Someone's got to pay the bills.'

'Doesn't Jay get any royalties?'

'Nothing significant. It's picked up since the band talked about a reunion. By the way, am I staying on till the death?'

'The death? Oh, you mean till the end of the show. Of course.'

'I thought you might have brought me here to fire me on the spot.'

'Why on earth would I do that? You need every penny you can get, don't you?'

He looked at his watch, frowned and asked the waiter for the bill. His concern at my impending economic downturn touched me. I walked the short distance back to the office with him and he bent to kiss my cheek. 'I'm sorry the show wasn't the success we'd hoped for, Pandora. But *we're* still good, aren't we?'

He looked sad and I wondered if he was feeling the same sorrow as me at the prospect of losing contact with a friend one was very fond of.

'Of course we're good,' I whispered. 'You'll always be a mate.'

But even as I said those words, I knew that from now on, finding a place in each other's lives would take a miracle.

* * *

When I got home, Jay wasn't around, so I took Fritz and Oscar for a long walk in the woods to clear my head. The meeting with Zac had churned me up. If only I hadn't slept with him at Christmas, I wouldn't be having all these mad thoughts of wishing I'd never got involved with Jay for the second time and had, instead, developed my relationship with him.

Forcing myself to think practical thoughts, I racked my brain for ideas about my next job. Cherry and Willow depended on me for rent and spending money so it had to be fairly lucrative, but by the time we crossed the road leading to the cottage, inspiration still hadn't struck.

Jay's car had appeared on the drive, so on the way in I took the letter out of my bag to show him. I found him in the living room, eyes closed, nursing the newspaper.

The past year had changed him. There were shadows under his eyes and his once silky, black hair was greying at the temples and seemed now to be a coarser texture. I'd suggested asking Rosemary for some elixir for him but he said he'd rather she used it on people like my half-brother, Theo, whose spinal injury was responding to the treatment.

This made me feel guilty, but I justified taking it myself for its general health-giving properties, and the need to look 'fresh' for the camera. The elixir had certainly lived up to its early promise of being an anti-ageing miracle and I found myself pretending to be younger than I was, to stop the people in Hair and Make-up asking for the name of the products I used.

'Are you interested in being featured in a book about musicians, Jay?' I said, as brightly as I could, feeling deeply ashamed for thinking those dark, disloyal thoughts: of wishing

I'd chosen Zac over him.

'What's that, babe?' he said, with a start.

'Did I tell you that Gina was asked to talk about Raymond Stone by a man who's writing his biography?'

Jay looked baffled and shook his head.

'Well anyway, he's written to me and he wants to know if you and the band are interested in being in his next book. Here, read it.'

Jay studied the letter and then went back to the beginning and read it again. 'What's he like, this bloke?'

'He's okay,' I said, trying to sound as if I'd scarcely noticed him. 'He's written quite a few books.'

A feeling of wanting to help Truman was pervading me, as it had when Gina was being difficult in the pub, but something told me if I was too enthusiastic, Jay would back away from doing it.

'What's this bit about tracking you down?' said Jay suspiciously.

'He's making a joke. Gina ignored his letter so he tracked her down to her local pub.'

'Did she tell him what he wanted to know?'

'She's not sure. They went to her place. After that it was a blur, apparently.'

'Sounds dodgy. He's not a rohypnol fiend, is he?'

Although he laughed when he said this, I detected a resistance to Truman. Maybe Jay suspected he was trying to get to me through him. Then my mind conjured an image of Truman's large, soulful eyes, which made me want to leap to his defence.

'I didn't believe her. She probably told him what he wanted, offered herself on a plate and he politely declined.'

'Made his excuses and left,' he said dryly, still watching for my reaction.

'Don't do it if you don't want to,' I said, taking a gamble that an attitude of indifference would indicate Truman was no threat.

Jay paused.

'Okay. Why not? Any publicity is—' He pointed his hands at me like a choir master signalling the chorus to come in.

'—good publicity,' I intoned, feeling a bit silly.

I went into the kitchen and started preparing the evening meal. Afterwards, when we were watching TV, I said, as nonchalantly as I could, 'Are you going to ring Andrew Truman?'

Jay yawned. 'It's too late now. I'll do it tomorrow – unless you want to? He's only asking for a yes or a no. You can do that, doll.'

We were side by side on the sofa and he snuggled my neck.

'You can pretend to be my PA if you like.'

'Okay, I'll ring him tomorrow,' I said, happy at the prospect of talking to Truman, but not sure why I was looking forward to it quite so much.

Chapter 7 – Cassiel

Jay got up from the table with a stretch of satisfaction. When I was around I always cooked him a breakfast fry-up; he was thin as a rake, so there was no excuse not to.

'I've been thinking, Andy. Better hold off ringing wotsisname till I check with Mick. You'd better give me the letter in case *he* wants to ring him.'

Owing to the band's recent burst of popularity, Jay's manager, Mick, now managed all of them. I felt a small pang of irritation that my letter was now being confiscated to show to him.

Hurriedly jotting down Truman's number on a pad, I gave the letter to Jay. 'Andrew Truman. That's his name.'

The look he gave me was contrite. 'Next time I'll remember it. I'll think of you, Andy, and Freddie Trueman, a great fast bowler. Word association – works every time.'

I should never underestimate Jay, I thought. His casual rock-dude exterior disguised a strong head and a sensitive heart. I kissed him goodbye and he went blithely off to join his gang in Hampstead.

I looked around for something to do. Having worked only six days in the last three weeks, I'd hoovered the fluff of ages from under all three beds, dusted the tops of all four wardrobes and scoured the grease off kitchen cabinets until there was no more scrubbing left to do. The solitude I'd sometimes craved at Four Seasons, where there was always something or someone to keep me busy, was mine at last in Phoenix Cottage. And I was bored.

Now you've got all this time on your hands, why don't you meditate? my inner life coach nagged.

But I'd got out of the habit. The early mornings and early nights that the show required, followed by the upheaval of the move, hadn't helped. More than that, though, I was suffering from a sort of spiritual *ennui* brought on by having to leave behind my precious healing spaces. Without the geodesic dome and the labyrinth – and the clients who came to me to benefit from them, I didn't have the heart to return to my healing, or any other spiritual practice for that matter.

These days I hardly even thought about the Violet Flame, whereas before I'd called upon it regularly. In fact, I'd used it all the time, silently invoking it to transmute negative energy as and when I came upon it – in public places, during family disagreements, as part of my clients' healing, and to combat my own negative feelings. You name it, I invoked the Violet Flame to transmute it: fear, anger, impatience, envy, depression were all blasted in violet fire and replaced, sometimes with difficulty, by thoughts of love and joy. If only I could regain that loving feeling but, to my shame, I'd let it slip away – temporarily, at least.

I was comforting myself with a mid-morning mug of hot chocolate, when Jay rang.

'Hey, darlin', that suggestion from *Andrew Truman...*' He emphasised the name and I was pleased he'd remembered. '...I ran it past the guys and they're all for it. Mick's keen too.'

'Good. So he's going to ring him, then?'

'He wants *you* to. He's got a busy schedule.'

'Either that or he can't be arsed.'

Jay sniggered. He was always amused when I used one of his expressions. 'So you'll do it?'

'Yes.'

'Sweet. And we've got some good news. A tour promoter's contacted Mick. For a reunion tour.'

Once upon a time this information would have caused a rush of blood to my head, but my present state of dejection meant it just got added to the heap of troubles weighing me down: like missing Willow, Rowan, Sharon, and the animals we couldn't bring with us; losing my job and having to look for another one; the unfinished business with Zac, etcetera, etcetera, etcetera.

'You mean a tour celebrating your reunion?'

'Yes and no. There's a few of us – all re-formed bands.'

'Sounds...interesting.'

'Yeah. We're stripping back some of our standards, then rebuilding them with some new arrangements. Letting them breathe.'

This sounded to me like pretentious jargon churned out by some publicity machine, so I answered in kind, adopting the accent of a Radio Four Arts interviewer. 'In the process of this reworking will you be bringing out facets of the songs that you hadn't previously known were there?'

'Abso-bloomin'-lutely. See you later, babe. Love you.'

'Yeah, wha'ever,' I said, in a bored teenager accent and he laughed.

I went into the study to find Truman's number. When he answered, I announced who I was and he thanked me for calling. I told him that Jay and the Jaylers would be happy to cooperate and he expressed his gratitude.

'Can we meet?' he said.

'You mean you and Jay?'

'No, you and me.'

I was taken aback and flattered in equal measure. 'Okay,' I said almost without hesitation.

I paused, waiting to hear the story that he'd no doubt devised as a pretext for us to meet. It'd be asking me to give him a few notes about Jay's early life, something like that. My mind worked like lightning as I waited for his reply, imagining further meetings, stolen kisses, inevitably leading to something even steamier in his pied-à-terre.

My massively inappropriate Mills & Boon fantasy was shattered by an announcement which took my breath away. 'I'm wearing my other hat today, speaking as Cassiel, the director of the Enoch Society Correspondence Course. As a graduate, you may want to help us. There's something I'd like to run past you.'

'Is this a joke?' I said, when I got my breath back.

'No. This is genuine. I'd prefer to explain in person. Can I come and see you?'

Disappointment and disbelief fought for supremacy as I struggled to comprehend what was happening. 'I suppose so. But how can you be Archangel Cassiel if you're Truman?'

'I'm his corporeal custodian at present. I'll explain everything when I see you.'

His voice had a hypnotic quality and I found myself inviting him to come at two o'clock and giving him directions to my home.

'Thanks. I'll need to transmit a download of data to put you in the picture. You'll feel as if you're in a trance, so please make sure, as far as possible, that we'll be undisturbed.'

'I will.'

He ended the phone call and I sat down to digest what had happened. Oscar came and sat beside me on the sofa and I kissed his silky head.

'How can an angel also be a flesh-and-blood man? And what on earth can he want me to do, Oscar?'

Oscar didn't have any explanation, but he offered up his tummy to be stroked, which calmed me down a bit. After a while, I went to my bureau and took out the folder which held the Enoch Society Correspondence Course. There had only been three levels, the most important of which was the third, entitled 'Renewal', which required me to meditate every night for two weeks from the new moon to the full moon, to anoint myself with sacred chrism and, hey presto, to emerge reborn like a phoenix with a responsibility to help and heal others. I started to read the letter that had accompanied the final unit. It was more than five years since I'd completed the course, and it felt as if I was reading parts of it for the first time.

The opening paragraph reminded me of how I'd felt after my second husband, Mike, had died and how the course had helped me overcome the sadness that had crushed me then. *This unit aims to connect you to higher planes of awareness, enabling you to complete the release from despair and depression suffered by those who are shackled to negative memories of the past.*

There followed details of the herbs used in the chrism: the same ones the phoenix gathered before self-immolating – the bird's new self rising from the ashes of the old.

If you anoint yourself with this chrism, as directed, your sadness will be replaced by hope. Your old, programmed ways of thinking and behaving will die and your new paradigm – your pattern of seeing the world – will emerge. You will have reached the position of an anointed one, anointed with chrism, from which the word 'Christ' comes.

But like all strong medicine it came with a warning.

Finally, before you make the decision to finish the course and proceed into a state of spiritual rebirth, please consider what you are taking on, for there comes with it a responsibility to help and heal others.

I had an attack of conscience when I read this. I could hardly call being a *Straight Talker* 'helping and healing' when most of it had turned out to be smarming over celebrities promoting their wares. So much for my idea of introducing subjects like mindfulness and alternative therapies – whenever I'd tried it, I'd been told to stay on message, in tune with the pre-show guidelines.

The next paragraph reminded me how I had to keep to my side of the bargain.

This does not mean you have to give up your life and go to work among the poor and suffering of the world. Although some have. No, there is no need to change your life radically. But you will be expected to consciously maintain your enlightened way of thinking and behaving by meditating regularly, eating healthily, exercising your physical body and avoiding alcohol and other addictive habits. Otherwise you risk sinking back into unhealthy ways of thinking and your newly achieved, ideal paradigm, will be compromised.

Oh, shoot, I thought, stalling on the 'meditating regularly' bit. *I wonder if Cassiel's been sent round to give me a talking-to on the dereliction of my divine duty.*

The sheet of paper I was holding began to tremble: I was experiencing a feeling close to the one I'd had when I thought Zac was going to prematurely sack me, only this sacking would probably keep me in Purgatory till the end of time.

I read on to the end, remembering how baffled I'd been at first about how I'd put the 'helping and healing' into practice.

Know that once you have become spiritually awakened, you must make a conscious effort to transform any difficult situations by your very presence. You will have the power to do this because you will be filled with light (en-lightened). Your function will be to raise the energy of any person or situation that crosses your path simply by focusing on your Oneness with All That Is. In this way, you will help others with their soul evolution.

All this will become clearer to you once the process has been accomplished.

I hope our correspondence has been, and will be, of help to you in your hour of need. It only remains for me to wish you Godspeed in your endeavours to bring harmony and balance into your life and into the lives of others.

Cassiel.

I'd contacted Enoch, the big kahuna himself, a few months after I'd performed the sixteen enlightenment meditations, to complain that, although I'd officially 'graduated', the course hadn't shown me exactly what I had to do to be a healer. He'd explained that enlightened individuals are expected to discover that for themselves. Nevertheless, he took pity on me and told me about the Violet Flame and how to apply it. Shortly afterwards, I chanced upon some information about sound healing, and those two healing methods had proved to be the answer. Once I'd sorted myself out and starting practising, I'd been very happy.

And then my mother had died; I'd got jealous of Jay working with *femme fatale* Gaby Laing; joined *Straight Talking* in retaliation; and it had sort of gone downhill from there.

I replaced the folder in the bureau drawer, put on my walking shoes and called the dogs. By the time I'd given them a run long enough to tire them out so they wouldn't disturb my 'download' with Truman, alias Cassiel, or whoever he was, the morning had gone.

* * *

The knock at the door came on the dot of two. Both dogs surged forward to see who it was but instead of barking at the stranger, they quietened down and trotted away to resume their sunbathing. As I greeted him, I caught the sweet aroma of cinnamon.

He was dressed more casually than he had been in the pub: a soft, blue shirt, light-brown chinos and navy linen jacket doing a lot more for him than the crumpled suit had. But now I knew he wasn't what he seemed, this was nothing more on my part than a neutral observation.

I took him into the living room and asked if he wanted a drink and he said he'd have some tea. My hands were shaking when I gave it to him.

My main experience of the invisible world had occurred not long after I was widowed, when I'd started receiving messages from Enoch, ending after a few months as quickly as it had begun. My only previous contact with Cassiel, who had worked in collaboration with Enoch, had been one phone call in answer to an advertisement for the correspondence course, followed by the course units, sent through the post, along with his written comments.

I'd accepted these incongruities then, because in my bones I'd felt them to be authentic. But believing that a flesh-and-blood human was also an angel was a different kettle of fish. I'd always understood that we were a completely different species.

Truman/Cassiel motioned me to sit down. 'You see me as a man but beneath this skin I am Archangel Cassiel.'

His voice sounded like Truman's but he was speaking with more authority.

'I'm confused. How can you be both? I don't see any feathers.'

'That's because we don't have any. Artists like El Greco gave us wings, presumably because they thought we needed them to fly back and forth to paradise.' He smiled. 'Ridiculous, of course, but artists deal in symbols, so quite understandable.'

'I knew that, I was just testing you.'

He nodded his head rapidly, as if willing me stop talking so he could get on with whatever it was he wanted to say. 'Let me explain. Archangels are God's means of interacting with the physical world. In exceptional circumstances, He will direct us to come to Earth to deliver a message or carry out a mission.'

'You mean like the Angel Gabriel when he visited Mary to tell her she would conceive the son of God?'

'Yes, he manifested into human form to deliver a brief message. But my embodiment is different. I must stay on Earth for some months until my mission is fulfilled. For that reason I had to take over someone's identity. This was so I could live as a human with ready-made documentation: a passport, driving licence, etcetera. And, of course, a place to live.'

'How does it work?' I asked, wondering if Cassiel was dosing Truman with a soma-like drug, galvanizing his body without his knowledge while he was 'asleep'.

Cassiel grasped his hands together and rested his elbows on the arms of the chair, holding my gaze steadily as if to capture every iota of my attention.

'While he slept, I took his spirit to rest in a place of tranquillity on the inner planes. Then my being occupied his body.'

I shuddered. This was beginning to sound like an *Invasion of the Body Snatchers* movie.

'What does your "being" look like? What would I see if you didn't have Truman's body?'

'Aah,' he said, his wide brow wrinkling slightly. 'Not everyone would be able to see an image, but you would probably perceive an orange orb of light. Other archangels have different-coloured rays.'

'And what about Truman, does his spirit know what's happening to him?'

'No. His essence is in a state of, for want of a better term, suspended animation.'

'Didn't his family notice any difference in him?'

'Not at all. I adopted his mannerisms, continued his normal life, his work. It's a condition of the embodiment that I do nothing to disrupt his life, his relationships...'

'But suppose he'd still been married? You'd have had to...'

I didn't quite know how to put it but Cassiel was surprisingly frank.

'Perform his marital duties. Yes. Why not? An act of love is wondrous to the angelic realm, in whatever form.'

The memory of Gina's words flashed into my mind. *I must have fallen asleep. When I woke up he wasn't there. What happened is anybody's guess.*

'Did you sleep with Gina?'

He looked surprised at the question, but nonetheless answered it.

'No. Sexual intercourse would not have been an expression of love on her part, and therefore not on mine.'

How ironic, I thought, that the irrational jealousy I'd felt at the thought of Truman and Gina together had been so totally misplaced.

'Well,' he said, getting up and fetching a chair from the kitchen, 'are you ready for the download?'

'What's it for, exactly?'

'You'll see,' he said, sitting me down and placing his hands on my shoulders. 'Close your eyes, empty your mind and focus on your third eye.'

Chapter 8 – Revelations

As Cassiel's words died away, I found myself sitting in a sort of cinema, watching scenes playing out on-screen like a newsreel. The scenes were shadowy: faces and places were blurred. But one thing was certain, I recognised myself as one of the players.

I saw a baby being taken from her birth mother. I watched that child growing up strong of limb, mind and spirit. I saw her advising on projects for a global health organisation and travelling the world as a peace ambassador. At this point the images faded and I felt myself sinking into sleep.

'You can wake up now, Pandora.'

Cassiel handed me a glass of water and some tissues which I used to dry my eyes. Finally, I was composed enough to speak. 'Is that some sort of alternative reality you've shown me?'

'It could be. No future is absolutely certain.'

I was so shaken at the very idea of what the 'newsreel' had demonstrated that I raised my voice in a way no polite person should to an angel.

'How can *I* possibly give birth? First of all, I've never been able to get pregnant, and second of all, I'm too old anyway. So what I saw is impossible – it'd have to be a double miracle.'

I half expected him to say, *I deal in miracles, that's why I'm here*, like a character in a bad movie. Instead, he looked up at the ceiling and smiled. 'St Elizabeth was past childbearing age when she conceived John the Baptist. A woman of your age gave birth to a child last year after IVF treatment and I believe your own mother had a second child some years after you were born.'

At his words, my original pain at the revelation that my mother had secretly given birth to a baby boy, leaving him in America with his father's wider family, re-emerged from the depths of my subconscious and clasped my chest like a vice.

'But I'm not like my mother,' I cried. 'Why would I want to go through all that and give the baby up?'

I started sobbing again at the idea that I could abandon a child as my mother had abandoned Theo. In response, Cassiel stood behind me and placed his hands on my forehead, uttering some unintelligible sounds which quickly had a soothing effect.

Once I was calmer, he told me that it was written that this child should be born in the Gregorian year 2009, of a woman who had undergone the process of enlightenment and a father of strong stock. Because the birth of this child was so important to the future of the planet, he had been given the job of ensuring that the prophecy came to pass.

'Are you saying that it matters more who the mother is, than the father?' I said.

'Up to a point. The requirement is that he's sound in mind and body. The child needs a good genetic blueprint so she can live a long and useful life. She'll inherit her spiritual legacy from her mother and also bring with her some knowledge from her stellar lineage. This will equip her for her own path to enlightenment, necessary for her work in raising the light of the world.'

He continued his story, telling me that he'd approached some young women, in the way Angel Gabriel had approached Mary, by appearing briefly in a vision. The first two had refused but the third, a young African woman living in Paris, had accepted. She stopped taking the contraceptive pill but failed to conceive. Time was running out, so he searched for another willing candidate. This time he found one in New Zealand, but she miscarried early in December 2008. Remembering me from the correspondence course, he attempted a visitation by means of a vision, but because I'd neglected my spiritual practice he couldn't get through to me to deliver the request.

'So,' he said, sounding serious. 'I had to refer to the Highest Authority to verify that the project could go ahead without your prior consent. Permission was granted because this child is destined to become a beacon of light whose actions will bring great blessings to planet Earth, assisting in its evolution and that of its population.'

'Stop right there,' I cried. 'The answer is no. I have no intention of having a child and giving her up.' My voice slid out of control, rising into a wail. 'And Jay would absolutely forbid it, anyway! Do you think he would stand by and let her go?'

He regarded me with a look of compassion.

'Do you not understand, Pandora? You are already pregnant. The sacred elixir prepared your body by healing the energy blockage in your reproductive system and rejuvenating your cells. Your womb is healthy and so is the child who rests within it.'

'How dare you!' I shouted, my mind almost exploding. 'How in God's name was this allowed to happen?' Realising, as I said it, that I was answering my own question.

Cassiel made some small movements with his hands, at the same time uttering more incomprehensible incantations, continuing until I'd calmed down enough to receive the next barrage of unwelcome news.

'You conceived on Christmas Eve.'

Christmas Eve? That was a good five months ago – no wonder my waistline had been expanding. My sex life with Jay had been deactivated at that time. There was only one other person I'd slept with, and that was after the Oven Ready Christmas party. I put my head in my hands and groaned.

'Then Zac must be the father.'

This realisation put me on the back foot, as I felt my cheeks grow hot, remembering that the God of the Old Testament hadn't been too keen on fornication. But Cassiel seemed unperturbed.

'Is he of good stock?'

I felt like saying, *No, he's a complete flake physically and mentally*, just so I could keep the baby, but I knew that wouldn't fool him.

'Yes. Probably better than Jay. I don't think Zac was ever an addict. Although Jay's been clean for years,' I added hastily, not wanting to sound too disloyal.

Cassiel stilled himself and appeared to be verifying this information. After a while he opened his eyes and nodded. 'It appears you chose wisely.'

'That's all very well, but I meant what I said before. If you *had* asked me in advance, I'd never have agreed to it. Now you've put me in an impossible position – forcing me to have a child which I'll have to give up, and destroying my relationship in the process.'

Cassiel had the grace to look embarrassed. 'We are extremely sorry for this lapse in protocol. When it became obvious that you couldn't be contacted by a vision, I was directed to embody on Earth. Once I found a suitable subject to inhabit, I was to make myself known to you and ask you to enter into a sacred contract: a promise from you to surrender the child at birth. But finding a suitable subject to occupy on the Earth plane took longer than expected. By the time I became the custodian of Andrew Truman's body, the conception had already taken place.'

The words 'surrender the child' burned like hot coals into my heart and every cell of that organ fought against the very suggestion of such a thing.

'Then if, as you say, I *am* pregnant, since I didn't agree in advance to give her up, how can you stop me from keeping her after she's born?'

Cassiel must have truly felt my heartache because the blood drained from his face. I thought he was going to faint so I gave him my glass of water to sip from. When he had composed himself he apologised for his weakness. 'I'm afraid I'm not fully used to the human emotions that sometimes grip Truman's senses. I have yet to master the art of observing his reactions without being overwhelmed by them.'

I wasn't surprised at what he was telling me. Being a different species with a natural existence in a rarefied atmosphere of love, peace and joy, he must find the emotional highs and lows experienced by humans to be quite incapacitating. After all, using Truman's body meant he had to deal with all the feelings locked into his cells as well. As a devotee of the Violet Flame, albeit a lapsed one, I understood that all too well.

'To answer your question,' he went on, when he'd finally got his, or rather Truman's, colour back, 'the conception itself was influenced, as you might say, by remote control. At the moment the egg was fertilised, the child you carry was endowed with special talents which raise her above the commonplace. She must be nurtured in an environment fit for her future position in the world. If you keep her, she won't have those necessary advantages.'

It wasn't the answer I wanted, yet I wasn't ready to give up easily. 'But if you tell me what she needs to realise her potential, I'll do everything to see she goes to the right school, the best university...'

Cassiel's raised hand brought me to a halt. 'You must think of her as a Western Dalai Lama: a child taken from the natural parents to be initiated from an early age into spiritual and temporal matters. The difference is, she will never know her true family.'

'Will you tell me where she goes?'

He shook his head and looked sad. 'I can only tell you that she is to be placed immediately after birth in the home of an enlightened one who holds high office. His wife is feigning pregnancy so the baby can be registered as theirs. It is important that she grows up in an environment where contact with luminaries from many spheres of influence is a natural occurrence. Her life will be dedicated to service – the service of humankind: their network of family connections and contacts will open many doors, enabling her work to spread more widely across the globe.'

'Why couldn't his wife have conceived the child? Isn't she enlightened enough?' I said, bitterly.

Cassiel gave me a look which conveyed that he considered sarcasm the lowest form of wit. 'She has a condition of the endometrium. They are childless.'

I suffered a pang of guilt then, but my blood was up. 'Suppose I decided to save my relationship with Jay and not have this child? What could you do about it?'

'Nothing,' he sighed. 'I only wish you had replied to my letter sooner. You're about to enter your twenty-fourth week of pregnancy. If you feel unable to go through with it because it would lead to an estrangement between you and your husband, you'll have to act quickly. You have only a few days left.'

When he said these words his eyes filled with tears and so did mine. That was when I knew I wanted to give birth to this baby, even if I had to give her up as soon as she was born.

'Jay's not my husband now. We were never officially remarried,' I said, hoarse from trying to hold back the sobs that the thought of aborting this child had triggered. 'I will go through with the birth. But I haven't a clue how I'm going to explain it all to him.'

'I cannot intercede for you,' he answered, his eyes dark with sympathy. 'When I meet him, I will be in the persona of Andrew Truman and our interaction will be strictly professional.'

'So what am I supposed to tell everyone?'

He looked perplexed and distressed in equal measure, and I actually found myself feeling sorry for him. Having finally tracked me down, instead of being acclaimed as the bearer of good tidings of great joy (in theory, I should have been ecstatic that the fruit of my womb was destined to be a saviour of the world), he'd brought a whole load of trouble to my door. 'I will need to take guidance on this matter. Earthbound as I am, I cannot see the bigger picture as my cohorts can. As soon as I know more, I will write to you. In the meantime, say nothing, but be assured that we are with you.'

When he stood up he seemed taller than before and his face

seemed to glow. 'Please be aware that our admiration for your courageous decision knows no bounds.'

I was prepared for further grandiloquence, resembling the lofty prose I'd transcribed from Enoch in my automatic writing days, but instead he issued me with a final instruction.

'When we speak in private, you may call me Cassiel. At all other times, please remember to address me as Andrew Truman.'

Then he gave an almost imperceptible shake of his shoulders, as if shrugging off a light cloak and resorted to being Truman, speaking his parting words in a completely different tone. 'Could you ask James to give me a ring? I have a place in London where we could meet to discuss what to include in the book.'

As soon as he'd gone I found a pregnancy calculator on the internet and typed December 24th in the box marked 'date of conception'. The due date came out as on or around September 16th. This meant I only had fifteen weeks to go. As Cassiel had said, the foetus was twenty-three weeks old. Further googling revealed her to be the size and shape of a small doll, weighing slightly over a pound. The scary bit was that in the next four weeks the baby's weight should double and from week twenty-seven the mother's weight-gain would really accelerate. *Uh-oh*, I thought, *how am I going to explain this away to friends, family and the yoga group?*

At first I considered confessing everything to Jay, but the idea of admitting that Zac had been the sperm donor put paid to that idea. Another option was to keep the pregnancy secret from him, but that would mean separating for the best part of four months and I couldn't think of any excuse acceptable enough to pull that off.

Conscious now of the true reason for my expanding belly, I dug out an apron and tied it loosely to conceal my little bump. When, in my innocence, I'd bemoaned my 'spare tyre' during our recent resumption of sexual relations, Jay had kissed it and said he liked it. Now it was the last thing I wanted to draw attention to.

While preparing dinner, I deliberately tuned the radio to a current affairs programme, something I could focus on to block out the yammer of possible scenarios over the coming months, each fighting for ascendancy in my head. When I heard Jay's car draw up, an unfamiliar feeling of dread seized me. He came into the kitchen and took a bottle of beer out of the fridge, kissing me on the cheek as he passed.

'Great news about the tour, babe. Even Eddie's getting excited. Did you contact Andrew Truman?'

'Yes,' I said brightly, trying to match the buoyancy of his mood. 'He wants you to ring him to arrange a meeting. He's got a place in London, so it should be easy.'

'Okay, no time like the present. Have you got his number? I left the letter at Donny's.'

'It's written on the pad, on my desk.'

Hearing Jay speaking to Truman and arranging to see him on Friday made me feel almost jealous. I desperately wanted Truman's body double, Cassiel, to confer with his mates 'upstairs' and get back to me a.s.a.p. to recommend my best course of action. It was all I could think of, especially as the evening ahead would be spent with the very person who was going to be the most injured by whatever action I ended up taking.

* * *

The next day was hard but I managed to get through it by offering to help Olivier. He was trying out some recipes for his next book so he set me the task of measuring out the ingredients and being second taster of the end products.

'Next time, Pandora, maybe just taste 'alf,' he advised, as I polished off a most delicious raspberry and violet cream mille-feuille. 'You are getting a "jelly belly", as Justin would say.'

I could almost feel my chin hit the ground. I'd purposely worn my shapewear jeans, bought when I first went up a size, combined with a loose-fitting tunic, topped off with the chef's apron that Olivier had given me. If my bump was still obvious, I might have to resort to belly binding. I'd stayed up quite late researching pregnancy on the internet so had become familiar with all sorts of previously unheard of gestation facts and practices.

While this was going through my mind, Olly was busy noting down our observations on the pastry we'd just sampled. When he looked up, he was met with the sight of me in tears. 'What's wrong? I didn't mean to upset you, darling.'

I shook my head. 'Don't take any notice of me, Olly, I'm hormonal.'

'Ah, I see. *La ménopause*. That's why your silhouette is changing.'

I didn't answer, so he continued.

'I thought perhaps you were overeating to compensate for Jay's insufficiency.'

This remark was accompanied by a purse of the lips and a knowing wink, but in my befuddled state, I had to think hard about what he was referring to. Then I recalled Jay repeating, in front of Olivier, what I'd said on *Straight Talking* – that he was a broken man who'd lost his home, his business and his libido.

'In the *boudoir*,' prompted Olivier.

'You mean about him being impotent? That's no longer true...not since the band got back together. There's even talk of a tour, so you were right to be optimistic about the reunion. The impossible actually seems possible now.'

(*In more ways than one*, I couldn't help thinking, gloomily.)

He beamed. 'Congratulations. I'm 'appy for you both.' He paused, presumably assessing how far he could go. 'You don't have to look elsewhere now.'

'What do you mean?'

I felt a flush creeping northwards from my neck, traversing my ears, and landing on my cheeks. Olivier was very astute and, having been around when I'd first fallen for Zac, knew our previous history.

'*Amour l'après-midi*? The day your hours were cut, you said you'd seen Zac in the afternoon. I noticed you were a little...preoccupied.'

'Okay, I admit we had just been together, but he was called back to the office because of the strike, so nothing really happened. Not on that day, anyway.'

He got up and opened one of the cupboards, revealing an array of alcoholic drinks. 'I think Jay's good news calls for a little snifter. What would you like?'

I was about to ask for a brandy and ginger ale, to calm my nerves, when I realised that I shouldn't be drinking at all. 'No thanks, Olly.'

He brought a bottle of Scotch whisky to the table and two glasses. 'If you change your mind,' he said, nodding towards the second glass.

In the wake of the Zac disclosure, the urge to confide further became too strong to deny, and I heard myself saying: 'I can't. I'm pregnant.'

Chapter 9 – Breathing In

I had to go to work on Friday. Gina wasn't in, so I was spared having to make excuses for not staying on afterwards. Bob, the only driver employed directly by Oven Ready Productions, drove me home to Phoenix Cottage and followed me indoors for his usual cup of tea to break up the journey. Fritz and Oscar greeted us as effusively as ever, and the sight of them set me off worrying about how they would cope if I had to go into hiding.

On the hall table, I found a note from Jay saying he'd cancelled his meeting with Andrew Truman today after Linden had called to say there was no hot water in their flat. Jay was quite a handyman and he could often work his magic on old boilers (no pun intended), leaky taps and the like. The note also told me that he'd walked the dogs. As I hadn't slept much the past couple of nights, for once I was pleased to be relieved of that duty.

'There won't be many more trips like this, miss,' said Bob, relaxing into an armchair in the living room, 'now *Straight Talking*'s been axed.'

Up to now, I'd only been aware of the show's demise as a strong possibility but Bob was talking about it as a done deal.

'Is it official?'

'So I've heard. Advertising's hit rock bottom. It won't be coming back in the autumn, that's for sure. According to the viewers, you panellists are too pale, stale and female.'

I was in the act of pouring the milk, my involuntary snort of laughter at his words jerking the jug forward so Bob's teacup now swam in a saucer of milk.

'Go easy, miss. It wasn't that funny.'

Swapping saucers, I offered him a biscuit, hoping to encourage further revelations. 'But we've got till the end of the month, haven't we?'

He nodded. 'Have you got anything lined up, miss?'

I could hardly tell him I'd be heavily involved in a production of my own, so I hedged the question.

'How do you know all this, Bob?'

He winked as he bit into his second Jammy Dodger. They were Jay's favourites and all I had. 'I drive Mr Willoughby and the directors all the time. They talk business in the back. They think I can't hear, but I've got ways and means.'

He tapped his nose and I wondered if Bob had the Mercedes bugged. 'I know a heck of a lot more than some o' them producers. Like who's for the chop and what's replacing the shows that turn out to be duds.'

'So are all the *Straight Talking* personnel for the chop, including Kay?'

'Every last one of 'em, from what I've heard. They've got a new soap in the pipeline to replace it, set in a London street. It's got a mixture of people, mellinge, they call it.'

'Mélange.'

'That's what I said. There's a Polish couple: he's a builder, she's a nanny. There's an illegal with forged documents working as a cleaner in a hospital, lodging with a lesbian school teacher who thinks he's a student.'

Bob dunked his Jammy Dodger and warmed to his theme.

'Then there's the investment banker and his family – they've got that Shakespearean actor, you know, the one that drinks, lined up for him. And there's a corner shop, run by Asians, naturally. There'll be all sorts in it. It's supposed to reflect the diversity of modern society.'

'Is it set in the East End?' I asked, feeling a bit miffed that Zac hadn't mentioned it to me.

'It's supposed to be round Notting Hill way.' He gave a pantomime wink. 'So nobody's toes get trodden on. They're calling it *Peeler Street*.'

The toes he was referring to belonged to the producers of *EastEnders*, a popular soap opera of many years' standing, on which *Straight Talker* Gary had served time.

'Maybe Gary could audition for it,' I said slyly, hoping for more gossip which I could pass on to my mates. 'Or even Gina. She can do accents. She could play posh or common.'

'They've already filmed a pilot episode so they've missed the boat,' he said dismissively. 'Anyway, the management's keen on bringing in "fresh new faces".'

He rose, picking up his chauffeur's cap from the hall table, his expression indicating that the *Straight Talking* chat show and its panel would soon be yesterday's news.

'Thanks for the tea, miss. See you next week.'

I was about to close the front door when I saw a postman approaching the house, so I waited to take the mail he brought. There was a plain white envelope addressed to me in familiar spidery handwriting which I opened with trepidation. As I'd guessed, the letter was from Cassiel.

Dear Pandora,

I have taken guidance from Head Office and their instructions are as follows:

Please resume meditating for both your own sake and that of the child.

Do not visit your family doctor. It is important that the child cannot be traced to you, so you must stay outside the National Health system.

We will therefore engage a midwife who will see you through your pregnancy and assist in the handover.

Please continue to take the elixir of life.

If necessary, remove yourself from any stressful situation while the foetus is developing in your womb.

Take care to confide only in trusted friends.

I have placed an advertisement for a midwife. In the meantime, your decision to tell your life partner of your pregnancy has to be considered carefully. Whatever you decide to do, it is imperative that you do not reveal my true identity to him. My mission is to stay on the material plane until the child has been safely delivered and this can only be achieved if I continue to 'be' Andrew Truman.

Once again, I can only apologise for the unhappy situation you find yourself in. Know that we are with you.

Blessings,

Cassiel

P.S. I have enclosed my card. Please text me your mobile phone number.

I put down the letter and considered the contents. It had answered some of my questions, but the biggest of all – whether and what to tell Jay – still remained a mystery.

I put the small card, inscribed with the name *Andrew Truman* and his personal phone number, in a card slot in my purse.

My phone rang. It was Olivier.

It was a relief to hear from him. I was beginning to worry that he thought I was deluded after I'd revealed all to him on Wednesday afternoon. But I'd felt I had to. The story wouldn't have made sense otherwise. At first he'd been sceptical about everything, especially Cassiel. But it helped that he'd read my novel, a thinly disguised autobiography about a woman who communicated with an ascended being via automatic writing and had, almost by accident, become enlightened. His next question had been how on earth, after all these years, I could have got pregnant. So I'd had to disobey Rosemary and come clean about the elixir of life. His eyes had gleamed at the thought of it, until I broke the news that she only gives it to people who are sick, or those who'd been present at the original ceremony.

'Hi, Olly, good to hear from you.'

'Hello, Pandora, or should I call you *Madonna* now?'

'Call me what you like, just don't ask me to sing "Like a Virgin".'

He guffawed in my ear. 'Are you all right?'

'Yes, not too bad. I've just had a letter from Cassiel. He's trying to arrange a private midwife. It's all got to be hush-hush and outside the system. Otherwise, if people see me pregnant and then there's no baby, they'll start asking awkward questions.'

'Don't worry, chérie, my lips are sealed, even from Justin. Have you told Jay anything yet?'

'No. I was waiting to hear from Cassiel. He doesn't seem too keen on Jay knowing I'm pregnant.'

'Well, if he does find out, remember, you can stay with us if he turns nasty.'

The idea of Jay turning nasty hadn't entered my head: going cool and distant, yes, but not violent. Although with all the stress of the past year, maybe this might be the tipping point. A vision of Jay upturning tables and chairs in a jealous rage provoked me to a swift decision.

'Thanks, sweetie, but he can't find out, so the only option is to leave before the bump becomes obvious.'

I heard myself saying these words as if I was talking about someone else. Olivier's intake of breath suggested that he was more shocked than I was. 'You mean, for always?'

'I hope not.'

'So when you come back, you'll say what?'

'I don't know. I'll have to think of something convincing.'

Olivier emitted a short, French articulation which came across as: *I doubt very much your ability to do that.*

'Staying isn't an option, Olly.'

'But where will you go?'

'Probably Glastonbury. I can't go to Charles because Jay would find me there. I could rent a house in the area, though.'

'But then you'd be seen by others. Jay's mother lives in Glastonbury, no?'

'Oh God, I forgot about Sharon.'

'Darling, you need to make a plan. At least you're not too *grosse*. You can get away with it for a couple more weeks.'

'Do you really think so? I'm beginning to feel like a pot-bellied pig.'

He laughed. 'More like a python who swallowed a football.'

This wasn't the assurance I was seeking. 'Whatever happens, I'll keep you posted. I'd better go. Cassiel said I had to start meditating again. Maybe inspiration will strike.'

'Bye-bye, chérie, promise me you'll ring if you need an emergency bed.'

That made me think of an Accident & Emergency unit, so I thrust that thought out of my mind, said goodbye and made for the study.

At first I couldn't find a candle, despite searching every drawer in the room, but then I remembered the glass Art Deco candlestick on the mantelpiece in the living room which held two pale blue candles. I carried it back to my desk and lit both. Normally it would have been just one but the *hausfrau* in me wanted to see the candles matched in length at the end of the session.

I switched off the overhead light, closed my eyes, emptied my mind and imagined a column of white light entering the crown of my head and extending down through my body deep into the centre of the earth.

Focusing on my breathing, I took my attention to the place between my eyebrows, 'watching' the retinal purple pigment slowly build up behind my closed lids. Once the backdrop was established, an ancient eye appeared. I'm used to seeing this eye. It looks like the eye of a bird, beadily opening and closing. On other occasions, when it opens wider, it's more like the big, beautiful eye of a horse. I try to focus on it but it never stays still long enough for me to get a good, uninterrupted look at it. An ophthalmologist could probably explain the image away but I like to think of it as the 'third eye'.

I stayed like that for half an hour until I was roused by the sound of Jay's car on the gravel. I certainly felt calmer but not much the wiser, although I knew from experience that insights don't always come in a flash. Sometimes they come later, when events have had a chance to unfold.

Jay was whistling when he came in. 'Look who I found at the flat.'

I came out of the study into the hall to find Jay's mother, Sharon, large as life, standing at the bottom of the stairs with two bulging carrier bags. Jay was on his way upstairs with her overnight bag.

'Sharon, what a surprise!' I cried, trying to sound welcoming.

Normally, I would have been pleased to see her but Sharon had eyes like a hawk. Consequently, I'd have to be vigilant about breathing in and engaging my core muscles whenever she looked in my direction.

As we embraced I leaned forward to avoid any contact at waist level. She panted that she was dying for a cup of coffee, so I took care of that and five minutes later we were sitting in the living room and they were telling me how they'd crossed paths. Sharon had decided yesterday to make a spur of the moment shopping trip, knowing there'd be a spare bed at the flat on a weekday. She'd intended to stay one night and travel back to Glastonbury today on the train, but when Jay turned up this morning to inspect the boiler, he suggested she came home with him.

'Pandora, I tell you, when I got under that freezing shower, I nearly had a heart attack. Soon as I've shown you what I've bought, I'm gonna take a long, hot bath.'

She then proceeded to empty the contents of the carrier bags and describe in great detail where and when she'd be wearing the items and their accessories. I didn't mind. It took my mind off the distress, sometime in the near future, I'd be inflicting upon her son. And it was good to have her company.

Jay and I had rarely been alone when we'd lived at Four Seasons, a state of affairs which hadn't always thrilled us. But since Sharon and the children had gone their separate ways, I sometimes fell prey to intense loneliness. I recognised the same thing in Jay, which was why I was glad that he'd palled up again with Donny. Being together wasn't enough to alleviate our sense of dislocation, because no one person could compensate for the loss of a beautiful home, and the land, the animals, and the people that went with it.

Once Sharon had finished her fashion parade and gone upstairs for a soak, Jay gave me the lowdown on the offending boiler and how he'd had to call a plumber who pronounced it dead on arrival.

'He reckons it'll cost over two thousand quid to supply and install a new one. He said he could do it next week. How are we fixed?'

I could tell he hated having to ask me whether there was enough money in the kitty, so I made light of it. With my guilty secret, keeping Jay sweet was a priority.

'No problem. You'd better ring him and give him the go-ahead. And you'll have to tell the girls there's no hot water in case they're thinking of staying there this weekend.'

'Okay, darlin', I'll do that.' He paused, looking forlorn. 'Now Sharon's here, I'd better tell Ash I can't make it to the Oval this weekend.'

'No, don't do that,' I said, the words out of my mouth before I knew it. 'I'll look after Sharon, don't worry.'

He kissed me and, with a big grin on his face, went into the study to make the calls. A plan was beginning to form in my mind and I realised that Sharon showing up was actually turning out to be something of a godsend.

* * *

Next morning, having bundled Fritz, Oscar and Sharon into my car, I set off for Glastonbury. We'd decided over dinner the night before, that with Jay being at the cricket match with his three sons on Saturday and Sunday, I might as well drive Sharon home and pay my honorary stepfather, Charles, a long overdue visit while I was there.

I couldn't avoid going to Glastonbury for much longer. I hadn't been near the place since we'd moved into Phoenix Cottage. The thought of being there made me sad now that my mother wasn't around – that, and the idea that Beau and Midnight and the goats, Bonnie and Clyde, might give me the cold shoulder for packing them off to Steve's farm.

After breakfast, I'd phoned Charles and arranged to meet for lunch in a restaurant in the town. He'd invited us to stay the night, which suited me. Jay had decided to brave the cold shower and stay overnight in London at the flat, so he wouldn't be at home anyway.

Then I'd phoned Rosemary and told her I needed enough elixir to carry me through till the end of September. She normally released only one month's supply at a time, making a fresh brew every full moon. She then posted it off to a handful of people, including me and my American half-brother, Theo, who lived in Los Angeles.

She could tell something was up from the way my voice shook when I said I'd explain when I saw her, so she asked me to come to see her straight after leaving Charles.

On the way down to Glastonbury, Sharon chatted away about her new life with Pete. 'My God, Pandora, it was hard to begin with. He wanted to do all the cooking – wouldn't let me in the kitchen, wouldn't let me change any of the decor. It was all so *dark*. I sat around wondering what the heck I was supposed to be doing all day. I gotta say, a couple of times I nearly packed my bag and came to you.'

When she said this my blood ran cold. Sharing Four Seasons with my ex mother-in-law had been unavoidable because she was already there when I moved back in, but the confines of Phoenix

Cottage would have afforded her no more purpose in life than Pete's place. Imagine, I thought, trying to manage my present dilemma with Sharon on the sidelines. It didn't bear thinking about.

I played the part of attentive listener as she catalogued the highs and lows of life with Pete, making sure I inserted the occasional 'hmm' or 'really?', until she finally ground to a halt.

'But you and Pete...you're all right now, aren't you?' I said, hoping she was taking root in Somerset soil.

'Let's just say, I'm getting him round to my way of doing things. It's been a lot better since I've been helping Charles at Gaia's Cave. I'm getting quite the expert at what those crystals mean. Every day I make it my business to learn about a new one.'

Relief washed over me. To keep events as private as possible, I needed everybody to be settled in their various billets for the next four months, until I'd successfully carried and delivered my precious cargo.

'What about you and Jay, dear? How's he coping?'

'Much better now he's back in touch with the band.'

'That's good. He took it hard, you know, not being the bread-winner anymore.'

'I won't be the breadwinner for much longer, actually. *Straight Talking*'s being pulled at the end of June.'

'You don't say!' Sharon's expression was one of horror. 'Well, just how are you two going to survive?'

'Don't worry about us, I've managed to save a bit. We'll be all right till Christmas and by then Jay will be earning. They're going on tour, you know.'

I was being positive for Sharon's sake but it had the added benefit of making me feel better about our financial situation, too. I did have enough to pay the bills on Phoenix Cottage and give the girls their monthly allowances for a few more months. What Jay got from royalties covered his day-to-day expenses, so there was no need to panic. Whether I left home or not, the direct debits would still be covered.

As we approached Pete's house, Oscar and Fritz became restless, sensing they were soon to be released from their confinement. Sharon made them worse by mentioning a friend of theirs.

'You're gonna see Milo, boys. Share his biccies...'

Milo greeted Fritz and Oscar joyfully. When we'd first had the *where to place the livestock* discussion, I'd hinted that three dogs would be too many for Phoenix Cottage so Sharon had suggested taking the smallest with her. He'd only lived with us a few months anyway. We'd been looking after him for Theo's girlfriend, who intended to come back for him one day.

'Hello, hello,' said Pete, ushering the dogs into the garden to restore a little order in his house.

I hadn't seen him for months, and I noticed his formerly whippet-thin figure was showing the beginnings of a paunch. 'Life with Sharon suits you, she's fattening you up,' I said, giving him a wink Sharon couldn't see.

'You're not looking so bad yourself,' he said, returning the wink, and I could have bitten my tongue. The last thing I wanted to draw attention to was *my* increased girth.

'Ah well, you know how it is, being chauffeured to work, it piles on the pounds.'

'Not for much longer, honey,' said Sharon, and she proceeded to bend his ear with the breaking news of my redundancy and the price of boilers in Fulham.

Sharon had already offered to look after the dogs while I met with Charles and Rosemary so, after a quick catch-up with Pete, I set off for the restaurant, which was a mere ten-minute walk away. Charles was already there and stood up to kiss me.

'Oh, Charles,' I exclaimed, blinking away the tears which had sprung as soon as I sat down. 'You're never going to believe this. Something totally embarrassing and incredibly problematic has happened. History has repeated itself.'

Chapter 10 – The Fountain of Life

We were approaching the end of the meal, although I'd hardly tasted my courgette and feta buckwheat crêpe, so engrossed had I been in opening my heart to Charles. After his initial surprise, he'd listened quite calmly, even though what I'd had to tell him included my infidelity with Zac and an Annunciation from an archangel akin to that of Gabriel's to the Virgin Mary.

'Do you believe all this, Charles?' I asked, scarcely even sure that I believed it myself.

Squeezing the last drop out of his pot of fennel tea, he gave his verdict. 'It has the ring of truth about it, Pandora. Otherwise, how could he have known about the elixir or your mother's second pregnancy? And he remembered you from the correspondence course. I should think that's proof enough.'

I nodded, feeling comforted that Charles trusted in Cassiel's provenance.

'I just can't get my head round being in the same boat as Frankie.'

He must have detected a note of criticism in my tone because his mouth tightened and his eyes grew cool. 'Well, try a little harder. I seem to remember you disapproved when Theo revealed the brevity of the relationship between your mother and his father. You even doubted it was possible for her to conceive a child because of her age, yet she was ten years younger than you are now.' He paused. 'Of course, unlike you, she was a single woman at the time.'

I blushed to my roots. He was right. I was being hypocritical. Whichever way you looked at it, it was my unfaithfulness to Jay which was causing the immediate problem.

I'm sure my mother would have taken my side, quoting 'sauce for the goose'. In contrast, while Charles was aware of Jay's chequered history, unlike Frankie, he didn't hold it against him.

'Believe me, Charles, the last thing I wanted was to hurt Jay. He's been through enough. Do you think I'd have slept with Zac if, for one moment, I thought this would happen?'

'Of course not,' he said, his expression softening. 'Pandora, I'm happy to help you through this in any way I can. As a member of the Circle of Isis that night, I'll take my share of responsibility for bringing the elixir of life into being in the first place.'

His words gave me a new perspective on the situation and I began to feel better. I was all for spreading the burden of blame.

'Although it's living up to its name in a way no one anticipated,' Charles continued. 'None of us imagined it would lead to the creation of a completely new life.'

It dawned on me then that Rosemary's other clients might have been affected, too. 'Who else is taking it, Charles?'

'None of the other circle members, apart from Theo. We all donate our supply to him and Rosemary's other patients.' He paused just long enough to make me feel uncomfortable. 'I understand Theo's deriving great benefit from it. He's almost pain free.'

I blushed, sensing that Charles had guessed I'd been taking the elixir as much for the cosmetic effect as for its energy-boosting properties.

'The elixir's certainly turned out to be a mixed blessing for me,' I muttered, defensively. 'Thank goodness Sharon didn't start taking it for her bad back. She might have got more than she bargained for.'

Charles allowed himself the glimmer of a smile.

'But it is one hell of a coincidence, isn't it, Charles – my mother giving birth to a secret child she immediately gave away to someone else to bring up, and a similar thing happening to me?'

'Yes, Pandora, but the comparison stops there. If Theo's birth had been preceded by an angelic messenger declaring he was being groomed for messianic greatness, I think I'd have heard about it.'

I felt a faint tickle in my left ear and Frankie's voice filled my eardrum. *Theo played the part of Christ for the church on Palm Sunday, though, didn't he? And it was his blood added to the first infusion in the chalice which transformed it into the elixir of life.*

I shook my head to dislodge her. I wasn't in the mood for a competitive-mom bragfest.

'As for the decisions you have to make,' Charles resumed, 'I suggest you ask Rosemary to give you some energy healing and see what comes through. She can get in touch with some pretty big guns and if it's advice you're after, you might as well go to the top.'

He had to get back to the shop so we went our separate ways, my next stop being Rosemary's place. I felt quite light of step as I walked to Apple Blossom Cottage. Being with people I was fond of buoyed me up. And then I realised something wonderful. I couldn't be alone while my daughter nestled inside me. The two of us were keeping each other company, day and night.

The front door opened before my hand even touched the knocker. Rosemary stood before me in her white tunic and dark trousers, looking every inch the dentist.

'I've got toothache and I've come for a filling,' I said, unable to resist.

'Wrong practice,' she said, as she kissed me. 'I deal with heartache here.'

She took me straight upstairs to the therapy room, a large and airy space, its high walls and ceiling painted a cool white, with a therapy table in the centre. We walked to the end of the room and sat down in the two easy chairs.

'I'm glad you've come to see me at last: you're due for an energy check-up. I was looking at your records, it's over six months since I've seen you. And what's all this about wanting four months' supply at once?'

It might have been something about the place, or possibly that I'd already run through my story with Charles, but the words just spilled from my lips while she listened, engrossed.

'Charles thinks it's a good idea for you to tune in and see what advice comes through,' I concluded, adding as an afterthought, '...and, of course, you need to know about the pregnancy in case the elixir could affect any other female patients.'

Rosemary placed her thumb and index finger on her third eye and began to gently massage it. 'I understand what's happened,' she said, after a few seconds. 'The patients I give the elixir to have chronic conditions and I always direct the elixir to their specific ailments, whereas, with you, I simply asked for your energy levels to be strengthened.'

'So the energy went where my body considered it was needed?'

She nodded and when she spoke again her voice was gentle. 'You've come to the right place, Pandora. As you know, the elixir has a guardian, the spirit of the Fountain of Life, and that's who I'm going to call on. But first I want to give you and the baby a health check.'

I followed her to the treatment table and Rosemary produced a crystal pendulum from her pocket which she held between her thumb and forefinger. She began to move the pendulum over my chakras, pausing to see in which direction the crystal swung. I was vaguely conscious of her progressing to other parts of my body; by the time she reached my crown chakra, my eyelids had become heavy and I fell into a deep sleep.

When I opened my eyes, I struggled to remember where I was. *This must be what it feels like to wake up after an operation,* I thought, and automatically felt my belly to make sure junior was still there. I turned my head to the left, recognising the apothecary chest where Rosemary's herbs and potions were kept. Pushing off the light blanket which covered me, I got up and went to the bathroom. I was familiar with the house, so had no trouble finding it.

Hearing the flush of the toilet, Rosemary appeared at the bottom of the stairs. I could smell cooking and wondered if I'd slept so long she'd started her evening meal.

'How long have I been asleep, Rosemary?' My eyes were still bleary and I felt like going back to the treatment bed and closing them again.

'About two hours. Do you need to ring anyone to tell them where you are?'

'Oh lord, yes. Sharon. I've left the dogs and my car there. How much longer will we be, Rosemary?'

'Not long. I've made some soup. While you're having it, I can tell you what came through.'

Five minutes later, I was seated at Rosemary's dining table, before me a brimming bowl of lentil and sweet potato soup, waiting to hear what the spirit of the Fountain of Life had decreed should be my course of action.

'The spirit feels like a feminine presence,' she began, 'so I'll call her "she". First of all, I'm happy to tell you that you, your womb and the baby are in excellent health.' She patted my hand as she said this, and I felt very comforted.

'To paraphrase the spirit's message,' Rosemary went on, 'she confirms all that your guardian, Cassiel, has already told you and gives me permission to supply the amount of elixir you asked for. She says you must contact Cassiel, leave the place you're living in now and ask the father of the child to provide you with somewhere peaceful to stay.'

I nearly choked on a lentil when Rosemary said that, but she shrugged in a *Don't shoot the messenger* way and carried on. 'She calls the baby a star seed from the constellation Lyra. We're entering a crucial phase in the evolution of our planet and these star seeds are being sent to Earth to use their special abilities to help us out of the cycle of destruction we're in – the way we're treating our environment, how people are making war on each other in the name of religion, all that. So it fits with what Cassiel showed you – that she'll be some sort of ambassador of peace.'

'That's lovely,' I said, beginning to feel excited and privileged to be part of it and thinking that if I'd been allowed to bring the baby up, I'd have called her Lyra.

'The spirit emphasises the importance of keeping the child a secret and she says you'll need to find a trustworthy companion, who'll stay with you until the birth.' Rosemary bent her head and put her hands in prayer position. 'That's it, I think. Does that cover what you wanted to know?'

I was on the point of protesting about having to reveal my tale to Zac, who was so agnostic – atheistic, even (I wasn't sure how far his disbelief went), that he'd never believe I'd been visited by an angel. But then I noticed how tired Rosemary looked so I held my peace. Channelling can drain a person and I'd taken up enough of her time. 'Yes. Thanks so much for everything, Rosemary. I'd better get the dogs. We're staying with Charles tonight.'

I got up and went upstairs to fetch my jacket. When I came down, Rosemary was completing my client record.

'How much do I owe you?'

She coloured. 'Nothing. Anything I can do to assist this little soul's safe passage into the world, is for love, not money. The full moon's tomorrow: I'll make some extra elixir for you then. Can you stay on one more night, so I can give it to you on Monday morning before you go?'

Luckily my next working day was Tuesday. 'I don't see why not. I'm sure Charles won't mind. Oh, by the way, not a word to Sharon about all this, in case she tells Jay.'

Up to now, Rosemary hadn't commented on poor old Jay and the effect it would have on him when I left, but when I mentioned his name, her eyes filled with tears in tune with mine. 'Collateral damage, I'm afraid. Let's hope you can put it right with him after it's all over.'

'I can't let myself even think about that,' I said, taking deep breaths to keep the tide of guilt from drowning me. 'I've got to avoid stress for the baby's sake. What Sharon and the children are going to think of me, I daren't even contemplate.'

* * *

When the dogs and I finally got to Charles's cottage, there was no answer to my knock, so we took the side path to the back door. Finding it unlocked, we walked through the kitchen to the living room and found Charles dead to the world in his rocking chair, the cat curled up on his lap. Anubis barely opened one eye when she saw us, paying me as little heed as she did the dogs.

Pete had, in Sharon's words, 'almost walked their legs off', so they soon settled down and joined the snoring chorus while I got my overnight bag from the car.

Having conducted a covert inspection of the bedding in the guest room, I went downstairs to discover them all exactly as I'd left them. Looking around for some reading matter, I finally chose a pocket guide to crystals and gemstones from a pile clustered on the narrow top shelf of a beautiful old mahogany chiffonier. Brushing the dust from the page edges, I searched the index for 'pregnancy', revelling in being able to do so without spectacles, another side benefit of taking the elixir.

There were three suggestions on the page: the first was moonstone, described as 'the divine feminine stone, good for preparing the womb for conception'. A bit late for that, I thought and moved on to the next, which was rose quartz, 'the stone of unconditional love, which creates a lasting bond between mother and child during pregnancy'. My heart fluttered uncertainly when I read that. Would it be fair to either of us to create too strong a bond, knowing we'd be separated almost as soon as she saw the light of day?

Moving on from these troubling thoughts, I studied the

picture of ukanite – a mottled green stone with some flashes of dark pink. It wasn't as attractive as the other two but I liked the description: 'a balancing stone that protects the health of the mother and child during pregnancy'.

Making a mental note to double-check this with Charles, I became conscious of a persistent compulsion, drilling at my head like a woodpecker, to get my finger out and do what the spirit of the elixir had said I had to: namely, get in touch with Cassiel and ask Zac to find me somewhere to stay.

'All right, all right,' I responded, putting the book down and taking my phone into the dining room, away from the sonorous yips and whimpers of the slumberers. 'Cassiel first,' I muttered to myself, 'so he can tell me if he's found a midwife yet.'

He answered immediately, barely giving me a chance to speak before delivering his news. 'Hello, Pandora, I've had one response to the advertisement. She's a very strong candidate.'

'Good-oh. What's she like?'

'She seems ideal. She's here on a student visa, doing a midwifery degree...just finished her second year. It's a perfect job for her because it corresponds with her university vacation.'

'So she's young, then?'

'I haven't seen her face to face. I didn't ask her age.'

'Single?'

'Yes.'

'And where's she from?'

'Colombia. She sounded very keen.'

Up to now, I'd pictured a home-grown earth-mother type, more of a doula than a careerist, healthcare professional, so I had to quickly adjust the image I had in my mind. I hoped she wouldn't take her job too seriously and order me about all the time.

'Where did you find her, anyway?'

'I placed an advertisement in an online midwifery magazine, using certain key words that only those at a certain level of spiritual attainment would understand and respond to.'

'I see. So what happens next?'

'I've given her your number and asked her to ring you so you can arrange a meeting. Her name's Viviana. If Jay's with you when she calls, just pretend it's a telemarketer.'

The mention of his name reminded me that Jay had cancelled his meeting with Truman. 'Did Jay ever reschedule his appointment with you?'

'Not yet. But it's not a priority for me at the moment. I'll certainly go ahead with it if necessary, but I used the book proposal as a ploy to get *you* to contact me, so I'll leave him to make the next move.'

Feeling slightly disappointed on Jay's behalf, I returned to the main topic.

'Anyway, if the midwife rings, it should be all right. I'm in Glastonbury till Monday.'

'Good.'

'I'm having to wait till Rosemary prepares the elixir tomorrow night. I'd have thought you'd have known that. Can you not see where I am?'

'Actually, no. Being in the body of a man rather limits my ability to detect your whereabouts. I thought you understood how limited my powers are on the earthly plane.'

My idea that Cassiel could, if he wanted, track me with celestial radar and even observe my movements was obviously well off the mark. 'So you don't know what the spirit of the elixir advised me to do?'

'No. How did you get in touch with *her*?'

'Through Rosemary. She said I had to contact you, and also Zac, so he can find me a place to live. And she confirmed that I needed a companion to live with me until the baby's born.'

'That's exactly what this candidate has agreed to.'

I told him my next call was going to be to Zac, so he rang off, after urging me to keep him informed because, he protested, he wasn't a mind-reader.

Before continuing, I tiptoed out of the dining room to check what Charles was up to. I didn't want him lumbering into the kitchen, clattering about and starting up a conversation when I was in the throes of one of the most difficult phone calls I'd ever had to make. He was still sleeping soundly, so I returned to my seat at the table and took a few deep breaths to quieten my mind, which had started bombarding me with possible outcomes.

What if the girl from New York is visiting? Suppose he doesn't answer? What if he ends the call when I tell him I'm pregnant?

It had been my habit in the past to take a drink, in the form of a small glass of sherry or port, before ringing a man I was involved with, but this avenue was closed to me now, courtesy of junior. So I adopted Plan B, shutting my eyes and taking several more slow, deep breaths. I sat like this for five minutes until I felt calm enough to press the dial button. I was rewarded with Zac's lyrical tones coming through loud and clear.

'Hello, Pandora. This is a nice surprise.'

'Hello, Zac. Sorry to interrupt your Saturday evening, but I wanted to let you know that I won't be able to work the last two weeks of June, I'm afraid.'

'Oh, I'm sorry to hear that. You'd better put it in writing to Human Resources, just to keep the paperwork straight. Are you going away?'

Here we go, I thought, taking a deep breath.

'Yes and no. I'm not taking off on holiday. I'm leaving Jay.'

There was a pause, while he took in what I'd said.

'Why, what's happened? I thought everything was all right between you now.'

'I'm afraid I've got myself into a bit of a mess. It's a long story. Can I explain when I see you? Right now, I need a massive favour. I can't stay with Jay but I haven't got anywhere to go. I wondered if you could help me find somewhere.'

I stopped. The logical hemisphere of my brain was telling me that unless I told him I was pregnant and he was the father, there wouldn't be any earthly reason for him to help me, yet my gut instinct was telling me to withhold the fact that he'd fathered a child I was carrying until I could tell him the whole story face to face.

'Yes. Okay.' His tone had changed. He was obviously worried. But was he worried for me or for himself? 'How urgent is it? I mean, is he violent?'

'God, no. Anyway, he doesn't even know I'm going yet. I won't tell him in advance. I'll leave a note or something. I have to leave soon, though.'

The phone shook in my hand at the thought of actually doing that to the man I'd intended to spend the rest of my life with, but I could see no other way.

'What's brought this on, then?'

'Oh, you know, we've been under a lot of strain lately...'

'And?'

I searched wildly for a more convincing reason. Then I remembered that I'd collected Truman's letter from Zac's office a few days ago. 'It's connected with that letter I picked up on Monday. The person who wrote it can help with the problem I've got but he can't provide accommodation.'

The sound of Charles clearing his throat wafted in from the living room.

'Look, I'm staying with an old friend this weekend so I can't really talk. I'll be working on Tuesday, can we meet up then? It's really important. I'd like to be out by next weekend if I can.'

'Tuesday. Let me think...I'll have to rearrange a meeting.'

I began to panic that I'd scared him off. Why would he want anything to do with a crazy woman who expected him to get involved in her relationship dramas?

'Please, Zac. The longer I leave it, the riskier it is.'

'Oh, Pandora, you're worrying me now. We're not talking STD, I hope.'

My addled brain refused to recognise this acronym and took refuge in the 1970s. 'What's Subscriber Trunk Dialling got to do with it?'

'Nothing. Seriously, has this person passed something on to you which you've passed on to Jay? And me?'

My brain was unable to comprehend this riddle until my mother turned up and enlightened me. *He's talking about Sexually Transmitted Diseases, Pan. Wake up to the 21st century, for goodness' sake. You're showing your age! That's the last thing you want to do with a younger man.*

Irritation at both Frankie and Zac made me snappy. 'Certainly not!' I fumed. 'What do you take me for? Anyway, it's worse than that.'

There was a silence, followed by a relieved laugh. 'What could be worse than that?'

'I mean, not worse, but more momentous.'

At that moment, Charles called from the kitchen. 'Tea or coffee, Pandora?'

'Tea, please,' I called back.

'So are we meeting or not?' I said, still smarting from Zac's suggestion that I might have caught something from a third man and passed it on to him and Jay, notwithstanding the fact that a few days ago I had, indeed, been fantasising about Andrew Truman as a possible lover.

'Yes, of course,' he said soothingly. 'Don't come to the office. I'll meet you outside the studios at one-thirty on Tuesday. You can tell me everything over lunch.'

'Thanks, Zac. And, please, don't breathe a word to a soul that I'm leaving Jay. Not Portia, or anyone at work. You'll understand when I tell you.'

'I can't wait. This is the stuff of drama, Pandora – you've ended this episode on a cliffhanger. I'll have to get you writing for *Peeler Street*.'

As I said goodbye, Charles brought the tea to the table and sat down. 'When you've drunk that you can tell me what happened this afternoon at Rosemary's.'

Chapter 11 – Old Friends

When I awoke on Sunday morning I got the notebook and pen I usually travelled with and wrote down the dream I'd had, afraid that if I left it till later, I wouldn't remember it at all.

I'm standing in a sort of temple. In the middle of this space is a pure white marble altar on which there rests a golden urn containing a vibrant violet flame. I move towards the altar and kneel in front of it. When I look up, an oriental female of great beauty, dressed in a flowing white robe and wearing a small, gold crown inlaid with shining amethysts, is standing a few feet away from me. Beside her is a cradle from which she takes a swaddled newborn baby, with golden hair. As she shows her to me, she says: 'I revealed to you that it was possible for you to become a mother. Soon it will be so.' She lays the baby down in the cradle and comes towards me. Then she places her right hand over my chest and I feel suffused with the love and compassion that comes pouring from her heart to mine. While she is doing this, a white dove comes to rest on her left shoulder. I stretch my arms towards the crib, silently imploring her to let me hold the baby, but she shakes her head. She moves towards the altar and the dove flies from her shoulder on to mine. I reach up and stroke its back and it starts to coo. The woman appears before me again, this time with a vase in her hand. I cup my hands but she pours the precious liquid on to my belly instead.

I tried to remember what happened next but all I recalled was a fleeting impression of being outside in one of the pagodas that surrounded the temple. I was so desperate to remember the last part of the dream that I got back into bed, closed my eyes and relived it, this time being the observer instead of the participant. As I'd hoped, the last, forgotten scene played out and was just as intriguing as my fragments of memory had suggested. When it ended I took up the pen and recorded it.

I see myself on the outside staircase of one of the twelve pagodas surrounding the central temple, which is higher than all the others and crowned by a golden dome. It is windy and the air is filled with tinkling and clanging from the numerous temple bells and wind chimes. The stairs lead me upwards to a door which opens to reveal a bedchamber containing an ornate Chinese four-poster bed dressed with red silk drapes. I watch myself approach the bed, curious to see who might be in it. The silk is sheer and a form is visible within. I raise my hands, pull the drapes apart and see a man lying beneath a gold- and silver-coloured eiderdown embroidered with Chinese characters. His eyes are shut. I move closer to look at his face and instantly recognise those features. It's Truman! 'Where am I?' he asks. 'Somewhere safe', I answer. He reaches for my hand and all the while he's holding it, I feel the grace of compassion flowing from my heart to his, like water from a bubbling spring. When he releases my hand, I thank him for making it possible for Cassiel to be present on Earth to help me through this difficult time, but he shows no reaction, having reverted to his immobile state. I leave the room, feeling sad that he is missing several months of his life for a cause he has no connection with.

Almost as soon as I'd written the last word, I heard Charles moving about below so I went down, taking my notes with me. Fritz and Oscar, still resting in their beds, lifted their heads in greeting when they saw me. I opened the back door and watched them stagger out to water the grass, still stiff from yesterday's marathon.

It was beginning to dawn on me that Oscar presented something of a problem. Fritz, a leggy pointer, had always been Jay's, but my late husband Mike had bought me Oscar, a handsome little chap of indeterminate ancestry. He'd be very hard to leave behind. But if wherever I ended up wasn't suitable for dogs, I'd have to entrust him to Jay.

'Come and have breakfast,' said Charles from the kitchen, and while I tackled a large bowl of muesli, he suggested that we went to his shop so I could look at some crystal jewellery.

'I'll let us in the back,' he decided. 'I don't do Sunday opening and I don't want anyone following us in if they see me unlock the front door.'

'Fine. I'll check to see if the midwife's been in touch.'

'You'd better switch your phone on, then,' said Charles, bringing me my bag, but there was no message.

The evening before, after I'd told Charles about my session with Rosemary, I'd phoned Jay to let him know I was staying an extra night so I could pick up this month's supply of elixir. He was full of the cricket and what a good time they'd had. In fact, the conversation had flowed and I was surprised at myself for being able to sound so natural, knowing that in a very short space of time I'd be breaking his heart.

'What have you got there?' asked Charles, nodding in the direction of my notebook.

'Some notes I made about a dream I had last night. Here, see what you make of it.'

He took the notebook from me and scanned what I'd written, pondered on it for a little while, and delivered his verdict. 'Most definitely Quan Yin, goddess of mercy – hence the Violet Flame. And bearer of the Water of Life, which she poured on to you.'

'That's what I thought. I remember Rosemary saying she was the goddess of fertility as well.'

'Mm, even more appropriate, considering where the liquid landed. But what's this about a previous revelation?'

'Rosemary channelled Quan Yin at my first healing, about six years ago, before I got back with Jay. She said that the words that came through were in a language of light and possessed healing properties, although she didn't understand it herself. The funny thing was, I did understand some of it. Quan Yin told me that I could still be a mother. I didn't say anything to Rosemary at the time because she might have thought I was showing off. And anyway, she'd just started treating me for the perimenopause.'

Charles nodded, his eyes misting over.

'The night before, your mother and I took you to a Harvest Moon ceremony. I remember it clearly.'

So did I. The image of Charles and Frankie performing a goat dance in Rosemary's back garden, fuelled with copious swigs from a communal chalice of strong cider was one I wouldn't forget in a hurry.

'Yes, well, when I got back from that visit, I rang Jay and soon after that we hooked up again. I happened to tell him what Quan Yin had said, and he asked me if I'd do him the honour of being a mother to his children, so I assumed that's what she meant.'

'Hmm. Interesting. So you were actually given the prophecy six years ago?'

'Yes, I misinterpreted it then, but it's coming true now. Quan Yin is the keeper of the Water of Life and last year we took part in the creation of the elixir of life – the same thing by any other name – which led to the pregnancy. I didn't stand a chance. I believe it was fated.'

Charles looked thoughtful. 'It comes down to how much of life is predetermined and how much free will we actually have, if any. It was a question the Greeks argued about for centuries. Leucippus believed that nothing occurred at random, whereas Pythagoras thought that human free will existed, tending to choose earthly pleasures rather than spiritual. I find the arguments that Epicurus put forward more convincing...'

'That's right,' I said, interrupting him by pretending to know what he was talking about. The last thing I needed was a philosophy lecture. 'And what about karma?' I said, to distract him. 'If you believe in that, you've got to believe that people wilfully choose the right or the wrong action.'

The truth was, I didn't know *what* I believed any more, having had a crisis of faith after my healing practice had crashed, along with Jay's finances. To my relief, on this rare occasion, my remark had gone in one ear and out the other. Charles didn't go to his study and unearth an ancient book explaining the Buddhist take on karma, free will and determinism. Instead, he returned to my dream.

'I must say, it does seem a bit back to front to me. You already know you're going to have a child and that you can't keep her. It would have made more sense if she'd appeared to you around the time of the conception.'

My thoughts turned back to Christmas and how easily I'd taken Zac into my bed. 'Cassiel said it was hard to get through to me then. I suppose because I'd strayed so far from the straight and narrow. Anyway, what about the second bit of it?'

'That's fairly clear. The essence of Truman is under Quan Yin's protection while Cassiel makes use of his body. She specialises in opening the heart to unconditional love and compassion – that's why she placed her hand on your heart chakra. I'm not sure why Truman felt the need to "top up", as it were, from you. Some sort of spiritual law of reciprocity, perhaps.'

Both dreams had saddened me. First, seeing a child I couldn't take in my arms and then, a man having his body invaded and his life lived for him because I needed a guardian.

'I suppose his spirit body or light body, whatever it's called, might have needed a boost,' I said sombrely. 'Now I've seen that aspect of him, I'm feeling horribly guilty that his spirit's being held in a sort of limbo because of Cassiel having to help me.'

Charles must have realised I was becoming maudlin so he terminated the conversation by clearing the table and washing up, after which we left for Gaia's Cave.

Once in the shop, I chose a delicate rose quartz pendant set in gold, and a ukanite bracelet. The bracelet was relatively cheap but the pendant was quite a bit more, due to the fine gold lattice on the front of the stone, in the shape of a four-petalled flower, its stamens forming a four-pointed star.

Charles had started pricing up some new stock while I was making my choice and I helped him by putting the crystals, small ornaments and pieces of jewellery on display. All this time, I kept an ear out for my ringtone, but it remained silent.

When we finished I offered Charles my credit card for the bracelet and pendant but he refused it, saying it was his contribution to the cause of mother and baby care. I was already wearing the bracelet and Charles threaded the pendant through some pale pink velvet cord so I could wear it until I could transfer it to a gold chain.

As we walked back, I mentioned to Charles that I'd like to see Beau and Midnight, so we took a detour via the lane at the back of the cottage to the farm. As we came in sight of the field, we saw them grazing with Flossy, the pony who'd welcomed them into her territory, and her daughter.

All four trotted over to the fence when they saw us. We had no treats for them so Flossy and the yearling wandered off while Midnight and Beau both put their noses out to me and the three of us snuffled our love for each other while Charles looked on in mock horror.

'How are you, Midnight?' I whispered. 'Do you like it here?'

Charles heard this and answered for her. 'Don't worry, Pandora, Jenny's taken her under her wing. She gets the same schooling as Flossy.'

'That's lovely,' I whispered. 'I'll tell the girls.'

'They already know,' said Charles, sounding surprised I wasn't aware of this. 'Clarrie drives down every so often with Rowan. Willow and Cherry usually come with them.'

I had a vague memory of Rowan saying something about him and his girlfriend, Clarrie, visiting Sharon but of more than that I had no recollection.

'Oh, Charles. I've been so wrapped up in keeping my job and worrying about Jay, I feel as if I've cut myself off from everything and everyone else. And now this *situation* has dropped on me like a ton of bricks, it might alienate them forever.'

'Now, now,' said Charles, awkwardly patting my back. 'You

know the drill: no wallowing. Remember, "No problem can be solved from the same level of consciousness that created it". Einstein knew what he was talking about.'

I nodded. Last night Charles had given me a pep talk about making an effort to feel joyful and grateful in order to be in what he called 'the positive field'. He said I mustn't slip into the negative field because assistance is never attracted to a negative state of mind and I needed to attract favourable outcomes to the difficulties I was facing.

While I was trying hard to see sunlight through the clouds, Beau had shouldered Midnight out of the way and stood scrutinising me with his big, dark eyes, ringed with white to match his nose, waiting for me to scratch his enormous ears.

A few minutes later, farmer Steve and his wife, Jenny, appeared. They'd seen us from the house and had come to invite us in for a chat. At the sight of them I exhaled, pulling my stomach in, hoping they wouldn't notice my fuller figure.

On the way to the house they told us that the goats, Bonnie and Clyde, had gone to a children's farm run by a friend of theirs and I felt reprieved. Now I wouldn't have to worry in case the sight of me stirred up memories of the disruption they'd suffered at leaving Four Seasons.

I was happy to let Steve and Jenny do most of the talking. It cheered me up to hear how quickly Midnight and Beau had settled in and how Midnight had slimmed down since Jenny had been putting her through her paces. She'd even been shown at a local event.

'Has Beau ever been back to the paddock?' I asked, having an urge to lead him back to the cottage paddock and sit with him for a while.

'No,' said Steve, looking puzzled.

'Could I take him to see Fritz and Oscar? They'd love to see him.'

Charles gave me a keen look. He knew there was more to my

suggestion than giving the dogs a trip down memory lane.

'Of course,' said Jenny, as though it was a perfectly under-standable request. 'I'll get his head collar.'

* * *

Once the paddock gate had closed, Beau made straight for his former shelter only to find his old hay rack empty of barley straw, so I made for the kitchen to get him a snack. As soon as I opened the back door, Oscar charged out to greet Beau, with Fritz following at a statelier pace. In response, Beau tossed his head and did a lap round the paddock with Oscar close behind.

I followed the dogs to witness their reunion, then wandered over to my mother's grave. The small white, wooden cross that marked it had been joined by a beautiful red rose bush planted by Charles on the anniversary of her death, earlier in the year. I can't say I felt particularly connected to that spot in the paddock though – after all, the important part of her had gone to join the Big Hippy in the sky.

So if she's been absorbed back into the Oneness, my inner sceptic nagged, *how come she still talks to you?*

Well, if people can channel goddesses and ascended masters, I argued, *why not their dearly departed mothers and fathers occasionally?*

My internal debate was interrupted by an impatient Poitou donkey poking me in the back with his muzzle, so I went inside and chopped some carrot and apple, holding out the bowl for Beau in one hand while throwing biscuits to the dogs with the other.

Charles had sat down on the garden seat next to the shelter and was looking towards the house.

'Are you hungry?' I said.

'Yes. Do you mind if I go in and get the meal going? It'll be ready in about an hour. I assume you want to spend some time

 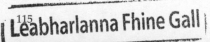

with Beau.'

'Thanks, Charles.'

When Beau had finished chomping, I started to stroke his neck, slowing my movements until his head rested on my shoulder. The last time I'd done this, it was to find out who had disturbed my mother's grave, but this time it was to make sure he was happy.

I closed my eyes, emptied my mind and waited to see if any images or feelings came through. The first impression I received was a wave of confusion and I guessed he was telling me how he'd felt when he'd had to leave Four Seasons and come to the farm.

'I'm sorry, darling,' I whispered, 'I had to go to a different place as well. We all did.'

Once we'd mutually commiserated, he moved on to his present circumstances. I got an impression of Jenny grooming him and leading him up and down the lane. This put my mind at rest. Midnight had the advantage of being rideable whereas Beau was a pet, so I was glad he wasn't being left too much to his own devices.

I stood there for a few minutes, drawing strength from this connection with such a sweet soul. The dogs came closer to us and settled down on the grass.

'I've been given a task to do,' I said, hoping they'd understand the meaning behind my words. 'If you don't see me for a while, don't worry. I promise I'll come back and we'll all be together again.'

* * *

Rosemary knocked bright and early Monday morning. I was already up, as I was eager to get on the road. I'd even loaded the car.

She was on her way to work so we talked in the hall. Handing me a box containing the phials of elixir, she wished me luck. 'Keep in touch, if you can. And if you need me, just call.'

'If I don't need you before the birth, I'll probably need you afterwards,' I wailed, suddenly overcome by panic at what I'd got myself into.

Rosemary hugged me and turned to go.

'You'll feel better when you've made the move.'

'In one way, I suppose, but I feel awful about the wreckage I'll be leaving behind me.'

'Just focus on the baby, that's all you can do at the moment. Have you got any idea when you'll be disappearing?'

'Not exactly. I'm seeing Zac on Tuesday. He knows I'm leaving Jay and need a place to stay, but that's all.'

'Good luck with that.'

I kissed her and she left the house, leaving me wondering what lay before me and whether I'd come out of it wounded beyond repair.

I called the dogs and we hit the road. Hoping to shut out my imaginings of how Jay and the family would react when I bolted, I turned on the radio, but it didn't stop my fevered mind circling round and round the subject.

Charles and I had met Sharon and Pete in The Flying Horse the evening before. She'd been exploring the possibilities of alternative employment for me when my *Straight Talking* stint ended and I'd felt a fraud as I pretended to consider her suggestions. She'd even asked Charles if I could join her in Gaia's Cave for part of the week.

'She can stay with us,' said Sharon, her eyes gleaming. 'We can decorate the spare bedroom. I can see it now...floral wallpaper with roosting birds and matching bedding.'

Pete, however, had looked less than pleased at the prospect of yet another corner of his home being Laura Ashleyed.

Charles's reaction to her proposal made me proud. It was seamless. 'Actually, I *have* been thinking of winding down. It's quite a commute but Pandora would be most welcome if she wanted to.'

Brightening at Charles's declaration of intent, Pete broke in excitedly. 'Any time you want to join me in a spot of fishing, old man, I'll gladly lend you my spare rod.'

I'd always known Charles to shy away from the subject of retirement but the dear man proceeded to lead the conversation up and down the highways and byways of potential leisure pursuits for long enough to distract Sharon from venturing any further down my career path.

When we got back, I asked him what he'd say to Sharon when the *ordure* hit the fan.

'I've been thinking about that. If I say it's a total surprise, she probably won't believe me. She'll presume you confided in me to some degree as I'm the nearest thing you've got to a relative. In this country, at least.'

He was right there. What with being domiciled in Los Angeles and the sad fact that I'd met him for the first time last year, my half-brother, Theo, was an unlikely confidant.

'So what have you got in mind?'

'You could write to us both.'

The thought of Sharon opening a letter from me with the news that I'd left her only child in the lurch for an indefinite period, sent shivers down my spine.

'Absolutely not, Charles! What could I say?'

He scratched his chin.

'Well just me, then. Post it to me on the day you go. Make it short. Er, along the lines of...you still love Jay but the combination of the trauma of the past year and losing your job has taken its toll. You need time and space to "find yourself" again. That might stop her—' He paused.

'—hating me?' I finished.

Charles's face sagged into more lines than I'd seen before, reminding me how difficult this deception must be for him. 'I was going to say, it might stop her thinking I knew any more than that.'

'It's a good idea,' I said gently, 'you can help me write it now. And I might as well do Jay's while I'm at it.'

Charles got me pen and paper and between us we concocted the letter that I would post to him the day before I left. The last sentence said that I was going abroad, on a long retreat, and wouldn't be contacting anyone until I felt ready to.

'Sharon's bound to be touchy that I wrote to you and not her, though,' I said, struck with remorse for putting him in an awkward situation.

Charles nodded his head wearily. 'My dear, I've known you far longer than I have her. If I have to remind her of that fact, I will.'

He went off to bed then, leaving me alone to compose my letter to Jay.

Chapter 12 – The Quickening

Jay was out front cleaning his car when we arrived back at Phoenix Cottage.

'Hey, you,' he said, giving me a bear hug while the dogs nudged him hello before disappearing inside. 'Did you get your fix?'

'Certainly did,' I said, clutching my box of elixir and wishing I could defend myself against what he probably thought was my vanity. Now that my TV stint was coming to an end, I could hardly use the excuse of taking the elixir to look fresh for the camera.

'Rosemary examined me. She says the elixir's doing me good and it's okay to keep taking it. You know, to keep my energy levels up.'

'Whatever you say, babe, I'm not complaining.' He looked me up and down, squinting like a farmer surveying a prize heifer. 'You're not bad for your age.'

'Wish I could say the same for you,' I purred, giving him all the excuse he needed to grab me again.

As he nuzzled my neck, he whispered, 'You know you love me just the way I am.'

He was right, actually. I loved every inch of him, but in the interests of healing the planet, I had to suspend my feelings and follow Rosemary's advice to focus on the star child.

We went inside and he gave me the lowdown on the boys, the cricket, the boiler, while I loaded the washing machine and emptied the dishwasher.

'The boiler guy's coming on Thursday, so I said I'd be there to let him in. I can go straight from Donny's and stay the night before. Which days are you working?'

'Tomorrow and Thursday.'

'You'll be all right here on your own Wednesday night, won't you, doll?'

More than all right, I thought. *This means one less evening in the throes of agonising guilt every time I look at you.*

Despite my feelings for Jay, the closer I got to my meeting with Zac, the stronger my desire to get away and get on with being pregnant, instead of being forced to hide it.

After I'd answered all Jay's questions about Charles, Midnight and Beau, I asked him if he was going to Donny's tomorrow.

Saying he'd ring to make sure, Jay went into the garden to make the call, returning with a wide grin on his face. 'We've got a festival gig. Mick pulled a few strings. It'll be fantastic practice for the tour.'

I was so pleased for him, I ran to him and kissed him full on the lips. As I did so, he picked me up and twirled me around.

'Fancy a lie-down?' he whispered, although there was no need to, as the only people around to hear were the dogs.

I hesitated. At night it was easier to get away with my expanding midriff but if he wanted to undress me in the full light of day, it might get embarrassing.

'I've got to make a shopping list,' I said, giving the corners of my mouth permission to droop. 'We've got nothing for dinner.'

'I'll make the list,' he said. 'Won't take me a minute.'

The only thing to do was to get into bed before him so as soon as he'd opened the fridge, I made for the stairs, climbing them two at a time. After closing the bedroom curtains, I swiftly got undressed, happy to be released from my underwear. My breasts were growing daily and none of my bras was coping.

He must have composed that list at lightning speed because it seemed only a couple of seconds later that he appeared at the foot of the bed. In the dim light, as he pulled off his clothes to reveal his slim, muscular frame, he could almost have been the young Jay I'd fallen for so many, many moons ago.

He got into bed and I immediately put my arms around him. I didn't want him to go all tantric on me and start slowly exploring my body, so I pressed my breasts firmly up against his chest. In fact I pressed a bit too hard, causing my new quartz pendant to dig into him, at which point he suspended operations and removed it from my neck. Mentally kicking myself for leaving it on, I surreptitiously removed the ukanite bracelet as well, resuming seduction before he went off the boil, by kissing him hard on the lips with plenty of tongue action. This achieved the desired effect and I didn't have to wait long before we docked, moving together in increasing vigour until he climaxed, uttering a shuddering gasp as he did so.

Normally I was quite happy to stay around for some afterplay but today, because I didn't want him scrutinising my body, I was willing him to leap out of bed and return to his car valeting. Instead, he lay on his back and pulled me over on to his chest, his eyes fixed on my breasts.

'That elixir's better than a boob job,' he said, pulling me closer.

'Are you suggesting I was flat-chested before?' I said, glad that he'd attributed their engorgement to the elixir.

'Perish the thought.'

As he said this he started slowly caressing my breasts, paying particular attention to the nipples.

Oh God, I thought, *what if there's some milk in there and it leaks out?*

I was saved by the bell. My mobile, which was downstairs, started ringing, so I jumped out of bed, grabbing my dressing gown on the way out, impervious to Jay's pleas for me to come back.

It was Cassiel. 'Hello, Pandora, can you talk?'

I walked into the study and closed the door. 'Jay's here, so it'll have to be quick.'

'I'm ringing for an update. Did Viviana contact you? I've tried to ring her, but her phone's going straight to voicemail and she's not replying to my messages.'

'No. She seems a bit unreliable, doesn't she? Do you think

you'll have to look for a replacement?'

'Possibly.'

'Anyway, I've got some news on the Zac front.' I lowered my voice to a whisper, even though I'd need to be shouting at the top of my voice for Jay to hear me in the bedroom. 'I'm seeing him tomorrow, after work. I told him I was leaving Jay and asked if he could help find me somewhere to live. He was in the office when I collected your letter, so I said the person who wrote it was going to help me.'

Cassiel sighed. 'This is proving far more difficult than I thought. I need to see you both so things can be moved along.'

The only place I could think of which wasn't too near the studios was the Raglan Arms, so I suggested that Zac and I meet him there.

'Is it safe? What if Gina comes in?'

'Don't worry. She's doing a voiceover for a Channel Five programme on welfare cheats so she'll be in Soho all day.'

'Fair enough,' he said. 'Make it the Raglan. I'll see you inside. What time?'

I could hear Jay moving about upstairs.

'About two o'clock.'

'I'll be there.'

'Wait. There's just one thing. Zac has a very logical mind and shies away from anything vaguely mystical. You're going to have to water it down for him.'

'Understood. I'll play it by ear. See you tomorrow.'

I waited for Jay to come down before I went back upstairs to get dressed, forestalling a question about who'd called, by lying through my teeth. 'It was the dentist's. Reminding me I've got a check-up on Wednesday.'

One cup of tea later, Jay resumed the beauty treatment he was giving his car, while I escaped to the shops, driving straight past the village supermarket and making for the nearest department store, where I hit the maternity section of the lingerie department to pick up the bump bandeau I'd seen online.

While I was mooching through the underwear, I came across a rail of swimwear. I'd read that swimming was good for pregnant mothers so I tried on a navy and white tankini which was just the job. The top piece was nicely ruched to allow plenty of room for expansion; if only they'd made the stripes vertical instead of horizontal, it would have been perfect.

I was having a look at the day-and-night maternity bras, more reminiscent of grannies than mammies, when I heard a voice behind me.

'Fancy seeing you here.'

I spun round to see Beverly, one of the group who attended the same yoga class as me in the village hall. There was no disguising the basket I was holding, or its cargo of maternity wear. I grinned back at her foolishly, trying to think up an excuse, but I'd left it too late.

'When's the happy event?'

'Have you got time for a coffee?' I said. 'After I pay for these.'

* * *

I'd met Beverly five months ago, when I'd enrolled in the yoga class at the beginning of January. We'd slipped into an easy friendship and had exchanged enough confidences up to now for me to announce, in the department store cafeteria, that I was, indeed, pregnant. I was about to elaborate when I realised she was regarding me with an odd expression.

'Has the pregnancy been confirmed, Pan?'

'What, you mean by a doctor? No.'

'Have you peed on a stick?'

I had no idea what she was talking about and my face must have showed it.

'Have you done a home pregnancy test?'

'No. I don't have to. I can see for myself. My stomach's

swollen, and my breasts, too.'

I felt a fluttering in my abdomen as I said this. 'And I can feel the baby move.'

She took my hand, her face full of sympathy.

'But you told me you couldn't have any children. And you said you'd entered the menopause. I was only joking when I asked you when the happy event was.'

I felt my face burn. In the spirit of revelation, believing my secret had been exposed, I'd confided in her. But she obviously thought I was deluded. I considered telling her about the healing power of the elixir; the look on her face, however, told me that she wouldn't have believed a word of it.

'It's true, look!' I babbled, grasping my tunic from the back so it stretched over my baby bump, paradoxically wishing it was bigger.

Her eyes told me she wasn't convinced. She leant forward, her voice low. 'Do you think it might be psychological? After the trauma of everything you've been through...it could be pseudo-cyesis.'

'What's that?' I said, feeling stupid.

'A phantom pregnancy.'

The laugh that shot out of my mouth sounded hysterical, even to me. It was the juxtaposition of 'pregnancy' and 'phantom' that did it, given that a sort of phantom had made it possible for my womb to function at all and another phantom had recently announced its occupation by an alien.

'I know of a good Cognitive Behavioural therapist,' she said, speaking slowly, her voice full of concern. 'Or you could go to your GP and get referred.'

My yoga buddy obviously thought I was off my head. The only thing to do was to go along with it, otherwise she might be knocking on my door next week enquiring after my mental health and being subjected to the third degree by Jay.

'Yes, you're right. I'll do the peeing on a stick thing, and I'll think about therapy. I have been feeling stressed lately. To top it all, my hours have been cut at work.'

Beverly looked relieved when she heard this. Problems like short-time working she could understand. I thought this was a good moment to make a move, so we kissed and went our separate ways, my way being to the big supermarket to stock up on a few days' supply of Jay's favourite foods. He was a mean cook and could easily look after himself, but I didn't want him to feel that I'd stopped caring about him.

While I was in the shopping mall I went to Boots and picked up a home pregnancy test, to satisfy my nagging, internal psychologist, who was telling me I was suffering from menopausal mania, of which hallucinating the Annunciation of the birth of a messianic child was a classic sign.

On my return, I let myself in quietly and peeped round the living-room door, pleased to see Jay asleep in his chair, the TV on in the background. Dumping the shopping in the hall, I shot upstairs to the bathroom with the test kit and did the necessary, after which I laid the test stick down beside the wash basin and prepared to wait two minutes for the result. But before even sixty seconds had elapsed, a blue plus sign appeared in the display window. And as it formed, so did my joy at being officially declared non-delusional by the *trial of the stick*, followed by another, more unexpected, leap of joy at finally being fruitful.

Pushing the stick back into its box, then into the pharmacy bag, I tiptoed downstairs and took it straight to the dustbin, shoving it far enough down to be swallowed by the contents of the topmost plastic bin bag.

Back in the living room, Jay was still snoozing, which meant I could unpack the shopping without him asking me why I'd bought so much. There had only been six items on the list he'd made on my behalf: an indication of his eagerness to have his wicked way with me.

He was in a great mood that evening, and just before we went to sleep he counted his blessings – which he'd recently read in *The Daily Record* was what everyone should do, last thing at night and first thing in the morning, to keep depression at bay.

'Me and the lads have got a new gig, my mojo's back, I've got a beautiful wife and great kids. Life is good again, Andy. Thanks for putting up with me. I know I've been a miserable git.'

I kissed him before he said any more, my guilty heart already slashed into enough ribbons. He fell asleep right away, but I lay awake for ages, sick at the thought of what I was about to do to him.

* * *

When the alarm rang at six, I just wanted to pull the covers over my head and stay there, but the studio car was coming at seven, so I hauled myself out of bed. Just as the car arrived, I remembered I'd be home later than usual. Scribbling a hurried note to Olivier asking him to let the dogs out at lunchtime if he was around, I posted it through the front door of The Cedars on our way past.

At one-thirty-five I was hovering downstairs in the studio reception area, trying to pretend I was calmly waiting for a friend, rather than seriously afraid I was being stood up.

The show had gone well. I suppose now we all knew we had nothing to lose, we were much more relaxed with each other and with the audience, who'd been responsive and warm, chanting 'Keep *Straight Talking*!' as we left the set.

'They'll cut that out,' muttered Kay as she made for her dressing room. 'Probably dub it with a chorus of "We want more daytime soaps!" as if we haven't got enough of the bloody things already.'

Zac finally arrived fifteen minutes late, by which time I was afraid my blood pressure might be about to blow. He didn't come in, but waved at me through the glass. When I joined him, he began walking briskly along Upper Ground towards Waterloo Bridge.

He was looking good: tall and athletic, his thick hair well cut, his complexion clear and lightly tanned. I couldn't help thinking that he was, indeed, the possessor of some very superior genes. *That's your father, Lyra,* I said silently, patting my tummy discreetly, as I trotted to keep up with him.

'I don't want to hang around here. Let's walk over the bridge and find a pub, that way we won't see anyone we know.' His voice had an edge to it which worried me.

'And hello to you, too,' I puffed.

'Sorry, Pandora,' he said, slowing down and pecking my cheek. 'I've had it up to here with disgruntled, soon-to-be-ex staff. It's bad enough them ringing up and badgering me for work, I don't think I could handle bumping into any of them.'

My heart sank. What was I doing, if not badgering him for a safe place to stay?

'We're going to the Raglan Arms in Charlotte Street,' I said, in my most soothing tone. 'We have to meet someone there.'

Rather than calming him, this shook Zac up even more, his face assuming the expression of a cornered beast.

'Oh, no. Don't tell me it's Jay.'

'Of course not. Do you really think I'd do that to you? It's the other person I told you about – the one who's helping me.'

I hailed a passing taxi and gave the driver our destination. Zac sat without saying a word, his head sunk on to his chest.

I tentatively touched his hands, calling up the energy with which I'd been so familiar once, but which I hadn't used for far too long. 'Put your hands in mine and I'll warm them.'

It was best not to say anything to Zac about energy healing because he didn't believe in what he couldn't see.

He smiled thinly and did as I asked. I was immediately taken aback at the sensation in the palms of my hands when he placed his hands on mine. It was like a hundred tiny dancing feet,

working up a fiery heat. And with the heat came an overwhelming feeling of wellbeing. From Zac's look of surprise I knew he felt it too, so I grasped his hands more tightly and the feeling grew in intensity. I closed my eyes and stayed like that until the bemused taxi driver craned round to see why we weren't budging now that he'd stopped.

'Raglan Arms,' he repeated, raising his voice and looking as affronted as if he'd caught us having sex in the back of his cab.

'Thanks, mate,' said Zac, giving him an unnecessarily large tip.

'You're too posh to be calling people "mate",' I said, on our way into the pub. 'Why do men like you always try to be mates with taxi drivers and builders?'

'For some reason, I'm in too good a mood to argue with you, Pandora. Go and find us a seat. I'll get the drinks.'

Chapter 13 – Disclosure

While Zac was at the bar I looked around for Cassiel. At first I couldn't see him, but when I moved further into the pub I found him alone in a booth reading a newspaper and nursing a pint of Guinness.

'Hello there,' he said, looking up a split second before I moved into his sight line.

I sat down and tuned in to which of his personalities was dominant at the moment.

'Hello, Prince Cassiel,' I said, remembering that Enoch had once described him as such, and he smiled. 'Zac's at the bar. How shall we play this, do you want me to stay while you fill him in, or not?'

'It might be better if you make yourself scarce. Have you told him yet why you're leaving Jay?'

'I was going to, but he got a bit twitchy when I said we were meeting someone else, so I got hold of his hands in the taxi, and it was the most incredible thing. The energy was like nothing I'd ever felt before. He felt it, too, and now he's much calmer.'

'Wonderful,' he said, beaming. 'You connected with the child and she obviously approves of her parents.'

At that moment a glass of mango and orange juice was placed before me and Zac sat down next to me in the booth.

'Zac, this is...well, I'll let him introduce himself.'

'Andrew Truman. I apologise for hijacking your lunch break, but Pandora wants me to tell you something quite important.' The expression he wore was calm and reassuring. 'Don't worry, it's surprising but not life threatening.'

Zac was putting on a brave face but I felt his body trembling beside me. 'Pandora's been quite mysterious, I'm not sure why. All she's told me is she's leaving home and wants me to find her a place to stay.'

With Truman happy to take over the role of narrator, I made my escape by volunteering to place our food order at the bar. On my way back, I was relieved to see that Zac was still there and hadn't denied paternity and run for his life. On the contrary, he was listening intently to what Truman was saying.

Reluctant to return before Truman had finished his peroration, I made a leisurely detour to the ladies' room. By the time I got back to the booth our sandwiches had been delivered, but the men had waited for me to return before starting to eat, proof of how well-mannered they both were.

'Are you done?' I asked.

Truman nodded, adding, 'Zac probably needs time to take it all in, so let's discuss it after we've eaten.'

I sat down beside Zac but he was so deep in thought he didn't lift his eyes from his plate. I was glad of the silence: it gave me a chance to reflect on each of them. I'd been quite besotted by Zac when I'd first met him but I'd thought I was well and truly over him until that fateful night in the hotel, after the Christmas party. I shifted slightly in my seat, remembering our afternoon in his apartment, surprised that I could still feel aroused at the thought of it.

To add to my confusion, the memory of the time I first met Truman in this pub was very much in the air, and I felt my face grow hot remembering how drawn I'd felt to him, and how jealous I'd been when he'd gone home with Gina.

Truman might not have been as classically handsome as Zac, but he had the same qualities: he was innately polite and considerate. What my Irish granny would have called 'a real gentleman'. Some women might find this a turn-off, but I found it incredibly attractive, possibly because my own origins were comparatively modest.

And then, of course, there was Jay, the third member of the trinity. Of course I still loved him, but compared to the other two he was a rough diamond: raffish and Estuary-accented, something he always exaggerated when playing the rock star.

Just at the moment when I was trying to decide who came out first, second and third, Zac revived, and announced he'd get us another drink. As soon as he was out of earshot, I fired a question at my companion. 'How did he take it?'

Zac hadn't looked me in the eye since his chat with Truman and I was beginning to worry that he'd returned to his previous restless mood.

'Very well, considering,' said Truman, morphing into Cassiel now we were alone, and becoming almost conspiratorial. 'Before I started I, um, sprinkled a little "angel dust" around, so he became very receptive to the whole idea of the pregnancy, once I'd explained about the potency of the elixir.'

Picturing Zac snorting an hallucinogenic drug supplied by a pusher who happened to be an angel, I sniggered, but I could see from my companion's bemused expression that he didn't get it. 'Sorry. Go on.'

'Obviously it was a shock at first, but he's agreed to protect you for as long as necessary. He's promised to sort somewhere out.'

'Great,' I said, awash with relief. 'Don't know what I would have done otherwise. What else...'

I was about to ask for a full rundown of what Zac had said, but he interrupted me. 'By the way, any word from Viviana?'

He looked around as if expecting her to appear in a puff of smoke.

'No. I thought you'd given up on her, anyway.'

Conscious of Zac being likely to appear soon with the drinks, I put the midwife situation on ice and attended to the question buzzing at the back of my brain. 'Tell me quickly, did he buy the fact that you're an archangel in a man's body?'

Cassiel looked sheepish. 'That would have been a bridge too far. I judged it best to say that I run a charitable society which can find a very good home for the baby, and you came to me for help when you realised you were pregnant. I called it the Enoch Society, by the way. I said what we couldn't provide is a safe house. So if he could organise that, once the birth is over, you can go back to your life with no harm done.'

'I think you cracked it. Respect, man,' I said, falling into Jay-speak. 'So I keep quiet about the baby being special and you being Archangel Cassiel. Right?' He nodded. 'And this way Zac won't be asking any awkward questions about Andrew Truman's spirit body being trapped in no-man's-land.'

I found my eyes had unexpectedly filled with tears at the thought of the essence of Truman lying dormant in one of Quan Yin's bedchambers, oblivious to what Cassiel was getting up to in his name. Seeing this, his double had the grace to look shame-faced.

Cassiel opened his mouth to speak but closed it again. I knew why when I felt a hand on my shoulder and looked up to see Zac, his eyes full of concern.

'Are you all right? Why are you crying?'

'I'm okay,' I said, swallowing hard. 'Just a bit...overwhelmed by what's happening to me. And to you. How does it feel to be an expectant father?'

As he sat down, his face momentarily twisted into such an expression of sorrow that I thought *he* was going to blub along with me, but he composed himself and took my hand.

'Don't worry, we'll get through it together. But I can't risk you staying at my place in Battersea in case Jay traces you, so I'll book you into a hotel until I can find a suitable place to rent.'

His words immediately cheered me up. It felt good to have a real, live, flesh-and-blood man dealing with the problem – someone who could make things happen quickly. Up to now, the archangel's efforts had been somewhat slow off the mark, to say the least.

'What about the midwife?' said Zac, looking at Truman. 'Will she have to be booked in as well?'

'I'll get back to you on that,' Truman said evenly. 'The important thing is to remove Pandora from her present situation as soon as possible – this week, preferably.'

'Could you be ready to roll in the next day or so?' said Zac.

This took me by surprise. I wasn't sure I was ready for quite such a speedy departure. But maybe it would turn out to be divine timing, since Jay was staying the night in Fulham tomorrow, thanks to Boilergate.

'Actually, Jay's away tomorrow night, so I suppose I could.'

'And how will you tell him?' said Zac, looking apprehensive.

'I'm leaving a letter. I've already written it.'

'Saying what?'

I wondered briefly whether, now I was under his protection, Zac felt he needed to know my every move. 'Saying that the past year has put me under immense pressure and losing my job is the last straw,' (Zac reddened at this), 'and I just have to get away so I'm going on an extended retreat abroad, and I'll be in touch when I get back. There's more, of course: financial stuff, and telling him I love him but I just need some space. Don't worry, I haven't dropped you in it.'

Zac's face fell and I immediately regretted the edge to my voice.

'Sorry, but ever since I wrote it I've been picturing him reading it, imagining how bad it'll make him feel. Just as he's coming out of his depression I'm probably going to plunge him back in. Only yesterday he was saying how good life was again.'

My voice failed and I had another attack of weeping. My two companions could only look on helplessly. To make matters worse, a woman came into the pub with a small, grey schnauzer which reminded me of another hurdle to be cleared.

'What am I going to do about Oscar? Should I take him with me or leave him with Jay?'

'Who's that again?' said Zac.

'My dog.'

'Bring him if you like,' said Zac, 'he's a nice little chap.' And I remembered how good he'd been with Oscar when we'd been an item.

'That might not be such a good idea,' said Truman. 'It'd make it harder for Jay to believe you're going abroad.'

'Anyway, hotels don't usually take dogs,' I said glumly. 'I can hardly leave and then go back for him when we've got a proper place, can I?'

Truman was looking at his watch and I wondered what he had to do that was so pressing. Then I remembered that he was required to regulate his life exactly as the real Truman would have done, as part of the 'deal' of being given permission to occupy his physical body.

'I have to go, I'm afraid. I've got an appointment with Raymond Stone's son. He's found some diaries of his father's he wants me to have a look at before I submit the final manuscript.'

That name rang a bell. A few seconds later I remembered why. Stone was the film director he'd come here to ask Gina about.

'Will you compare what Gina told you with what *he* has to say?' I said, unable to disguise my distrust of anything Gina said.

Choosing not to comment, he simply smiled and produced a business card from his jacket pocket, which he gave to Zac, who read it in surprise. 'So you're a biographer. I thought you'd be a minister or whatever the equivalent is in your organisation.'

'A man of the cloth? No, no. My ministry is something I do outside working hours. You can ring me at any time if you need to.'

Once Truman had gone, Zac moved a little closer to me and lowered his voice. 'I'm not sure getting a companion midwife for a woman of your age is going to be enough. Don't you think you should be seeing a doctor, getting booked into a hospital, all that sort of thing? My sister was always back and forth when she was expecting hers.'

Choosing to ignore his reference to my years on Earth, I said,

'The elixir Truman told you about should keep me fit and healthy.' I searched Zac's face for any hint of disbelief but the 'angel dust' must have done the trick because his only reaction was to shrug his shoulders in acceptance. 'Andrew says it'll be easier to place the baby if I keep out of the system. Then the adoptive parents can register the baby as their own. That way there's no paper trail back to us.'

'Because of Jay finding out,' he said flatly.

'Yes. And because it's better for the child not to be wondering who her birth parents are.'

'I suppose I don't have any say in the matter,' he said, his voice taking on a sullen tone.

Remembering how hysterically I'd reacted on hearing I wasn't allowed to keep the child, I couldn't blame him for feeling this way. Especially as, unlike me, Zac had no idea how important this baby was. Since I was under strict instructions to keep that information from him, if that made me seem hardhearted, then that's how it had to be.

'I'm afraid not. It's different for you, you have nothing to lose. But I want to go back to Jay after all this, if he'll have me. And if Jay or his family got to know what was really going on, they'd probably turn their backs on me. I don't want to end up a sad singleton, all alone at Christmas with a single chicken leg for company.'

'I'm sure that would never happen,' he said, his eyes suddenly all soft. '*I'd* never let it happen. There is another option. Why don't we get together and raise the child ourselves?'

The gasp of panic which escaped my lips wasn't lost on him. A flush rising from his neck suffused his face and he hurried on. 'Or maybe my sister could step in. You could visit...'

'That would be too upsetting. We've got to be grown up about this, Zac. You can't tell anyone, especially your sister.'

He stared at me for a few seconds and in that gaze I read a dawning realisation of what we were both giving up.

'If you want to back out, please say so now. Cass...' Turning my slip of the tongue into a cough, I continued. 'Andrew might have a Plan B.'

'No need, no need. You're right. Has to be a clean break. Don't worry, my lips are sealed.'

Despite his assurances, I couldn't suppress a niggling doubt. Had Rosemary got the message from the spirit of the elixir wrong? She'd told me that I had to leave the place I'm living in now and ask the father of the child to provide me with somewhere peaceful to stay, so how come the father of the child had just made a suggestion which would put a massive spanner in the works?

'I should be getting back,' I said, as gently as I could. 'I've got to start packing.'

This excuse even sounded feeble to me, given that all I'd be needing was some baggy clothing, toiletries, my laptop and the elixir. But I was itching to get out of the noisy pub.

Zac got to his feet. A little reluctantly, it seemed, but maybe I was imagining it. 'I should be getting back, too. Come on, let's walk until we see a taxi.'

The walk gave me a chance to think about the next two days. I was happy to spend tomorrow pottering about at home, just me and the dogs. As I was due to be working on Thursday, it seemed logical for me to check in to the hotel straight from work that day. Jay wouldn't be back from Fulham until late afternoon, so it'd be safe to leave the letter on the hall table for him to find when he came in.

By the time a taxi for hire finally appeared, I was too close to Marylebone station to need a lift. We'd agreed that once he let me know which hotel I was staying at, he'd keep a safe distance from me, just in case Jay got suspicious and followed him. When he moved in to kiss me goodbye, I offered my cheek and he complied without targeting my lips.

Once aboard the train, I checked my phone for messages.

There was still nothing from any midwife. I began to wonder how to get my car to the hotel on Thursday. I'd either have to cancel the studio car and drive myself, which would be tough as I hated driving in London, or...or what? I couldn't think of another alternative. All I knew was, by the time Jay came home on Thursday, my car and I needed to be well clear of Phoenix Cottage.

I decided to ring Olivier. I needed to check if he was free to be dog guardian on Thursday. He answered immediately and told me he was working from his office in The Cedars and the dogs were with him.

'Thanks, Olly, I'll come and fetch them as soon as I get back. I'm on the train. Will you have time for a quick chat? I've just seen Zac.'

'Of course. I can't wait to hear all about it. Has he proposed yet?'

Since I needed a favour, I resisted the urge to scold him for his deplorable lack of tact, ringing off quickly because I was just about to get off the train and board a taxi.

Twenty-five minutes later I let myself in the back door of his house and made for his office. Before I got there I was met by two overexcited dogs, convinced I'd appeared with the prime purpose of rushing them straight out for a walk. Luckily I'd stopped off at the cottage first to get some venison chews, which distracted them while I took my seat the other side of Olivier's vast, Victorian partners' desk, the surface of which was covered with photographs of his confections.

'What do you think, Pandora, the summer berry pavé with white chocolate ganache or the croquembouche stack, swathed in spun sugar?'

'What's it for?'

'*Good Housekeeping* magazine. I gave them three recipes – now they want one more.'

'I don't know, but if you've got any samples I'll taste-test them for you.'

'*Bof!*' he said, sweeping the photos to one side.

I could see his task was making him irritable, so I came down on the side of the pavé. I then broke the news of my imminent departure, outlining what my letter to Jay would say, and giving him a résumé of my meeting with Zac and Truman. Last of all, I announced my dilemma with the dogs.

'My goodness, Pandora, suddenly things are moving fast.'

'That's why I have to try to sort things out quickly. I can't bear the thought of Oscar and Fritz being left alone for hours.'

'You're talking about Thursday, no? That's no problem. But I'll return them to the cottage early. I don't want to be around when Jay gets back. And I'll make sure Justin and I are "out with friends" all evening.'

'Thanks, Olly. As far as Jay's concerned, I haven't told you anything and you know nothing, okay?'

He mimed zipping up his mouth and we high-fived, which wasn't easy given the width of the desk between us. Catching the atmosphere of goodwill, Oscar and Fritz bounded up to me, which set off all of my protective impulses. 'I'm so worried about what's going to happen to them after I go.'

I wanted Olly to assure me he'd take them in and treat them as his own; his face, however, wore an expression of benign regret. 'If Jay asks me, I will help as far as I can. But once you're gone he'll have to take responsibility for them. Don't you trust him?'

My head cleared then, and I realised he was right. I'd supported Jay through his crisis, now that I was having one of my own he'd have to be man enough to do the same for me and take up the reins while I was gone.

'I'll have to trust him, won't I? I suppose I've got too used to protecting him. Ever since he lost everything...'

'Not everything, Pandora. He never lost you or his family. They might be scattered, but what family isn't? It has to 'appen some time.'

'He doesn't like living alone, though. I wouldn't be surprised if he moved to London. Donny's place, maybe.'

Olivier shrugged, but I caught a look of sadness as he leaned down to pat Oscar, and I realised that departures cause ripples more far-reaching than one may ever know.

'Can I phone you to see how he is? And how the dogs are?'

'Of course. Better still, I could visit you, if you like.'

My spirits leapt. The prospect of being isolated from everyone I knew and loved for the fourteen weeks until my due date had been preying on my mind. And common sense told me that I couldn't possibly make a reappearance until I'd got back into shape, especially as I'd supposedly be returning from a retreat where mind, body and spirit had been detoxed, reconditioned and retuned. So it was likely to be sixteen weeks or so before I'd be properly out of purdah.

'That would be fantastic.'

'We'll wait a decent interval, just in case Jay pins a tail on all your friends.'

I giggled. Olly and Justin were fond of detective movies but he hadn't quite got the jargon off to a 'T'.

'Do you think you could shake it off if there's a car chase?'

Before he could answer, the phone rang. It was a business call which sounded as if it was going to be lengthy, so I waved him goodbye, miming that I'd ring him when I was in a permanent place.

Chapter 14 – Viviana

Jay and I spent the evening as we usually did. I cooked, we chatted about what we'd both been doing that day – in my case an expurgated version of events and, for all I knew, in Jay's case too. I was happy to sit and watch TV with Jay but pretty soon the effects of too little sleep and too much drama (personal as well as televisual) took its toll and before I knew it Jay was standing over me, gently shaking my shoulder, telling me to go to bed.

He pulled me up out of the chair and, half-asleep, I instinctively put my arms round his neck and kissed him full on the mouth.

'I'll come up with you,' he whispered, but by then I'd come to my senses enough to remember that I had to keep my baby bump and its binding out of sight.

'Sorry, darling, I'm shattered...don't think I could stay awake long enough.'

'Okay, babe,' he said, escorting me to the bottom of the stairs. 'Sweet dreams.'

I changed into my night things, taking off my bandeau and hiding it in my underwear drawer. Then I flopped into bed and slept right through till eight o'clock the next morning when Jay brought me a cup of tea, taking a seat on the French boudoir chair while I drank it.

The chair was one of the few things we'd brought with us from Four Seasons. I'd picked it up for a song at an auction. Once the seat and heart-shaped back had been reupholstered in rose pink and cream striped silk, and its slim, mahogany legs restained, it had taken pride of place in my home dressing room. Now it sat in the corner of this rather overcrowded bedroom, fighting with the laundry basket for a place of its own.

'Any plans for today?' he asked.

'Oh, a bit of light cleaning. I might hit the shops, treat myself to a new feather duster.'

He smiled. 'Why not come with me to Donny's? He suggested it the other day. This chick he's living with at the moment, she's cool. You'd like her. Then we could go on to Fulham, take Ash and Linden out for dinner. Stay the night there. What do you say?'

My limbic system instantly fizzed with excitement at the prospect of a day out somewhere new, until my logical brain intervened with a bucket of cold water, reminding me that if I wanted to leave my lover I should stay put, or else risk bungling the whole operation.

'What about the dogs?'

'They could come with us – they love the heath.'

'But I'm working tomorrow.'

'No problem. You can go to work from Fulham.'

Inside I was floundering, at a loss to come up with a water-tight excuse and half-tempted to forget my troubles for a day and go with him. Oddly enough, Jay solved the problem for me.

'Hang on, didn't you say something about the dentist? You'll have to cancel.'

This was news to me until I remembered the lie I'd told on Monday, to cover up Cassiel's call. 'Oh yes, I nearly forgot. It's too late to cancel now.' I made an unhappy face which should have been convincing because that's just how I felt.

'Can't you say you don't feel well?'

'I would, but I've got a bit of toothache...it comes on when I have a cold drink.'

He looked concerned. 'What time's your appointment?'

'Two o'clock.'

'Ring them and see if they'll bring it forward.'

'They won't be able to do that, hon. They're always fully booked. Sorry.'

He got up and took my cup, disappointment written all over him. 'Never mind. Next time, eh?' he said, sloping away, leaving me to contemplate how much I hated hurting him, yet how easily the lies had dropped from my lips.

When I went downstairs, I found him cooking breakfast.

'This is an unexpected pleasure, what have I done to deserve this?' I said, as he placed a plate of bacon, egg, sausages and baked beans in front of me.

'Just a small token of my appreciation. I wouldn't have got through the last year without you, Andy.'

He sat down opposite me and unleashed the full beam of his big, brown eyes. 'I want you to know that when I go on the road, when I'm with the boys, you don't have to worry about what I'm up to.'

At one time this declaration would have been Mozart to my ears but my present situation precluded brooding on any doubts I had about Jay's fidelity, alcohol intake or use of recreational drugs once he hit the road with the Jaylers. All I could think of was getting through this final hour or so before he took himself off to Donny's so I could then concentrate on my unborn child and all the preparations necessary for a successful birth. Beside that, much as I loved Jay, my old fears and preoccupations about him paled in comparison.

'I'm not worried,' I said lightly, and he looked surprised. 'I trust you,' I added, remembering what Olivier had said.

And then, much to *my* surprise, one of those declarations I sometimes came out with – that somehow seemed to bypass my mind – slipped out. 'The time has come for you to step into your power, take responsibility for your actions. This phase in your life will test you to the limit; it will show what you're made of. If you survive the trials ahead, you will find a reward you never dreamed of.'

Jay was staring at me open-mouthed. 'Where did that come from?'

I laughed, knowing I had to play it down. Talk of being 'tested to the limit' and 'trials ahead' was too close to the truth to be bandied about the day before I walked out on him. 'I think I must be channelling Obi-Wan Kenobi.'

'That makes me Luke Skywalker.'

'Yup. It's time to grasp the lightsaber and become a Jedi knight.'

'Jay and the Jedis, hmmm.'

A telltale twitch of his lips indicated that a joke was coming. 'A nice ring, has that got...yes. For a name change, it could be time.'

'Button it, Yoda,' I replied. 'The name stays.'

Jay had adopted a mock innocent expression. 'I never said a word...must have been channelling.'

Reassured that he'd regarded my message as a joke, I finished my breakfast and started loading the dishwasher.

Jay was still at the table, reading a newspaper, and I couldn't resist kissing the back of his neck for the last time before who knew when.

'I'm taking the dogs out now,' I said, softly. 'Will you be gone when I get back?'

'Probably,' he said, getting up and taking me in his arms. 'Ooh,' he murmured, as he snuggled into me, 'you're so cuddly, I could stay here all day.'

I waited a decent interval before pulling away. Much as I was enjoying our embrace, guilt and grief were beginning to overwhelm me and I didn't know how much longer I could keep a brave face going. 'Say hello to Donny for me and give my love to Ash and Linden. Take care, darling. May the Force be with you.'

My final memory of him on that day was his laughing face as he wished me the same, at which point I whistled the dogs and made my escape. I was so glad to have the woods close by because my eyes ran with tears all the way through the walk, which didn't really matter because we didn't pass close enough to anyone else for them to notice.

* * *

The rest of the morning passed quickly enough. I'd made a to-do list, top of which was to withdraw enough cash from my account so I wouldn't have to use any ATMs, which would show I was still in the country. Second on the list, was to post the letter to Charles that he and I had concocted to back up my alibi.

It took me less time than usual to pack, because most of my clothes didn't fit me anyway. Even my shoes seemed to have got tighter. As I filled each bag, I put it in the boot of my car, just in case Jay reappeared unexpectedly and found my luggage in the hall.

I couldn't stop my unruly mind imagining worst-possible scenarios, like his car breaking down, or him forgetting something, and then turning up here catching me *in flagrante*, with a boot full of essentials for a top secret four-month vacation.

After lunch, I was about to call Charles and Rosemary to warn them that D-Day was scheduled for tomorrow and that I'd keep in touch, when my mobile phone rang.

The voice that spoke was unknown to me. 'Hello, is that Mrs Pandora Armstrong?'

'Yes.'

'My name is Viviana Moreno. I applied to Mr Truman for the job of midwife and companion.'

My brain froze for a moment. I'd filed the midwife question away into the deeper recesses of my mind, trusting that if the elusive Viviana couldn't make it, then Cassiel would hook a second candidate by placing another of his special ads. After all, that's how he'd enticed *me* into taking the Enoch Society Correspondence Course in the first place. If it hadn't been for the transformation that took place as a result of that, I wouldn't have been eligible to carry this child.

'Hello, Viviana. I expected to hear from you sooner.'

I deliberately paused so she could explain why she hadn't

been in touch. After a short silence, she spoke. 'Something unexpected came up, but I'm free now. I just rang Mr Truman and he told me to ring you to arrange a meeting.'

'Well,' I said, a bit at sea because I didn't know myself where I'd be based after today. 'I'm waiting for some more information. Shall I ring you back when I can give you an address?'

'Where are you now, Mrs Armstrong?'

'I'm at my home.'

'Can I come and see you?'

This was unexpected but, in view of Jay's absence, perfectly feasible.

'Um, I suppose so.'

I gave her the details and told her I'd pick her up from the station. She said she could get to Marylebone station in half an hour and would contact me when she was on the train.

When she rang off I phoned Cassiel quickly to tell him that Viviana was on her way to see me. While he was pleased that she'd finally turned up, he was concerned that Zac hadn't come up with a hotel yet.

'I wonder if it's connected with what he said yesterday.' I was worried now that Zac had gone rogue and decided to bail out.

'What do you mean?'

'Well, after you left, he suggested that he and I could keep the child. I told him that was impossible and he seemed to agree but maybe he's had second thoughts.'

Cassiel sighed deeply. 'That's the danger of revealing only half the story. Give me his number. I'll have to tell him the truth about her.'

'No, that's not the answer. He'd think it's all nonsense. In fact it'd probably make him insist on keeping her.'

My voice had risen quite a bit at the thought of Cassiel putting his foot in it. He must have got the message that he was stressing me out because when he replied, his tone was soothing. 'Very well, Pandora, as you wish. I'll have to contact him, but I promise

I'll be careful what I say.'

After reluctantly giving him Zac's number, I said goodbye and went to the study to switch on the desktop computer. I needed to delete my browsing history in case Jay checked it and found several hits on pregnancy websites and belly binders. Once I'd done that, I switched it off and sat quietly, with Oscar at my feet. Slowly, a picture of Mike came into view. Mike Armstrong was my second husband. He'd bought Oscar for me when we first got married and I wondered if Oscar was thinking about him too.

Mike was as different from Jay as chalk from cheese. While Jay was tall, dark and lean, Mike had been sporty and muscular with piercing blue eyes. In later life he was a very successful businessman, but I'd first met him when he was a young van driver. We rediscovered each other at the time of the new millennium, got married and lived in bliss, here in Phoenix Cottage, for three years until he'd died suddenly of a heart attack. We'd also bought The Cedars at the same time, for me to run as a conference and workshop centre, but when I got back with Jay, I sold it to Olivier and Justin and moved to Four Seasons.

As Mike's eyes began to hypnotise me, I was drawn back to the feelings I'd had when I was with him. They presented themselves to me in the form of hazy layers which surged up and down, intermingling with each other. At the base was a feeling of security, above that was trust, commitment, closeness and passion.

Then I heard the words, *Nobody will ever love you like I do, Andy*, which confused me, as they'd been spoken by Jay, not Mike. I knew this because Mike had always preferred to call me Suze, after Suzy Wong, because I'd been wearing a Chinese-style dress on the night we revived our romance.

My phone's ringtone cut into my daydream. It was Viviana.

'Hello, Mrs Armstrong? My train gets in at three-twenty-five.'

'Okay, I'll be near the barrier. I've got shoulder-length, dark hair and I'll be wearing a pale-green shift dress.'

Viviana was waiting at the barrier when I got there. She was short and stocky with a face which owed more to an Amerindian heritage than the Spanish conquistadors. It was hard to assess her age because her hair, tied back in a low ponytail, was still black and her olive skin only faintly lined, yet she had an air of maturity, augmented by sensible sandals and a boxy dress in a dull navy. She held out her hand and bobbed down when I took it, as if she were curtseying to me. 'Pleased to meet you, Mrs Armstrong.'

A suitcase was placed near her on the ground and I thought it must belong to someone else until she got hold of it and followed me out of the station. When we got to the car, I had to unload some of my own things, so her suitcase could lie flat. I bent down to pick it up but she stopped me and lifted it easily into the boot as if it was half the weight.

Once we were on the road, I saw no reason to beat about the bush and started to question her. As a result, by the time I pulled up outside Phoenix Cottage, I'd learned that she was able and willing to cook, shop, drive, clean, do laundry and generally keep house, as well as monitor my progress, and the baby's.

Once we were inside the house, I broached the subject of her suitcase. 'Are you expecting to stay with me from now on?'

'I understand that is what Mr Truman requires.'

'Oh.'

I would have preferred to have given her the okay today, and waved her on her way until the house was arranged. The idea of sharing a double hotel room with a virtual stranger held little appeal.

'You know we'll have to be in a hotel until we find a more permanent place. And that you can't tell anyone where you are.'

'Yes, of course.'

'And you still want to come with me tomorrow? You don't

want to wait until we've found a house and come straight there?'

'I have left my accommodation, madam. I can't go back there now.'

'Viviana, there's no need to call me madam. My name's Pandora.'

'Are you Pandora Fry from *Straight Talking*?'

This took me by surprise. I suppose I'd assumed that a person who'd come here to study wouldn't be watching much British TV.

'Yes I am. But Armstrong is the name I use privately. I don't much like my first name. You can call me Andy if you like.'

She wrinkled her nose. 'It is not my custom to call my mamás by their Christian names. To me you are Mrs Armstrong, or madam.'

'That's a bit formal,' I said, expecting her to capitulate, but she didn't.

'I could call you madre Armstrong or mamá Armstrong if you like.'

'No thanks. That makes me sound like your mother.'

I waited for her to offer an alternative, but none was forthcoming, so, feeling irritated, I told her I was going to ring my friend to let him know she'd arrived. Having excused myself and gone into the study to make the call in private, I scrolled to Zac, but his number went straight to voicemail, so I left a message.

'Hello, Zac. I'm with Viviana the midwife, now. Could you book a double room with twin beds, please, and let me know as soon as possible which hotel it is. Just reminding you that once I leave tomorrow morning I can't come back here. Bye.'

I returned to the living room but Viviana had disappeared. I finally found her out front giving my old Volvo hatchback the once-over.

'You've got a current driving licence, haven't you?' I said, crossing my fingers. 'Will you be able to drive that?'

'Give me the keys, mam, and I'll see.'

Conceding that 'mam' was marginally better than 'madam', I

did as she asked and off she went, past The Cedars and out on to the main road, reappearing five minutes later looking as if she'd been driving it for years.

It was then it dawned on me that tomorrow I could leave the car with Viviana and go off to work in the studio car. She could spend the morning here, then drive straight to the hotel.

I was about to run this past her when a taxi drew up and Andrew Truman got out.

Chapter 15 – Settling In

'Two unexpected visitors in one day,' I said, taken aback by Truman's appearance on my drive. 'Wonders will never cease.'

Nodding in my direction, he strode over to Viviana and shook her hand. 'Pleased to meet you, at last.'

Viviana performed the same bobbing curtsey to him as she had to me, managing to utter the word 'Sir' before shyly averting her gaze.

The dogs led us through the house to the conservatory.

'I've not long picked up Viviana from the station. If I'd known you were coming, I could have waited,' I said, but Truman wasn't interested in small talk.

Once we'd sat down, he composed himself for a moment and then made his announcement. 'I've had some bad news about Zac. After speaking to you, I tried to contact him, with no luck, so I rang his office and his PA told me he'd been involved in a road accident when he was riding home from work on his bike yesterday.'

I pictured Zac lying bleeding in the road, his bike a snarl of twisted metal, while the rush-hour traffic roared round him.

'Is he in hospital?' I said, trying to contain my distress in Viviana's presence.

'They kept him in overnight. His sister collected him today and took him off to her place in Kent.'

'It's his place, actually,' I said. 'He lets her and her family live there.'

Truman gave me a 'not relevant' frown. I couldn't blame him: I didn't know why I'd said it, either.

'I'm surprised Portia told you all that,' I said, still veering off the point. 'Usually she's very cagey about his whereabouts.'

'I invented a meeting he hadn't turned up for. Made it sound like business, so she had to come up with an explanation.'

I steeled myself and asked the question I'd been avoiding. 'How badly hurt is he?'

'Hard to say.'

Fear about the extent of Zac's injuries was gripping my chest but I fought it off by taking deep breaths, instinctively aware I should protect the star child from too intense a reaction, especially as it was her father who'd been hurt.

Truman must have recognised my struggle, because his tone was calming. 'If he's been discharged he can't be too bad.'

'But was he run over?'

While Truman was assuring me that, according to Portia, Zac had been knocked off his bike on to the pavement, rather than pitched headlong into the oncoming traffic, Viviana got up and crossed the room, pausing at the door to ask if we wanted tea, coffee or a cold drink.

When she was gone, relief at this news gave way to an urgent need to share my views on the newly arrived midwife. 'She's not a bit how I thought she'd be,' I whispered. 'She's older and she acts more like a servant...won't call me by my name. And,' I continued, warming to my theme, 'she's brought her suitcase with her and left her accommodation...I feel I've been steam-rollered into giving her the job.'

Truman shrugged his shoulders, as if to say, *What's the problem?*

Seeing I was getting nowhere fast, I decided to trust the archangel's judgement on the midwife issue and get down to brass tacks. 'So what happens now? Will *I* have to find somewhere for us to stay?'

I was more than a little worried at the effect on my bank balance of the cost of a double hotel room for an unspecified number of days, or, heaven forbid, weeks, so I was hoping the answer would be in the negative.

'No, you won't. You can come to my apartment tomorrow. It'll only be temporary, of course, till we can see more clearly how the land lies with Zac.'

'Thank goodness for that,' I said, feeling my shoulders loosen for the first time in days.

Money was a tricky subject. What I'd saved from my time at *Straight Talking* was earmarked to pay the direct debits for the cottage while I was away, as well as Willow and Cherry's allowances. Taking into account my own living expenses, I couldn't afford to fritter too much away on lodgings.

'How soon do you think I can ring Zac?'

'Perhaps best to leave it till tomorrow.'

He reached into his breast pocket and drew out two address cards, leaving one on the coffee table for Viviana. 'Come over tomorrow afternoon, as soon as you've finished filming.'

The card showed a South Kensington address, and a picture of the sort of mansion block he lived in formed in my mind. For a brief period, as a teenager, I'd stayed in Mulberry Walk with my mother and her artist boyfriend, who'd inherited a townhouse. Property in that area cost a fortune and I vaguely remembered that Truman also had a house somewhere else, so he must be writing bestsellers.

I was about to ask about his books when Viviana appeared with our drinks order and some dark-chocolate Florentines from Harrods that I'd been keeping for a special occasion. *She must have a sniffer dog's nose for chocolate,* I thought, feeling a little unsettled at the way she'd so swiftly commandeered my teapot and my best biscuits.

Viviana looked as if she was about to escape back to the kitchen but I asked her to sit down so I could raise the question of her willingness to drive to London. When she said that would be no problem, Truman told her to ring him when she arrived and he would bring her out a resident's permit so she could park in his bay, as he didn't keep a car in London. He asked us to leave our luggage in the car and just bring an overnight bag into the apartment, as space was limited. He explained that his second bedroom was very small so he'd sleep in there tomorrow night and we could have his bedroom.

I was still feeling curious about Truman's second house, so I made an excuse and went to the study to find the notes I'd made about him the first day we'd met, when I'd been interested enough to search for his name on the internet.

Andrew Truman: born 28 July 1953 (55 yrs old)
Education: Bristol University, History degree.
Career: publishing until 1992, left to pursue a full-time career as ghostwriter and biographer, specialising in creative artists: actors, musicians, directors, authors.
Family: married 1980, one son, divorced 2005.
Resides: Reigate, Surrey, and S. W. London.
Hobbies: sailing, fishing, squash.

After reading the notes, I began to wonder if, as Truman was divorced, we could stay at his place in Surrey. His London apartment was obviously too cramped for three of us.

'Well,' said Truman, rising to his feet when I returned, 'I'd better be getting back.'

'I'll give you a lift to the station,' I said quickly, before Viviana could offer. 'You don't mind being on your own for a little while, do you?'

'No, mam. Do you have a bag I can use for overnight? I need to get some things out of my suitcase.'

I found her a holdall and opened the boot of my car, so she could hoist her case out.

'So, Cassiel,' I said, once we were on our way. 'I can call you Cassiel, can I, now we're alone?'

He nodded, seemingly unaware I was being faintly ironic.

'Truman must be quite well-heeled to live in South Ken.'

Cassiel had shaken off the cloak of Truman so successfully that he answered my questions without any prevarication. 'Not really. It's rented from an aged aunt at a peppercorn rent.'

'But he's got another house in Surrey. Couldn't Viviana and I go there?'

'It wouldn't be practical. His son, Harry, lives there.'

'That's a shame. I mean, I know he's got a son but I thought he might be living elsewhere. Maybe with his mother.'

'No. His mother lives in France.'

'Anyone else around?'

'Not at the moment.'

'So he hasn't got a lady friend?'

This was something I'd been wondering about and had at last found an excuse for asking the question. There was still a part of my heart that was drawn to him and therefore interested in his romantic life. When I say 'him' I mean the man Cassiel was impersonating, not Cassiel himself. That would have been weird.

'No one special at present.'

'But did he have a girlfriend at the time he left his body?'

'Yes.'

Hearing this revelation, I had a consuming desire to find out if Cassiel had made love to her, in order to fulfil his earthly 'contract' of living Truman's life as he would have lived it.

'Did you have to continue the relationship?'

I'd half expected him to tell me to mind my own business but he favoured me with an angelic smile. 'Yes, for some weeks. She was living in the house, so it was unavoidable.'

'You kept that quiet,' I burst out, almost running a red traffic light in my agitation – an agitation which I had no right to be feeling.

'Pandora, I explained to you before, it's an accepted part of our embodiment duties. Truman was attracted to her, so nature took its course. He was, shall we say, quite *active* in that sphere before my embodiment. It was his dalliances that led to his divorce in the first place.'

'So how did it end?'

'When I first embodied, I was preoccupied with getting to grips with Truman's workload and finding a way to contact you. Before he left his body his girlfriend had asked for more commitment but he hadn't given her an answer. It was not within my remit to make life-changing decisions on his behalf, only to continue his daily life in the way he had before.'

'You mean she wanted a ring on her finger?'

'She did indeed.'

'And what about his son, did he have any opinion on the matter?'

'Let's say he's glad she's no longer on the scene.'

We were approaching the station drop-off point, so I had one last try.

'So there's no chance Viviana and I could stay at Truman's house in Reigate if Zac can't come up with a place?'

'I'm afraid not. Harry has a girlfriend himself. She's there a lot of the time.'

'It's in the hands of fate, then,' I said, bringing the car to a halt.

'Yes. We'll have to wait and see. By the way, don't forget your passport.'

'Why, will I need it?' I said, wondering now if Cassiel had thoughts of shipping midwife and mother off to a cheaper part of the world where board and lodging would cost peanuts in comparison to the home counties.

'Your passport is the first thing Jay will look for,' he said, opening the car door. 'He'll want to know if you really have gone abroad. We want him to believe you have, so he doesn't start searching for you here.'

'Okay, I'll do that as soon as I get back. See you tomorrow,' I said, observing Cassiel's retreating figure in a whole new light.

* * *

Truman's apartment was, in the end, a bit of a disappointment.

This wasn't one of those portered developments with a gym, spa and laundry service. Both the building and the apartment were more shabby than chic, our temporary home harbouring a mixture of vintage and MFI furniture (circa 1980), although the curtains and upholstery looked clean enough.

When I arrived from work at two-thirty, Viviana was already settled in. The kitchen was tiny; the only dining table was in the living room but instead of place mats and a vase of flowers, it was strewn with Truman's papers. In fact, he was sitting at that very table typing away on his computer keyboard, so engrossed in his work that he barely lifted his head to greet me when I entered the room.

Viviana showed me to our bedroom where she'd left my overnight bag. Thanking her, I closed the door and lay down on the double bed to rest for a few minutes. I wasn't used to sharing a bed with anyone but Jay; I just hoped Viviana didn't have any noisy nocturnal habits.

It had been a long morning. I'd said goodbye to Oscar and Fritz at seven o'clock when the studio car collected me. I'd had to pretend I was having an attack of hay fever, so red were my eyes from weeping.

My hopes that Gina wouldn't be on the panel today were dashed when I entered the Hair and Make-up suite to see her with a head full of rollers, already in full flow on the subject of how unfair our dismissal was. I'd been hoping to duck out of the post-show rundown but she had a bee in her bonnet about organising an end-of-show party and wanted everyone to go to the pub and start planning it after the meeting. Luckily, when we all flooded out on to the pavement there was a party of Italian schoolchildren approaching from the opposite direction and, in the ensuing melee, I managed to make my escape.

Before hailing a taxi, I'd walked until I found a postbox so I could mail my letter to the Oven Ready HR department saying that, due to stress, I was unavailable to work for the foreseeable future. That way, if Jay contacted them, they'd confirm my story.

I'd made my phone calls to Charles and Rosemary last night. I hadn't wanted to worry them with a tale of woe, so I kept quiet about Zac's accident. I tried to keep my tone positive: the midwife was now by my side and we were staying temporarily with Cassiel/Truman until we found more permanent quarters.

My call to Olivier was more honest. I told him about Zac's accident and our temporary accommodation crisis and warned him that Viviana would be in Phoenix Cottage all morning. I'd had a vision of Olly letting himself in to take the dogs for a walk and Viviana knocking him for six with a frying pan.

I looked at my watch. I'd been resting for longer than I'd thought. It was now four o'clock. I got up and went into the living room where I found Truman still working and Viviana in an armchair, knitting.

'Shall I make some tea, Andrew?' I said.

'If you like.'

His answer was accompanied by a pained expression, making me all too aware that I'd interrupted his train of thought.

When he took a breather to drink his tea, I grabbed the opportunity to ask him if I should ring Zac.

'If you really want to. Although, if he's well enough to talk, surely he'd have contacted you by now. And if he's still recovering, booking hotels won't be uppermost in his mind.'

I agreed with the logic of this but, provisional or not, I'd been given the holy go-ahead, so I went back to the bedroom and called his number. This time, however, I didn't even get voicemail. Zac's phone was now completely dead.

Filled with a mixture of frustration and concern, I called the Oven Ready office. When Portia answered, I decided I had to mention the crash, otherwise she'd fob me off with her usual 'he's out of the office' line.

'Hello, Portia. I was wondering how Zac's doing after the accident.'

There was a pause while I could almost hear her brain ticking over.

'How did you hear about it?'

'Oh, you know, a mutual friend. I need to speak to Zac but his phone's off.'

'I believe it got lost in the accident.'

'Oh, right. So how is he now?'

'I understand he's feeling better. He hopes to be back at work sometime next week. You can contact him then.'

'I need to speak to him before then. Could you give me his sister's number, please. That's where he's staying, isn't it?'

'Sorry, I'm not supposed to...'

I imagined myself brandishing a violet flame-thrower – something I hadn't done for ages – and summoned all the authority I could muster.

'I can assure you it's a matter of urgency.'

'Oh well, seeing it's you. Just don't say where you got it from.'

Portia's speedy capitulation gave my confidence a boost, but failed to stop my hands shaking when I tapped in the number. The call was answered by a male voice but it wasn't Zac's.

'Hello, could I speak to Zac, please.'

'I'm not sure if he's asleep. Who should I say's calling...if he's awake?'

His tone was guarded which didn't surprise me. The family was probably trying to shield him from callers who might tire him out. Of which, unfortunately, I was one, although I couldn't admit that.

'Pandora Armstrong. I'm a friend of his.'

Shortly afterwards the same voice spoke down the line. 'He said he'll speak to you. He's on the extension upstairs.'

There was a click followed by Zac's urbane drawl, the sound of which warmed the cockles of my heart. 'Hello, Pandora. Nice bit of detective work. How on earth did you get this number?'

'From Portia, but I'm not supposed to say.'

'I'm impressed. My sister gave her strict instructions not to dish it out. In fact, if she'd been here you wouldn't have got past her.'

'Who answered the phone?' I said, delighted that he sounded in good spirits.

'My brother-in-law, Chris.'

'So, how are you?'

'Not too bad. Pulled in too close to an HGV when I was turning left...got bumped off my bike and my head caught the curb. Next thing I knew I was in an ambulance and a guy was telling me off for not wearing a helmet.'

There was a pause while I wondered if he'd got concussion and suffered memory loss as a result. What would I do if he had no recollection of what Truman and I had told him on Tuesday?

'I left you a voicemail message about the midwife turning up.'

'Did you? That's good. God knows where my phone ended up – probably down some drain. How's all that going? Have you left home yet?'

How's all that going? was hardly the response I expected.

'Yes. We're at Andrew Truman's place but it's very cramped. I don't know how long we'll be able to stay here.'

'I was supposed to arrange a place, wasn't I? Sorry, I'm not much use at the moment. I want to buy a new phone but Rachel won't let me. She's enforcing a digital detox whether I like it or not. Look, give me your mobile number. I've got an idea.'

I dictated my number and as he was repeating it his voice speeded up. 'Sorry, have to go. Rachel's back. I'll be in touch.'

Chapter 16 – Loving Angels

Viviana had been itching to cook dinner but there was nothing much in Truman's fridge and I didn't fancy going out to find a supermarket. The hour was approaching when Jay would come home and read my letter, the part of the whole business I'd been dreading the most. Because I was nervous that he'd keep on ringing, I switched off my phone so I wouldn't hear it if he did. I couldn't bring myself to block his number, but I'd steeled myself not to talk to him until after the baby was born.

We ended up ordering an Indian takeaway. As we waited for it to be delivered, watching the news on Truman's surprisingly smart TV, which was perched on an old-fashioned, wood-veneered corner unit, I imagined Jay opening the letter. Would he start shouting, swearing – sobbing, even, at my desertion, upsetting the dogs as he raged? Or would he sit quietly weeping, his head in his hands, with Oscar and Fritz licking his face to comfort him? My stomach churned at the thought and I cast around for a distraction, to stop my mind churning over and over as well.

'What do you usually do in the evening?' I asked Truman, when he'd polished off the last samosa.

'Depends,' he said. 'Sometimes I carry on writing. Or I might go to the local pub, see a film, watch TV, read the paper...'

'I wouldn't mind going to the cinema. Is there anything on?'

He switched on his computer and showed me the list of films that were showing locally. There was one about the Illuminati versus the Roman Catholic Church called *Angels and Demons* which seemed appropriate at the present time. I wondered out loud whether the presence of an angel would automatically attract a demon but neither Truman nor Viviana responded, so I shut up.

Viviana wanted to watch a TV programme she followed, so it

was just Truman and I who caught the bus to see Tom Hanks.

'I see you're Cassiel, now we're alone,' I said, as we waited at the bus stop.

'How can you tell?'

'A tiny halo of orange light is leaking out around your head.'

I also detected the sweet, woody aroma of cinnamon but that could have been Truman's aftershave.

He smiled. 'Most people wouldn't notice it, but thanks for the warning. I'll be more careful in future.'

'There's something I want to ask you,' I said, screwing up my courage. 'But I think it's going to embarrass both of us.'

'"Embarrass" is a word unknown in the Enochian lexicon, Pandora.'

I must have looked puzzled, because he elaborated. 'The Enochian language is the language of angels. What was it you wanted to ask?'

'Okay, I'll be frank. In my head, I'm involved with three men at the moment.'

'Three?'

I hesitated. Should I just leave it as Jay and Zac and blame my maths?

'Go on, Pandora,' he said in a kindly, persuasive tone and I blundered on.

'The third is Andrew Truman. When I first met him, against my better judgement, I fancied him. Do you know what that means?'

He nodded, his eyes revealing a glimmer of amusement.

'I even felt jealous when he went home with Gina. Then, once you told me he was, I mean, *you* were Cassiel, I thought I'd stopped feeling like that. But I had a dream where I saw Truman's spirit in a pagoda temple, under the protection of QuanYin, and I felt a sort of loving compassion for him. He woke up from his coma and took my hand and I could feel the life-force energy passing from me to him. Since then, my feelings for him seem to have come back. It happened again on Tuesday, in the Raglan Arms. The fact is, when you're being Truman, I'm attracted to you...to *him*.'

At that moment our bus arrived and we went upstairs where it was less crowded, so we could continue our conversation.

'I think you should meditate upon the nature of love,' he said in a low voice, once we were seated. 'Love is of a higher vibration than other emotions: love is spiritual energy. To reduce it to the merely physical is like buying a Porsche and only driving it to the supermarket.'

'But I didn't say I *loved* Truman.'

'Then examine why you were considering a sexual relationship with him.'

I wanted to deny this, but he was right, I had fantasised about Truman as a lover. Cassiel was waiting for me to speak, so I dug deep and came up with a passable explanation, even though it made me sound as shallow as a puddle. 'I suppose it's because the idea of starting a relationship with someone is exciting. He intrigues me and he's so different from Jay. And,' I added, glancing at him to see his reaction, 'the attraction seemed to be mutual when I first met him. If someone shows an interest in you, it often makes them more intriguing.'

His facial expression gave nothing away which was why his next remark surprised me. 'So all you wanted was the novelty of a new sexual partner who flattered you by flirting with you?'

When he put it like that, my opinion of myself took a further nosedive, but star baby Lyra delivered a hefty kick at that point, and I took it as a sign that she was encouraging her mum to defend herself. 'No, it was more than that. I suppose it was a longing for someone who ticks all the boxes: a perfect match. Jay's been unfaithful in the past. We both have, but him much more than me. Once that happens it's never quite the same.'

'True love survives betrayal. In your case, it survived betrayal and divorce. Could a new love compete with that?'

I racked my brains for an answer, but all I had was questions. 'I do still love Jay, but if my love for him was as strong as before, I wouldn't be tempted by Zac and Truman, surely?'

Cassiel gave me a compassionate smile. This topic obviously held an appeal for him. 'What you describe is a very human perception of love. You yearn for romance to compensate for what you feel are the deficiencies in your present relationship. This longing for an ideal lover has been stimulated by your dissatisfaction with life and your lack of trust in your partner.'

I thought back to the spring of last year when Gaby Laing had come on the scene and I'd started torturing myself with the idea that she and Jay were sexually involved. And then, later in the year, how angry I'd felt on discovering he'd kept me in the dark about his financial dealings, which had brought us within a hair's breadth of insolvency. 'I did blame Jay for the way he put his head in the sand about the money he owed. Maybe I'm not as over it as I thought I was.'

Cassiel nodded his head sagely, like an agony uncle.

'And I do feel guilty about sleeping with Zac, especially now that Jay's more like his old self and being so loving again. But my attraction to Truman is mixed up with sympathy for him being in a cryogenic coma on my account.'

'Not just on your account,' he said, looking at the bigger picture. Lyra chose that moment to perform a victory roll around my womb, so I took it she agreed with him.

I started thinking about Lyra's future then, and we didn't speak for a minute or two. Cassiel broke the silence with one of his pearls of wisdom. 'Humans mostly love in order to be loved, but angels love for the sake of love itself.'

I was puzzling out why he should mention this, when he fired his arrow. 'Have you thought you might have been attracted, not so much to Truman, but to the angel within him?'

I glanced at him in surprise. As he returned my gaze I felt something like an electric charge pass between us and quickly looked away.

'Just remember, Pandora, the heart is the seat of the soul. Be careful who you give yours to. There should be passion in your life but it doesn't have to be of the kind which leads to jealousy and mistrust.'

I stared out of the window, unwilling to look him in the eye again.

'This is our stop,' he said, getting up. I followed him down the stairs to Kensington High Street, where we waited in the cinema queue in silence.

On the journey back, our conversation was limited to the film's shortcomings. I didn't feel I could return to the subject of Truman because I didn't want to revisit the subject of loving angels. Being attracted to a blob of orange light was too extraterrestrial even for me.

We were five minutes away from our stop when Cassiel rescued the situation by returning to the subject of my dream. 'Your dream was valid. When I took Truman's spirit body to the inner planes, Quan Yin came forward to claim him.'

'So when exactly are you going to *reclaim* him and make him whole again?' I asked, relieved that the awkwardness I'd felt had abated.

'When the child is safely in the hands of her new parents. Then I will repeat the process in reverse. He'll wake up one morning and never know a thing about it.'

'But what about when he had to pretend to Zac that he was director of the Enoch Society? And having Viviana and me as guests? Will he remember any of that?'

'No. All episodes connected with the star-child mission will be expunged from his memory. But he'll retain everything connected with his everyday life and work, so he *will* have memories of you and Gina that afternoon in the pub and, of course, Jay and any of his fellow band members he might meet.'

Feeling glad that I wouldn't be completely deleted from

Truman's memory, I turned the conversation to the midwife.

'How much does Viviana know?'

'I told her only that Truman's organisation was providing a good family to adopt the baby and that your pregnancy had to be concealed from your husband so you can return to him after the birth.'

'Right. She recognised me from *Straight Talking*, you know. Is that a problem?'

'Not unless she wants to blackmail you,' he said, smiling.

Cassiel wasn't usually so droll and I had a suspicion that Truman might have surfaced briefly. But I didn't find his remark humorous: I knew very little about Viviana, so therefore would put nothing past her.

'Does she know who the father is?'

'That's none of her concern.'

'Did you talk to her about the key words you used in the ad to attract someone who was spiritually aware?'

'No. People don't always consciously recognise that about themselves. It's innate. Her desire to respond would have been instinctive. Just as your response to the Enoch Society Correspondence Course was.'

'Mmm.'

I didn't reveal any more of what was on my mind: that I hadn't seen any evidence of spiritual depth on her part. But it was early days and she was certainly eager to serve, so maybe that counted.

Viviana had already turned in for the night when we got back so I undressed in the bathroom and tiptoed into the bedroom. Against all my expectations, I fell quickly into eight hours of unbroken sleep and woke up feeling relaxed and relieved that I'd managed to leave Jay without the world crashing down about my ears.

* * *

The next three days slipped by in the way they do when you're in a new environment and you suspend your normal routines. Being in Truman's apartment was like being on holiday, only with none of the benefits of sand or sea. The day after we arrived he left us to our own devices, going off in the afternoon to spend the weekend at his house in Reigate. This gave Viviana the chance to attack all the nooks and crannies that Truman's cleaner, who'd been given paid leave while we were there, had missed. When I could tear her away from her mop and bucket, we found a supermarket and stocked up on enough provisions to avoid having to resort to another takeaway, which hadn't been to Viviana's liking. We also bought some vitamin-D tablets, which she said I should be taking.

She'd given me a brief examination that first evening, when she stayed at Phoenix Cottage, and pronounced everything to be in the right place. But I hadn't been worried because Rosemary had already told me that the baby and I were in fine fettle, the weekend before.

I'd been keeping my phone switched off for most of the day in case Jay called, switching it on briefly late in the evening to check for messages or missed calls, but there was nothing important. I couldn't even bring myself to look at my emails until Sunday night, when I was thankful to find that there was nothing from him in the inbox. This didn't prevent me wanting to know how he'd taken the news and I longed to ring Olivier, but the danger that I'd ring when he was with Jay stopped me – my overactive imagination picturing Olly's phone ringing and his face giving the game away that it was me.

Truman arrived back at one o'clock on Monday and immediately replaced all the books and papers on the table which Viviana had removed from the surface when she'd polished it. Nevertheless, she cleared a space and insisted that Truman and I sat there while she served us lunch. Despite our protests, she ate hers in the kitchen.

'Anything to report?' he asked, as we supped our homemade bean-and-tomato soup.

'No. Not a word from Jay or Zac.'

'Let's hope Zac's back at work today...better leave it till tomorrow to contact him, though.'

'Yes, I don't want to hassle him, but it must be hard for you having us here, invading your space.'

He smiled, raising his eyebrows in a way that seemed to say, *What else can we do?*

'Did you have a good weekend?' he asked.

We chatted on. I told him we'd visited Hyde Park and Kensington Gardens and he told me he'd been to his sailing club. I didn't mention that I'd asked Viviana if she'd like to meditate with me and she'd said 'no thank you', because she was within earshot.

She had prescribed a rest for me every day after lunch and as she was clearing the table she reminded me of this, so I duly complied and withdrew to the bedroom, leaving Truman to get on with his research and Viviana her knitting.

I closed my eyes and managed to doze off, when the sound of voices broke into my sleep. The bedroom was the first room on the right in the hall, close to the front door; snatches of Truman's dialogue with another man were filtering through to me.

'Afraid my cleaner's here...not such a good time.'

'...arrange something...come to Hampstead?'

'...get out of here...go for a drink.'

I lay as if frozen, afraid to breathe, wondering if I'd left any evidence of my presence where Jay could see it. For it was he. His was the voice addressing Truman. And all that separated us was a bedroom wall and a wooden door.

Truman's voice got fainter as he moved away from the front door. I assumed he was talking to Viviana because I still sensed Jay's presence very close by. Soon after that I heard Truman muttering something to Jay, accompanied by the sound of the front door banging shut.

I hadn't realised my heart had been racing so fast until it began to quieten down. Unsure whether the coast was completely clear, I was thankful to hear a tap on the door followed by Viviana carrying a cup of herbal tea.

'Who was that?' I asked, bursting with curiosity to know what Truman had told her.

'A gentleman without an appointment. Mr Truman took him to the pub and asked me to bring you a cup of tea when they'd gone.'

I got up and took my tea into the living room, scouring the room for anything which Jay might have recognised as mine. The only thing I could see was my raspberry-pink laptop, but that was on a corner table and, unless he'd brought a periscope with him, out of his sight line.

'Didn't the man come in and sit down, Viviana? They seemed to be talking in the hall. That's what woke me.'

'No, mam. Mr Truman was in the bathroom when the doorbell rang. I answered the door, but Mr Truman rushed out and talked to him in the hall.'

Imagining Truman's panic when he saw Jay brought a smile to my lips. I could see the lighter side now that the danger had been averted. At least, I assumed it had. Surely Jay had just stopped by to arrange a session with Truman for his book on old rockers or, as Truman had put it, 'groups popular in recent decades'. On the other hand, it seemed strange that he'd turned up unannounced. Why hadn't he phoned first?

I pretended to study one of Truman's reference books, bringing the topic to an end. Viviana's attitude to me had set the pattern of our relationship. Hard as I'd tried to establish a friendly rapport, she had determinedly kept me at arm's length. I wouldn't even describe it as a patient-nurse relationship, more like employer-employee. So I'd decided to respect her wishes and follow her example. If she wanted to act as my maid, then so be it.

I could hardly wait for Truman to come back and tell me all about their meeting but in the meantime, secure in the knowledge that Jay was safely out of the vicinity of Chace Standen, I had a golden opportunity to ring Olivier. I went into the bedroom, switched on my phone, and called his number. He answered at once, his tone businesslike.

'Hello. I'm with a client at the moment. Could I ring you back in ten minutes?'

'Of course, Olly. We'll speak then.'

True to his word, he rang back promptly. He told me was at the Cool Cake Boutique, and had been taking an order from a bride for a very expensive wedding cake.

'Anyway, how are you, chérie? I've been thinking about you and hoping you weren't stuck in a cheap hotel somewhere.'

'No, don't worry. We're still with Truman. He's given us his bedroom and he's got a cubby hole, poor man. I've spoken to Zac. He's still getting over the accident, but I'm crossing my fingers he'll come up with something. I haven't heard from Jay at all. Have you seen him, Olly?'

'Yes, but not the way I expected. You know I said I was going to be hard to find on Thursday night? Well I was anticipating a phone call at least, but nothing. Then on Friday he came over and said he was spending the day at home and he'd trim my hedges while he was doing his own. But he never mentioned you at all. When he finished he let himself in the back door to tell me he'd done them, which wasn't necessary as I could see that. I had the feeling he was checking the place out, in case I was hiding you.'

'How peculiar,' I said, not sure whether to be glad or sad.

If he'd been completely devastated by my letter, I reflected, surely he'd have been beating his breast and gnashing his teeth, wouldn't he?

'Where are the dogs today, Olly?'

'I don't know. He didn't ask me to check on them. I've been

here all day. I don't know where *he* is, either.'

'I do. He's in a pub down the road. You're not going to believe this. He came to Truman's flat about half an hour ago. Luckily I was having a rest so he didn't see me.'

'*Mon dieu*! Why would he do that?'

'Because Truman's cover story for getting in touch with me in the first place was that he wanted Jay and the band to feature in his next book. He turned up out of the blue, without ringing first, so I'm beginning to wonder if he's doing the rounds of anywhere he thinks I might be.'

'He certainly seems to have his Hercule Poirot hat on, darling. Who do you think is next to be investigated?'

'Probably Zac. But I can't warn him because he lost his mobile in the accident. I'm having to wait for him to contact *me*. I wouldn't be surprised if the Oven Ready offices are next on Jay's list. Or maybe he's been there already.'

Olivier gave a shout of laughter and I joined in. Sometimes things are so bad you just have to laugh.

'Zac doesn't know what's coming!' he wheezed.

'I don't want to ring the office again. Portia would start to smell a rat. Anyway, I doubt she'd let me speak to him now I'm not on their books,' I said, sobering up at the thought of a tense scene between Zac and an irate Jay. 'Zac's already had a knock on the head: if Jay gets physical he could do a lot of damage.'

'Maybe I could help you there. I have to talk to Zac about my next TV show. I could slip in a little warning.'

'Oh, Olly, could you? That'd be wonderful. I'll ring off so you can do that now. Call or text me if you get through to him.'

'Okay, darling, *salut*.'

I went into the living room and sat at the table with my laptop, reading an online newspaper. I'd heard Viviana go out when I was ringing Olivier. On occasions she went to the car to get something from her suitcase – Truman still insisted we kept most of our luggage in the boot – but other times she disappeared for hours. I felt it would be rude to ask where she was going or where she'd been. Maybe she went to browse the shops in Oxford Street. I didn't disapprove, it was easy to get cabin fever in such confined conditions, but it would have given us something to chat about.

Truman returned at just after four so I turned off my phone, even though I hadn't heard from Olivier, just in case Jay tried to call. I waited for him to sit down and then asked him the obvious question.

'Did he say why he came here out of the blue?'

He lowered his head and exhaled as if exhausted. Viviana was still out, so I detected that Cassiel was in the ascendant.

'Not really. I suppose he thought because he'd cancelled his previous appointment it was up to him to make another one.'

'But that still doesn't explain why he turned up without ringing you first.'

'Exactly.'

'So you're of the same mind as me. He came here unannounced because he thought I might be here.'

'It would seem so.'

'Tell me what he said. Did he mention me?'

'No. He wants me to go to Hampstead tomorrow to meet the rest of them. I'll be there all day. They've got some old photographs they want to give me.'

'It was a close thing, though wasn't it?' I exclaimed. 'If I'd still been sitting at the table, he'd have probably seen me. I rang our neighbour, Olivier, and he said something similar happened to him. Jay made a surprise visit to The Cedars which was obviously a reconnaissance mission to see if I was there.'

Cassiel had frowned at the mention of Olivier.

'Don't worry, he's a good friend and he's sworn to secrecy. He knows Zac, as well, and he said he'd try to warn him that Jay might pay him a visit.'

The sound of a key in the lock prompted Cassiel to don his

Truman skin. 'Pandora, would you like to type up some handwritten notes I've made on that blues-based rock band we were talking about? I want to give each of them a copy tomorrow and they can confirm dates, etc., and recommend alterations and additions. It's always best to give subjects somewhere to start from.'

I was very happy indeed to spend the rest of the afternoon typing up Truman's notes on Jay and the Jaylers. Any discrepancies I noticed, I left in, working on the theory that if it was all too perfect, there'd be nothing for them to do.

Chapter 17 – Moving On

On Tuesday, after Truman left for his rendezvous with Jay and the Jaylers, and Viviana went out on one of her trips to who knew where, I thought I should ring Charles to see if Jay had been in touch. When I switched on my phone I found a voicemail from Gina, asking me where the hell I was, one from Beverly asking why I hadn't been to yoga, and a text from Olivier which was brief and to the point.

Zac not at work when I rang. Have you got his sister's no? xx

I had to ignore Gina's message, as I was under strict instructions to maintain radio silence with all but a trusted few. Olly was one of the few, so I texted him the number, crossing my fingers that he'd get past Zac's sister, Rachel.

As for Beverly, much as I liked her, I didn't want to risk a phone conversation in case of awkward questions, so I wrote her a card saying as I wasn't working at the moment, I'd decided to go on a long, relaxing holiday and would be in touch when I got back. I made sure this message filled the space on the card because I didn't want to pretend the pregnancy test had shown negative. I felt it might be tempting fate to deny Lyra's existence.

I went out immediately to post it, then hurried back to ring Charles. I'd been worried that Sharon might be within range if he was at his shop when I rang, but luckily he was home alone and eager to know how things were going. I told him we were still at Truman's and that Zac would be finding us somewhere more permanent soon but had been held up by a minor accident. I wasn't sure of this last fact – who knows what lasting effects can come from a bump on the head – but was keeping my tone upbeat so Charles wouldn't worry. For the same reason, I didn't mention that Jay had shown up at the flat.

When I asked him if he'd heard from Jay, his answer didn't surprise me. 'No, my dear, not a dicky-bird. I'd half expected him to come down in person. I got your letter, by the way...had it all ready to show him.'

'Do you know if he's contacted Sharon yet?'

'I'd say absolutely not. She was working in the shop yesterday but no sign of anything amiss. I think I'd have heard all about it if he'd told her.'

'He hasn't said anything to Olivier either. Maybe he's keeping it quiet because he doesn't want people to think I've left him for good.'

'Well, that's understandable.'

'So you might as well tear up the letter, Charles, as he didn't break your door down to find out where I was, in the end, did he?'

'Well, in that case, at some stage, I'll have to ring him to say I haven't heard from you. Three weeks, say?'

'That sounds about right. Look, Charles, I'm so sorry for all this deception I've involved you in. I know it's not your style.'

'Needs must when the Devil drives, Pandora, or in this case, the archangel. Don't worry about any of us, you're the one who's got the biggest part to play in this drama. How's the midwife shaping up?'

I tried to give a balanced view of Viviana, but ended up confessing that I wished she was someone I could be friends with instead of someone who was more comfortable in the role of my carer.

'Perhaps it's for the best. After all, she's the one who'll be taking the baby away from you. She's trying to maintain a professional relationship, from the sound of it.'

I wanted to say that all the cooking and cleaning and curtseying wasn't doing it for me but instead I agreed with him and we said goodbye, with a mutual promise to keep in touch.

Truman got back from Hampstead in the late afternoon, quite exhausted from being with Jay, the four Jaylers and their manager, Mick, who'd sat in on the meeting to make sure nothing was disclosed which might sully the band's carefully restructured public image.

'So, are you happy with what they gave you?' I said.

'Yes. Once they started talking they wouldn't stop. I've got plenty of material for the section they'll be in, so I won't have to meet them again. A bit further down the line I'll let Mick see the draft, but I don't intend to do an exposé, so he should rubber-stamp it.'

Viviana was in the room so I couldn't ask the questions I wanted to. I had to wait till she went to bed before I broached the subject of Jay, asking how he'd behaved and what he'd said.

'He was quieter than the others, but then we'd already chatted about the group's history in the pub yesterday, so—'

'How did he look?' I interrupted, almost willing him to be a pale shadow of himself from pining for me. His lack of public outrage had initially been welcome, but was beginning to smack of indifference.

'The same as yesterday. It's only the second time I've met him, remember.'

'Did you get any impression that the others were feeling sorry for him?'

'No. The dogs were there, by the way. He was out with them for most of the afternoon.'

I immediately formed a mental picture of Jay, Oscar and Fritz running in slow motion through the dappled sunlight of the heath, their ears and his hair fluttering in the breeze, without a care in the world.

'Pandora, has it occurred to you that perhaps he's accepted the reasons you gave in your letter, which were perfectly under-standable, given the turmoil of the past year. Perhaps it's time to stop thinking about what's going on in *his* life and focus on what has to be accomplished in *yours*.'

Flipping heck, I thought, *brought up short by Cassiel's honesty. If the archangel himself thinks I'm banging on too much about Jay, maybe it's time to drop the subject and move on.*

* * *

It wasn't until the weekend that things finally began to happen, by which time I was thoroughly sick of Truman's pied-à-terre and ready to book myself and the midwife a cheap package holiday to Majorca, just to get a change of scenery.

It turned out that Olivier *had* been able to get past the Rachel radar and warn Zac that Jay might pay him a call. It was then he decided not to go back to the Oven Ready office for the current week but to work from home.

Olly had texted me this news, with the message that Zac would soon be in touch. In the end, it was Truman who Zac actually made contact with.

'Good news, Pandora,' Cassiel announced on Friday morning.

I'd just arrived back from a supermarket spree with Viviana, who was parking the car in the underground car park. I'd been craving liquorice, but Viviana was limiting me to small amounts: in fact, she never let me go out alone to shop in case I accidentally overdosed on some forbidden substance. 'Don't tell me, we're all going sailing this weekend.'

He looked puzzled. Irony was something the Cassiel part of him hadn't quite mastered. 'No, I'm visiting Truman's aunt in Gloucestershire.'

'Only joking. So what's the good news?'

'Zac says you can use an apartment in the grounds of his house.'

'But isn't that risky, if Jay's still playing private eye?'

'Well, Zac's pretty sure his accident has provided him with a good enough alibi to satisfy Jay, so he thinks you'll be safe there.'

'What about his sister and her family? How's he going to explain us away to them?'

'I'm not sure. You'll certainly have to adopt another identity.'

'But if any of them watch *Straight Talking*, they'll recognise me.'

'Perhaps you could change your appearance.'

'It's a bit late for plastic surgery.'

Viviana was just coming through the door with the shopping and must have caught his words about changing my appearance. She usually took little part in the exchanges I had with Truman but she parked the bags and studied me closely.

'I can cut your hair, mam. And maybe change the colour, too.'

I struggled to keep the alarm out of my voice but it wormed its way in. 'No! I mean, sorry, but I always get my hair done at the same place.'

Viviana's lips had tightened enough for Truman to notice and intervene. 'You can't go to your usual hairdresser, Pandora, it's too risky.'

An image of Viviana placing a pudding basin on my head, a pair of kitchen scissors clutched in her short, stubby fingers, just wouldn't go away. 'Well then, what about a salon around here?'

'The problem is your public profile. If you're recognised, others could get to hear of it. And, uh, your condition's becoming noticeable now.'

Thanks a bunch, I thought. *It's one thing feeling like a Teletubby, but quite another being told I'm beginning to resemble one.*

Helping herself to some paper from Truman's printer tray, Viviana took one of the pens scattered about the table, and drew a head-and-shoulders image of a bald woman with an oval face and no features.

'This is your face shape, mam. Now look.'

She sketched a pixie cut on to the head as if she'd been designing hair for years.

'I think we lighten the colour, then apply a rich copper with strawberry-blonde highlights.'

'My goodness, Viviana!' I said, getting interested. 'Could you really do that?'

'Of course. I was a hairdresser in Bogotá before—'

She stopped, as if reluctant to disclose any more of her personal history than absolutely necessary.

'Well, no time like the present,' said Truman, looking pleased. 'Zac says you can move in tomorrow so you'd better get on with it.'

'I have to buy scissors as well as the dye,' said Viviana quickly.

This prompted me to get my purse, but Truman beat me to it, producing a fifty-pound note from his wallet.

'Will this cover it?'

It was far too much but Viviana took it without batting an eyelid and within thirty minutes had returned with everything necessary to turn me from a cool brunette into a fiery redhead.

While she was out, I bemoaned the fact to Cassiel that I hadn't been able to make friends with Viviana because she seemed to want to keep the relationship strictly professional.

'Well, you must respect her position, if that's what she wants,' he said, making me wonder whether this reaction was from a male human point of view or an angelic one. To me, they appeared identical.

'I suppose so. But she never talks about her life, or asks me about mine. It's like a jaded marriage – two people sharing a bed with nothing in common and even less to talk about, apart from what our next meal's going to consist of.'

He allowed himself a shy smile. 'I've checked with Zac. There are two bedrooms in the apartment so, from tomorrow, your sharing days are over. You can take heart from that, at least.'

* * *

Before he left us, later that day, Truman urged us to get to Weald House, Zac's place in Kent, as close to twelve noon as possible because Rachel would be out riding with her daughter at that time. Zac would meet us at the gate and take us to the apartment, then explain what he'd told his sister so we could get our stories straight before we met her. I was looking forward to being billeted in a place with a garden. And to seeing him, too.

I woke early on Saturday morning and headed for the bathroom, taken by surprise at my reflection in the mirror. The transformation had been successful: I hardly recognised myself. Viviana had cut my hair beautifully and lightened and tinted it to a rich, coppery auburn. The highlights were subtle but added texture and depth; in fact, I had to admit that her skill matched that of any hairdresser I'd ever handed over a small fortune to.

We'd done most of our packing the evening before, so the few hours before we left seemed to me interminable. Finally, it was time to leave. In my impatience to get to our destination, I took the wheel, even though I could sense that Viviana had antici-pated driving rather than navigating.

Weald House was in the district of Sevenoaks, a mile or so outside the nearest village, and as we turned right on to a private track, there was Zac waiting for us with a lively Border terrier by his side, who barked his own greeting when I wound down the window to say hello. I wouldn't have been surprised to see a locked electric gate and intercom, but it was a traditional, wooden five-bar gate which Zac unlatched for us, an expression of surprise on his face.

For a moment I was mystified, until I remembered that my hair had been interfered with since last we'd met.

'It's not a wig, Zac. Viviana's given me a makeover.'

'Ah,' he said, his eyes panning to Viviana and then back to me.

'How are you?' I said, sensing a certain awkwardness on his part. 'How's your head?'

'Fine. Follow me and we'll talk when we get inside.'

The gravel drive wasn't as long as the one at Four Seasons and the house was less imposing, but it was still a sizeable property, painted white with a black, round-topped front door. An old

Jaguar saloon was parked at the front, so someone must have been at home, unless it belonged to Zac. He walked quickly past the main entrance and round the side of the house towards a double garage with an upper storey. There was a black BMW convertible outside one of the garages, which I assumed to be his, and he motioned me to park beside it. When we unfurled ourselves from the car, he came and kissed me on both cheeks.

'Sorry it's taken so long to get you out of London. I hope this'll be all right for you.'

'I'm sure it will. Thanks for springing us out of Andrew's place. I was beginning to think we'd have to leave the country to get a room each.'

We stood for a moment gazing at each other and then I remembered my manners.

'This is my midwife, Viviana. Viviana, this is Zac, my...friend.'

Viviana bobbed her usual curtsey before turning away from his extended hand and going to open the boot. Zac gave me an enquiring look and I responded with what I hoped was a subtle eye signal which conveyed, *Don't expect any more from her because you won't get it.*

Zac took one of the suitcases which Viviana had already unloaded and headed to the side of the building, where an entrance door opened on to a staircase leading up to the apartment. One more trip and the boot of my car was finally clear of luggage – for the first time since leaving Phoenix Cottage.

While Zac gave us a quick tour, I told him about Truman's embargo on us having anything but an overnight bag and how we'd had to travel to and from the car to get a change of clothes. He smiled at this, which was encouraging, as up to now he'd seemed edgy.

The tour didn't take long. The main room was a combined open-plan kitchen-diner and living room. There was an intercom for answering the door and a telephone which Zac said we could use, within reason.

'So no calls to Colombia,' I said, catching his drift, at the same time winking at Viviana so she knew I was joking. But she shrugged her shoulders as if to say, *Don't make me the butt of your jokes*.

The remaining space contained a bathroom, linen cupboard and two identical bedrooms, not much more than three metres square. We dumped our bags in the bedrooms while Zac made us a cup of tea, explaining that he'd started us off with some basic provisions and giving us directions to the nearest small supermarket.

As he talked, I sensed that he was feeling nervous about us being so close to his family home. Maybe he was worried we expected to eat with him this evening in 'the big house'. He was on to his third description of food shops in the area when I interrupted him. I wanted to get down to the nitty-gritty of what he'd told his family about us.

'Don't worry, Zac, we won't go hungry. Now, can you tell us who we're supposed to be and where we're allowed to go, please?'

'Where you're allowed to go?' he repeated, nervously.

'Can we explore the garden or are we confined to quarters?'

'Er, I haven't thought that through yet. I'll have to run it past Rachel. We've never let this place out before, so there's no precedent. I had it built when the family started expanding. I sleep here when I'm around and sometimes the kids and their friends use it when I'm away.'

'So where are you sleeping now?' I said, worried he'd have to spend the weekends at his other place in Battersea and I'd never see him.

'Don't worry,' he said, sounding pleased at my concern. 'When I had the accident, Rachel put me in the attic room so she could keep an eye on me. Had to fight my way through the cobwebs, but it's all shipshape now.'

'That's good. You will remember to mention the garden, won't you?'

'Point taken,' he said, a trifle impatiently. 'As I said, I'll run it past Rachel.'

'Okay,' I said, making allowances for his failure to draw up a detailed tenancy agreement because of the knock he'd taken on his head. 'So who am I?'

He looked uneasy, as if I were a doctor asking him to name the current prime minister.

'Who did you tell your sister I was?' I prompted.

'Oh, I see. I said your husband's working in America. You were over here on an extended visit, seeing your family, when you unexpectedly found out you were pregnant. You've decided to have the baby here so it has British nationality.'

I felt doubtful of the reliability of this part of the tale. Surely, it should be the other way round. Wouldn't it be more beneficial to the child to be born in the United States and so be eligible for dual nationality?

Zac got up and rummaged in a drawer, from which he extracted a plaited tug toy, whereupon his dog launched himself from one of the armchairs and fastened his jaws round it.

'How did you and I get in touch, then?' I continued, determined to square our stories.

'I said I used to work with your husband and he happened to mention your situation to me the last time I was in the States. I was over in LA for a conference fairly recently, so that rings true.' He tugged at the toy, fixed firmly between the dog's jaws. 'Come on, Max. What a strong boy you are!'

The play growling was getting quite loud so I had to raise my voice. 'Is he supposed to be an actor, director? What? Where do we live?'

Zac was on his hands and knees now and beginning to irritate me. 'I don't know. You choose.'

I said nothing, hoping my pointed silence would shame him

into coming up with some suggestions, but the tug of war continued with renewed gusto, rendering my silence pointless.

'What's most important, Zac,' I said at last, trying not to sound as exasperated as I felt, 'is why I need accommodation at all. Why can't I stay with one of these family members you said I came over to visit?'

He sat back on his heels and contemplated the question. 'Because you don't want to impose on their hospitality?'

I groaned. The holes in the story he'd concocted were so vast, you could drive a truck through them. I'd just have to pray that no member of Zac's family was curious enough to ask me any searching questions on the subject of my current circumstances.

'Didn't your sister think it was odd when you told her?'

'Not really. She's used to weird and wonderful things going on in my business. Like the picket line, for instance.'

His mention of one of my less-than-sensible moments struck home, so I judged it best to back down. 'Okay then. By the way, have you given anyone a name? Me, or this husband?'

'No.'

'Well, we'd better think up some identities now, don't you think?'

I was quiet for a few moments; Zac, on the other hand, started a new game of tossing the tug toy around the room for Max to chase.

An idea for a name popped into my mind almost immediately. My mother's sister, Maggie, had married a man named Ken Scott. I'd always liked her name. They were both dead now, so it wouldn't hurt to borrow them.

'I'm Maggie Scott and my husband's called Kenny. He's a sound technician. That's more anonymous than an actor or director, so nobody will expect to have heard of him.'

Zac stopped cavorting with the dog and made a note of this in a small notebook he produced from his shirt pocket.

'I'm glad that's settled,' I said. 'And what about Viviana? Did you tell your sister and her husband there'd be two of us?'

'Uh, yes. I said your niece would be with you.'

'What!'

Viviana, who'd been busying herself inspecting the kitchen cupboards, visibly stiffened at my scandalised tone.

'We look nothing like each other,' I said, my voice sharp with impatience. 'What on earth made you say that?'

'Well, it sounded more believable than a midwife. They don't normally come into the picture till the last minute, do they?'

He looked so much like a little boy who didn't know why his mummy was cross with him, that my exasperation began to subside. It was beginning to dawn on me why he'd looked so disconcerted when we'd arrived at the gate. With the elixir rejuvenating me by a good decade and Viviana's old-fashioned air, she looked more like a youngish aunt than my niece.

'Zac, can you show me where the fuse box is before you go?' I said, winking at him so he'd know I wanted a quiet word.

We went downstairs to the garage, the dog hard on our heels. Zac opened the fuse box and started pointing out what was what.

'Yes, yes,' I said briskly. 'It's all self-explanatory. I just wanted to get away from Viviana so we could discuss her role.'

'Oh, I see,' he said, looking crestfallen.

It occurred to me that maybe he thought I wanted to get him on his own, which made me blush, embarrassment adding an edge to my voice.

'How are we going to solve the problem of who she is? No way could she ever be my niece. What possessed you?'

Zac's complexion coloured to match mine. 'Your friend Andrew Truman said she was free during the summer because she's doing a midwifery degree. How did I know she'd turn out to be a mature student from another continent?'

I paused, regretting my outburst, as I remembered how surprised I'd been myself when I'd first met her. 'My story's going to be that she's a nurse I've engaged because I'm a mature gravida, in case there are any complications.'

'Okay,' he said, extracting the notebook and jotting it down. I knew he'd never heard of a mature gravida in his life but he was probably too frightened to ask in case I bit his head off again. When he'd finished writing he gazed at me apprehensively. 'Sorry, Pandora. I haven't prepared very well for this, have I?'

He looked like a chastened schoolboy being taken to task for not doing his homework. My heart softened. He really was out of his depth. You'd think a fifty-year-old man would be able to carry off a bit of subterfuge but it really didn't come naturally.

You've got a nice dad, I said soundlessly to the star child and received a tingle in my hands in return, which I passed on to Zac by taking his hands in mine.

'Don't worry. I'm sure it'll be all right.'

He didn't say whether he felt the connection with our daughter, but his face relaxed.

'I'd better go. Rachel's due back. I don't want her coming here to find me.'

'As an excuse to check out the new tenants?' I said, smiling.

'Probably,' he said ruefully, making for the door, where he paused, as if unwilling to say goodbye. 'Look, I'd like nothing more than to have a catch-up but it'd seem a bit strange if I stayed any longer. We're supposed to be strangers.'

I felt suddenly sad. Maybe because I was carrying his child, who knows why, but I wanted to be with him. On second thoughts, maybe *she* wanted to be with him.

'So we'll have to meet off the premises,' I said, hoping he wouldn't disagree.

'Yes, that would work. I'm going back to London tomorrow morning.'

His brow wrinkled.

'How can we organise this? Chris usually gives me a lift to the station.'

'You don't take your car?'

'No. Once I'm in town, two wheels is my preferred form of transport.'

Some sort of awakened maternal instinct provoked a quick retort from me. 'Don't you dare get on a bike so soon after your accident.'

He gave an embarrassed laugh. 'I didn't know you cared.'

This was supposed to be a joke but it fell a bit flat for me. After Cassiel's bus-top lecture, I really wasn't sure myself how deeply I cared for him. How much of what I felt was physical attraction, how much him being the father of our child, and how much, if any, the selfless Love with a capital 'L' which apparently every angel (but very few humans) felt?

I couldn't come up with a glib riposte so I took refuge in the details of our arrangements. 'I can pick you up from the station, can't I?'

'No need. We can go to the Dog and Duck, opposite the station. Park in the pub car park and I'll meet you there. I'll ring the apartment landline just before we leave.'

'Okay,' I said, trying to be cool to disguise the excitement I felt.

'It'll be about eleven. I usually stay here till the afternoon but they're taking Chris out for Father's Day.'

'As long as they don't end up in the Dog and Duck,' I said, and he leaned forward and gave me a soft kiss on the mouth.

* * *

That night, I lay in bed wishing Zac hadn't mentioned it was Father's Day tomorrow. I kept thinking of Jay getting together with the children and them asking him where I was. What would he say? Even if he gave them the official line – that I'd gone on a retreat – the two younger ones, and maybe Cherry as well, would feel I'd abandoned *them* as much as their father. I tried to push away the awful fear that I'd never see any of them again: never see Ashley as a fully qualified doctor; nor see any of the other four making careers for themselves; getting married; having children of their own. Where would I be when they were celebrating their triumphs or needing comfort for their sorrows?

Chapter 18 – Shifting Roles

It was two o'clock. Zac and I had been in the Dog and Duck for almost three hours. We'd begun with fruit cordial for me and Pimms for him, laced with gossip about what was going on at Oven Ready Productions, then progressed to a Sunday roast, seasoned with my account of life with Andrew Truman and Viviana. Now we'd hit dessert, Zac was quizzing me about the Enoch Society.

The Society's purpose was to lead men and women to enlightenment, but I couldn't explain that to Zac in any way he'd accept. In preparation for the moment when he asked about it, I'd decided to describe it as 'a non-denominational charitable organisation with a mission to assist those who ask for their help'.

'That's rather a wide remit,' he said, laughing. 'Can't say I've ever heard of it.'

'It's a pretty well-kept secret,' I said (truthfully), 'known about in healing circles.'

His eyes twinkled. 'Does that mean Andrew Truman's into all that woo-woo stuff? Although he doesn't strike me as new-ageist in the least. Just the opposite, in fact.'

If only you knew the half of it, I thought. But it was better he didn't. As long as he viewed Truman as Mr Stiff Upper Lip it made my life that much easier.

'He's more of an organiser. Someone who knows his way around the systems,' I said, pouring the last half inch of water from the carafe into my glass.

Zac took the hint and ordered coffee for himself and more water for me. I'd hoped this diversion would bring our Truman conversation to an end but I didn't get off that lightly.

'So,' he said, leaning forward and lowering his voice. 'Has he told you who the baby's going to?'

I instinctively put my hands on my bump when he said that,

as if to cover the star child's ears.

'Is she moving?' he asked, his eyes shining.

She was being quiet, actually, but I nodded because that's what he wanted to hear.

He was waiting for me to answer his first question. This time I told the truth. 'He'll never tell me that, just in case I turn up and spill the beans when she's older.'

I had a feeling he was testing me with these questions, to see whether it upset me to talk about giving the baby up, so I forced a weak smile.

'And where are you having the baby?' he persisted.

'I'm not sure yet. Andrew's arranging everything, don't worry.'

That seemed to satisfy him and he moved on to deliver a piece of welcome news. It turned out that his sister and her husband had said we should feel free to use the garden any time we liked.

'In fact, Rachel said she'd like to meet you. So don't be surprised if she asks you over to the house.'

* * *

As Zac had predicted, a couple of days later, his sister rang the apartment to invite me and my 'niece' to the house. Viviana had taken the car and gone off on one of her unexplained sorties, so I said she was out and I'd come over on my own.

As I came in sight of Weald House I noticed the old Jag had gone, replaced by a dusty Range Rover, presumably Rachel's runabout. The house looked very peaceful in the June sunlight. It had two impressive chimneys, one at each end, lending it an air of importance. On closer inspection, however, the stucco revealed itself to be in need of a fresh coat of paint, the window ledges had begun to peel and the front door knocker and letter plate were crying out for some brass polish.

My knock was answered by Max's barking, shortly followed

by Rachel appearing at the door and proffering her hand. 'Hello, Maggie.'

I opened my mouth to correct her, in the nick of time remembering that this was, in fact, my alias.

She led me through the house, past a sizeable drawing room, to a large kitchen with oak cupboards and a massive rectangular central 'island', popular in the 1990s. My passing glimpse of the drawing room had revealed a well-worn Persian carpet and sofas strewn with throws. I'd been curious to see inside the house, expecting it to be a bit of a show home – Zac's Battersea apartment had an interior designer's fingerprints all over it – but his sister was obviously happy with the vintage look.

'What would you like? Coffee, tea? Tisane?'

When it was ready, she showed me into the morning room, which led to a terrace with a metal garden table and chairs. Rachel asked whether I'd like to stay in or go outside. I'd had enough of being indoors lately, so I chose the terrace, which overlooked a landscaped garden of lawns and flower beds.

She didn't start fishing for information immediately. She began by talking about her children and then her husband, a solicitor in a local practice.

'*Your* husband's a friend of my brother's, I understand,' she said silkily.

With her blue eyes, sun-streaked hair and aquiline nose, she almost looked like Zac in drag. But whereas he was pretty much a *what you see is what you get* character, the female version was more devious.

'Yes, they worked together on something or other. I suppose your brother's told you I'm staying in the UK until I've had the baby.'

She nodded vigorously, making evident her eagerness for further revelations.

'Kenny doesn't want me to fly in this condition.'

For some reason, when I said that, my unruly mind provided

a picture of a pregnant me flying like a pot-bellied Tinker Bell in pursuit of Peter Pan in Never Land.

'It's not your first, though, is it?' Rachel said quickly, as if trying to catch me out.

Some beads of sweat formed on my brow but I managed to rally. 'It is, actually. It came as a huge surprise to both of us.'

After that I kept talking so she wouldn't ask any awkward questions like how old I was. My biological clock might be going backwards, but I was still no spring chicken. 'By the way, if you're wondering who Viviana is, she's a midwife I've hired as sort of companion. She's Colombian.'

Rachel's mouth dropped open in surprise. 'Oh well, that must be reassuring for you. But where are you having it?'

I had no idea, but I could see from her face that on no account would plastic sheeting and wet towels be allowed to sully her brother's desirable residence.

'In hospital,' I said.

She mentioned a local NHS hospital but I managed to satisfy her by telling her it was a private hospital. Luckily, she didn't ask which one.

'When's it due?'

'I've got about twelve weeks to go.'

'So you've had your scans?'

I only had a vague idea of the procedures a pregnant mother in the system would have to undergo. For the sake of my own peace of mind, I'd steered clear of all that, trusting that Viviana would be watching for any signs of trouble.

I said I had, hoping that would shut her up.

'Do you know if it's a boy or a girl? After three boys, I was so hoping for a girl, that I had to know. So when they said it was, I bought some pink paint and went to town on the nursery.'

'I'm having a girl, too,' I said, wishing I could be preparing a lovely room and shopping for tiny dresses and nursery furniture instead of shutting my mind off from her life after birth. All

Viviana had let me buy was a pack of sleepsuits for just after she was born and a blanket to wrap her in.

'I expect your husband's taking care of the baby's room,' she said, still digging.

I didn't want to venture down any more fictitious freeways so I gave a pantomime shrug in a *hope so* kind of way and asked her how old the house was. She told me it was Edwardian, left to her brother by a great uncle. I knew this already but reacted with sufficient interest to satisfy her.

'Do you work?' I asked, keeping the spotlight fixed firmly on her.

'Not now, I used to write for a magazine, but the deadlines were hell. If Zac hadn't offered us this place, I'd have to be doing something, but, thank goodness, I don't. God bless Great Uncle Stanley.'

'So your brother isn't married, then?'

I couldn't resist stirring the pot a little. It was his house, after all, and if he wanted a family of his own, why shouldn't he claim it for himself and his wife?

'*No,*' she said, emphasising and elongating the word as if what I'd suggested was preposterous. 'He's more of a serial monogamist...has one girlfriend at a time but never manages to pop the question.' She paused, looking thoughtful. 'Although things might change. His present girlfriend's in America but she's managed to wangle a transfer to her firm's London office, so we'll see what happens when she comes over.'

At the news of Lauren being known in the family as Zac's *girlfriend*, I experienced a sort of prickly heat from my head to my toes. Dismayed, I got to my feet, feeling an urge to escape before I heard any more bad tidings. Seeing Rachel's surprise, I pretended I was feeling a little faint.

'Wouldn't it be better to sit down again, then?' she said, sounding like a sensible head girl talking to a scatty twelve-year-old.

I took several deep breaths, concentrating on the word 'calm' and told her I felt much better.

'Good,' she said, getting up. 'I'll walk back with you just to be on the safe side. And I can show you the garden at the same time.'

We had to descend six wide stone steps to get to the path which skirted the lawn. After passing a fish pond with more weed than fish, we came upon an orchard with apple and pear trees, some pink and white blossom still visible in the upper branches of the apple trees.

As we got farther away from the house, the garden became wilder, with mature trees and shrubs taking over. Emerging from a copse, we passed a wooden summer house with rocking chairs and a veranda which she said we were welcome to use. By this time I was disoriented, not knowing where we were in relation to the apartment, but it proved to be nearer than I thought. Having shown me how to get there without retracing our steps, Rachel left me at the door with a cheery wave.

Viviana arrived back shortly afterwards and I took her to the summer house so we could have a proper talk without her fidgeting about, doing unnecessary housework just to keep busy.

When I'd got back from the Dog and Duck on Sunday, I'd found her ironing towels, just for something to do, which made me wonder whether she was suffering from obsessive compulsive disorder. Yesterday she'd moped about the place, too fed up even to pick up her knitting, and this morning at breakfast she'd hardly spoken a word, save to ask if she could use the car.

We took two white rocking chairs from the summer house and sat down on the veranda. I was glad of the padded cushions because I hadn't managed to shake off the niggling pain in my back that I'd woken up with.

'Do you like it here, Viviana?' I said, getting straight to the point.

'Yes, mam. Better than Mr Truman's.'

'Good. But I'm just a bit worried that you're getting bored. I thought you might have some summer reading to keep you busy. Did they not give you a reading list for your next semester?'

Her eyes flickered and she nodded slowly. 'I get the books from the university library when I need them. They're too expensive to buy.'

'I can give you the money to buy them if it would help.'

'I haven't got the book list with me.'

Extracting any details from Viviana about her life before we met was like pulling teeth, but I persevered. 'Where is it, then?'

'I rented a room in a private house. The landlady let me leave some things with her. The list must be there.'

We seemed to have hit a brick wall but then I had an idea. 'Why don't you go to your landlady's house and get it? You could make a day of it. The change would do you good.'

'She's on holiday, mam,' she said, with a hint of mutinous teenager in her tone.

I didn't believe this for a minute but her attitude was beginning to wear me out so I closed my eyes and concentrated instead on feeling thankful for being in a lovely garden on a lovely day. I'd read that it was very good for the baby when the mother was calm and at peace – common sense, really, but important for me to remember, as this pregnancy was the source of more stress than I'd ever have wished.

'I like to be busy.'

I opened my eyes, surprised that Viviana had actually initiated a conversation that wasn't connected with food, housework or pregnancy. 'And there's not enough to keep you busy here, is there?'

The look on her face told me she was torn between keeping her thoughts to herself and being honest with me, so I prompted her. 'You can tell me. I'm already bored stiff, so I won't be surprised if you are too.'

I was exaggerating slightly but the thirteen days since I'd left Phoenix Cottage was beginning to feel like a lifetime.

She sighed, which was unusual for her, as she typically remained poker-faced in almost all circumstances.

'Yes. I can't sleep very well at night because I don't do enough in the day. For you, you need to rest for the baby, but for me, the days are too long.'

I took her hand and tried to tune into her state of mind, but there seemed to be a barrier I couldn't breach. 'Viviana, I don't think either of us can stand this routine for the next twelve weeks without going mad. Can you think of any way round it? Have you got any friends you want to go and visit for a few days? You don't have to stay by my side all the time. But you understand why I have to remain here, don't you?'

She nodded. Cassiel had told her that I had to stay away from my home, family and friends so my husband wouldn't find out about the pregnancy, and that she would be instrumental in getting the baby to its adoptive parents. It was a strange situation. I knew what she'd been told but the two of us had never discussed it.

Viviana raised her dark eyes to reveal an expression that was almost pleading. 'Mr Truman said I must stay with you. But today I saw a notice in a café for help in the kitchen over the summer. I spoke to them and they said I could have the job. Would you give me permission to take it?'

Only my aching back stopped me from jumping up and performing a dance of joy at the prospect of being free of my restless companion for the whole of the summer. 'Of course I will. Come on,' I said, heaving myself out of the rocker. 'We'll both go. I can tell them what a good worker you are.'

* * *

Once Viviana started at the café, life began to look up. I willingly gave her a lift in the morning and picked her up in the late afternoon. While she was gone I occupied myself with all the tasks she had formerly insisted on performing, but at a slower and more sedate pace, naturally.

In the morning I hoovered, tidied, shopped, or did laundry, as necessary. Once or twice a week I went to the swimming baths at the nearest leisure centre. In the afternoon I took myself into the garden, meditated in the summer house and strolled around the two acres until I felt tired. Occasionally I caught sight of Rachel's children, who ranged from an eleven-year-old girl to a young man who'd started work, but we simply smiled at each other and kept our distance. I imagine they'd been told not to disturb the tenants.

At other times I read, listened to soothing music, watched television or browsed on my laptop. My last domestic task was preparing the evening meal, after which I went to get Viviana. Our roles had altered and it suited us both fine.

When I rang Cassiel with the news of our regime change, slightly to my surprise, he applauded it. He said he could see that Viviana and I needed more activity and it was a good solution for both of us. I asked if we could expect a visit from him but he said he preferred to keep a low profile and, anyway, he had his work cut out maintaining Truman's workload along with his home and social life.

Wondering if he was deliberately avoiding me in case I started lusting after him in his Truman persona, the devil in me asked if any more of Truman's lady friends had been in touch. He answered with a curt 'no' and I felt duly reprimanded.

I was sorry that he was too busy to come and visit. I wanted him to see how difficult it would be to have the baby in our present accommodation, it being so close to the family house, and how Zac's sister wouldn't take kindly to a home birth. When I finished explaining this, he said, in that case, he would make arrangements for me to be admitted to the nearest private hospital.

'But won't they ask for medical records?' I said. 'Wouldn't it be simpler to find another place to live and have a home birth?'

'Not really. It's easier and safer to do it this way. No doubt I'll be able to find someone who is, shall we say, sympathetic to the cause, who will book you in without all the usual bureaucracy. When the time comes, you'll just have to say your records are in another country.'

I had a fleeting vision of Cassiel appearing to a medical secretary and giving her the *Archangel with a Message* treatment.

'Okay, I'll leave it in your hands,' I said, slightly peeved that Andrew Truman's life was receiving rather more attention than mine. 'Don't forget, my stage name is Maggie Scott and, if you need it, my husband is Kenneth.'

* * *

It was soon after Viviana started work that I heard from Charles. True to his word, he'd contacted Jay three weeks after I'd left, to say that he hadn't heard from me and I hadn't responded to a message. My heart almost stopped as I waited to hear what Jay's reaction had been.

'He was as cool as a cucumber. Just told me the story of you needing to go on a long retreat, the stress of losing your job being the last straw, etc. He embroidered it a bit...said he'd had one phone call and you'd sent your love to everyone and apologised for leaving so abruptly. That's not true, is it?'

Charles waited for my reply, but Jay's generosity in not publicly condemning my behaviour had produced a lump in my throat the size of a pigeon's egg, thus restricting my speech to a squeak.

'Hello, Pandora. Are you still there?'

I was so full of gratitude and admiration for Jay supporting me, in spite of how devastated he must have been, that I had to swallow hard before continuing. 'No, I haven't had any contact with him.'

'I didn't think you had. Anyway, in response I made all the right noises: "she seemed stressed the last time she was here", etc. Then he talked about the band. They've got the festival gig coming up next weekend. He can't wait to go on tour in August.'

Charles made it sound so matter of fact that the egg in my throat miraculously shrank, along with the extent of my compassion for Jay.

'He doesn't sound too upset. I'm glad of that,' I added, not really meaning it. 'How are the children taking it, and has he told Sharon yet?'

'He said they were fine and he'd mentioned your sabbatical to Sharon but asked her to keep it to herself.'

'That must be awkward for you.'

'Not really. She told me "in confidence" the other day...sounded quite sympathetic. She expects to see you later in the year.'

'So all the agonising I did, over how worried and offended everybody would be, has turned out to be a waste of energy, hasn't it? Although I still can't work out what Jay's game is.'

'Why does he need to have a game? Maybe he truly believes you'll come back to him when you're ready. That's your plan, isn't it?'

'Yes, of course,' I said, quickly deleting images of Zac and Truman which had appeared on my inner screen, one either side of Jay, like some bizarre triptych.

* * *

A couple of Saturdays later, Olivier came to visit. We had a lovely day and met Zac for a drink in the Dog and Duck before Olivier went home. I'd already grilled him about Jay's comings and goings. All Olly knew was that he was still living at Phoenix Cottage with the dogs and disappearing most days, presumably to London, taking them with him. He'd said nothing about where

I was; in fact, they saw each other so infrequently that the subject of my absence just hadn't come up.

At the weekends, Zac would come round to the garages to pick up his car to go out somewhere – usually the golf course. When he came back, he always buzzed the apartment and I'd come down and we'd wander to the summerhouse for a chat. Sometimes he brought Max round as an excuse to walk in the garden together. I didn't broach the subject of Lauren at all, waiting to see if he'd mention her.

It was at the end of the third week in August, when I was in the final month of my pregnancy looking like Tweedledum and Tweedledee rolled into one, before he did. Olivier was planning to come to see me again and I asked Zac if he'd be around. He studied his shoes, then looked me straight in the eye. 'Sorry, I'm away next weekend. Lauren's in town. She wants to do something for my birthday so we're going to Paris.'

I felt the pressure of molten jealousy in my vitals. *What right have you got to feel like this?* I reproached myself, but my head was burning with indignation. It took every ounce of self-control to keep my voice steady. 'Your sister mentioned that she was coming to London. Is it a permanent arrangement?'

He looked embarrassed.

'When did Rachel tell you that?'

'Ages ago, when we first came,' I said, trying to sound nonchalant, but inside the volcano continued to bubble.

When his eyes searched mine for a reaction he must have seen the fire in their depths because his tone was apologetic. 'She got the transfer she wanted and she's staying in my apartment till she finds a place of her own. I've managed to keep her away from here so far,' he said, as if he deserved a medal. 'I told her we were short of space because we've got tenants. It's actually easier to take her to Paris than bring her here for the weekend, with things as they are.'

'So you're shacked up together and you never thought to

mention it?' I shouted. 'Couldn't you at least have had the decency to wait till after your child was born?'

I'd been clasping my ukanite bracelet with one hand, wishing desperately for some serenity to descend from heaven, but it was too late. My emotions had got the better of me and hot tears were erupting from my eyes.

Unsurprisingly, after my outburst, Zac wasn't in a placating mood. 'I could hardly expect her to stay anywhere else, could I? Anyway, I'm a single man.'

He spoke the last words with a tone and a look indicating that I'd had my chance and rejected his offer, so why should I care?

I turned on my heel and fled upstairs, slamming the front door shut in case he tried to follow me, then throwing myself on my bed and sobbing into my pillow, heartbroken and acutely embarrassed, in turn. Fortunately, Viviana was in the orchard picking apples with Rachel and didn't witness any of this. When I heard her footsteps on the stairs, I slipped quickly into the bathroom for a shower, so when I emerged my red eyes could be explained away by an excess of shampoo.

Chapter 19 – Nearly There

Viviana's casual job in the café finished at the end of August. Her course resumed in October, so she wouldn't be missing any lectures because the baby was due on September sixteenth.

I was glad when the weather started to get cooler after the August Bank Holiday. I was carrying an extra thirty-two pounds and my feet and ankles had become swollen. In fact, my hands had puffed up so much, I couldn't get my ring on. It was my original wedding ring from Jay and I wondered if my finger would ever be small enough for it to fit again.

Viviana told me to keep off my feet as much as possible and drink lots of water, but that only gave me heartburn. I suppose this was when Viviana came into her own, because it was an effort even to wash and dress, so she more or less waited on me hand and swollen foot.

When Truman phoned for an update, I heard Viviana assure him that all was going well, so I wasn't worried, just fed up and praying for it to be all over soon.

Now that my due date was only one week away, I forced myself to think about what I'd do straight afterwards. I'd be having to cope with my star baby being snatched away from me in the midst of a tide of ebbing and flowing hormones, so I was going to need somewhere to grieve and recuperate before approaching Jay.

Up to now I hadn't emailed anyone or ordered anything online because I didn't want to leave any electronic 'footprints' which would place me elsewhere from the remote retreat centre where I'd told Jay I'd gone to 'find myself'.

But it was time to make some plans, so I switched on the laptop so I could book myself into a hotel I liked, a few miles from Chace Standen. It had a spa where I could relax and regenerate to my heart's content. The list of treatments even included postnatal massage.

I hesitated when I had to choose which day to begin my stay. I'd have to risk losing my payment if, heaven forbid, the baby came late. To make matters worse, I'd woken up with a muzzy head which even my daily dose of two precious drops of elixir had not dispelled. I was still trying to decide, when the landline rang.

The ringing of the apartment phone always caused my heart to leap in case it was Zac. He'd been in the habit of calling from his office, although I hadn't seen or heard from him for two weeks – ever since he'd told me Lauren was living with him.

Over the Bank Holiday weekend, my fevered imagination had been inventing several Parisian scenarios, one of which was a tearful break-up, with Lauren packing her bags and hightailing it back to America, and another involving a sparkling diamond engagement ring followed by the lovers arranging a wedding date at Chelsea Register Office as soon as they landed.

Rachel had said she didn't think Zac was the marrying kind, but I'd been wondering if his thwarted paternal instincts might propel him into a hasty marriage so he could have a child to call his own.

As I was contemplating this, I heard a familiar voice in my left ear. *If you really loved him you'd want him to be happy and if that means being with Lauren and starting a family of his own, then you should rejoice for him.*

At first, I thought the voice belonged to my mother, although she'd been unusually quiet since I'd discovered I was pregnant, probably because she'd been there, done that, and didn't particularly want to relive the experience through her daughter. If it wasn't Frankie, then it must be the Big Yin – my higher self, higher consciousness, the inner voice of reason. Whatever it's called, it's usually right.

Naturally, as a graduate of the Enoch Society school of enlightenment, I had to admit the truth of these words, but I was nevertheless hoping Zac would be back at Weald House this coming weekend. With this in mind, I'd asked Viviana to trim and dye my hair so I was looking my best – that's as good a 'best' as a woman resembling a Michelin Man could ever look.

I lumbered to the phone, but instead of Zac's voice, it was Rachel's, wanting me to come over to look at some curtain material samples with her. This late-onset interest in soft furnishings had sprung from her quizzing me about where I'd lived before my husband got a job in America. I had to say something, so I described Four Seasons, placing it in a different county to protect my cover. This had sparked off the dormant Martha Stewart in her and, with the help of a stack of *House Beautiful* magazines, she'd been spending Zac's money on reupholstery, lighting, tie blinds and swags like there was no tomorrow.

I said I'd better check with Viviana first, assuming she'd say no, but Viv said a change of scene would do me good. It had been raining in the night so it was with some reluctance, and an umbrella, that I traipsed round to Weald House.

* * *

'I'm going to miss you, Maggie,' said Rachel, as she closed the sample book. 'But you will keep in touch, won't you? You'll have to give me your address. Although I don't suppose you'll stay in the States for too long. Your husband's bound to want to come back after a couple of years. They always do. Something about the beer.'

With my head full of whether I'd be back home with Jay within the space of two or three weeks, it was hard to keep going with my story of rejoining an invented husband, but I managed to mumble a promise to keep in touch.

So far I'd just referred vaguely to a rented apartment in Los Angeles, but my knowledge of the place was sketchy, having only been to LA once, on a short trip to see my half-brother. I hadn't expected Rachel to want to exchange addresses. What with this and my, by now, aching head, I felt it was time to bring the visit to a close. 'Rachel, I'm sorry...feeling a bit under the weather, would you mind if I toddled off?'

'Of course not,' she said, studying me closely. 'Your face is a bit flushed. Have you got any contractions?'

'No, no,' I said, worried she might set the cat among the pigeons by calling an NHS ambulance. 'Don't worry. Viviana's keeping an eye on me. She'll probably prescribe an ice pack and a darkened room.'

By now, the weather had improved so, hoping the fresh air would clear my head, I said I'd take the garden route and walked through the morning room to the terrace, leaving Rachel to ring the interior-design service and order the curtains.

I was beginning to feel slightly dizzy, so I was careful where I put my feet, since the steps were still wet. Using the umbrella as a walking stick, I had reached the third step when a feeling of intense nausea swept over me, forcing me to drop to my knees and retch, bringing up not only the tea Rachel had given me, but my breakfast as well. This was followed by a gut-wrenching pain which kept me on my knees, frantically clutching my belly.

In my terror that my baby was going to die if I didn't get help, I attempted to crawl back up, at the same time calling Rachel's name, but far too feebly for her to hear. I had nearly reached the terrace when the black rim at the edge of my field of vision expanded until I could see nothing. Then my body slumped and dropped backwards on to the granite steps.

Chapter 20 – At the Crossroads

As soon as I lost consciousness, I felt part of myself floating upwards to a point where I could watch the scene below me. The lightness and freedom from pain was so sweet, I wanted nothing more than to remain in this state.

I had a bird's-eye view of my supine body, spread-eagled across the steps, a trickle of blood dripping on to the bottom step, on which my head had come to rest.

I wondered if I was dead or alive, but so all-embracing was the peace and freedom I was experiencing in this new form, that I felt I would greet either state with the same equanimity.

The answer came from the glow of luminous light around my body which surely indicated that the heart was still beating. This aura was at its weakest point around my swollen abdomen and it was then it hit me that the baby would stand little chance of survival unless I was rescued. No sooner had this thought arisen, than I experienced a tug, as if I were a kite being played, and found myself in the apartment with Viviana, who was in the act of polishing her sensible leather pumps with a shoe-shine sponge.

I glided down to ground level to see if I could attract her attention but she looked right through me. Out of curiosity, I went to the bathroom mirror to see if I had any form of visibility at all – as a spark of light, maybe, or a small orb, but even though I dived around like Tinker Bell, there was nothing to see.

That's because you're pure consciousness, said a baritone voice behind me.

I searched in the mirror but all I caught was the fragrance of frankincense.

'I can hear you but I can't see you,' I said, hoping this would turn out to be a friendly supernatural.

Patience, the voice said. *Is that better?*

I turned to see a shimmering hologram of a bearded man in a spotless white turban topped off with a short, brown fez. The rest of his outfit was equally exotic: a brown suede waistcoat, piped in gold, over a golden robe tied with an orange sash, with white, billowing trousers tucked into knee-high brown boots. This vision, who looked as if he hailed from ancient Araby, was smiling at me with deep, dark twinkling eyes.

I was so engrossed in admiring his gold earring, the rings on his fingers and the talismans around his neck that I forgot about Viviana until I heard the front door bang shut.

'Quick,' I said. 'I've got to get her to the house so she can find me and get me to the right hospital. Can you help me?'

I half expected him to bow and say, *Your wish is my command*, but instead he instantly transported us to my car, which Viviana was just approaching. I don't know how he did it, but the keys she had in her hand suddenly disappeared without her seeming to notice. When she went to unlock the car door she looked in astonishment first at her hand, then at the ground, after which she tipped the contents of her bag on to the gravel. I'd retained enough of my Spanish to be shocked at some of the expletives she was using in accompaniment to this.

We followed her as she retraced her steps, but she couldn't get into the apartment because the front-door key was on the same key ring as the car key. We then observed her making a phone call. I assumed she was calling my number to ask me to come back to let her into the apartment. Getting no response, she rang another number. This time the call was answered.

'Hello, Miss Rachel? It's Viviana. Is Miss Maggie, there? I can't find my keys and I can't get in.'

There followed an exchange between the two women which, luckily for me, led to Viviana asking Rachel to double-check whether I was still in the vicinity of the house.

After a short time, we heard Rachel speaking in an urgent tone at the other end of the line and Viviana saying, 'No, please.

I'll do that. The ambulance must come from our hospital. Don't move her. I'm coming over right away.'

The 'genie' must have engaged warp drive again because, in a trice, we were hovering above the garden steps in time to see Rachel crossing the terrace with a blanket, which she spread over my body. As she did so, she touched my wrists and neck as if searching for a sign of life.

'Am I dead?' I asked my companion. He shook his head but didn't elaborate. There was more I wanted to ask, so I thought if I introduced myself it might stimulate further conversation. 'I'm Pandora, by the way. Thanks for helping me...and my baby.'

He smiled. *I know who you are. My name is Melchior. In my life on Earth I was a magus: a seer, astrologer and healer. Archangel Cassiel asked me to watch over the coming birth of the star child. That is why I was near.*

This answered the question in my mind of whether his rescue work had been random or targeted. It felt good to know that baby Lyra had a celestial bodyguard. Because, after all, *she* was the important factor in all this. I was merely the vessel from which she would emerge. The corollary of that, of course, was that my body was expendable.

'Will I die in childbirth?' I asked, not really caring what the verdict was, as long as the baby was all right.

My question hung in the air, unanswered. He'd started chanting and, as his chanting grew faster, I found myself pulled back into my body at such great speed that when my eyes shot open, Rachel was so shocked, she almost fell on top of me.

By the time the ambulance turned up, the reassembled me had managed, with Viviana's help, to sit upright and reassure all present that no bones felt broken. My headache had returned with a vengeance, however, so I gladly put myself in the hands of the paramedics, who fitted me with a neck brace and whisked me off to wherever it was that Cassiel had arranged I should go.

* * *

Viviana drove herself to the hospital in my car, the keys having reappeared miraculously in her jacket pocket, and from the moment she arrived, stayed by my side like a shadow. The back of my head was sore and bruised but mercifully the CT scan had shown no internal bleeding. My blood pressure, on the other hand, was sky high so they did some tests and found I had pre-eclampsia, which I'd never heard of, but seemed to require urgent attention.

'I'm afraid, Mrs Scott, that we'll have to perform a caesarean section.'

The doctor who stood at the end of my bed was charming and I had every faith in his establishment, but although Viviana had told me she'd informed Truman I was in hospital, I hadn't had a chance to speak to him and didn't know how this new development would fit in with Cassiel's master plan.

'Oh dear. That's a bit of a bombshell. Will the baby be all right? I mean, it'll be more than a week early. Could we delay it, perhaps for a few days? I could go home and put my feet up till then.'

The doctor's smile looked strained. 'I don't want to alarm you, Mrs Scott, but this condition is potentially very serious, both for you and the baby, especially as it's your first pregnancy, and in view of your age...'

I wished I could tell him that it was all right, that the elixir had specially tuned up my gynaecological apparatus to meet the challenge, but of course I couldn't.

At that moment a wave of nausea washed over me and a small niggle of doubt began to take hold. I really did feel weak and ill. Surely the elixir wouldn't fail me...*us*...at the final hurdle? I made one last effort to object, but it sounded unconvincing, even to my ears. 'It just seems rather drastic considering I've been mostly fine throughout the pregnancy, except for the last

couple of days.'

'Well, in the absence of any antenatal records, we've only got your assistant's word for that,' he said tersely, giving Viviana a look of deep disapproval. 'We don't even have the name of your obstetrician.'

'I haven't got one in this country.'

I was going to spin him the same yarn I'd spun the ward clerk earlier, but he waved an irritated hand at me. 'Mrs Scott, regardless of how well you've been feeling up to now, pre-eclampsia can strike suddenly, often in the last month. We can't wait, I'm afraid. Nurse will get you prepared for surgery and we'll perform a caesarean section this afternoon.'

* * *

This time, when my soul left my body, I was in a surgical delivery room surrounded by medical staff in blue scrubs and face masks. Queasy by nature, I didn't want to hang around for the first cut, so I called Melchior's name and the faint scent of frankincense told me he was beside me. *I am here. We are going to a place where you can restore your spirits. Come, let us travel towards the light.*

I let myself be guided by him and as we got nearer, I began to distinguish green hills and valleys in the distance. When we finally left the darkness behind, Melchior slowed down, bringing us to rest in a beautiful garden.

'Hey, I've got a body now,' I cried, almost squealing with delight.

Looking down, I could see a pretty turquoise dress with a sweetheart neckline, identical to one I'd worn in my twenties. I ran over to the sparkling pond, lush with water lilies, koi carp and mandarin ducks, to check my reflection. My hair was long and thick and I was very slim. It was like looking at an old photograph.

'Gosh, thanks for giving me a retro look,' I said, laughing in

delight. 'Is there any chance I could go back like this?'

Melchior had taken a seat under a spreading maple tree, its canopy of leaves a vibrant red, and invited me to sit next to him. At each side of the tree stood a large screen which I assumed was some sort of windbreak. Around us were all manner of attractive creatures: baby deer, rabbits, raccoons, red squirrels, birds of all plumage. It was almost Disneyesque.

These forms you see now, he said, pointing to himself and to me, *are an illusion. It makes it easier for me to communicate with one such as you, who has not yet completely left her body.*

'What about all this?' I said, gesturing towards the garden and its abundant fountains, flora and fauna.

Yes. That, too, is an illusion. What you would experience if you had truly passed over, is in a wholly different dimension. I cannot show you that because once there, you could never bear to leave. And you must return if you want to complete your life's mission.

I'd been feeling disappointed that the surrounding scene was a mirage, but at the mention of a mission, I was all attention. I'd been primed by my spiritual mentor, Enoch, on this subject. He'd told me that my life's mission was to raise the energy of any person or situation that crossed my path and in that way I'd be helping their souls to evolve. That was why I'd become a healer. 'I've already been told my mission is to help and heal others. I'm doing that by giving birth to the star child, aren't I? She'll be doing the same sort of thing but on a far grander scale. According to Cassiel, she'll be going global.'

He nodded.

'Well, surely, if the baby's going to be born in the surgical unit and taken away from me almost immediately anyway, that particular mission's more or less completed, isn't it?'

Melchior put his fingers together to form a church steeple. *Yes and no.*

This answer was just as confusing to me as my presence here. I'd returned to my body successfully once already today, and was struggling to understand why it had happened again. Unless...

'This isn't Purgatory, is it?' I said, panicking. If Melchior left the garden I'd have only the bunnies and bluebirds for company. I was no Robinson Crusoe: there's only so much free time an individual can endure without a stack of books or a laptop with a wi-fi connection.

He shook his head. *Just as there are crossroads in our human lives...times when we have to choose which path to take, so there are crossroads in our spiritual lives. This is your crossroads.*

'Are you telling me my physical body has given up the ghost?' I said, trying to sound calm.

Not yet. But during this time, when your physical body is separated from your spiritual self, you can leave Earth, if you so desire.

'But suppose my body revives?'

The doctors are doing all they can but there is a chance that your physical body will fail after giving birth.

'And if that happens, will I go to that ineffable paradise you mentioned?'

Yes. Your spirit will be absorbed into the Body of Light.

'And would I feel the same euphoria I felt when I left my body for the first time, on the terrace?'

More...by a thousandfold.

'So are you saying I can either go now or wait to see if I lose my life naturally?'

Yes. If you choose to return, the outcome will depend on your will to live and the strength of your body. You may die or you may live. It is not known which.

My overwhelming reaction was, *Let me go now!* What better escape from the misery that was bound to consume me after the baby was taken away, compounded, no doubt, by Jay's rejection. It could all be avoided if I quietly expired on the operating table. Jay could get on with resurrecting his career and Zac with his love life. The rest of them had managed without me for four months, so my eternal absence probably wouldn't make much difference to them.

'Okay,' I said, 'I've made my choice. Take me home – I mean home to the Body of Light, not back to Earth.'

Melchior's holographic image quivered. *Are you sure?* he said, his formerly serene expression breaking up.

'Absolutely. I've had enough of life on Earth. Just when I thought I was doing okay – had the enlightenment thing cracked – not only did I lose my home but my healing touch as well. I don't have the strength to go back and grovel to Jay. As long as you can promise me I'll go straight there, that's my decision.'

Melchior looked towards one of the screens and back to me. *Your ultimate decision will, of course, be respected. But there is a process we have to complete first. You are entitled to see three potential futures to help you decide. But remember, these are not set in stone. The actions arising from your free will, and the free will of others, could determine a different outcome.*

Half of me was intrigued and the other half indifferent. I'd already made up my mind. What could be better than eternal peace? Why torment myself further?

Just then the figure of my mother appeared, dressed in a long, white, linen robe, similar to the one she'd worn at the Circle of Isis meetings. *Think carefully, Pandora. Don't make any hasty decisions you might regret.*

'Hello, Mum,' I said, happy to see her. Usually all I got was a disembodied voice in my left ear with a tendency to nag. 'Don't you want me to come and keep you company?'

As her image faded, I heard the voice of my best beloved. *If she doesn't, I do.*

In front of me stood Mike, the darling husband who'd died too soon. I put out my arms to embrace him but his form dissolved, leaving me alone again.

I'm sorry, said Melchior, *your loved ones are only allowed to say one thing to you.*

I groaned, and my new body slumped in the chair. 'I want to

be with Mike. Can't I go now?'

But even as I spoke, a tableau had begun playing on the screen to the left of the tree. I saw Zac with a cute little girl of about four years old, who was wearing a red and white polka dot hat and dress. They were playing in the garden at Weald House. A swing had been installed on the lawn and the girl was shouting at him to push her higher. He was laughing and teasing her. I was inside the house with Rachel. It looked as if we were planning the week's menus. I didn't look very happy. In fact, my body language suggested frustration and discontent.

When that screen went blank, the one on the right of the tree took over. This showed Andrew Truman's Kensington apartment. He and I appeared to be living together – I figured that out when he brought me a cup of tea and got into bed beside me. Then the scene shifted to a larger place, presumably his house in Reigate, where he was making love to someone who definitely wasn't me. The next scene was set in a marquee at what looked like a literary festival where he was giving a talk about his biography of Raymond Stone. I was in the audience, looking more engaged than I had in the Zac tableau. Then he gave me a mention as his 'indispensable assistant without whom the whole process of researching and editing would have taken twice as long' and I saw myself look down at my hands in embarrassment as the audience clapped politely.

Well, that's it, then, I thought. *I don't particularly fancy either of those futures.*

In the first situation, it looked as if Zac got his way and kept the baby, installing me in his house and obliging me to dance to Rachel's tune, having presumably revealed to her my true identity and the reason for the subterfuge.

In the second situation, I hooked up with Andrew Truman and ended up as his typist-researcher and bit on the side. In either case I'd be playing second fiddle which has never been my favourite place in the orchestra.

You're allowed one more, said Melchior.

I shrugged, imagining this would show me back with Jay in a broken relationship because I'd hurt him so badly by leaving that he couldn't forgive me.

I was right about one thing. The last tableau did feature Jay. At the end of the showing I sat quietly, letting what I'd seen sink in.

Melchior's deep, kindly voice cut through my thoughts. *Have you made a decision?*

'Yes, I have, thank you. I think I'd better go home. I mean home to Earth.'

Chapter 21 – Lying In

Melchior smiled and his whole form sparkled and danced with light. *Follow me. We're going back the way we came.*

This time the light at the end of the darkness revealed itself to be a recovery room in which I was still asleep from the anaesthetic.

Don't open your eyes immediately, whispered Melchior. *Think yourself back in gently.*

I did as he suggested and opened my eyes a fraction to get used to the light and noise, which seemed too bright and too loud. *I'm alive. At least, for the time being,* I thought, still not sure whether to laugh or cry. But what I perceived when my eyes and ears adjusted made me glad to be alive with all my heart and soul.

Viviana was sitting to my left. In her arms, she held a baby whose head was covered with a down of golden hair. Opposite her, dressed in an identical pink and white sleepsuit, another baby – this one with fine, dark hair, was being held awkwardly by Truman. Both babies were exercising their lungs on a grand scale.

I moved my arms to indicate to them that I was coming to, and heard Truman's deep sigh of relief.

'Hello,' I said drowsily.

'You have two babies, mam,' said Viviana, in an unusually animated tone. 'Both of them healthy.'

'Congratulations,' said Truman. 'I hope this pleases you.'

It pleased me so much that if I hadn't been stitched across the middle, I'd have leapt out of bed and performed several cartwheels of joy.

At that moment a nurse came into the room to take my temperature and blood pressure.

'Well, Mrs Scott, what a surprise for you. And for us. The

second little one was hiding, wasn't she?'

Reluctant to become involved in yet another conversation about the absence of scans, examinations by a specialist, etc., I lay back on my pillow with what I hoped was a beatific smile, nodded and closed my eyes.

'They weighed in at five pounds ten ounces and six pounds two ounces. They've been checked over by the paediatrician and they're fine – no need for them to go into the neonatal unit,' she said, raising her voice over the racket. 'So, if you just let me get you and the babies into position, they can take their first feed.'

To protect my modesty, she positioned a screen around the bed before she helped me into a semi-upright position and placed the babies, each supported by a large pillow, next to a breast.

'Would Father like to come and see his daughters having their first drink?' she called, but Truman had left the room, probably to avoid doing just that.

Looking down on two tiny heads, I watched the nurse guiding their mouths to a nipple and giving a cheer when first Blondie, then her smaller sister, latched on.

'There they are, up and away. I'll stay with you, don't worry,' she said kindly. 'This is your first time breastfeeding, isn't it?'

'Yes.'

I couldn't say any more. I hadn't anticipated actually breastfeeding and I was lost in a surge of love for these two little creatures as they guzzled away. I felt I would die for them. I remembered Cassiel's words: *humans mostly love in order to be loved, but angels love for the sake of love itself,* and I realised that the love I felt for them wasn't dependant on them loving me back. At their age they wouldn't know the meaning of the word anyway; they were too busy trying to stay alive outside the safety of the womb.

When the dark-haired one gave a tiny whimper and fell asleep on my breast, the nurse put her into a cot. Her sister suckled for longer.

'Keep going, darling, you need to be strong,' I whispered and she snuffled like a little cub until she, too, fell sound asleep.

When the nurse put the second baby in her cot I began to feel cold and thirsty and the nurse fetched me a blanket and some water which she told me to sip.

'What's that?' I said, feeling a tube under the sheets.

'Don't worry, it's just a catheter. It saves you getting up to go to the toilet. We'll whip it out tomorrow.'

Shuddering at the thought, I pulled the blanket up to my chin while the nurse removed the screen, asking if I wanted any pain relief. By now, the anaesthetic was beginning to wear off and my wound was throbbing but I said only if it didn't stop me breastfeeding. She went off to get the medication and shortly afterwards Truman sidled back into the room and closed the door.

'Hello, Father Andrew,' I said. 'That's got a certain ring to it. Are you masquerading as my significant other, by any chance? If so, you've got the wrong colour hair.'

'I'm afraid so,' he said, smiling. 'I said I was the father of the child...children. Otherwise I probably wouldn't have been allowed in the recovery room. Thought I'd better let you know.'

'Anyway, while we're alone, you can stop being Truman and tell me about Melchior. I suppose you know I was with him during the operation?'

'Yes,' he said, morphing into Cassiel. 'I'm fully aware of what happened. He's still around, acting as her protector. And yours as well, for as long as she's with you.'

I inwardly thanked Melchior, giving him an imaginary high five in celebration of my safe return to terra firma.

'Which one's the star child?' I asked.

'That's her,' he said, pointing to my fair-haired daughter.

I wasn't surprised at this. The young woman in the 'newsreel' had been a natural blonde, like Zac.

'She's the firstborn,' he continued. 'As you can see, they're not identical.'

'How do you know which one was born first?'

'Because I was there. I got here just in time.'

'What about Viviana? Was she there too?'

He frowned.

'Yes.'

'Where is she now?'

'She's gone back to the apartment. She'll be based there until you and the babies are discharged.'

'When will that be?'

'The doctor told me you'll have your stitches removed in four or five days. You can't leave till then.'

'Does that make it difficult for you with the handover?'

'No.'

I found giving up Lyra a hard subject to talk about so I was glad to see the nurse appear with some painkillers. 'Are you over the moon to be the father of twins?' she said to Truman, as she poured me some more water.

She seemed to be almost flirting with him and I wondered whether he gave off a particular pheromone which made him attractive to women. Whatever the reason, I knew the feeling all too well.

He smiled shyly. 'It'll be a challenge but I'm sure we'll manage.'

'You're taking them back to America, I hear.'

He paused and I guessed that the archangel part of him found the lying difficult. 'As soon as they're up to it,' he said, managing another smile.

'Did the doctor talk you through the next few days?' she said, her eyes still fixed on his, rather than mine.

'The stitches, you mean?'

'Yes, they'll probably come out on Saturday. Your wife should be up and about tomorrow, and the babies will have their full examination on Wednesday. The paediatrician likes the father to be present if possible.'

'Of course,' said Truman. 'What time?'

She asked him to go with her to the office to consult the computer for an appointment. Left alone, I started thinking about the tableau I'd seen of Truman and me in bed together, quickly erasing it from my mind on his return.

'The doctor will be asking questions about any childhood problems in our families – that's why he wants to see us both,' he said. 'That's no problem for you, but I'm wondering if I should get in touch with Zac to check if there's anything in his family's medical history I should mention.'

My immediate reaction was horror, remembering the first tableau, with Zac and our daughter in the garden.

'No, you can't! Suppose he comes here and insists *he's* the father. It'd only take a DNA test to prove him right. He might get a court order for custody or something awful like that.'

Then my fuzzy, postpartum brain finally figured something else out. 'Viviana's gone back to the apartment, so when Rachel sees the car, she might insist on coming to see me. Then she could tell him where I am!'

The more agitated I got, the harder I breathed and the more my wound hurt. Seeing this, Cassiel moved forward and placed his hands on my forehead, uttering some sounds which immediately had a soothing effect on me, just as he'd done the day he told me I was pregnant and had to give up the baby.

I closed my eyes and must have drifted off, only to be awakened by the motion of my bed being wheeled along a corridor and into a lift, ending up in the room I'd started off in.

'Where are my babies?' I asked the porters sleepily.

'Beside you, love,' one of them said, and there they were, one either side of my bed.

Cassiel then loomed over me, saying he was going and would be back the following afternoon.

'I'm hungry,' I murmured, when a nurse came into the room to take the babies to the nursery for the night.

I was dying for a warm bacon baguette followed by a blueberry muffin and hot chocolate, but my dreams were soon dashed when a solitary bowl of thin soup appeared with the explanation that I was on liquids only, until the next day.

The soup revived me enough, however, to ask a nurse to look in my bedside locker and show me what was there. Viviana had brought the maternity holdall which had been packed weeks ago with nightwear, toiletries, baby clothes, a baby blanket, etc. I searched in the toiletry bag for my phial of elixir, but it wasn't there, so I asked for my handbag, got my phone, and rang Viviana.

There was no reply to my call so I texted her to please bring the phial, my phone charger and some chocolate.

* * *

Viviana turned up the next morning with the items I'd asked for. I'd never discussed what was in the phial, which I kept in the bathroom, so when she gave it to me I said it was vitamins in liquid form, and fortunately she showed no interest whatsoever.

'Have you seen Rachel?' I said, trying to sound casual.

'No, mam.'

'You *are* staying at the apartment, though, aren't you?'

'Yes. But I went to the cinema last night.'

The nearest cinema was miles away and Viviana had never expressed a desire to see a film before, but as our association was reaching an end – I didn't expect, or want, to see her again after she'd carried out her final duty – I couldn't be bothered to fake interest by asking her what she'd gone to see. 'Oh. Well, if Rachel does ask, just say I had the baby and I've left hospital. Don't say anything about twins. If she wants to know why you're still there, say your student accommodation isn't ready till the weekend.'

Viviana nodded distractedly, giving me the impression she felt the same as I did, that this rather tedious period in our lives was nearing its end and she couldn't wait to get away from here and back to her normal life.

'Does Mr Truman know when he wants us to take the babies away, mam?'

As I was in the process of breastfeeding both my daughters, I thought this question insensitive, to say the least. 'Baby, not babies. I'm keeping this one.'

By admitting this, I realised that the story about rehoming the baby so my husband wouldn't find out I'd been unfaithful no longer made sense, but she just blinked, still preoccupied with her own thoughts.

'The baby can't go before I do,' I continued, 'and that won't be before Saturday. So you'll have to pack up all my stuff and bring it here, and take yours when you leave with Mr Truman in his car.'

A nurse entered the room at that point, to see how the babies were feeding. Although I'd stopped speaking when I saw her, she must have caught the last word. 'You'll need two car seats with twins, don't forget.'

I hadn't even given it a thought, probably because I hadn't expected to be driving anywhere with a baby. This meant that Truman would need one, although he'd have to be careful not to let his son see a baby seat in his car.

Once the nurse had left, having suggested that Viviana could help me take a shower, I asked Viviana if she'd warned him about needing a car seat.

She hesitated. 'I thought I could carry the baby on my lap.'

'No!' I cried, incensed that she would even have considered putting my flesh and blood in danger.

For a moment, I thought she was going to bite back, but she restrained herself.

'Mr Truman's coming this afternoon,' I said, frostily, 'so I'll let him know about it then.'

In silence, she helped me get out of bed and into the toilet, the catheter having been removed first thing. Then she supported me in the shower and lathered my hair carefully (my head was still sore from the fall), while I held on to the shower rail. I hated the look of my body. My belly was decorated with a long row of stitches like a badly sewn rugby ball above which hung two inflated beach balls, sagging under the weight of the excess milk I was producing. I swear I could have fed quadruplets if I'd had them. Being vertical gave me a dragging pain so I was eager to get off my feet, but Viviana insisted on walking me around the room a few times before she helped me back to bed.

'Thanks, Viviana,' I said, feeling ashamed of my earlier outburst. 'I expect you'll be as glad as I am when it's all over.'

'Yes, mam,' she replied. 'It's hard for you, but it's good you have another little one.'

At that, my eyes filled with tears.

'The baby will be safe, don't worry,' she said, speaking with such conviction that I grew sure Cassiel must have let her in on his plans. He'd told me only that she was going to a couple in a high position, the woman feigning pregnancy so that the baby could be registered as theirs.

'Do you know where she's going?' I said, excitedly.

'No, no,' she said hurriedly, looking flustered.

My heart sank, soon to be raised by the appearance of solid food. As I tucked into sole mornay and creamed potatoes, Viviana excused herself, saying she'd be back tomorrow with my laptop and some magazines.

The food, and the fact that my sleep had been broken by a nurse taking my temperature at intervals throughout the night, made me drowsy. I slept till the middle of the afternoon and woke up to the sight of Cassiel sitting with Lyra, rocking her from side to side. 'She started crying,' he said, smiling. 'I didn't want her to disturb you.'

'Is Lucy awake, too?' I yawned.

The name had slipped out unconsciously. Up to then, she'd been 'the dark-haired one'.

'Lucy means "light". It's a good choice for her,' he said, his own light radiating a good three inches from Truman's skull.

I pointed at my own head to alert him to the leakage so he could adjust it before anyone came in.

'I call *her* Lyra,' I said, nodding at the baby he was holding, 'because of where she's from. And her eyes are so big, when they catch the light, it seems she has stars in her eyes.'

He looked sad, probably because he perceived the extent of my love for her. 'I've had a word with the doctor,' he said. 'If everything heals as it should, he'll remove the stitches on Saturday morning and you and the twins can be discharged then.'

'Right. Let's aim for Saturday morning. I'll let Viviana know. Have you told her where you're going?''

He shook his head. 'I've told her nothing about our desti-nation.'

So I was wrong, I thought.

'By the way, I'd like to give Lyra this,' I said, touching the rose quartz pendant I was wearing. It was so dainty, even a little girl could wear it.

'Very appropriate,' he said, examining the gold lattice flower which overlaid the rose quartz, its stamens forming a four-pointed star. 'We can give it to the new parents to keep for her but you do understand...'

'Yes,' I sighed, 'she'll never know it's from me. I'm resigned to that. I want her to have it anyway.'

Then I remembered the car-seat dilemma. 'The nurse pointed out the baby needs a car seat. Viviana seemed to think it was all right for her to carry the baby on her lap!'

He looked rather more irritated than one would have thought possible for an archangel, so I guessed that Truman's emotions had momentarily risen to the surface. 'I'm sadly disappointed in Viviana's overall performance. Apart from being far too withdrawn to be a true companion, she neither spotted the warning signs of your illness, nor flagged up this important detail.' He fished Truman's mobile phone out of his inside jacket pocket to do an internet search. 'Luckily, there's a store not too far away. I'll have to get one fitted on my way here on Saturday.'

'Well, I did tell you early on that she wasn't what I expected.'

There were one or two other issues which had occurred to me, so I didn't linger on what could easily have turned into an *I told you so* lecture.

'Lyra will need a passport if you're leaving the country.'

'Not necessary. We're taking her to an embassy.'

I'd love to have known which one but it would have been useless to ask.

'Why do you need Viviana with you?'

'Because I couldn't help the baby if she was in distress. She needs someone next to her...for feeding, changing, etcetera.'

Accepting the logic of that, I continued. 'Will you drop Viviana off afterwards?'

'Yes, at a station or wherever she asks to go, within reason.'

'And where shall *I* go on Saturday? I can hardly turn up at my house. Jay would have a fit. In fact, I don't think I'm allowed to drive, anyway.'

Having been interrupted when I was about to book the hotel, I was open to any other board and lodging which might be on offer.

'I'm sorry,' he said gravely. 'I'm afraid I cannot help. Truman will be back soon, with no recollection of any meeting with you apart from the first. So staying in his apartment is not an option.'

'Yes, I understand that. I just thought you might have delayed his arrival for a week so I could rest and recuperate without spending a fortune.'

So much for feeling sorry for him languishing in the pagoda, my conscience nagged. *Now you want to delay his re-entry.*

I took the point, but my newly maternal brain had transformed into that of a lioness, intent, above all else, on finding a den for her young.

'I'm sorry, Pandora, it's too risky. Particularly as I'm duty bound under Cosmic Law to reunite the body of my host with his soul as quickly as possible after the mission has been completed.'

'But Truman *will* remember writing to me about giving Jay and his band a chapter in the book, won't he?' Cassiel nodded. I realised then that I didn't know how well that was going. 'Have you seen Jay lately, by the way?'

'We don't meet. We have the occasional telephone conversation.'

'Did he mention the tour?'

'He said it was a great boost for them. They've got more bookings and a contract for a new album. He asked if it wasn't too late to mention that in their chapter.'

'And did you?'

'Yes. Does it make you happy to hear of his success?'

'Very.'

I remained silent for a time, thinking about how much I'd love to be taking the baby home to him – if only it had been *our* baby and not mine and Zac's.

'What about your French friend, can he help?' said Cassiel.

'That's who I was thinking of. I'll ring Olivier. If he can't pick us up, I'll get a taxi. I'll probably go to a hotel for a few days.'

'Will you need help getting your luggage from the apartment?'

'Viviana can bring it here on Friday. She'll have to leave my car at Weald House and get a taxi to the hospital on Saturday.' There was something else I wanted to run past him. 'While I'm at the hotel, I'll get in touch with Jay. Is that a good plan?'

Cassiel smiled, but his words were determinedly non-committal. 'As you wish.'

He got up, saying he had some work to do but would be back the next day for the twins' examination. I said goodbye but then called him back. 'Cassiel! There's one thing I keep meaning to ask you. Why did the elixir fail me and allow me to get ill? I thought it was protecting me so I'd deliver the star child safely.'

He stopped in his tracks and turned to face me, Truman's blood draining from his face. 'Did Melchior tell you about the spiritual crossroads you had reached, one where you had the choice of life or death?'

'Yes, I wasn't really sure what he meant by that.'

Cassiel came to my bedside and sat down, taking my hand. 'This was a terrible mistake on my part. I was so intent on finding a womb for the star child, that I failed to check your lifespan records. These are not immutable, but the seventh day of September 2009 was the date on which your spirit was provisionally timed to separate from your physical body.'

'You mean I was supposed to flatline on Monday – the day the twins were born?'

'Put crudely, yes.'

'How?'

'Who knows? An accident of some kind; a blood clot, perhaps. The cause of death is never specified.'

'So is that why I got ill?'

'It is. Unfortunately, when that day came, your life-expectancy estimate overrode the effects of the elixir.'

'But surely, if my body was programmed to die on that day, I shouldn't have had the choice to come back.'

'Usually, yes. But because your cellular blueprint had been altered for the better, both by the elixir and the presence within you of the star child, there was a strong possibility that you would survive the birth.'

'And when did you find all this out? '

He looked sad and his voice shook. 'I had no idea until Monday, when Melchior brought it to my attention. I can only offer you my deepest regrets for what you have suffered since we met.'

I interrupted him because he seemed to be on the verge of tears. 'Don't be sorry, Cassiel. Look on the bright side. I've got you and the elixir to thank for being alive today. And for giving me two beautiful daughters.'

A nurse walked in on the conversation at that moment and approached me with a blood-pressure machine.

'I'm going to have to borrow your wife for a little while, I'm afraid,' she said, her face soft with pleasure at the sight of us holding hands. 'It must be wonderful for you both, at your time of life, to finally have these two little treasures.'

At which point, both Cassiel and I burst into tears.

Chapter 22 – Missing

Three days later, on Friday evening, when the nurse took the babies away for their final night in the nursery, I settled down to sleep, willing myself to drop off quickly. But, as always, the more I focused on sleep, the more my thoughts rampaged.

After putting everything on hold for the fifteen weeks since Cassiel's Annunciation, I couldn't wait to be me again. I'd finally booked myself and the baby into the hotel for a week, and Olivier had jumped at the chance of picking us up from the hospital and driving us there. He was as excited as I was about there being a child I could actually keep, and didn't turn a hair at having to get a baby seat.

'If Jay turns his back on you, chérie, you can live with me and Justin, *en famille*. And Oscar too, of course'.

His words were a great comfort. I *had* been wondering where I'd go to in this eventuality, especially as I couldn't afford to stay any longer than a week at the hotel. This would be my last extravagance, before officially becoming an unemployed, intentionally homeless, single mother.

Cassiel hadn't visited today, as he'd been finishing off some of Truman's work, but Viviana had come, bearing all my luggage, which she'd piled up in one corner of the room.

I'd given her a list of essentials for Lucy's hotel debut which included, at her suggestion, the supplying and fitting of a baby seat, even though there was no hurry for that as I'd been advised not to drive for at least three weeks. I planned to leave my car at Weald House and pay a driving service to deliver it to the hotel, sometime next week.

I was short of cash so I asked if she could pay for the things on her own card and I'd give her a cheque. I was taken aback when she said she didn't have a bank account and began to wonder if this was a ruse to get her hands on my debit card. But then she told me there was an ATM downstairs in the hospital shop, so I changed out of my nightdress and got her the cash. I'd managed to avoid using an ATM so far but I was so close to getting back to 'normal' that surely it wouldn't matter now.

I told Viviana I'd be expressing some milk for the baby before they left for the embassy the next day. Cassiel had phoned to say they should be leaving around ten o'clock and the journey would take at least an hour. Lyra would probably sleep through it but I couldn't bear to think she might be hungry if they were delayed in traffic.

When the nurse told me, later in the day, that the twins had passed their health screenings she'd added, 'Their next check's due in six to eight weeks. And you should have one, too.'

I was grateful for this information, because it alerted me to the need for booking an appointment with my GP in Chace Standen. I anticipated that this would involve a rather sensitive conversation about why I hadn't contacted them before the birth. I'd have to make sure I saw nice old Dr Guest who was the one most likely to fall for the *I didn't know I was pregnant till I had it* line I planned to feed him.

The nurse asked me if we'd decided on names for the twins so she could put them on their health-record books. I told her Lyra and Lucy, hoping that her new parents might see the name on Lyra's book, love it, and keep it.

When she gave me the two red books, I saw she'd written 'Scott' as their surname. This, of course, was the name on the hospital records – which had been just what we'd wanted originally, to keep Lyra's identity a secret. But for Lucy, it was disastrous.

I had to think quickly, so I said the first thing that came into my head.

'My name isn't really Scott. We're not actually married.'

'Oh,' she smiled. 'That happens all the time. Usually it's the other way round. Mothers book into hospital under their own names and the fathers want it changed to theirs.'

I began to feel a glimmer of hope.

'So it can be changed. That's good. Will it mean a new book?'

'No, just do it yourself – strike it out and write in the name you want the baby registered in. Otherwise it would mean transferring all the entries made so far.'

I felt myself beaming, even more so when I noticed a National Health number beneath their names. This was irrelevant for Lyra but essential for Lucy.

'I wasn't sure they'd be given an NHS number, as it's a private hospital.'

'Oh yes, it's automatic. And you'll need it if the babies have to be treated while you're still in the country, or if you come back to live here. I'll give you a leaflet about registering the births before you go.'

After the nurse had gone, I powered up my laptop and looked up registering a birth. One of the requirements was the baby's place and date of birth and another was the birth date of the parent registering the child. The hospital records would show Lucy's mother as Margaret Scott, ten years younger than me, with a completely different date of birth. I didn't know whether the registrar's office ever checked up on the hospital records, but I couldn't afford to run that risk.

This was what was keeping me awake. My only hope was Cassiel. Could he persuade the person 'sympathetic to the cause' who had originally booked me in without the necessary paperwork, to amend the hospital records so they showed Pandora Armstrong, aged fifty-seven, as having given birth to a single baby girl?

* * *

The next morning I woke to the sound of a hungry baby. The noise was coming from Lucy's cot, so after a dash to the loo, I picked her up and waited for the nurse to bring Lyra. In the meantime, Lucy was so hungry she was snuffling at my breast so I lay back and let her get on with it, my thoughts turning to the day's coming events.

After about five minutes there was still no sign of Lyra, so I pressed the call button next to my bed. A nurse I hadn't seen before appeared at the door with a determined smile as if she thought the busy morning feed time wasn't the best moment to be pressing one's buzzer.

'Are you all right, Mrs Scott?'

'Could I have the other twin, please? They usually feed together.'

She looked puzzled.

'Sorry, I'll go and check in the nursery.'

Another five minutes dragged by until she came back. She was holding a phone with shaking hands.

'The night nurse says your assistant came to the nursery just before she went off duty, and said she'd take the babies in to you. Here, she's on the line.'

I moved Lucy over from the left to the right breast and took the phone. The voice at the other end sounded as alarmed as her colleague looked. She told me that Viviana had been a regular visitor to the nursery – something I hadn't been aware of, having assumed that when she left my room, she'd gone back to the apartment – and when she'd turned up at ten to six this morning, she'd had no qualms about letting her take the twins to me for their feed. She last saw her wheeling a cot towards my room.

I knew my brain had to work quickly before I said anything, so I wouldn't say too much, but it was frozen with fear. My eyes were glued to the clock over the door which showed six-thirty: by now Viviana would be well on the way to wherever she planned to take the baby.

While my maternal instincts cried out for a dragnet across the whole of southeast England to rescue my child from the clutches of a rogue midwife, I had to work out what the repercussions might be for all of us, including Lyra, if the hospital reported a kidnapping to the police and the press got involved. The first thing to do was to check with Cassiel in case this was part of his plan, however unlikely that may be.

'Um, okay,' I said, forcing my face into a mask of calm. 'Well, if it was Viviana who took her, it should be all right. We're due to be discharged today, anyway. There's bound to be an explanation. We've only got one car seat, so maybe she's coming back for me and Lucy once I've had my stitches out.'

I gave the phone back to the nurse who was observing me with mute surprise. She'd probably expected to have to slap the hysterics out of me.

'Could you pass me my mobile phone, please? It's in my bag.'

I switched on my phone and rang Viviana's number. As I anticipated, it went straight to voicemail.

Observing this, the nurse moved anxiously towards the door. I put up my hand to stop her. 'I'm going to ring the baby's father now. There's no need to tell anyone else until I speak to him. He might have asked Viviana to collect her.'

The nurse flushed, nodded and left the room. Maybe she suspected I was in the middle of a break-up, dividing everything down the middle, including the kids.

I called Cassiel and he answered immediately. 'Viviana's taken Lyra but Lucy's still here,' I said. Now I was alone in the room I gave myself up to panic, which gripped my throat and made my voice shrill. 'It happened just before six o'clock this morning. She's not answering her phone.'

'I know. Melchior has been in touch. Don't worry. I'll be with you soon. Don't let anyone ring the police.'

'What shall I say, though? The nurse knows I didn't give Viviana permission to take Lyra.'

'Tell the nurse she's a bit eccentric but quite harmless. And she's just turned up at your husband's hotel with the baby. Say that's where you'll all be staying until the babies get their passports.'

This still didn't explain Viviana's actions, but I couldn't think of any better story, so I marched to the nurses' station and delivered the news, shaking my head and throwing my eyes to heaven quite a lot, making sure to convey that I was rather surprised, though, that the twins had been handed over to a non-staff member.

I must have been convincing, because when Cassiel arrived, the nurse brought us both a cup of tea and apologised for the 'misunderstanding'.

When we were alone, Cassiel told me that Melchior had alerted him when he observed Viviana going into the nursery, wheeling Lucy into my room and the star child to the lift, after parking the empty cot outside another woman's room. Once at ground level, she put the baby in my car and drove away.

'Did she feed her any formula before that?' I said, thinking how hungry the little mite would be.

Cassiel's expression told me that any halfwit would know that an offender is only interested in getting as far away from the crime scene as quickly as possible.

'So where are they now?' I agonised. 'And why has she kidnapped Lyra?'

'She's heading for London. We don't know what she's up to, but we suspect she's not who she said she was.'

'No shit, Sherlock.'

His shocked expression told me that while he may not understand the reference, he recognised the sarcasm. But I was past caring.

'All this "don't know" and "suspect"! If a bloody archangel and one of the three wise men are so incompetent they failed to perform basic background checks on a crucial employee, no wonder the world's in such an almighty mess!'

I was shouting but I couldn't put the brake on. 'I said all along she didn't ring true. Why didn't you check her out properly instead of using "certain key words" in the ad? She hasn't even got a bank account in her name. Key words my backside!'

We were both sitting in easy chairs and he got up, with the obvious intention of placing his hands on my forehead and soothing me with some angel gobbledegook, but I was so incensed I paid him the great insult of putting my arms in a cross in front of me, as if warding off the Devil himself.

'Don't touch me!' I screamed. 'If one hair of Lyra's head is harmed, I will never forgive you. And if you know where she is, why are you here? Why aren't you following her?'

Cassiel sat back down and started intoning under his breath. Whether I liked it or not, this did have the effect of pacifying me, but not enough to take back what I'd said.

'I'll ask you again,' I said, breaking into his chant. 'Why aren't you following and intercepting her?'

He looked relieved that I was finally speaking at normal volume.

'Pandora, you know I can't use Truman's body to do anything which might lead to involvement with the police or other officials, and it was highly unlikely that I would have caught up with her anyway. But I've alerted others who can help.'

'Well, I hope they make a better fist of it than you have so far. Strikes me you've been squatting in Truman's body with very little to show for it. Except a massive cock-up.'

Looking shocked, he soldiered on. 'I'm in touch with a network of what are commonly known as "lightworkers" – men and women who have dedicated their lives to raising the collective consciousness of humanity with the aim of creating a peaceful and loving world. You, of course, can be counted among their number.' (He spoke these last few words in a slightly admonitory tone, as if to say, *but you don't very often act like one*.) 'I was able to pass the details of your car to our contacts immediately. We've got two people following her now, one driving, the other keeping me informed. Five minutes ago, they entered the Blackwall Tunnel. As you yourself pointed out, the child can't leave the country without a passport.'

Almost as an afterthought, he added, 'Try not to worry.'

Even he couldn't make these words sound convincing and I felt my anger rising again. 'This reminds me of that old joke,' I said bitterly. 'How do you make God laugh?'

Cassiel looked blank.

'Tell him your plans.'

I paused for hollow laughter but, naturally, none came so I continued. 'Except, according to you, that's whose orders you're carrying out. So why isn't everything going swimmingly?'

There followed a sermon on free will, and how humanity's exercise of it can hurl all sorts of spanners into the divine works, which reminded me of an inconclusive conversation on the same subject I'd had with Charles.

Happily for me, this was interrupted by a nurse popping her head round the door to tell me that the doctor would be with me around nine o'clock to remove my stitches.

I'd almost forgotten about that. It was what I'd been longing for, so I could get the dreaded parting from Lyra over and done with and escape with Olivier back into the real world. But now I felt paralysed, capable only of waiting in this room until I knew she was safe.

'Can't you ring your contact to see what's happening?'

'Let's be patient,' he said softly. 'You're overwrought and it isn't good for Lucy.'

At this point I burst into tears and this time I allowed him to calm me down with his angel magic. When he'd finished, he asked me how I felt.

'Desolate. I can't bear the thought of Lyra being in the hands of people who'll prevent her from doing what she came into the world to do. I want to know who Viviana really is and why she's behaving like this. What address did she give you?'

Cassiel looked embarrassed. 'None. Her address wasn't relevant.'

'She told me she didn't have a bank account, so how did you pay her?'

'She asked for cash. I gave her half the agreed sum in advance and the rest was due when we completed the handover.'

I shook my head in disbelief at the utter laxity of his security arrangements. 'It's obvious she's untraceable. I suggest you get your secret light cavalry to hack the records of the Colombian embassy to see if the real Viviana Moreno exists. Maybe she saw your ad and mentioned it to someone else.'

Cassiel's phone rang before he could agree, or disagree, with my suggestion. I'd like to have heard what the caller was saying but I pieced together the gist of it from Cassiel's replies. 'Did you get the registration? Can you text me that and the name of the road. Is the abandoned car parked on a yellow line? That's good.'

When the call ended, Cassiel regarded me with a lighter expression than before. 'She's switched cars. The second one was driven by a man. It doesn't look as if they're heading for an airport.'

'Can one of your contacts trace the owner from the car number plate?'

'I should think so.'

'Let's hope they don't pass Lyra on to someone else before they're identified,' I said, my imagination running riot with a fresh car in every town between wherever they were and Dover, going on to board a fishing vessel to France.

Something Viviana had said to me on Tuesday floated into my head – *The baby will be safe, don't worry*, but I couldn't get any comfort from it because no matter who Viviana gave Lyra to, she'd be in the wrong place.

'Where did they leave my car?'

'Somewhere called Stamford Hill, in north London. I can go there but I'll need a driver with me who can deliver your car to the hotel. Do you know anyone who would do it?'

I could only think of Olivier, but how could I ask him to do that and then come back here again?

There was a knock on the door. I assumed it was the lady with the breakfast trolley.

'Come in.'

'Hello, Pandora, hello, Andrew,' said Zac. 'Sorry to barge in on you so early. I just wanted to catch a glimpse of the baby before you left.'

Chapter 23 – Unconfined

Painfully conscious of my tear-stained, unshowered self, I dived back into bed and motioned Zac to sit in the chair I'd vacated.

He was looking his tall, tanned, blue-eyed best, his body language and softness of pitch indicating that he'd come in peace. I was lost for words. There was so much I hadn't wanted him to know. I should have been feeling horror that he'd turned up in the middle of this major crisis; instead, I felt intense relief that he was here, a flesh-and-blood man, in my opinion worth a hundred angels.

He was regarding me expectantly, but I could only look towards Cassiel, afraid to open my mouth in case I spoke out of turn.

Lucy gave a little cry. I don't think he'd noticed her until then, her cot camouflaged by the piled-up luggage behind it.

'Oh, she's here,' he said, striding over and peering down at her. 'She looks like you.'

'Pick her up if you like,' I said, lost for more words than that.

While he was walking round the room with Lucy in his arms, gazing into her eyes, I struggled to gather my thoughts. The question was, how much to tell him? At some point in the future he'd be bound to find out that I'd kept Lucy, in which case he'd have to be told I'd given birth to twins. Or should I pretend I'd had only one and, at the last minute, decided to keep her?

I got out of bed and wrapped myself in a dressing gown.

'Zac, would you excuse us a minute, we have some paperwork to sign. It won't take long.'

'Sure,' he said, uncertainly. 'Will she scream when you go?'

Assuring him that, as she wasn't hungry, it was highly unlikely, I led Cassiel down the corridor until we were out of earshot.

'How did he find us, and how did he know Lyra was due to

go today?'

'His sister must have told him you'd gone into labour. He rang me last night to ask if you and the baby were all right. I told him you were probably being discharged today.'

'Why didn't you tell me?'

'It didn't seem important in view of recent events. And he never said anything about coming here.'

'Shall we tell him there are two babies? And should we mention what's going on with Lyra?'

Cassiel shook his head in bemusement. 'I don't think we can mention anything about the abduction. I'll be reverting to my Truman persona, so there can be no talk of Melchior, or light-workers in pursuit.'

'So shall we say Lyra's already been taken to her new family?'

'Yes. I think we'll have to.'

'So I'll tell him I had twins and I'm keeping Lucy.'

'He might not take too kindly to that. You have to remember the reason you gave for getting rid of the child. You said once the birth was over, you wanted to go back to your life with Jay.'

'Well, I'll say I've changed my mind.'

'But, logically, if you've changed your mind about that, why didn't you keep both of them? Zac doesn't know anything about her being a star child.'

'You're right. And suppose he wants to claim joint custody?'

My head felt blazing hot, but the rest of me had started shivering with fear at what might go wrong. Seeing this, Cassiel got hold of my arm and steered me back to the room. 'Don't worry, I'll handle it,' he whispered, just before we crossed the threshold.

He helped me into bed and supported my back with pillows so I could sit up and eat breakfast, which had arrived in my absence.

Taking Lucy smoothly from Zac, he put her in her cot.

'Pandora's got to get ready – having a visit from the doctor quite soon. Do you fancy having breakfast downstairs?'

Zac allowed himself to be led from the room, turning back to me on his way out.

'She's beautiful,' he said softly, and if it hadn't been for Melchior's picture show, I'd have probably asked him, then and there, if he still wanted us to raise our child together.

* * *

An hour later, Cassiel phoned me from the restaurant to disclose what he'd told Zac over breakfast. He'd broken the news that I'd unexpectedly given birth to twins and that I'd considered giving both babies up to the new parents, so they wouldn't be separated. But my lifelong yearning for a child of my own had prevailed and, after great soul-searching, I'd decided to honour the agreement with the new parents by giving them the firstborn child but to keep the 'bonus' baby a secret from them. And to bring up Lucy myself.

'And I emphasised that, even though you're keeping Lucy, you're still hoping for a reunion with Jay,' he concluded.

'What did he say to that?' I gasped, feeling half grateful, half disappointed that Cassiel had taken it upon himself to burn my bridges with Zac.

'He said he wished it could have been otherwise but understood why you wanted to return to your life with Jay. He asked me if you were going to reveal to Jay who the baby's father was. I said that was up to you.'

'But who else could I say it was – some random bloke at the Oven Ready Christmas party? That would be worse than telling him the truth. At least I've had previous history with Zac.'

'Quite.'

'Did he wonder why Lyra had gone so quickly?'

'I got in first and said he'd just missed her...the transfer had been arranged for a certain time, etc. He asked if you'd taken a picture of her. Have you?'

I hadn't. I'd been waiting till the last minute so my memory of her would be as she was when I last saw her.

'No,' I said, my voice cracking. 'There were three things I wanted to do today: take a photo, put her baby-record book in her baby bag, and enclose the pendant with it.'

I stopped, engulfed by grief. This time I didn't cry. I'd gone beyond that into a wasteland of hopelessness.

'Pandora. Are you still there?'

'Yes,' I said, dully, glad that Cassiel couldn't see my descent into the deadly sin of despair.

'I told Zac I got held up and couldn't make it in time so Viviana had to drive to London alone,' he continued. 'I said the new parents arranged to meet her close to where she lives and she's left your car nearby. Anyway, he volunteered to come with me to drive your car back. I gave him the name of your hotel and he says he knows where it is.'

So, he remembers, I thought. I'd taken him there for a drink to celebrate signing The Cedars' location contract for a new cooking show, in which Olivier made his debut appearance. After my second glass of champagne, I told Zac I'd been married to James Jay but we'd divorced because I couldn't get pregnant. Later that evening we'd ended up in bed together. Who'd have thought that six years later I'd be returning with our daughter.

'That was clever of you, Cassiel,' I said, pushing away thoughts of Zac and I in the master bedroom at Phoenix Cottage. 'You're turning into a credible liar. Where's Zac now?'

'He's taking his car back to Weald House. I'm just about to pick him up from there.'

He rang off and I flicked through some magazines in a desultory fashion, unable to concentrate on the text which accompanied the pictures of plastic celebrities, photoshopped and spray-tanned to infinity.

At last the doctor came to take out my stitches and pronounce me healed enough to leave hospital. Now that Cassiel was receiving all the intelligence concerning Lyra's whereabouts from his light crew, I couldn't see any reason to hang around, so I rang Olivier to tell him we were ready to roll, deciding to keep quiet about the kidnapping until I saw him face to face.

When he turned up, holding a cuddly grey and white toy puppy which looked just like Oscar, I was almost mad with impatience to leave.

'I've got so much to tell you,' I said, 'but I'm dying to get out of here. Let's talk in the car.'

Olivier made two journeys outside with my bags and then came back to escort me and Lucy, who was dressed in a fancy new sleepsuit covered in butterflies and apple blossom, a tiny, white, quilted jacket, and a white cotton hat with a large pink bow at the back, to his car. It was the first time she'd been outside and the September sun was just right for her: mild enough to warm her and soft enough not to dazzle her.

After Olly had expertly demonstrated how to strap the baby into her seat in the back of his car, I climbed in the front and proceeded to bend his ear with the latest on Zac, Viviana, and Cassiel.

I didn't dwell too much on Lyra's abduction, because I didn't want to upset Lucy. She might only be six days old, but she'd spent thirty-seven weeks in the same womb and must have been missing her as well.

'So your instinct about the midwife was right,' he said. 'But it sounds like the angel man has it under control. That's good.'

When I told him about my out-of-body experiences and how Melchior had taken me to a beautiful place to reveal that I'd escaped death, and that he'd helped track Viviana's movements, his delighted laughter woke up Lucy, who gave a polite cough and settled back to sleep.

'My God, Pandora,' he chuckled, 'you move in strange circles. You 'ave one foot in this world and the other 'oo knows where.

You'd be a parapsychologist's dream!'

We left the motorway and were soon driving along a private road which wound across the hotel golf course. Crossing the bridge, which spanned a small river, we pulled up outside Reception and unpacked the boot, waiting till the last minute to release the sleeping baby, who I carried into the building, followed by Olivier with my bags.

I gave the receptionist my name and she handed over a room key, asking me to wait for the porter. Out of the corner of my eye I saw a man in one of the easy chairs in the lounge behind Reception put down his paper and move towards us.

'It's in the nearest car park,' said Zac, kissing me on the cheek and handing me my car keys while I shifted the baby on my hip to put the keys in my shoulder bag.

I felt embarrassed to look him in the eye, knowing that after his tête à tête with Cassiel in the hospital restaurant, he now knew that I'd given birth to twins, given the firstborn away, decided to keep Lucy, and wanted to get back with Jay. Yet he'd still been gentleman enough to drive my car here for me. I wondered why he hadn't just left my car keys at the desk.

'Thanks,' I said, wishing I could tell him the truth about why Lyra had to go to someone else. The awful worry about where she was and what they intended to do with her was something else I couldn't share with him, even though he was her father.

'It was good of you to wait,' I said.

Olivier had just walked in after parking his car and Zac was now kissing *him* on the cheek.

'How are you getting home?' asked Olly.

'Andrew's on his way. He said he didn't mind driving me back. I thought he'd be here by now.'

I blushed then, for thinking he'd waited to see us, when he'd actually been waiting for Truman.

Lucy had acquired her own little suitcase since Viviana's shopping expeditions. I bent down to reach its handle when a porter came to pick up my heavier luggage, groaning as I experienced a jab of pain where the stitches had been.

'Let me,' said Zac, picking up his daughter's case, and the three of us followed Olly and the porter to a room on the first floor of the west wing, overlooking a walled garden.

The room was spacious, with two easy chairs, a desk, and a massive television, though I wasn't sure how much TV the baby would sleep through. A cot was set up next to the king-size bed, but my daughter was wide awake now and declaring her hunger to the world so there was no point putting her in it.

'You'll have to excuse me, gents,' I said, over the din. 'I'll be in the bathroom.'

While Olly was busy finding a rugby match on the TV, Zac asked me if I needed anything, so I handed him the baby while I located the changing paraphernalia. There was already a stool in the bathroom and I was touched by his thoughtfulness when he brought me a cushion for my back.

As he was closing the bathroom door, he asked if I wanted tea but I shook my head. I was dying for a cup but I wasn't ready for anyone other than a medical professional to see me with my breasts out.

In the middle of feeding Lucy, I heard my phone ring. I'd thrown my bag on the bed, so I couldn't get to it for obvious reasons. Then I heard a different ring which I assumed was the room phone. Zac answered it. I didn't catch every word, but the gist of it was that he'd come down and show someone the way, so I assumed Cassiel had arrived. Although, of course, with the others here, I'd have to call him Andrew. Soon after that I heard a knock on the main door, followed by Zac introducing Andrew Truman to Olivier Dubois.

The baby and I finally emerged from the bathroom to the sight of three men glued to the Sky Sports channel. Truman looked just as interested as the others, which was enough to remind me that he couldn't tell me anything about Lyra while

Zac was present, since as far as he was concerned, she'd already been delivered to the correct address.

That makes her sound like a parcel, said my inner voice, and I sighed, which made them all look up.

'Hello, Andrew. Thanks for the car retrieval.' There was little else to say to him – it was his Cassiel persona I desperately wanted to speak to.

As it turned out, Zac's appetite came to my rescue. 'Is anyone else hungry?' he said, as I put a very full and sleepy Lucy in the cot. 'Shall we ring room service?'

Olly was all for it but all I wanted was some fresh air and said that if they were going to be watching the match, would they mind if I took a walk around the grounds. Zac and Olly looked nervously towards the cot but relaxed when I said they could ring me if Lucy started crying.

Truman said that he'd already had something to eat on the way over. I held my breath, wondering if he'd take the hint and join me, as Cassiel, or continue watching the rugby, as Truman.

'Actually,' he said, getting up, 'after all that driving, I could do with stretching my legs.'

* * *

Cassiel and I walked downstairs and along sunny corridors hung with modern art, in agreeable contrast to the Grade-II listed building itself, until we found a way out into the garden. We'd barely left the room before I started grilling him.

'What's the latest news? Where's Lyra?'

'She's quite safe. She's at Viviana's house. Although she's not called Viviana. You were right about her. She *is* an imposter. Her real name is Adriana Smith.'

'Thank God you've found her!' Then the rest of what he'd said began to sink in. 'Smith?'

'She's married to an Englishman.'

'Oh, that explains why she knew how to drive my car...and why she recognised me from *Straight Talking*.'

'And probably why she used to disappear when you were staying with me in London.'

'Mm. So where does she live? How did you find this out? Does she know you're on to her? Talk to me, Cassiel! I want to know everything.'

We were just approaching the small restaurant at one end of the walled garden. I was still dying for a cup of tea so we ordered some and sat on the terrace, where Cassiel revealed what had happened after Viviana, or rather, Adriana, had switched cars.

'The man who picked them up is her husband. His name is Joseph Smith. They live in Crouch End. The team member who was following them lost him. Smith was driving very fast.'

I thought of my tiny daughter's life being put at risk by this child snatcher and visualised what I would do to him if I could get my hands round his throat. Cassiel must have sensed my dark thoughts and made a swirling motion in the air with his hands, as if to disperse them.

'Luckily, one of the lightworkers I was telling you about is in a position to access car-registration details. That's how we got the husband's name and address. The next step was easy. He looked them up on the electoral register and found Joseph and Adriana Smith and a person called Viviana Garcia listed for that address. He, er, investigated further—'

'You mean hacked into some records,' I said, thankful from the bottom of my heart that this flesh-and-blood lightworker had taken the required action even if it did break some man-made law.

Cassiel avoided my gaze and continued. '—and found that Viviana Garcia is lodging with them while she completes her midwifery degree. The Smith residence is registered with the Colombian embassy as a place students can board.'

'It sounds as if the real Viviana answered your ad in the first place and then Adriana took over. She pretended to be Viviana, but with a false last name so she couldn't be traced.'

Cassiel nodded, looking sheepish.

'But didn't you notice the voices were different?'

'Can't say I did. It was a few days between conversations.'

'So is Adriana a midwife or not?'

He looked at the table, then up at the sky, as if searching for an answer, which made me suspect it was 'not'.

'Don't tell me. I bet she's a hairdresser.'

He nodded.

'Ye gods! She was supposed to be officiating at the birth originally.'

He stirred some sugar into his tea anticlockwise, very slowly, as if by doing that he'd calm me down. 'It's not as bad as that. She *was* a midwife in Colombia but hasn't practised here.'

The words she'd said to me in the hospital came back and echoed in my head: *The baby will be safe, don't worry.* All I could hope was that someone whose work had been devoted to mothers and babies wouldn't hand over a child to a stranger.

But isn't that what you're doing? my inner voice whispered. *No it isn't*, I answered, my blood up. *This ultimate sacrifice is my gift to the world, so put that in your pipe and smoke it!*

'Do you know why she wanted Lyra?' I demanded.

When he answered, his tone was almost hypnotic and I knew he'd gone further into pacifying-Pandora mode. 'Not yet. But let me tell you what happened next. As soon as we discovered Smith's address, two female team members in that area took over and drove to the house. They witnessed the couple going in with the child.'

'What time was that?'

'About an hour ago.'

'So did they go and rescue Lyra?'

He shifted uncomfortably in his seat.

'That's not how it's done. We can't do anything that would set us against the law. They have no more right to take possession of the child than the Smiths.'

'Your team seems to have a dispensation for hacking, though.'

'Intelligence gathering is a different matter – if the information is there, and it's crucial, the team may access and make full use of it.'

'But you employed her, surely you're entitled to intervene. Why aren't *you* round there now, sorting it out?'

'I still don't have any legal right to remove the child. And I can't risk Truman being involved with the authorities.'

'So what are you saying?'

'It has to be a parent. If they refuse to give her up, you'd be justified in calling the police. You should take some proof with you.'

I had a horrible vision of the kidnapping of the century being played out on the front pages of the tabloids, followed by a court case prosecuting Mr and Mrs Smith. I could hear her statement: *The mother didn't want the baby, so I was giving it to someone who did.* I could see the headlines: *TV panellist abandons newborn.* Or, even worse: *James Jay's partner gives up other man's child.*

'But how can I? I've got Lucy and I can't even drive at the moment.'

'I'll do the driving. We can't bring Lucy, there's only one car seat and that's needed for taking the star child to the embassy. Perhaps Olivier will babysit?'

'Or Zac,' I said. 'He's her father.'

'Then we'd have to tell him that Lyra's been kidnapped.'

'He's got a right to know. Go to the room and tell them what happened this morning – Olly knows most of it anyway. I'll get the baby seat out of my car. Then we can get going.'

Chapter 24 – To the Rescue

I deliberately dawdled my way back to the room, to give the men a chance to digest the information that even I was finding difficult to process. Every new fact raised more questions. What did Adriana intend to do with Lyra? Was the real Viviana in on it? My old self wanted to speed to Lyra's side to do battle, but the fragile self I was at the moment felt terrified of entering the lion's den, especially with the risk of a painful savaging by the press if the story got out.

Lucy was due for her next feed at three o'clock, so the first question I asked when I got back to the bedroom was how long we'd be.

'It'll take about an hour from here,' said Truman. 'Then, assuming they give her up, I'll take the child straight to the embassy.'

'Just you?' I said. 'I thought you wanted someone to sit in the back with her.'

'It's a much shorter trip to the embassy from there. As long as she's not hungry, it'll be fine.'

'So what do you expect me to do while you're doing that?'

I was more than a bit hurt at him still excluding me from knowing which embassy she was going to and it leaked into my tone.

'I suggest we go in two cars,' said Olivier, easing the tension. 'I have a baby seat, remember? You and Lucy can come with me. Andrew can follow. Once you give him the baby, we can come back here.'

That sounded like a good solution, so I went into the bathroom to express some milk in case Lucy needed it on the way back. It was one o'clock now so she probably would.

I put the feeding bottle in a tote bag and then fetched Lyra's red book from my luggage, along with the pendant which I'd put in its original box. One set of Lucy's new clothes had come in a pretty drawstring bag which was just the right size to hold these two items.

'Okay, I'm ready. I left the seat next to your car, Andrew. Olivier can fit it for you.'

Zac was staring at his hands, like a boy who hadn't been picked for anyone's team.

'Sorry, Zac. I expect you're dying to get home. I'd offer you my car, but Rachel would find it pretty weird if you arrived home in that. Did you have something planned with Lauren today?'

At my mention of that name, his mouth tightened.

'No. She's doing her own thing this weekend.'

Truman swiftly intervened before I started quizzing Zac about the state of his relationship.

'I'll come back for you, Zac. You'll be all right here, won't you?'

'I could come with you,' he said, in a low voice, lifting his head and giving me an entreating stare. 'Then I could see her.'

I searched Truman's face. It was as neutral as Switzerland, so I made the decision myself.

'Why not? It'd be good to have back-up. If necessary, I can even say I've decided to keep her.'

I could have bitten my tongue, in case he thought that was what I was proposing, but the droop of his shoulders suggested otherwise.

'Okay,' said Truman, making for the door, 'probably best if you all ride together. If you get to their house first, wait for me to arrive before you go in. I'll stay in my car, ready to get going.'

Once Olivier had set the satnav for the Smiths' address, off we went on our second road trip of the day. Zac sat in the front and I went in the back with the baby, who seemed mesmerised by this whole new world rushing by.

* * *

Olivier drew up outside a row of nondescript terraced houses in an anonymous cul de sac. Apart from an occasional difference in the colour of the front doors, all the houses had identical black window frames, sideways-facing brick porches like sentry boxes, and the same wooden gates and low front fences, enclosing a narrow strip of grass. There was a long row of garages opposite, which Olivier said was good because no one from that side of the road was going to be observing us.

'There he is,' said Olly, as Truman passed us, turning round at the end of the cul de sac and coming to a halt on the opposite side of the road about fifty yards further up.

'All ready for a quick getaway,' I said, hoping that would be the case.

Truman had told us to wait for his call before going in. When my phone rang, it made me jump, even though I knew it would be Truman. I put it on speaker so Olly and Zac could hear it too.

'Hello, Pandora, my contacts report that there's no exit from the back garden and nobody has left the house since they arrived just before noon. They have, er, disabled Smith's car, so it's all systems go.'

I presumed Truman's special agents to be the two women in tracksuits sitting in a car a few yards behind us and I imagined one of them surreptitiously slashing Smith's tyres with a flick knife concealed in the sole of her Nikes, as she jogged by.

'Right. There's just one thing. We never did tell Adriana who the baby's father was, so do you agree that it's best to keep quiet about that?'

From my position in the back seat I was surprised to see the back of Zac's neck turn red.

'Let's play it by ear,' Zac muttered, at exactly the same time as Truman was taking the same line.

Having reassured Olly that it was too early for Lucy to feel hungry and that if she cried he could sit in the back and distract her with Puppy, I got out and joined Zac on the pavement. He had insisted on coming with me in case the Smiths turned 'awkward'.

'It is number eleven, isn't it?' I said, struggling to see it because it was sideways on.

Zac didn't reply and a glance at him revealed a clenched jaw and hands curling into fists.

When we reached the front door I took a deep breath and rang the bell. The net curtain of the downstairs window twitched but no one opened the door.

Zac bent down, opened the letter-box flap and shouted through it.

'Open up, Mr Smith, or I'll call the police!'

The door didn't open but a man's voice shouted, 'What do you want? We don't open the door to strangers.'

'I want the child you stole, you bastard,' screamed Zac as he proceeded to aim a series of violent kicks at the door, causing the surface to splinter and cave. 'And if you don't open this fucking door, when I get my hands on you I'll fucking kill you both with my bare hands!'

I don't know about Mr Smith, but I was scared to death, worrying that somebody in the adjoining houses might be witnessing the scene and ringing the police at that very moment.

Zac paused for a few seconds, steadying himself for his next onslaught. This time he changed tactic, crashing the door open with a shoulder charge. As he fell into the hallway, he collided with the woman who had stolen our child.

Zac's rage proved infectious because when I saw her, I pushed my way into the hall and grabbed her by her ponytail, pulling her head back until she had to look me in the eyes.

'Where is my daughter?' I shouted in her face.

She didn't need to answer, as the cries of a hungry baby filled the air. They were coming from upstairs.

'Zac!' I cried, running up the stairs. 'Find the husband and I'll get the baby.'

Zac had taken over where I'd left off with Adriana and was giving her the third degree as to his whereabouts.

'In the garden,' I heard her gasp, as I pushed open the door of a small bedroom where Lyra lay enfolded in a swaddle blanket in a large cardboard box, which rested on a bare mattress. Her face was contorted in distress. She was so hungry she was sucking her little pink fist.

'It's all right, darling, Mama's here,' I crooned, throwing off my jacket. There was no chair in the room so I picked her up, knocked the box to the floor and manoeuvred myself on to the bed, wincing as the wound across my belly gave me a stab of pain. Having wedged my back against the wooden headboard, I undid my bra with one hand, lifted her to my breast, and let her drink.

The bedroom was at the back of the house and I could hear a scuffle going on below, where I assumed the garden to be, but I couldn't get to the window for fear of disturbing Lyra. This was followed by wails from Adriana from inside the house and a few short, sharp words from Zac. Then I heard footsteps on the stairs and Zac came into the room, dragging Adriana with him.

Lyra had already been moved from the right to the left breast, so it wouldn't be long before she'd had her fill.

'She was starving,' I said, spitting the words accusingly at Adriana. 'How could you treat her like this?'

Adriana broke down into more sobs, which I ignored by asking Zac what had been going on downstairs.

'I found him in the garden trying to climb the fence so I pulled him down and knocked him out. Couldn't run the risk of him escaping and getting reinforcements.'

'You haven't killed him, have you? Shouldn't you go and check on him?'

The last time I'd seen Zac naked, he'd been in good shape, muscular and lean – powerful enough to deal anyone a fatal blow, I'd say.

'Of course not. I know what I'm doing. He wasn't very big so I hit him on the chin. He won't be out for long.'

'Where is he now?' I said, aware that Zac was staring at Lyra with a look of wonder.

'Locked in the shed.' He held up a small key. 'I'm taking it with me.'

Hearing this, Adriana started wringing her hands and moaning and I began to feel a smidgeon of sympathy for her.

'Nearly there,' I said glancing at Lyra and back at Zac. Transferring my gaze to Adriana, I embarked on the interrogation. 'Tell me why you took her.'

'Oh mam, mam,' she sobbed. 'I would never hurt her. I have no children...always miscarriages.'

'So you wanted to keep her yourself?'

She nodded, giving me a look of supplication. 'We tried to adopt a baby last year but they said we were too old. They wanted us to take an older child. But Joe...he wouldn't...'

'And do you think that justified stealing my child without a word of explanation? No note, no call. How do you think I felt this morning when she wasn't there?'

'But you were giving her to someone else. I didn't think it mattered who it was.'

'You didn't think it mattered? You must be mad! Do you honestly think I'd give her up to just anybody? The people she's going to...the life she'll have...will be more special than you or I could ever give her. She can shine her brightest with them. It beggars belief that you could have deprived the world of the person she's going to be.'

Adriana, of course, didn't know what I was talking about and I realised, as I said it, that this was news to Zac as well.

To cap it all, Frankie showed up in my left ear to deliver a reality check. *Who are you trying to convince, Pandora, this woman or yourself?*

That's rich, Mother, coming from you, I silently retorted. *You gave up my little brother, remember?*

Never judge others, Pan. You can't see what's in their hearts. Theo had a better life than I could have given him.

But I feel so guilty, Mum.

Don't waste your life grieving for Lyra. She'll be fine. Concentrate on Lucy. You'll know more joy than you've ever known before. I love you.

She was gone before I could tell her that I loved her too.

Blinking away the tears, I cuddled the little golden-haired girl I'd fed for the last time, patting her back as the nurse had taught me. My wound made getting off the bed painful, so I asked Zac to hold her while I stood up. He took her as if she were made of fine china but when she snuggled into him he relaxed and began to stroke her hair. Adriana observed this scene with a shrewd look and I wondered whether she'd ever harboured any suspicions about him being the father.

'I need to change her,' I said. 'Can you give me her things, please?'

Adriana put a changing mat on the bed and brought me Lyra's holdall with her spare clothes and the rest of the changing kit. She took away the dirty nappy and showed me the bathroom where I could wash my hands. I changed Lyra into a fresh sleepsuit, and sat on the edge of the bed with her on my lap while Adriana sat next to me, speaking in a low, urgent tone.

'Believe me, mam, I tried to give her some formula, but she wouldn't take it. I was just going out to get a different brand when you came.'

I immediately wished she hadn't told me that, because that set me worrying about how her new mother would cope.

'Well, she's full up now, that's the main thing,' I said, trying to be positive. 'I know you wouldn't intentionally harm her, Viv...Adriana. I just feel sad that all the time we were together you were planning to take her away. You were living a lie, weren't you? You adopted your lodger's identity. She's the one doing the midwifery course, isn't she?'

Her head jerked back when I said that and she looked scared. 'Who told you that?'

'Mr Truman knows people in high places: that's how we found you so quickly,' I said, seeing a way to ensure that neither Mr nor Mrs Smith would try to sell the story to any dodgy newspapers. 'If this gets out you and your husband, and the real Viviana, will be in big trouble. You kidnapped a child and she'll be seen as an accomplice. How else would you have known about the advertisement?'

Adriana put her hands together in supplication.

'Mrs Armstrong, please. She is my cousin's daughter. She doesn't know what I did; she's not even here. She told me about the job but then she had to go back to Colombia urgently because her father was taken ill, so she asked me to contact Mr Truman.'

'And the rest is larceny,' I muttered under my breath.

'I wish I had just delivered the message,' she sobbed, 'but something made me take the job instead.'

'You must be crazy to think you'd ever get away with it. How were you going to explain the baby?'

'That we adopted her through a charity.'

'But what about registering her birth? You haven't got any paperwork.'

Her face flushed and her lip twisted guiltily, suggesting that faked documents would have been no problem. Not that I was whiter than white in that respect. A reckless part of me wanted to ask for the forger's name and address, so I could make Lucy legal without having to ask Cassiel for angelic intervention which, quite frankly, hadn't been much cop up to now.

While Adriana and I were talking, Zac got his phone out. Lyra was drowsy, but not yet asleep. When I saw what he was doing, I jiggled her about a little bit so she'd open her eyes for the photos. As he took them, I whispered soft words to her.

'You're gorgeous, *such* a beautiful little girl. Smile for...' I nearly said 'Daddy' but luckily the sound of my ringtone stopped me just in time. The last thing I wanted to do was confirm Adriana's suspicions with a last-minute newsflash.

I passed Lyra to Zac, and got my phone from my jacket. It was Truman.

'Is everything all right? You've been in there for nearly thirty minutes.'

'It wasn't all right to begin with, but it is now. I've fed the baby, so she's ready for you. See you soon.'

I did a quick scan of the room to make sure we had everything and hurried downstairs, with Zac behind me, carrying Lyra, and Adriana bringing up the rear.

Feeling that I couldn't end it like this, I forced myself to say goodbye. 'I'm sorry you haven't got a baby of your own, Adriana. I never thought *I* would. If it's meant to be, perhaps someday you will.'

She shrugged, the expression in her eyes showing she was unconvinced. I didn't blame her. Who was I to dish out platitudes when my life was such a mess?

Adriana turned her attention to Zac. 'Mr Willoughby. What about my husband, suppose he's hurt? Please, let me have the key.'

Ignoring her, Zac walked out of the house and straight to Truman's car while I stopped off at Olivier's car to get the little muslin bag containing Lyra's red book and pendant, which I slipped into her holdall. Olivier had taken Lucy out of her seat and was holding her but she was hungry and beginning to complain, so I took her from him.

'Sorry we were so long, Olly, we'll tell you all about it when we get going. Won't be a sec...just got to say goodbye.'

'No problem, chérie. I won't lie – I'm very glad to see you back,' he said, as he got out of the car and stretched his arms and legs, his face a picture of relief.

Lyra was still in Zac's arms when Lucy and I arrived at

Truman's car, so I moved in close to them, the four of us a family unit for the first and last time. One by one, we kissed her goodbye. When I positioned Lucy so her lips touched Lyra's cheek, both babies stopped moving and went very still. Once Lyra was in her baby seat, I gave Truman all her worldly goods, kissed her one last time and whispered, 'Goodbye, my heart,' then strode off in the opposite direction without looking back, so I wouldn't see the car pull away.

'Could you email me those pictures? I never got a chance to take any,' I said to Zac, as we crossed the road, turning my head to brush the tears away. 'I'm glad you got to see her.'

'So am I. They're not alike, are they? One looks like you and—' He stopped, as if unsure whether he should be the one to say it.

'And the other just like you,' I confirmed, looking straight ahead so he wouldn't know I'd seen the tears in *his* eyes.

When we reached the car, I got in the back with Lucy and removed her bottle from the tote bag. As soon as I touched her mouth with the silicone teat, she grasped it so vigorously that I was glad it was that teat she was sucking, rather than mine, which had taken quite a bashing from Lyra.

'Hey, what's going on?' said Olly.

He'd started the engine but, instead of joining him in the front, Zac was making for the Smiths' house. He pushed something through the letter box, then sprinted back to the car and got in the front.

'Had second thoughts about the shed key. Let's get out of here.'

Chapter 25 – Tracked Down

'Well, if you could just do that for me, Cassiel, it would set my mind at rest.'

Cassiel and I were on the terrace in the walled garden, enjoying the autumn sunshine with Lucy. We were seated on rattan chairs and she was between us, stretched out in a brand-new baby stroller which Olly had kindly presented her with on Monday. I'd been happy to manage with the simple baby sling I'd brought with me, but he'd insisted on something with wheels and I'm glad he had. She loved observing the world from her new carriage – better than the view obstructed by Mama's upper body, any day.

Cassiel had come to say goodbye and his parting gift to me was the promise that his secret agent would wave his or her (he didn't say which) magic wand and alter the hospital records so if Lucy, or anyone else, ever delved into her family history, they wouldn't 'discover' her mother was a woman called Margaret Scott who'd given birth to twins.

I still hadn't decided what to do about naming the father.

After hightailing it out of Crouch End on Saturday afternoon, once Olly had been fully apprised of the fracas between us and the Smiths, we'd all fallen quiet on the journey back to the hotel. I'd been so intent on rescuing Lyra that I'd been unprepared for the harrowing sense of bereavement which inevitably followed our parting, and which I'm sure Zac was feeling too.

Exhausted by the whole experience, I'd joined Lucy in a nap, waking up with a start at the slam of the front passenger door and the crunch of gravel as Zac strode off to the lounge to wait for Truman, with only a muttered goodbye.

It was Wednesday now and I still hadn't heard from him.

The arrival of a waiter brought me back to the present. I'd had breakfast and lunch but was ravenous again. According to the gospel of the internet, it was breastfeeding that made mums hungry. Breastfeeding was also supposed to encourage a swift flattening of the tummy but I hadn't noticed much of that yet.

'I've got to lose weight before I contact Jay,' I said, my jaws clamped around a scone, loaded with jam and clotted cream.

Cassiel smiled. 'Can you afford to stay here that long?'

The unexpectedness of this joke made me snort with laughter, sending crumbs flying out of my mouth in all directions.

'Sorry. I think Truman's sense of humour must have seeped into your feathers.'

He shook his head.

'Cancel that. You did tell me you haven't got any.'

'No feathers, or no sense of humour?'

'Feathers. But I haven't heard you crack many jokes either. What's happened to you today? Are you demob happy?'

He looked puzzled, in a good-natured way.

'It means you haven't a care in the world because your job is finished.'

He put his hands together in a church steeple. 'Not quite finished. I have to return Andrew Truman's body to him tonight.'

I pictured Truman's spirit resting in Quan Yin's temple and hoped the transfer would go well. 'How long have you been in his body, Cassiel?'

'Almost six months. It has been very interesting – at times exhausting, on other occasions enlivening.'

I caught a twinkle in his eye and wondered if he was referring to his lovemaking with Truman's girlfriend.

'I expect by now Truman will have got over his girlfriend leaving him. He'll be looking for a replacement.'

'No doubt,' he said, taking one of Lucy's tiny hands while she kicked and cooed at him.

'Are you sure he won't have any inkling at all of what you've been doing in his name while he's been away?' I said, taking her other hand.

'Quite sure. He'll only remember the work and family activities.'

'So he'll have absolutely no memory of his dealings with Zac and Adriana?'

'*He* won't, but *they* will. Which hardly matters because he's never likely to bump into Adriana again. Or Zac, for that matter.'

'But they've both got his mobile phone number, haven't they?'

'Yes. I'm glad you reminded me. I'll dispose of that phone tonight. It's the spare I keep for matters concerning the star child.'

'Which number did you give Jay?'

'Truman's authentic one.'

'And which have I got?'

'The one I'll be throwing away tonight.'

For a moment, a fragment of my heart throbbed, until I remembered the second tableau, starring Truman, that Melchior had shown me.

'That's probably for the best,' I said.

Cassiel picked up his cup and finished his tea. I guessed he was avoiding making a comment in order to maintain his neutrality.

He was getting ready to move on, so I surreptitiously consulted the list in the pocket of my smock. I didn't have access to my normal clothes – they were all at Phoenix Cottage – but it didn't matter anyway as I was still too vast to fit into them.

There were two things on the list left to ask him.

'Will Melchior still be keeping an eye on Lyra?'

When I spoke her name, my lip started trembling and Cassiel patted my hand. 'Yes. His last report showed her feeding well and bonding with her new mother and father.'

An involuntary pang of jealousy appeared in reply to this news, which I forced out of my heart to make room for the glow of gratitude which replaced it.

There was no point in asking him for any more details because he'd already explained that the Lyra files were forever closed to me, so I continued to my last question. 'Just one more thing, Cassiel. I got into this whole situation because I followed your enlightenment programme. That's why you chose me. But let's face it, when the chips were down last year and we lost everything, I wasn't strong enough to cope, was I? I mean, I completely abandoned my meditation and healing practice. Where did I go wrong?'

'Don't confuse enlightenment with spiritual perfection, Pandora. No one is asking you to be perfect. You're human, after all.' He smiled shyly. 'Having experienced being a human for six months I know just how difficult it can be.'

He pushed back his chair to get up, but I wasn't satisfied. Before he ascended into heaven I badly wanted him to give me the key to fixing my life – in every aspect: physical, mental, emotional, spiritual and whatever else there was. If *he* didn't have the answer, who did?

'Cassiel, what can I do to become the person you and Enoch wanted me to be?'

We stood facing each other. His gaze, benevolent and wise, beamed into my eyes.

'Learn to love the life you have, Pandora. It is when you feel you can only be happy if a person or situation changes that you become conflicted. Constantly wishing for things to be different only results in anxiety and disillusionment. As a wise man said, "The greatness of a man's power is the measure of his surrender". Surrender to a willingness to love the life you have. This is true enlightenment.'

I stood still, feeling my hands grow hot. This was always a sign that something worth listening to was in the air. 'You mean let go and go with the flow?'

'Exactly,' he said. 'Deep within yourself you know all this. You've had a brief lapse of memory, quite understandable in the circumstances.'

'I feel a bit like Truman – as if I've been asleep and I'm just waking up.'

He looked at his watch. 'I have to go.'

'To sing your praise with the stars' majestic choir, dance the streets of heaven and touch the face of God?'

I don't know where this came from, only that I was paraphrasing a poem I'd once read.

'Something like that,' he said, waving goodbye as he crossed the garden, heading for the massive gate which led to the car parks.

'Give my love to Melchior,' I shouted after him.

And then he was gone.

I pushed Lucy back to the room, feeling as if my best friend and supporter had forsaken me. Fetching my tankini from the bathroom, where it had been spread over a towel to dry, I made for the swimming pool. Lucy was too young to be allowed in the water but they let me park her stroller in a corner while I swam. Gradually the physical activity sent my mood from forlorn to accepting. A few more lengths and I was counting my blessings and planning what I was going to order from room service for dinner.

* * *

Charles rang me on Thursday morning to see if I'd contacted Jay. He was concerned about how much money I was spending on my accommodation. 'You should be convalescing in your own home, not a five-star hotel. You need to conserve what money you've got,' he scolded.

'But, Charles, I can't go home without speaking to Jay first. In the meantime, what better place than this? I don't have to lift a finger, apart from seeing to your granddaughter at all times of the day and night.'

'When am I going to meet her?'

He sounded pleased that I'd referred to her as his granddaughter. He and my mother, Frankie, had never sealed the knot but he was my stepfather as far as I was concerned and, as neither Zac nor I had a living parent between us, the only grandparent Lucy had.

'Let me get my call to Jay out of the way, then we can arrange something.'

'But you *are* checking out on Saturday morning, aren't you? For goodness' sake don't do anything silly like booking another week.'

'I don't have to. Olly says I'm welcome to stay at his.'

'That's better than the hotel but you and the baby need some stability. I don't see why you haven't been in touch with Jay yet.'

I couldn't tell Charles that, apart from dreading having to admit to sleeping with Zac, I was so ashamed of my body shape at the moment that I couldn't bear the idea of Jay seeing me. I uttered a long sigh, and Charles's tone became less impatient.

'Do you want me to ring him?'

It was tempting, but as Jay had been telling everyone I was away on a retreat, if Charles rang and told him I was a few miles away and hadn't been in touch, he'd have every right to feel affronted.

'Thanks for the offer, but it should be me.'

'In that case, no time like the present, Pandora.'

At the thought of it, I was overwhelmed by a fear which made my voice break when I said goodbye. On hearing this, Charles called out 'Wait!' so I wouldn't ring off.

'Be strong, Pandora. Remember, courage is not the absence of fear. It's the ability to act in spite of it.'

He was right. I'd felt afraid every day for the last four months and the only way to deal with it was to come clean to Jay and move on. Whether that was towards him or away from him remained to be seen. But whatever happened, I would at last be free of the gnawing fear of the unknown.

While I was screwing up my courage, Cassiel's last words,

about accepting life as it is, came to me. I had to wake up to the fact that there might never be a thinner me: that I might never again have a twenty-six-inch waist.

As I steeled myself to ring Jay's number, my heart beating like a drum, I prayed that he would accept that I'd slept with Zac, and that Lucy was the result.

You're not asking much, are you? my inner critic jeered, but I pressed the call button just the same.

I let it ring but there was no answer and no voicemail, not that I would have left a message anyway, in case he ignored it. But he'd see it as a missed call from my number. If he called back, that would mean we were on speaking terms. I couldn't bear to think what it would mean if he didn't.

Ten minutes later my phone rang.

'Hello, Pandora, how are you?'

My disappointment at not hearing Jay's voice was tempered by my relief at hearing Zac's.

'Not too bad. Still as fat as ever. Lucy's doing well.' I paused, but he didn't speak so I added, 'It's good to hear from you.'

'I should have been in touch sooner...been a bit down. Lauren's not too happy with me at the moment, either. I can't tell her what's wrong...think she's about to dump me.'

'Oh, Zac, I'm sorry.'

I forced myself to say this but I couldn't ignore the little leap of happiness in my breast, especially when he added, 'It'll be a relief, really.'

Choosing to focus on his loss of Lyra rather than Lauren, I tackled that subject head on.

'Zac, I felt terrible, too. But we mustn't agonise about the baby because I can guarantee she's with a wonderful family. Andrew Truman said she's happy and healthy and bonding with them. And you won't forget to send me those pictures you took of her, will you? Andrew made me promise never to mention her to anyone, so I'll never say who the photos are of. We have to respect the agreement with her new family.'

I went on like this for a few minutes, hoping that my gratefulness that she was safe and well would rub off on him. I longed to say he could come and see Lucy whenever he wanted but I was wary of committing to this before I'd got back in contact with Jay, so I suggested he went away on a golfing trip with his pals to take his mind off the kidnapping trauma.

'I'm not in the mood for a holiday. Have you decided where you're going when you leave the hotel?'

'Either Olivier's or back to the cottage, I'm not sure. I haven't spoken to Jay yet.'

'I don't envy you that.'

'I'm going to tell him you're the baby's father.'

'Are you sure? I'm not exactly his favourite person, am I?'

'Well I didn't sleep with anyone else,' I retorted, 'and I'm certainly not going to invent a one-night stand with a random Oven Ready employee whose name I can't remember.'

'Of course not. So will you tell him I know about the birth?'

'Yes, but obviously I won't tell him I stayed at your place. And I won't say you've seen her. That reminds me. If you want your name on the birth certificate, you'll need to fill in a form beforehand, then I can give it to the registrar.'

'Can I think about that?'

'Whatever you decide is fine with me. But you're her father and you have a right to have that recorded. If you want to.'

'That's decent of you, Pandora. You're a good egg.'

I laughed. 'That just about describes my shape at the moment.'

I heard voices in the background and Zac told me he had to go.

'Okay. I feel much better now you've called. I'll tell Lucy when she wakes up.'

He laughed and I hoped that wasn't the last I'd ever hear from him. For Lucy's sake, of course.

As soon as he'd rung off, I started to obsess about Jay ringing. I felt far too fidgety to sit in the room and wait for his call, so I put Lucy in the baby sling and took her to the spa. I'd invested in a postnatal body massage on Monday and had really felt as if my innards were starting to retreat back to where they should be. Luckily, I found a therapist who was free to dish me out a second helping on the spot, so the treatment began while Lucy watched. As before, the therapist gave her a little massage afterwards, which she loved.

Since the spa wasn't busy, our therapist said we could visit the tropical room which was usually restricted to children over ten. This was an area with palm trees and special lighting which made you feel as if you were outside. I was partial to the foot spa, where you could dangle your feet in effervescent bubbles, and the vitality pool, which was a fancy name for a Jacuzzi. As a bonus, there was a beach bar with free herbal teas and a conveniently empty bathroom next to the tropical shower where I fed and changed Lucy.

We stayed there until a group of women came in and stretched out on the loungers, looking all set for some quiet time. Taking the hint, I scooped up Lucy and walked back to the room. She dozed off on the journey back, so I put her in the cot and checked my phone for the umpteenth time. Still no missed calls or messages.

The newspaper, which was delivered to the room every morning, was still unopened, so I settled down with it in one of the armchairs. Lucy had woken early this morning so it wasn't long before I felt my own eyelids closing.

While asleep, I was dimly aware of the tone of the room phone, but couldn't rouse myself enough to answer it. When I finally came to, at the sound of Lucy crying, I gave her a little pre-boiled water in a bottle, which she gulped down, burped her and put her down again while I went to the bathroom. As I came out, I noticed a piece of paper which must have been pushed under the door while I was asleep. It was a document the hotel used to inform guests of telephone messages received in their absence, with spaces left for the name of the caller and the time the message was left. Except this time, the caller had appeared in person.

Today *17 Sept 2009* at *2.30 pm* you received a ~~call~~ *visit* from *Mr Jay.*
Message: *He is waiting for you in the Lounge.*

It was now three-thirty so I raced to the room phone and dialled Reception.

'Hello, it's room one-four-six, Mrs Armstrong. I've just found a note from you. Is Mr Jay still waiting for me? He said he'd be in the lounge.'

The receptionist sounded blank, as if she'd never heard of such a thing, and asked me to hang on while she investigated. Lucy had started crying again and I dangled Puppy in front of her but she wasn't in the mood for diversion. She was hungry.

'Hello.'

'Yes,' I said, putting my hand over the mouthpiece to prevent my daughter's cries from filtering down the line in case Jay had followed her to the desk.

'He is still here. Will you be able to join him?'

I calculated how long it would take to feed Lucy, dress her up, and primp myself. Forty-five minutes at least – fifty-five by the time I'd wheeled her to Reception.

'It'd be easier if he came to me. You can give him my room number.'

'Hold on please.'

The hotel lounge was actually a series of interconnecting rooms giving the impression of private drawing rooms; he must have positioned himself in the furthest one because it was an age before she picked up the phone.

'He's on his way.'

I didn't know what to do first: change out of my baggy trousers and top, hide the washing, put on some make-up, or spray some dry shampoo on my hair, which had relaxed to the point of limpness on the massage table, in sympathy with my body's soft tissue.

But the decision was taken out of my hands when Lucy's cries reached a crescendo. I was still wearing the baby sling so I slipped her into that to calm her. Almost simultaneously came a knock on the door. Following Cassiel's precept of going with the flow, I opened it.

The expression in Jay's eyes, as he surveyed the sight that met him, changed instantly from eagerness to bewilderment.

'Sorry,' he said, shifting his rangy frame from one foot to the other. 'I must have the wrong room.'

I wondered whether this was an elaborate joke, and that in a minute he'd start laughing, forgive me everything and take me home. Then I realised Lucy's head must have partially obscured my face.

'It is me,' I said. 'Come in.'

He stood stock still, staring at the papoose I was wearing on my chest. For a moment I thought he was going to turn and run, but he crossed the threshold and walked into the room, avoiding the wire clothes dryer I'd borrowed from Housekeeping draped with baby vests and sleepsuits, and sank down in an armchair. He hadn't greeted me with a kiss but I suppose you couldn't blame him after the shock he'd had.

His manager, Mick, must have engaged a stylist for the band because his hair was cut shorter than I'd ever seen it, which was a great improvement now the salt was overtaking the black pepper at his temples. He'd ditched his blue jeans for black, slim-fit chinos and topped them with a white t-shirt and a zipped jacket.

I felt myself staring at him, coming back to reality when Lucy started bawling again.

'Sorry, I'll have to feed her. I fell asleep, so I've only just seen the note. Then the baby woke up...that's why I didn't come down to the lounge. How's Oscar? And Fritz.'

Looking out the window while I removed the sling, he mumbled that the dogs were fine. I sat down in the other armchair, positioning it so he didn't get a full-on eyeful of my inflated mammary glands. If Lucy had been his, I probably would have been less coy. As it was, I depended on my baggy clothing and the baby sling to hide as much as possible.

'Did you really not recognise me?' I said, still not sure how much he knew or what was going on in his head.

'It's your hair,' he said, with more than a touch of disapproval. 'What have you done to it?'

I could hardly say that a woman who was supposed to be my midwife cut it and dyed it red so I wouldn't be recognised as Pandora Fry off the telly.

'I fancied a change. It'll grow out,' I said, feeling at a disadvantage with him looking so good and me like a beached whale who'd fallen victim to an oil slick.

'Where've you been?'

This was a question I'd prepared myself for earlier. Originally, I'd had vague thoughts about saying I'd been on an ashram in India. Trouble was, I'd never visited the country and I wasn't sure I could get away with it by picking Google's brains. But if not there, where? I absolutely, definitely couldn't confess to occupying Zac's garage extension.

So I'd searched the internet for retreat centres in Kent and come across a Catholic one run by the Daughters of Mary and Joseph, which was pretty appropriate in the circumstances, Mary having given birth but Joseph not being the father. And being in the same county, it tied in with the hospital. The fact that it was twenty miles between centre and hospital would, I hoped, go unnoticed.

'A retreat centre near Dartford. Some nuns run it.'

'Did they cut off your hair and lock you away in the laundry?'

I laughed. His dark humour always got me.

'Is that where you had the baby?'

'Of course not. It wasn't a home for unmarried mothers. I had her in a private hospital.' It occurred to me then that I should mention my operation in case he was wondering why I was lounging about in this swanky hotel. 'I had to have a caesarean, so I can't drive or anything. I wasn't sure where to go after being discharged. I thought a week here would be like a convalescence.'

I glimpsed a flash of concern in his eyes, rapidly replaced by one of suspicion.

'But I passed your car in the car park. How did it get here?'

Good question, I thought. *How did it get here?*

Somehow or other, I managed to cobble together an answer. 'I made friends with a woman at the retreat centre. She came to see me in hospital. She drove us here in my car and her husband followed and took her back.'

As I said this, for some reason the image of Adriana came into my mind. It wasn't an image I welcomed, but at least it gave my story a touch of conviction.

He seemed satisfied with this, so I turned my attention to the job in hand. Lucy's legs were pressing on my wound so I asked Jay to hand me a cushion to place under her. He took the one that was in his own chair and approached me with it.

'Could you just put it there, please,' I said, lifting her up.

He placed it gently on my middle and I lowered Lucy on to it. As he bent down I caught the earthy scent of vetiver and I wondered whether he was wearing the expensive cologne Gaby had bought him at the end of the tour they did together.

'I've put on so much weight,' I said softly. I'd got used to talking in a low voice around Lucy but it sounded as if I was talking intimately to him.

'Nothing wrong with that,' he said, quietly.

I followed his gaze to my left hand.

'I can't get my wedding ring on, my fingers are still swollen.'

'As long as you haven't thrown it away,' he said.

I was about to assure him I'd never do that when the baby rolled off my breast, having nodded off too soon. Still embarrassed by my swollen body, I turned away while I guided her mouth to my other breast. When I looked up, he'd returned to his seat.

'How did you find me, Jay?

'Before we go there, is there anything else you'd like to tell me,' he said coldly, nodding towards the baby.

My heart sank. The forgive-and-forget scenario I'd been banking on was a bit slow in coming. I was thirsty, so I played for time. 'You couldn't make me a cup of tea, could you? I'm parched.'

He did as I asked and while he was fiddling with water for the kettle, warming the pot, wrestling with the tiny milk pots and letting the teabags brew, I racked my brains for a way to rescue the situation. Now I'd seen him, I knew in my bones that I wanted to spend the rest of my life with him. But there was an enormous hurdle to surmount first, and it began with 'Z'. *Or*, said that pesky inner voice of mine, *does it begin with 'I.'*?

Jay put a cup of tea on the desk, averting his gaze from the feeding baby.

'I was going to order afternoon tea for us if you'd come down.'

The sadness and reproach in his voice made my heart bleed and all I wanted to do was uncouple Lucy and clasp him to my breast instead, covering his lovely, sorrowful face with all the kisses he'd missed since we'd been apart.

'Jay,' I said soothingly. 'Let me tell you what happened from the beginning.'

Chapter 26 – Home Truths

Seeing how genuine Jay's distress was at the sight of me with a newborn baby, I was convinced now that neither Charles, nor anyone else, had warned him in advance. One thing I'd tried to do in the past few days, usually when I couldn't get to sleep after one of Lucy's night feeds, was to work out what I would tell him and what I'd leave out. Most importantly, there'd be no mention of Lyra or her status as a star child. And therefore no mention of Adriana, alias Viviana.

I was glad Cassiel had made it clear that Lyra was subject to a sort of spiritual Official Secrets Act because it took the responsibility off my shoulders. He'd made it plain to me and Olivier that we could never reveal her existence. I'd passed this 'memo' on to Charles and he'd passed it on to Rosemary – not that they would have leaked it anyway. Truman and I had given Zac the message in a watered-down form, so that was that. Lucy would never know she had a twin sister.

The only thing I wasn't going to lie about was who Lucy's father was. But for Jay, that was going to be the most hurtful truth of all.

So I began by telling him about the elixir. 'That's the only explanation for it. It made my whole body younger and healed it as well. But, of course, I didn't realise that.'

Jay nodded. He'd been in on the planning of the very first elixir-creating ceremony, so believing this didn't present any problems to him.

'I only wish it could have happened years ago,' I said, wanting him to know that I would have cherished having a child with him.

'She's not very old, is she?' he said, dismissing my comment with a distracted shake of his head.

'Ten days.'

He was clearly trying to calculate the date of conception. So I saved him the trouble.

'It happened after the Oven Ready Christmas party. Too much alcohol...I stayed in London. But, believe me, it wasn't planned.'

Jay's deep brown eyes, full of pain, watched as I laid the baby in the cot. I sensed he'd felt excluded by the physical contact between Lucy and me and I needed him to feel close to me when he inevitably asked the next question.

'Who was it?'

'Zac.'

'Bastard!'

He got up and paced back and forth, as far as the clothes horse would allow.

'I'm sorry, Jay.'

'Wasn't I enough for you?' He kept his voice low because of the sleeping child, which gave his voice a menacing air. 'I know we weren't sleeping together at the time, but there's such a thing as loyalty.'

'Perhaps you should have thought of that when you were having it off with Debbie,' I said, resenting his tone. 'What loyalty did you show *me*?' Throwing caution to the wind, I dealt him a blow below the belt. 'What goes around comes around.'

'Are you saying this was a revenge shag?' he said, his eyes blazing. 'I thought you were better than that.'

'Of course it wasn't,' I hissed. 'It was more like a *well at least someone wants to sleep with me* shag. You didn't have the monopoly on feeling depressed. You weren't the only one grieving for our old life, missing Willow and Rowan and the others. Sleeping with Zac was a mistake. If I hadn't got pregnant, you'd never have known about it and we'd be fine. I haven't done anything you didn't do every time you went on tour.'

He couldn't defend himself because he'd confessed as much to me when we'd got back together. Instead, he ignored what I'd said and continued with his cross examination.

'How many times did you have sex with him?'

This was awkward.

'How many?' he repeated, raising his pitch.

If I'd been strictly truthful, I'd have mentioned our afternoon of *nearly but not quite* passion. It wasn't just *my* reputation I needed to guard, though, it was Lucy's father's too.

'Only that once,' I said, hoping Jay would see my blush as shame at being unfaithful to him, rather than shame at lying to him. Strictly speaking, I could get off on a technicality anyway, come Judgement Day.

Jay's face relaxed and I began to see a ray of hope for us.

'Does he know about the baby?'

I was beginning to feel like a contestant in a quiz show, desperate to answer each new question correctly so I could go on to the next round and not be sent packing.

'Yes.'

'So you told him but not me?'

From the hurt in his eyes, I saw that this might be the sticking point. And yet I could never tell Jay the real truth – that I was instructed to involve Zac by order of a heavenly diktat.

'Why did you have to tell *him*? Did you see yourself walking off into the sunset with lover boy? Is that the real reason you're not wearing your ring?'

Jay had stopped pacing and was standing over me, his eyes boring into mine.

'I just felt he had a right to know. But I told him I wanted to get back with you after the baby was born. And he's got a girlfriend anyway,' I finished, lamely.

This was another half-truth. It was on the cards that the relationship was over. But Zac had said he *thought* she was going to dump him, not that she had. The memory of how happy I'd been to hear this brought a fresh blush to my cheeks.

Jay frowned and sat down heavily, as if all the wind had been knocked out of him.

'Why didn't you just tell me? Do you honestly think I'd have kicked you out?'

'Well that's what I did to you when you got Debbie pregnant.'

Into my mind came a movie of the day I'd got the anonymous letter...years ago, but as clear as yesterday. When he'd admitted it, I'd packed his things and had them couriered to the recording studio with a note telling him not to come back. Then I'd had the locks changed and after that was so comatose with grief I'd taken to my bed for a week.

The memory of it overwhelmed me and I started crying – not ladylike tears glistening on my cheeks but body-wracking, nose-running, eye-reddening sobs. The old Jay would have comforted me but this one remained in his seat.

'To t-top it all,' I blubbed. 'You wanted to keep us both on. If anyone's been a bastard, it's you.'

Jay had got up and was fidgeting from one leg to another, seemingly uncertain whether to stay or go. I might have got away with it if I'd stopped there, but I had to open my big mouth and bring up Gabygate.

'And what about Gaby Laing?' I shouted. 'How do I know you weren't up to your old tricks with her as well?'

'Well, if that's what you think of me,' he said grimly, 'you can get the fuck back to golden boy. See if he'll have you.'

The shock of what he'd said brought me to my senses like a shower of ice cold water. This wasn't the result I'd been hoping for. Jay was heading for the door. I searched frantically for a way to delay him.

'You never told me how you knew I was here.'

'Easy,' he said, his eyes steely. 'You left your bank details in your desk. I logged on to your bank account every few days. Apart from the direct debits, there was no activity until nine days ago when you made an advance payment to this hotel, followed by an ATM withdrawal of five hundred pounds two days later. You're close to being overdrawn, by the way. So, if I were you, I'd get on to golden boy for child support.'

Stung by his harshness, I lashed out myself. 'Those direct debits are paying allowances to your daughters and the bills on *my* house. I'm moving back in on Monday and if you don't like it, you can pack your bags!'

The door slammed, waking Lucy. I picked her up and took her into the bathroom to change her nappy, determinedly refusing to shed another tear. *She* was my priority now and anyone who didn't want her, wouldn't have me.

* * *

Olivier came to pick us up on Saturday morning, bringing Justin with him, who drove my car back to The Cedars. I'd phoned Olly on Thursday, soon after Jay had gone, and given him a blow-by-blow account of the conversation. His verdict hadn't done anything to cheer me up.

'I'm sorry to hear that, chérie, but not surprised. Put yourself in his place. His old love rival has walked in and taken you. What's a man to do?'

'But he hasn't taken me, Olly. I'm not with him. I want to be with Jay.'

'You misunderstand me, Pandora. I mean "taken" in the sense of "had". It's the worst thing that can happen to a man.'

'You're sounding very heterosexual today, Olly.'

'I 'ave a man's brain, my dear,' he'd said, laughing. 'That's why I can park better than you.'

When we arrived at the house, Olivier told me to choose a bedroom. As The Cedars was a wedding venue as well as a location for the Oven Ready cooking shows, all the guest bedrooms looked like hotel rooms, complete with en-suite bathrooms. Being a former owner, and familiar with the layout, I made straight for the bedroom with a window looking on to a side view of Phoenix Cottage. I could see the front drive, on which Jay's car was parked.

'Thanks, Justin,' I said when he handed me my car keys. 'Where did you put it?'

He gave me a wink.

'Round the back where he won't see it.'

'Thanks,' I said brightly. I guessed he thought he was protecting me from an angry, cuckolded man, but most of me wanted Jay to know I was here.

We were in the kitchen. Olivier was preparing a light lunch of tuna carpaccio, I was sitting on a high stool at a massive L-shaped counter and Lucy was lying in a Moses basket on a stand, which was Justin's gift to us. Justin was a good-looking chap of forty-two, a bit younger than Olly. He came from a large family and seemed to have more idea of what babies needed than I did.

'So you're only staying the weekend with us?' he said, sounding disappointed.

'That'll probably be long enough for you. She wakes up roaring at least twice in the night.'

'Don't worry, our bedroom is soundproofed,' said Olivier.

Seeing my startled expression, Justin added quickly, 'In case we disturb the guests when we watch late-night movies.'

Olivier continued dressing the salad while Justin sliced a baguette. As he placed the carpaccio on my plate, Olly played the matchmaker card.

'So, are you going to call on Jay?' Justin's forehead wrinkled in disapproval. Ignoring that, Olly continued. 'His car's there.'

I desperately wanted to see Oscar and Fritz and had briefly considered letting myself into the cottage, announcing I'd come to take them for a walk. But a mixture of pride and apprehension wouldn't let me. 'I don't think he'd be very pleased to see me after what I said to him.'

Olly shook his head, looking sidelong at Justin. 'We all say things we shouldn't. It's not the end of the world.'

'I told him to pack his bags, remember.'

'Where would he go?'

'Now I'm back, I'll be taking over the responsibility of the dogs, so he's a free agent.'

'He'd probably bed-hop at the homes of his friends,' said Olivier. He loved to show off the odd bits of slang he picked up, usually from Justin.

'Sofa-surf,' said Justin quickly.

Olly smiled fondly at him and I stared down at my plate, the tears which had sprung at the thought of Jay having nowhere to go falling on to the beautiful lunch Olly had prepared.

* * *

Although Jay's car had stayed put all day Saturday, it was gone by the time I opened the curtains on Sunday morning. Normally I'd have been overjoyed that Lucy and I had overslept, but when I saw the empty drive outside Phoenix Cottage, my heart sank to my bare feet. Now I'd never know whether he'd loaded the car with his things or just gone out for the day.

When it got to lunchtime, I started worrying that he might have left the dogs at home, so I asked Olivier to check. He wasn't keen to do this in case there was someone in the house, but when he saw how stressed I was, he reluctantly agreed.

'No sign of any dogs,' he said, when he returned five minutes later.

'Is the place in a state?'

'It's just the same as usual.'

His reply hadn't told me much.

'Does it look empty?'

He shook his head.

'Did you look in his wardrobe? Are his clothes gone?'

'Pandora, what do you take me for? Of course I didn't.'

I immediately became convinced that Jay's wardrobe was bare and Olly was just protecting me by pretending not to have looked.

'Come and relax, Pandora,' he said, leading me to the living room on the first floor. It had very comfortable chairs and three Sunday newspapers which Justin had bought from the village shop when he'd taken Lucy out in her stroller.

Olivier went off to get me a cup of tea and when he came back, he said, 'If you really want to know what he's up to, why don't you ring him?'

But I couldn't bring myself to, for fear he wouldn't answer or would cut me off.

When I turned in for the night at ten o'clock, Jay's car still hadn't returned. Convinced he'd packed up and left, I fell into a pit of remorse. I shouldn't have brought up the Debbie business. I shouldn't have mentioned paying Willow and Cherry's allowances as if I resented it. And I certainly shouldn't have told him to get out of 'my house'.

Early Monday morning, as I lay in bed, wide awake at four a.m., wondering whether I'd signed the death warrant on my relationship with Jay, I re-ran the scene that Melchior had shown me in the beautiful garden: the one featuring Jay, which had prompted me to return to Earth.

That's probably their standard procedure, I thought. They show you an attractive, but highly unlikely, future to lure you back and then cover themselves by saying: *The situation isn't set in stone and the actions arising from your free will, and the free will of others, could determine a different outcome.*

Then a replay of Cassiel's pronouncement, delivered on the day he showed me the newsreel of Lyra's life, started hip-hopping round my skull until I despaired of any hope of a good outcome to my present unhappy situation. *No future is absolutely certain, No future is absolutely certain, No future is absolutely certain.*

I was like a zombie at breakfast. Justin had given Lucy her bath and dressed her in her finest sleepsuit because he wanted her to look her best when she crossed the threshold of her home for the first time. I took a quick shower and emerged in my usual uniform of baggy top and bottoms to match my baggy body.

When Olly saw me he tutted his disapproval. 'You can't go out looking like that. Suppose Jay turns up. He's got to bring the dogs back.'

I could feel my face fall. 'Has he called you? Has he moved out?'

'No, no. I don't know. Here, put this on.'

Olivier produced a floaty, scoop-necked dress in a swirly copper and silver pattern, which worked remarkably well. The sleeves were long and gathered at the wrist and the bodice was pleated, with a row of mother-of-pearl buttons in the centre.

I took it upstairs and tried it on. It was a good length, just below the knee. My legs were still tanned from sitting in the garden at Weald House so all I needed was the pair of faux snakeskin wedge sandals I had in my shoe rack next door.

I'd assumed my belly would spoil the line, but the bodice was long enough and wide enough to skim it. I skipped downstairs to show the boys.

'Olly, I love it. It makes me look human again. Where on earth did you get it?'

'One of the guests left it behind. I found it in a closet. No one claimed it.'

'That's what all the cross-dressers say,' I quipped, and Justin tittered.

I felt so happy to be out of my maternity uniform that I kissed each man on the cheek. 'You're our fairy godfathers. I love you.'

It didn't take long for Justin to drive my car round to the cottage and unload the bags I'd packed fifteen weeks before. It was a mild and sunny September day so I pushed Lucy round to the cottage in the stroller and put her out in the back garden for some fresh air while I unpacked the bags and sorted the clothes into piles for washing.

As Olly had said, the house looked very much as I'd left it. I waited till he and Justin had gone off to start their working days before running upstairs and pulling the door of Jay's wardrobe open. It wasn't bare inside but there were fewer clothes than there had been before I'd left. *Inconclusive*, I thought, filing away the fear that he wasn't coming back into 'matters to be agonised over later'.

I went downstairs and inspected the fridge. I'd planned to walk with Lucy to the village shop for the basics and order the rest online, but inside there was milk, butter, eggs, cheese and salad. I even found some bread in the freezer, among the ready meals Jay must have been living on. I was surprised at seeing these, knowing how much he enjoyed cooking.

At first, I hoped the full fridge was a positive sign but then I convinced myself that he was just returning the favour – hadn't I left the place well-stocked with food for him when *I* had left?

Relieved of the burden of shopping, I turned my attention to the washing. The weather was warm for the time of year so I was able to peg the clothes on the line as they came out of the machine. I'd had enough of living out of a suitcase and couldn't wait to get back to normal life as quickly as possible.

In the afternoon, I set up the ironing board in the conservatory with Lucy in her Moses basket beside me. I put on the radio and sang along, wielding the iron in time to the music. I didn't bother to press the baggy tops and trousers because they were going to the charity shop anyway.

After everything had been hung up and put away, I fed and changed Lucy and put her back in her Moses basket. I sat down to continue reading a book that Olivier had lent me but the feverish energy I'd been running on was draining fast. Feeling the effects of being awake since four a.m., I closed my eyes.

Some time later, I had no idea how long, I was roused by a hysterical dog, trying to jump in my lap.

Whoozy with sleep, I screamed, clutching my scar, and I heard a man's voice calling Oscar off. Still not sure where I was,

I recognised Jay leaning over me and instinctively put my arms up to him. He responded by kissing me gently on the lips.

'I'm tired, Jay, so tired,' I whispered.

I was dimly aware of being helped to my feet and up to bed.

Twice in the night, Lucy was placed in my arms and I fed her. But as soon as she was taken from me, I fell back to sleep again.

It wasn't till six o'clock the next morning that I woke up properly. But I wasn't in the bedroom I usually shared with Jay. He'd put me in the middle one, where Rowan slept when he stayed. Lucy was nowhere to be seen. I got out of bed and went to the bathroom. I was wearing a long t-shirt which I had no recollection of putting on. When I squinted into the bathroom mirror, the face looking back at me showed a streaked complexion and a pair of panda eyes. Unfortunately, all my cleansers and moisturisers were in the en-suite bathroom in the master bedroom, so I did what I could with a wet tissue and soap.

I went downstairs to see who was up and about. The dogs were in the conservatory and woke when they heard me. I closed the door behind me so Oscar's ecstatic greeting wouldn't wake the house. Responding to Fritz's quieter welcome, I let them out into the garden.

Hurrying back upstairs, I stood outside the closed door of the master bedroom. The small, third bedroom was empty, so this was the only place Lucy could be. I opened the door an inch. Jay was fast asleep, his long frame spread diagonally across the bed. Lucy was beside the bed in her Moses basket, her eyes still tight shut.

I took the opportunity of having a bath while she was still asleep. Getting dressed was a problem, as most of my clothes were in the big bedroom. I had, however, been in the habit of storing items I rarely wore, but couldn't bring myself to get rid of, in the other two rooms. Searching the chest of drawers in the room I'd slept in, I found some silk underwear, a floaty top with batwing sleeves, and a pair of palazzo pants in a red and white abstract print with a drawstring waist just wide enough to contain my middle. It was a shame that the top was an orange and pink paisley print, but it was that or an Athens 2004 Olympic t-shirt, so I chose the lesser of the two evils.

I thought I heard Lucy stirring. I didn't want her to wake Jay, so I opened the door as quietly as I could. And there, in front of me, was the tableau that Melchior had shown me. Jay was sitting on the side of the bed with his back to me, his dark head close to Lucy's, cradling her in his arms while she gurgled as he softly sang to her.

Chapter 27 – Going with the Flow

I stood watching the pair of them, rapt. I'd never seen Jay with a baby before, but he'd had five of them with Debbie so, in fact, he was miles more experienced than I was.

Something must have given my presence away, because he turned his head.

'So you're alive then,' he said, with a hint of a smile as he looked me up and down. 'I see you got dressed in the dark.'

Ignoring his jibe at my outfit, I asked him what had happened.

'You were almost comatose when I found you last night. It's a good job I came back when I did.'

I wanted to ask if that meant he'd decided to leave me and then changed his mind, but I wasn't sure I could deal with the answer at the moment so I put that on hold for later.

'I think I overdid it a bit. Thanks for taking over.'

At the sound of my voice, Lucy opened her mouth and let me know how hungry she suddenly was, so I took her from him and sat down on the boudoir chair to feed her, managing to do it without revealing too much flesh. Meanwhile, Jay had returned to bed and was sitting up watching us.

'Don't worry,' he said, after I'd latched her on. 'It's nothing I haven't seen before.'

'Did Debbie breastfeed?' I said, deliberately misunderstanding him.

He groaned. 'Why are you bringing her up after all this time? I thought we'd put that subject to bed years ago.'

'Sorry. I think it must be the effect of the anaesthetic. Old memories are resurfacing...like Debbie being able to give you children when I couldn't.' Against my will, my eyes were filling up. 'I've got what I always dreamed of, a child of my own. But...'

I couldn't bring myself to finish my sentence with: *she's not yours*, because I felt it'd be implying that Lucy was second best, but he caught my drift.

'Well, you took my five kids on.'

'But they were a lot older. It's a bit different from bringing up someone else's baby.'

Hearing our voices, the dogs had come upstairs. Fritz jumped on the bed and Oscar draped himself over my feet.

'He shouldn't be on there,' I said, seeing an army of bacteria waiting to pounce on my baby when she had her night feeds.

'He's okay. You'll be in the other room anyway.' Jay looked so serious I actually believed him until he started to chuckle. 'Your face...' he said, at the same time pushing Fritz off the bed.

Jay got up and stretched.

'No peace for the wicked. Come on, boys, let's leave the girls to it. See you downstairs. I'm making breakfast.'

* * *

Jay didn't leave us at all that day. He said that I should stay in, too, because if anyone saw me in that outfit, they'd call the style police.

Over breakfast, he told me that on Saturday morning he'd phoned Charles, who'd invited him to spend Sunday with him. Knowing I couldn't drive yet, Jay suspected I was staying at The Cedars. He'd walked round to the car park, seen my car and stayed home for the rest of the day waiting for me to pay him a call. When I didn't, he presumed that I didn't want any more to do with him and we were finished.

The next day, he told Charles he intended to leave because I couldn't forgive him, even after all these years. Plus he couldn't stand the thought of me sleeping with another man, especially Zac of all people. But Charles fought my corner: reminded him of what I'd been through, pointed out that hormone shifts can put words in your mouth you don't really mean. Jay ended up staying the night in Glastonbury, which was why he and the dogs weren't there on Monday morning.

Then Olly got in on the act. He rang Jay early on Monday and asked him what was going on...told him how much I wanted him to stay and how I shouldn't be struggling on my own, so soon after an operation. Jay still wasn't sure if that's what I wanted, so he decided to go and see Zac.

When he said that name, my mouth went dry and my heart almost bounced out of my chest. 'What, you went to his office?'

'No. We went to some pub he suggested.'

I hoped against hope it wasn't the Raglan Arms, in case Zac had taken one drink too many and blabbed about how he'd once met a man from a charity there, who'd offered to rehome the baby.

'You didn't have the dogs with you, did you?'

'No, I left them at Donny's and went in by tube.'

Jay ladled some more porridge into my bowl, assuring me it was good for lactating mothers. Bowing to his greater experience, I forced it down, but I hardly tasted it, so nervous was I of what he might tell me.

Jay filled the porridge pan with cold water and resumed his tale. 'Once we'd got past the unfriendly bit, we got down to logistics.'

I imagined Jay threatening Zac with a proposition of what he'd do to his wedding tackle if he touched me again, and shuddered.

'I asked him if he'd offered to stand by you.'

I sat immobile, my nerves in shreds. He had, and I'd said no, but I'd been madly attracted to him at the time, nonetheless.

'He said you weren't interested.'

Taking a deep draught of air, I secretly thanked Zac with all my heart, remembering how I'd thrown myself on the bed in floods of tears when he told me Lauren had come to town.

Your daddy is a gentleman, I said silently to Lucy, and she waved her arms.

'Is that it?' I said, as Jay fell silent.

'Not quite. He wanted to know if there was any chance he could see her once in a while.'

I looked over at Lucy and thought what a great responsibility it was, that we had the power to make decisions for her which would affect her whole life.

'What did you say?'

He tossed his head and ran his fingers through his hair, in the way he did when he was nervous. 'I said I'd ask you. It's not really up to me.'

He was staring at me intently. I sensed he'd prefer it if I said no, but I couldn't.

'I wouldn't mind. I don't want Lucy to say we kept her away from her father.'

His face clouded. 'So who would I be?' he said, the same expression in his eyes as when he'd first seen me feeding Lucy. 'What would she call me?'

'Anything you like. What difference does it make? Names, titles, they're just words. She'll love you as much as him. Probably more.'

* * *

Later that day, Jay took Lucy into the garden to watch while he played with his latest garden toy, a machine called a 'scarifier'. It was September 22nd, the autumnal equinox, and Jay's gardening calendar had told him it was time to aerate the soil and remove the dead grass and moss.

While I had some time on my own, I went to the study and switched on the computer.

Hanging on the wall above my desk, my own calendar was still showing June so I turned the pages to September. Beneath a picture of a beautiful spreading maple tree, its leaves a vibrant shade of red, just like the one I'd seen in the beautiful garden with Melchior, I read the following words.

The cycles of Nature are reflected in your life.
Autumn is the perfect time to release old cares to make way for new
growth.
Be like the trees whose leaves must fall. Allow your true nature to be
laid bare.

My hands felt very warm when I read this. The lines were reminiscent of Cassiel's guidance, to let go and go with the flow. It was great advice, if only Jay and I could pull it off.

I turned my attention to the screen before me. I was still waiting for Zac to send the pictures of Lyra. The last time I'd checked, he hadn't, but this time I found an email from him with the subject line 'Hi', even though there was no text in the body of the email. I opened the attachment to find three pictures. One of them showed her cradled in my right arm; in the other two I was supporting her body so she could face the camera. There was nothing to show that the person holding her was me, possibly because Zac had cropped the pictures.

I thought I'd feel sad when I saw her image, but my heart was gladdened by it. She had such a lovely, peaceful look on her face, and the light had caught her eyes so they sparkled. I wondered whether Zac would print them out and keep one in his wallet, something I could never do because Jay was always looking in my purse for change.

I surfed the net for a little while, then reclaimed Lucy from the garden and brought her into the kitchen to keep me company while I prepared some vegetables for later.

When Jay came in he looked satisfied in the way he used to when he'd been working in the organic garden at Four Seasons.

'That's the scarifying done, young lady,' he said, sitting at the kitchen table and pulling the Moses basket nearer so he could tickle her toes.

He was in a good mood so I thought it was time to stand up for Children's Rights. 'I hope you didn't scarify Zac too much. You of all people should support children being in contact with their parents.' I softened my tone, seeing a look in his eyes I couldn't identify. 'You never got to meet your own father, did you?'

'I'm over it,' he said, finally. 'It's not that. How old is golden boy?'

Zac had turned fifty-one in August but Jay would be suspicious if I knew too much about him so I said, 'About fifty, I think.'

'Do I look my age, Andy?'

I hadn't expected this and a surprised laugh escaped before I could stop it. 'You know you don't, mostly courtesy of my moisturiser. You're costing me a fortune, that stuff costs £75 a pot. Why are you asking?'

'I'll be sixty-six when she goes to school. Too old for any little girl to be calling me "Daddy".'

My heart went out to him but he had a point. I could get by as an older mum with the help of the elixir, and Zac looked young and clean-cut enough to be Lucy's dad, whereas Jay was of a craggier vintage.

'Why don't we ask Rosemary for some elixir for you?'

He shook his head. 'That's never going to make me her dad.' He sighed. 'Of course she can see him. And she can call him whatever she wants.'

'You're a good man,' I said, putting down my knife and planting a kiss on the top of his head, adding, in case his head swelled, 'despite what they say.'

'Who knows,' he went on, gloomily, too sorry for himself to joke back. 'By that time one of my lot might have knocked out a grandkid.'

I laughed at how he saw that as a minor tragedy. 'When that day comes you'll have to make the big decision – "Granddad" or "Grandpa".'

He adopted an expression of horror. 'Neither. Never. Ever. I've got my reconstructed rock-star image to protect.'

He was being ironic for my benefit but I knew he meant it.

'Unless you want her to call you "Surrogate Daddy", looks like it'll have to be "Jay" then,' I said, picking up Lucy and giving her a cuddle. Jay got up and put his arms around us and we had a group hug.

When he kissed her on the cheek, my heart went into a spasm of sorrow as I remembered how Zac, Lucy and I had kissed Lyra goodbye.

'Are you all right, Pandora?' said Jay, seeing my teary eyes.

'Yes, I'm fine. Why are you calling me that?'

'I don't know. It kind of suits you now. Reckon you've grown into it.'

'Why, thank you. In that case would you like me to call you James from now on?'

I suddenly found myself out of my body, looking down on the scene below. I thought of Melchior and he immediately appeared beside me, shimmering and smiling as he told me that Lyra was in the safest hands on Earth and I shouldn't ever worry about her.

Lyra is your gift to the world, Pandora, and Lucy is Quan Yin's gift to you. Remember your dream? You saw a golden-haired child and a dove. The child was Lyra and the dove was Lucy. The Water of Life which Quan Yin gave you fell through your hands on to the part of your body enclosing your womb. As above, so below. This was orchestrated from above before you were even conscious of it. All has happened just as it should. And will continue to do so if you take Cassiel's advice: to trust the current of life. Align with that and you will always be in tune with your divine nature.

I must only have been gone for an instant because when I dived back into my body, Jay was saying, 'Whatever you say, Momma, your wish is my command.'

Taking Lucy from me, he did a slow waltz round the room, holding her head protectively like the old hand he was. She was looking up at him, entranced.

Please, God, we all stay around long enough to see her through adulthood and beyond, I prayed, as they danced out into the sun, the dogs following in their trail.

Other Books in the Pandora Series

Transforming Pandora
Pandora Series – Book One
978-1-78099-745-2

Showcased by The People's Book Prize 2014

Attempting to come to terms with her husband's death, Pandora is searching for love and meaning in her life. After reluctantly attending an evening of clairvoyance, she is visited by a mysterious spirit who sets her on a new path. He offers her the chance of enlightenment, but will she choose love or light – or can she have both?

This charming novel blends romance with spirituality. Carolyn Mathews is a talented writer, adroitly balancing the emotional and spiritual themes that drive this multi-layered metaphysical romance. A rich cast of characters supplement the basic love story and keep the plot moving. Whether you're looking for romance or spiritual guidance, this well-written novel of love and rebirth satisfies both.
~P. J. Swanwick, Fiction for a New Age

Well-written and engaging, *Transforming Pandora* is an enjoyable read. I highly recommend it.
~Alice Berger, Berger Book Reviews

Inventive and accomplished use of language and assured handling of the different elements of the story, make for a great read.
~Lois Keith, author of *A Different Life* and *Out of Place*

Transforming Pandora is engaging, meticulously observed, grace-

fully written, bubbly and touching.
~Joseph Laredo, translator of *The Outsider* by Albert Camus, Penguin Modern Classics

Fascinating, interesting, introspective and well written, this could be your story or someone else's, but regardless, it is a story about coming of age, at whatever age that may be! A great read.
~Ian Banks, Blue Wolf Reviews

Squaring Circles
Pandora Series – Book Two
978-1-78279-705-0

Free spirit Pandora is shaken by the sudden death of her mother and puzzled by the appearance of a young stranger at her funeral. When her mother's grave is disturbed, she turns detective and finds herself drawn into a world of intrigue, centring round a plot to exploit a healing circle for money. Along the way, she faces a choice between the comfortable *status quo* of her healing practice or a more stimulating alternative. Will her partner's collaboration with an attractive singer and her own encounter with an old flame change their lives irrevocably?

Carolyn's writing is elegantly stylish, fluid and easy-flowing, with a good helping of wit and beautiful, unforced dialogue which adds to the richness and depth of its characters. A thoroughly entertaining read.
~Ella Medler, author of *Martin Little, Resurrected*

Squaring Circles is a rich and delicious slice of modern British life, topped off with an intriguing dollop of paranormal whipped cream. This brilliant novel captivated me from the black-humor-filled opening scene until the last sizzling paragraph. The writing is masterful throughout, each sentence thumping with energy and flowing with great momentum, with sparkles of humor sprinkled generously throughout. This is a sequel to *Transforming Pandora*, and like the first instalment, this is a novel of many characters and almost non-stop conversation, delightfully narrated by the protagonist, Pandora. Carolyn Mathews' rare literary artistry will leave readers blessed and uplifted, not to mention highly entertained. This is a delightful book!

~Ram Das Batchelder, author of *Rising in Love: My Wild and Crazy Ride to Here and Now, with Amma, the Hugging Saint*

This story has it all: family secrets, family crises, intrigue, duplicity, legend, magic, mystery... I love the way the author has cleverly blended the many and varied forms of spirituality into the everyday lives of the characters, skilfully demonstrating how thin are the veils between this world and the dimensions beyond. Carolyn Mathews' writing is fast-paced and beautifully readable, with a great sense of place and a cast of truly believable characters. I was hooked from the first page and genuinely sorry when I reached the end. By that time, I felt as though the characters had become firm friends, and they will stay with me for a long time. Highly recommended.

~Sue Barnard, author of *Nice Girls Don't* and *The Ghostly Father*

References

Chapter 25

'The greatest of a man's power is the measure of his surrender.'
~William Booth

The Blind Man Flies ~ by Cuthbert Hicks, concludes with the lines:
'For I have danced the streets of heaven,
And touched the face of God.'

Carolyn enjoys writing, dog walking, being with friends and family, following her local football team, trying to find the meaning of life. But not necessarily in that order.

Find her at: http://carolynmathews.co.uk

Tweet her: @Carolyn_Mathews

http://www.johnhuntpublishing.com/authors/carolyn-mathews

At Roundfire we publish great stories. We lean towards the spiritual and thought-provoking. But whether it's literary or popular, a gentle tale or a pulsating thriller, the connecting theme in all Roundfire fiction titles is that once you pick them up you won't want to put them down.